JEWELS OF CLAY

Diminishing Magic
Book One

CAT COLLINS

For more information, or to book an évent, contact :
Web@CatCollinsBooks.com
http://www.CatCollinsBooks.com

Original Cover design by GetCovers.com ; New cover by Dramatic Tuba Designs, a division of Dramatic Tuba Books by Cat Collins
ISBN - Paperback: 979-8-9870363-0-3
First Edition, January 2023

JEWELS OF CLAY

Diminishing Magic
Book One

CAT COLLINS

Is it weird to dedicate your spicy book to your children?

Probably.

Eh, I'm doing it anyway.

To C. For every conversation that started with "What if…"
To H. For introducing me as a writer to your friends.
Neither of you ever read chapters 23, 27, 33, or 36.

And to my husband P. For putting up with me throughout this
whole process. And, you know, our whole lives together.
Feel free to read those chapters.

I couldn't believe I'd done it: cash-apped a sketchy leprechaun two-hundred bucks for intel on the location of the closest fairy ring. In my defense, I was running out of time, and catching fae wasn't illegal by definition; just frowned upon by most Magicals.

Good thing I was *half* magical.

I laid my oversized purse onto the kitchen counter, careful not to jostle the contents inside the small carved trunk or scatter the cooking utensils I'd laid out in preparation for this. The food was in the fridge, the recipes picked. I'd even grown and picked the vegetables with my Earth magic that morning and pre-rinsed them for good measure. Rinsing veggies was easy. It was the fairy's job to do the hard stuff.

Taking a deep breath, I removed the box, eager to see if giving up the last of my savings account for the ride-share it took to get to the ring and back was worth it. I didn't have a choice. Not if I wanted a roof over my head. Throw in months of bank notices, unopened letters from bill collectors, and stacks of Gram's unpaid medical bills, and my situation added up to be one big pile of suck.

Nabbing a fairy was the only way I could see out of it.

The lid creaked as the fairy burst out, cerulean wings fluttering as he sailed around the kitchen. He was easy to track because he wore what had to be Polly Pocket clothes from the eighties—bright pink shorts and a neon yellow and green tank. He whizzed by, almost colliding into the antique rack full of banged-up pots and pans before passing behind Gram's lace curtains that were now more cream-colored than their original white.

He finally flapped toward me and hovered a few inches from my face, coughing in the most exaggerated way as his shaggy mess of blonde hair flopped. "What in the name of the Mage did you let die in that bag? It smells like pig's feet and donkey ass!"

I stuck my nose inside the purse, picking up the scent of leather and breath mints. "No, it doesn't."

He pointed toward his nose. "Trust me. You'll appreciate my overdeveloped sense of smell after you taste what I make for you. That's what you said when you ripped me from my home: I'm here to cook. Right?" His voice was pleading and hopeful, and a nugget of guilt lodged in my gut. I quickly assured myself that Magicals had probably captured fae for much worse things than cooking. "Yes, I need this meal to be perfect." Mage knew I wasn't going to chance this very important meal on my culinary skills or lack thereof. I could barely make toast.

"Well, you nabbed the right fairy, Babycakes." I raised an eyebrow at the nickname, but it didn't slow him down a bit. "In Aetheria I was known for my skill with the culinary arts. Have you tried roasted strix? I know it's hard for some to stomach eating something that eats human flesh, but once you get past that, they're delicious. Though, I guess I'd have to pop over to the Mediterranean to get some. I could be back in a day, maybe two. Where are we, anyway? I was in that trunk for a few hours. Are we still in Oregon?"

"We're in Eugene. My deceased Gram's house. In a retirement village." I checked my phone, nervous titters swirling through me. Six hours and counting. No time for strix hunting. "I need you to understand: an entire species of Magicals is at stake here."

Not to mention my accommodations, living expenses, food on my table. Or, again, lack thereof. I couldn't survive on tomatoes and carrots I'd grown in my garden. Vegan was more of a dirty word than a way of life for me. And I'd had enough ramen noodles for two lifetimes already.

I kept mum about how I was about to be kicked out of my home and had no real job outside of a seasonal gig at the garden center and part-time meal delivery service driver, where I'd skimmed a few fries off the top every now and then. He didn't need to know how desperate I was.

"A whole species? Sounds ominous." He dropped to a lounging position on the counter, crossing his legs and throwing his muscled arms behind his head. "As the humans say, spill the coffee."

Already, he was getting under my skin, and he'd been there less than five minutes.

I shook my head. "Spill the *tea*, not coffee."

"What-the-fuck-ever. I try to steer clear of humans as much as possible."

Same. Which was weird considering I was half-human. But truth be told, I stayed away from just about everyone, human or magical. If I'd had a middle name, it would've been hermit. That was mostly due to circumstance. It was hard to form relationships, friend or otherwise, when you spent all your time caring for an ill, unstable person. Once my Gram died, I didn't even know where to start to look for people to socialize with outside of work, so I didn't.

I took a deep breath. It seemed like a point of no return-moment, but

I needed the fairy to fall in line. "We're petitioning to join the Conclave."

I'd sold Gram's car to Liam for information on the leader and how the petition process worked. Which meant I was no longer going to make food deliveries. Another gamble that could've left me homeless if it didn't play out as I'd planned.

Even at his small size, the fairy's deep throaty laugh filled the entire kitchen. "I'm impressed you got anything on the Conclave, but they haven't let a species join in hundreds of years. The last one was gargoyles. That ended *so* well for them."

Thanks for the reminder about how high the odds were stacked against me.

I grabbed a dish towel and threw it at him, which he dodged like a professional…dodger.

Douchehead.

"We've got more to offer than gargoyles and we wouldn't let being in the Conclave go to our heads like they did." I sounded lame, even to myself. I was more worried about my personal stake in this than getting my species in the Conclave. They'd managed millennia without the protection and privileges the Conclave offered. Me? I had another week or two, tops before I was out on my ass.

Helping gnomes into the Conclave was the only way to get to Aetheria, the birthplace of magic—my true purpose for all of this nonsense. In Aetheria, there would be no hiding from humans, no taxes or monetary system to worry about, and oceans of ambient magic, free for the taking. It sounded like the perfect place to be. Besides, I had no ties keeping me in this realm since Gram had died two years ago, leaving me a house I couldn't pay for and no inheritance whatsoever. I couldn't even afford to change the old-lady lace curtains or, Mage help me, the wall-to-wall gold shag carpet.

The fairy took me in with his crystalline blue eyes, which matched his flittering wings. "So, what species are you? No, don't tell me." He surveyed me, trying to pinpoint my species.

My pulse raced under his scrutiny because being in the spotlight was not my thing. It unnerved me. Enough that I went straight to goading him. "What? Your super sniffer failing you now?"

I folded my arms across my chest. Not my most mature moment, but he was wasting my time and frying the last remnants of my nerves. Again, he laughed. Then, he sailed off the counter and made swirling circles around my neck. I didn't have to hear or see him to know he was sniffing me.

Sniffing. Me.

Though, in all fairness, I basically invited him to take a whiff.

In response, he grunted. Not sure if it was a good or a bad kind. I almost grabbed the fly swatter, but I stopped short.

Slow your roll, Terra. You need him.

He flitted around my head, picking up a strand of hair before he nearly landed on my nose. "Plain brown hair, so you aren't a pixie; dark eyes instead of gold, so gryphon's out…too small to be Valkyrie…Who else isn't in the Conclave like us lowly fae?" He said with a hint of bitterness in his voice, then landed back on the counter, cocking his head. "You smell of buttery gold and rich soil after a rain. And there's something else, but maybe just your own personal aroma."

"Can we just get—"

"Wait. Oh, my Mage. Are you…no way, you can't be!"

There it was.

He slapped his own knee laughing and nearly rolled into the jar of flour he should've been using to cook my meal. "You're a gnome, aren't you? An elusive gnome. This just keeps getting better."

Among Magicals, not even trolls got the amount of ridicule that gnomes did. We didn't deserve that but having so little magic made a difference in our world. I released a slow breath. I didn't have time for his nonsense.

I slammed my hand on the counter for emphasis, setting my features into a cold stare. Letting him know I meant business. "Yes, I'm half-gnome. You've got three seconds to stop laughing and get busy. Or did you forget? I captured you, so I own your ass."

At least I thought so. Liam was a little loose with the details on that.

"Yes ma'am." He managed to pick himself and assemble what resembled a serious expression, then ruined it by turning and slapping his own butt. "This ass is yours."

What had I done?

I'd gambled the remnants of my savings, not to mention my future, on a flippant, smartass fairy.

To his credit, he didn't even blink at the half-gnome comment. Being half-blood had cursed my entire life. Most Magicals did a one-eighty when they found out about it. And, of course, I couldn't tell any human friends about my magical half. If I'd had any. I guess if you counted co-workers who occasionally ate in the same breakroom and had conversations about last night's tv shows count as friends, I did.

Yup. Terra Hermit Youngblood had a nice ring to it.

I turned my back on the fairy. The pressure was getting to me, and I didn't want to lose my shit in front of him. There was too much riding on this.

He pricked my shoulder with his tiny finger. "Oh good, I thought you were turning into a statue. You know, like a garden gnome. Get it? Garden gnome!"

Anger rocketed through me. I grabbed a dirty glass containing the remains of my breakfast milk from the sink and slapped it down over the fairy, capturing him in one swift motion. Droplets of souring milk dripped onto his head, splashing on his shiny hair. He did not like that.

As he flapped and gagged and made a fool of himself trying to escape, I tapped my foot. "I'm sorry, what? I can't quite hear you. Did you need something?"

Juvenile behavior — two. Maturity — zero.

I was overreacting. But Gram's gnome pride was ingrained deep. I even refused to sell the garden gnome statues at work. I let my co-workers think I was freaked out by them, so I didn't have to face the insult head-on.

When the fairy quieted down and sat cross-legged on the counter, I let him free. He raced to the sink, hit the nozzle and took a little fairy shower. When he had the milk removed, he shook his head like a dog.

I could've sworn the ancient cuckoo clock hanging in the dining room ramped the volume up to eleven.

Tick. Tick. Tick.

If he didn't start cooking soon, it would all be for nothing.

"Sorry about the milk. I'm just nervous," I admitted.

Not that I owed him an apology because from where I stood, he started the whole mess, but I was desperate, and anxious. Though, I understood the big question mark that accompanied the word, gnome. I may have forgotten all about that part of my lineage if not for my frantic need to provide for myself.

To appease some of his questions and get his ass in gear, I went with the simple explanation my dear ole gnome-proud Gram gave me when she told me what I was. "Yes, the cheesy garden gnomes are based on our species. No, we don't all have pointy red hats." Though my favorite beanie was red, but that didn't count. "We're an ancient, cunning, and noble guardian species formed by the Mage to guard the palace jewels for the Fae Kings of Court. We're experts at hiding and protecting valuables."

If it was someone else's, not our own, but he didn't need to know that part. There were other things too, but I wasn't going to share them with a fairy. Before she went loco and died of some unknown disease no human or Magical doctor could pinpoint, Gram had told me fae couldn't be trusted.

She also said trolls were the best lovers and she'd spoken to the Mage many times and he replied because he was her bestie. She was full cuckoo at the end, my Gram. I'd filled an entire journal with her harebrained ramblings because they made me laugh. *Gramisms*, I called it.

"Gnome. Okay." He side-eyed me like he was trying to make sense of my existence. Been doing that for twenty-two years and hadn't come up with much yet, so good luck, Bud. He sailed off the counter, buzzing around my head. "Gnomes are alchemists, right? So, you could make some edible gold leaf for the meal if I asked?"

If only.

Most gnomes were great at alchemy, but I sucked at it.

I assumed I didn't have enough magic in me, thanks to my human mother. Not that I could've kept the gold for myself anyway. Magical rules and all that B.S. I *did* have some that Gram had made tucked away though. I nodded at the fairy. "Yeah. How much will you need?"

He rifled through the pile of recipe cards and clapped his hands. "A quarter-cup should work. Now, I have dishes to prepare. Go somewhere else and deal with your nerves, get laid or something."

Not an abysmal idea, but I didn't have the time to dedicate to that endeavor. Besides, who was I going to sleep with? I had no prospects on the horizon. My life had been about prepping for that night, not Terra's personal plan to hook up with the hottest guy I could dig up.

Which was usually how my encounters were. One-night stands or occasional sexy liaisons that lasted a few days or weeks. Because even though I was a solitary soul by nature and by circumstance, I still had...needs. Though getting laid would have to take a back seat, at least until I got into the Conclave. Maybe then I'd find a sexy elf or gryphon in

Aetheria that caught my eye. Until then, ix-nay on the ex-say for me.

I tromped down the stairs to my basement suite. The rich brown walls reminded me of the soil when I tunneled. It was dark, cool, and enveloped me like a hug. I was safe there. Protected. Throwing myself down on my comfy and unmade bed, I wrapped my homemade green comforter around me and glanced at my bedside table.

Out of instinct I reached for my Gram's Magic 8-Ball. It was a silly human toy she'd bought for my father when he was young, but after her mind started to go, she used it every day when she wanted to *consult the Mage.*

I had to swallow down the lump in my throat. I missed her so much. So much that I made a point to ask the thing at least one question a day, just to keep her memory alive. Since the fairy had put the thought in my head, I went with the obvious question. "Magic 8-Ball, will I get laid anytime soon?"

Reply hazy, please try again.

That's what I figured. I needed to stay the course and see my plans through. There would be time for all the hook-ups in Aetheria as soon as I got gnomes into the Conclave. Obviously Magic 8-ball agreed.

Reluctantly, I set the 8-ball back in its place and pulled myself off the bed. There was work to do. I went over to the tiny water closet where my ever-so-seventies gold tub and toilet were located and started the shower. Thanks to the practically-prehistoric water heater, it would take about ten minutes for the water to heat to a bearable level, so while it warmed, I pulled my Gram's battered old trunk from under my bed.

Inside were the last fragments of my Gram's gold stash. She hadn't made gold in quite some time before her passing, but I'd kept the last of her supply just in case I needed to sell it. Turned out I had exactly a quarter-cup.

I swore when I died and went to Netheria—that is, if a half-magical person's soul were even permitted in the resting place of Magicals—I'd ask the Mage why he'd made gnomes incapable of keeping any treasures or riches for ourselves. That sick trick of nature was responsible for a lot of pain. Though, in fairness, my human side didn't seem to be that great at holding on to my own money either.

After I showered, I dressed in my black dress pants and fitted black sweater, attempting to look as put-together and professional as I could. Out of habit, I reached for the vial that contained soil from my birthplace. It hung from a black cord, and I only took it off to shower. I even slept in it.

Gram was too deep into her delusions to ask where the soil was from when I discovered the vial tucked in her jewelry box with a note saying *"Terra, this is the soil from where you were born. It will ground you and guide you."*

It didn't matter where I was born. What was important was that I had something that connected me to who I was, to Gram. I put it on, feeling the familiar silk cord, the weight of the vial against my chest, and stared at myself in the mirror. I instantly calmed. The vial *did* ground me. But I was still waiting for the guide part to kick in. Maybe it and the Magic 8-Ball needed to get together.

The cord looked fine with my outfit, but something about having dirt hanging from your neck screamed weak and desperate. Okay, I was weak and desperate, but they didn't have to know that, so I pulled the vial off and hung it over my mirror.

I poured the last sprinkles of Gram's gold into a bowl, then headed upstairs, where the fairy forbade me from helping him. Great idea on his part. I almost burned my whole house down making French fries in the oven.

Teach me to try and be healthy.

I set the table as best I could, using gold-plated utensils that I hoped wouldn't be too obvious because it was all I had. The tablecloth and napkins were made of gold silk I picked up at a thrift store and I added a sprinkling of gold leaf down the center of the table. It looked majestic and elegant. That's what I was going for. The Conclave was all about formality, tradition, and sticking to magic rules. It's how Magicals had survived undetected by humans for so long, according to Liam the leprechaun.

I gathered the rest of the gold leaf in a bowl and pushed the swinging kitchen door open. "Here's your go—" The glass bowl slipped from my hands and tumbled to the floor. "Oh, my Mage!"

The fairy was standing at the sink with his back turned. He didn't even react to the shattering glass. "Oh, my Mage, what?"

He'd turned into a full adult-sized man—no wings.

Also, no clothes.

JEWELS OF CLAY

Y ou're naked!" I squeaked my voice more than a little shrieky.

He was wearing my half-apron, which was tied in a bow low on his back, making his killer butt like a freaking gift to be unwrapped.

"Oh yeah. You didn't think to stop for some big boy pants now did you, Babycakes?"

"Um, no. I didn't know fae could…" I paused, searching for the right word, but my brain was spiraling at the sight of him, it was hard to find one. "…enlarge."

"You have no idea," he snickered, capitalizing on the innuendo I inadvertently served up. "You captured me in my natural state, but most fairies can be any size we want, wings or no. I needed to manipulate the oven and utensils, so I went for human-size." He turned and held out his spoon. "Wanna taste?"

He didn't care one tiny bit about flaunting his naked body in front of me. In all honesty, he shouldn't have. Who knew fairies worked out? He was ripped. As the sauce dripped from his spoon, he smirked, no doubt because he noticed I was checking him all the way out, cursing the stupid apron in my head.

Then cursing myself for thinking it.

"Do. You. Want. A. Taste?"

"Um. Yes?"

I managed to gather myself together enough to walk over to the sink. I was inches from tasting whatever it was, but he yanked the spoon back at the last second. "Hey!"

"Changed my mind. It's not ready yet."

Jerkhead.

He shoved the bowl into the fridge and retrieved a head of lettuce. "Tear this for salad. Cutting makes it taste funny."

I did what I was told, while he took a knife and cut vegetables. To my surprise, the act of tearing lettuce released some pent-up nervous energy and helped to distract me from the apron-clad dude standing next to me. By the time I finished the third one, I wasn't even thinking about anything and that was a relief.

"I'm Tristan, by the way. What's your name?"

Shit.

I didn't want to know anything about him, including his name. Our arrangement was business, a means to an end, not a way to make friends. It took me a few seconds to respond, but I gave in because I didn't have much choice. I supposed it wouldn't hurt. The least I could do was be civil to him. "I'm Terra, with an e and two r's, Youngblood."

"Ha! Terra means Earth. And gnomes are Earth elementals."

"Yes, my parents, Mage rest their souls, were apparently very literal."

"Nice to meet you, Terra." His smile was huge and genuine. It tugged on my heart and that wasn't good at all. Annoying as he was, I was starting to like the sucker.

He was there for one meal. That was all. No attachments.

We got into a groove of working together. For over an hour, he gave me the easy jobs and I marveled as he did all the complicated ones. When I'd finished stirring the bacon glaze for the hundredth time, he ran out of simple tasks. Pulling up one of the mismatched bar stools and patting it with his hand, he gave me a command like I was working for him, not the other way around. "Sit."

"I'm not a dog."

"Trust me, I know." He bit his lower lip, his meaning clear, and it struck me low in the gut. He was super attractive. I tried very hard to picture him in his miniaturized form, like a mini-Ken doll with smooth junk and wings dripping in sour milk.

It didn't work. And I needed to put my guard up because he was as charming as he was annoying, and he was looking at me like I was on the menu. "Who's heading the Conclave these days? I can create a sauce tailored to their species. Please don't say Desdemona is still in charge, because a fish sauce would ruin the entree."

"Desdemona? Where have you been? The Water elemental term ended decades ago." I said it like I hadn't just learned it from Liam myself.

Gram had told me mermaids are notoriously hard to please and difficult to work with. Werewolves, however, were a little more flexible. Especially a couple of days after their monthly sabbaticals. At that time, they're particularly hungry and as long as you feed them, they're agreeable.

It's why I chose that night. And that menu.

Assuming the intel I had was accurate. And that my Gram was right about werewolves being reasonable. "Mateo Coran, Alpha of the Northern Region leads the Conclave now. He's bringing his four beta wolves with him tonight."

Tristan paused; a weird look crossed his face before he went back to stirring. "So that's why you're not doing a vegetarian option. Got it." He busied himself making some kind of meaty gravy. It smelled delicious, but he wouldn't let me taste it. He was using very little actual magic, favoring his culinary skills over '*cheating*' as he put it. I would have chopped off half my arm doing what he was doing with those knives.

It occurred to me that maybe I had trouble tapping into my gnome magic and making gold was because alchemy was a lot like cooking. Even if you got the ingredients correct, if you baked it at the wrong temp, your souffle would fall.

Or something. Never attempted to cook a souffle.

Tristan paused chopping, eyeing me up and down, fixating a little too long on my breasts. "I'm sure you've got your petition all worked out, but maybe use the warring species angle. All the in-fighting is causing a strain on magic. Or so I've heard. If gnomes could help with that, he'd be a fool to deny you."

"There's fighting between species?" After my monthlong obsession with *Twilight*, Gram had confirmed the cliché of vampires and wolves not getting along, but she never said anything as concrete as actual fighting was occurring. "How do you know that?"

"Just something I heard a vampire say not long ago. You know, vamps are so gloomy and emu sometimes."

It might work if I could figure out how gnomes would help with the fighting. "*Emo*, not emu." He shrugged and I got the impression he didn't care if he got human idioms correct or not.

The clock ringing six cuckoos struck me down to the core. Two hours to go. I got up and began pacing around the kitchen, glancing at the clock every minute for half an hour. My lungs began to feel like there was too much oxygen in them. I tried to exhale, and it came out in ragged puffs.

This had to work.

"You need to relax."

"Hm?"

Tristan grabbed me by the shoulders, pinning me with his hypnotic blue peepers. I wondered how many had fallen under his spell. "Maybe this will help with your nerves: ask yourself, what's the worst thing that could happen tonight?"

I'd done that a hundred times in the past twenty-four hours.

"Mateo chokes on the food, denies us membership on the Conclave, then I get thrown out on my—"

I didn't get to finish my sentence because Tristan stopped me.

By shoving me against the refrigerator. "Terra, you know you want to kiss me."

Holy Mage.

Where did *that* come from?

It *had* crossed my mind. Several times. That didn't mean I would go through with the idea. I was capable of reigning in my hormones when necessary. Mostly. "Whoa. I can't think about that right now. They'll be here soon."

He was insistent. "Come on Terra. Kiss me. You know you'll feel better once you do."

He was probably right. I mean, why not? He was gorgeous, standing there in nothing but an apron and I was a grown woman. There was no harm in it if was consensual.

I leaned up, brushing my lips against his. He groaned and wasted no time deepening the kiss. Then his hands were in my hair, all over my body, touching all the right places and making me wonder why it had been so long since I'd done this with a guy.

As soon as I managed to calculate the eleven-month dry spell I'd been rocking, my need surged. I jerked the apron string, exposing him completely. He caught me staring at him and smirked as he grabbed himself. "You want this, don't you, Terra?"

In my lust-driven haze, I forgot all about Mateo, the dinner, and truth be told, any other being in existence. I wanted him, more than I'd wanted

21

anyone and that was all I could think about. He leaned forward, pressing his hard length against me and biting my earlobe. "Now, Terra, I want you to get on your knees and—"

Hold it.

Hold it a damn minute.

"What did you just say?"

"Well, I didn't get to finish, but I was about to say, Terra, I want you to suck my—"

Oh, my Mage. It was like ice water had been injected into my veins. I couldn't believe I'd been so stupid. He'd just said my name over and over. More times than was natural. There was only one reason why a person would do that. I shoved him, pushing him as far away as I could as I came to my senses. "Did you just try to use Name magic to get me to screw you?"

A normal person may have made some kind of effort to deny it, given how wrong it was. Not Tristan. He laughed. "Guilty. Don't be mad. You're hot and I did it to help you."

Uh, nope. It was an assault and so wrong. I didn't care how attractive he was, I wasn't going to lose my senses over a man. Ever. "How would fucking you help me?"

He shrugged. "You needed to relax and that's the best and most fun way to do it."

Technically, not wrong. Still, it was akin to molestation in my mind, and I was seething. I grabbed the apron and shoved it at him. "Put this on and get back to work, you little shit. It's almost time."

My knees were weak as I went downstairs to think. If Gram hadn't shown me how to perform Name magic, I wouldn't have recognized it. I didn't even know how two Earth elementals like Gram and I could even perform Wind magic, but she'd made sure I could.

Regular Elemental magic is easy to manipulate, but special magic like

Name magic needs a driving force to work. The secret for Name magic is having clear intention. Once you have that solidified in your mind, all you needed was to say the person's name, gather air in your lungs, and release as you think about what you want them to do.

Tristan had been very deft at it, which makes sense given he was a Wind elemental.

Mage. I almost gave in to it.

As I paced around my room, the tiniest part of me regretted not going ahead with it. It would've taken the responsibility off me, absolved me of any future guilt if I was under a spell and had sex with him. But the very last thing I needed was to get closer to him. Things were precarious enough and I was starting to doubt I had the nerve to go through with the evening as I'd prepared.

But, if I was going to get to Aetheria, I had no choice but to continue with my plan.

I grabbed the Magic 8-Ball, shaking it as I circled my room trying to calm down. I didn't bother to pose a question. I'd already asked the big one hundreds of times.

Will gnomes get in the Conclave?

It gave me a different answer each time. Not that I believed it held the actual answer, but it would've been nice to have some inkling of what I was walking into, given my grand plans to get in the Conclave and travel to Aetheria to save myself. I had no clue if the wolf leader of the Conclave was a reasonable guy. Or what the betas would be like. Or what would happen when I served the meal I'd diligently planned to help my cause?

I hated the unknown. But that didn't matter because the doorbell rang. It was time to feed the wolves.

JEWELS OF CLAY

Wild but regal, Mateo Coran, alpha and Conclave Leader, with long slicked-back hair tied at the nape and shoulders as wide as a tank arrived as the cuckoo crowed eight. His face was pock-marked with age or battle scars—I couldn't be sure which. He and his party of betas filled the dining room to the rafters with masculine musk and thick disdain.

They didn't want to be there.

Not at all.

A tremor of insecurity ran through me. It was odd to see five beasts squeeze into the small dining room between the curio cabinet and card table I'd disguised with a quilt and white out-of-season lilies I'd grown with my Earth magic. Not that they'd know that or be impressed by it.

They certainly weren't impressed by the threadbare rug I'd borrowed from the neighbor that was hiding as much of that hideous shag as I could. Half of them were staring at it like it would jump up and bite them. The other half were trying to look anywhere else.

For a second, I was offended on my Gram's behalf. I mean, the carpet and furniture weren't high-end, but they were hers and those beasts needed to check themselves if they were going to insult my Gram or her lack of taste. She had no money either, thanks to the gnome thing. She'd always said her style was retro, not old.

I glanced over to her cane which I'd lodged in the bare corner to give it a little life. It was a gnarled old branch from the tree outside and I felt instantly connected to her as I stood there with my knees trembling.

Mateo formally introduced me to the betas, but I was hyper-focused on their intimidating appearances, so I didn't retain many of their names. The one with the lightest brown hair started with G, and I think the one with curls was Ace? I was pretty sure the one with tatted arms and man bun was Ben. They looked like I'd expect werewolves to look—muscular, dark, and brooding. Hot didn't even come close to describing them. Looking from one to the next made me dizzy.

Until I got to the surly beta standing to the right of Mateo. He was something else. His hair was dark and just a smidge too long, so it did that flippy, sexy thing over his ears that just isn't fair to people who are into males. He was rocking everything a dude could rock—full lips, chiseled jaw with bad boy stubble, insane eyelashes. And his eyes? Mage help me, they were an alluring lavender, and it was other-worldly the way he took everything in with them.

Who has purple eyes?

That guy.

I wasn't sure if I should thank the Mage or curse him for putting a second panty-melting dude in my presence in the same day. Though Tristan's appeal had lessened since he'd tried to seduce me with magic. I struggled to think anything this guy could do would diminish his physical appeal. Though he was probably a jerkhole. Guys who looked like him usually were, human or magical.

His name was Wells, which struck me as too civilized for something so savage looking. He was wearing a heather green Henley, and his chest, his arms, shoulders—stretching that shirt to its maximum limits.

He was the muscle. Which says a lot when you're looking at a roomful of animals who could snap someone in half between their fingers, or their teeth—depending on which form they took.

I went straight to business because I wasn't going to give him any reasons to discount me. Plus, I wanted to get Wells' eyes off of me as soon as I could. They may have been pretty, but his stare was unsettling.

"Sir, I've done some digging and I think…what I mean to say, I know gnomes have a lot to offer if you'll give us—me—a chance to show you…"

I was choking. I'd completely forgot the entire speech I'd planned and rehearsed for days until I was hoarse. This was all my idea and if I failed, it was all over. For me and for all other gnomes, none of which had any idea I was trying to pull this stunt. What was I thinking trying something so risky?

Deep breath, Terra. You got this.

Or you don't, but at least you may be able to outrun them long enough to get outside to the back yard where you can tunnel your ass away from them, gnome-style.

"Sir, gnomes have a lot to offer the Conclave, especially now with whispers of clashing species." He winced, emitting a low gnarl. Okay. Sore subject. Thanks for nothing, Tristan.

I scrambled to recover. "We're alchemists, so if you need money, we can turn things to gold for you. And while gnome magic is seen as one of the weakest, you'd be surprised what we can do if given the chance."

He nodded for me to continue. There we were: on the edge of insanity. I'd plunged in with every insane idea I'd had in the process, might as well go all in on the last one.

No one could resist a sob story, right?

I gestured for them to take their seats at the table, then I positioned myself at the end across from Mateo. "Before she died, my grandmother's fondest wish was for gnomes to be part of the Conclave. She was going to make the petition herself when she was younger, but when my parents died, she was forced to care for me. A few years later, she got ill and deteriorated until she died a two years ago."

I stopped for a second. An unexpected lump formed in my throat. Though I was laying it on thick for the wolf, I wasn't immune to my own story. Her death still affected me in a deep way. "She cared for me until the last breath left her body. She made sure to tell me to make a special tribute meal to show you my respect for traditions and perhaps foster the transition into the Conclave. She really wanted this. It was the last thing she said."

Okay, so Liam's the one who told me about the Conclave tradition and Gram's last words were *'the Mage has a beard,'* but Mateo didn't have to know that. Gram had wanted me to join the Conclave based on all the babbling she'd done about Aetheria, so I was twisting the truth, not lying.

Mateo's face was a stone façade. He didn't give two shits about me or my Gram. He was there fulfilling his duty and nothing more. He nodded politely, looking to the kitchen, eager to get on with the meal.

Right. Time to serve.

Bon Appetit!

The hors d'oevers course consisted of caramelized maple figs with smoky bacon on top. They smelled delicious but were on the tiny side. Wells' eye-roll over only having one to eat was epic, so I rushed back into the kitchen to hurry the next course along.

Tristan had shrunken down to his small frame in case one of the wolves got nosy and he needed to duck inside a coffee mug to hide. I didn't want any of them knowing I'd used a lowly fairy to help me. They would've dismissed me instantly. I didn't know how it was in Aetheria, but fae were jokes to every magical creature in our world, stripped from the Conclave millennia ago, but not sentenced to Netheria like gargoyles and cupids had been. I think that would've been a kinder fate, in a way.

When I set the plate of caprese garlic bread with bacon glaze in front of the wolves, I got a look of satisfaction from the curly-haired beta, but the others stuffed their mouths without even glancing in my direction.

They made small talk amongst themselves, ignoring me and all my efforts, but when I brought out the salad with lemon garlic vinaigrette, I had to say something. "I grew the lemons and garlic yesterday with my Earth magic."

The one who started with G—Gabriel maybe—raised an eyebrow and glanced in the direction of manbun before he spoke. "You grew lemons in October?"

Finally, maybe someone would see my value. "Yes. Gnomes are resourceful like that. I could set up an exchange, like a farmer's market, if you like. I could supply the pack with vegetables."

Manbun grunted. "We don't need food. Lemons and garlic are easy to get."

Okay then.

I'd used Gram's recipe for beef bourguignons and when I brought it out, Wells slid forward in his seat, eyeing the meat like the carnivore he was. He'd stirred his food around the plate politely so far, but he was there for the beef. They all seemed to like it and I had Tristan to thank for cooking so perfectly and adding whatever sauce he'd concocted. Maybe I'd see the solution to my poverty by the end of the night. Hope was blooming in my chest.

When it was time for the last course, Mateo leaned back, the wooden chair creaking under his weight. "The meal was pleasant. You've done gnomes proud." My knees wobbled. I'd lived this moment before. Countless times for countless reasons.

There was a *but* coming.

"But I don't see what you have to offer in exchange for Conclave membership. I regret I must deny your petition."

I couldn't help but notice the beta wolves had varying looks of relief on their faces. They were ready to get out and forget I existed. The whole evening had been a charade, a duty for them to fulfill, and nothing more. "Sir, if you'd just give me a chance."

He shook his head. "You've done your research—obviously this meal was done in the old tradition, and I appreciate that. However, as you alluded to, these are troubling times, and the Conclave must move forward in order for us to survive. Gnomes offer nothing to help us accomplish that."

"But—"

I was tanking fast. Mateo was all but out the door.

To back up his position, he offered me some insight. "We've done our research too. As soon as I received your letter of petition, I sent a scout to observe you for some time, to learn your strengths and weaknesses. It says something that I agreed to this meal. Other gnomes and different species haven't made it past the scouting phase."

"You spied on me?" I spat, anger dripping from my words. I was shocked, offended, and not down for that kind of scrutiny. I was just trying to help myself out. They held all the cards in this arrangement, and they still had to spy on me. What if they'd seen me trap Tristan? Could that be the real reason he was denying me? Had I screwed myself? I could barely contain my rage and fear. They roared around inside me like a tornado. "What do you think you've learned about me?"

Mateo glanced at the betas. None of them looked like they wanted to offer any insight, so he continued, "You're a caring person. And you've overcome many tragedies in your life, showing you're strong in character. It goes without saying you've shown some fierce determination to get this far. But, you're weak in magical potential. You've done very little with the ambient magic all Magicals here in this realm have access to. I mean no offense; I must consider many factors in this decision. I'm afraid the Conclave would gain nothing from gnomes, so, as I said, I have to deny your petition."

This was it.

Now or never.

I had to make a move to show we were worthy. That *I* was worthy.

I had to use my failsafe. It turned my stomach, but I hoped it would get Mateo's attention and make him change his mind. I dared to lay a hand on his arm. He bristled. "At least have dessert before you leave."

I didn't give him time to refuse. I rushed back into the kitchen, drawing a deep breath. I looked at Tristan and I swear I felt his touch on my body, like he'd left permanent fingerprints there.

I should've just slept with him.

It would've been the least I could do.

I lowered my voice. "Quick, hide in here. He was looking toward the kitchen." I raised the metal cloche lid, and he dove in. Just as I'd done in the glass earlier, I trapped him inside.

This time he stayed still because he wanted to help me.

Whispering "Thank you," I grabbed the chocolate and gold flake sauce Tristan had melted, then took the platter into the dining room and presented it to Mateo, bowing low. Couldn't hurt, right? Plus, it gave me something to do while I tried to hold the vomit in check. "I'll hope you'll reconsider. Gnomes are fantastic at guarding treasure. For example, I've guarded your special dessert all day."

I raised the lid. Tristan sat still and cross-legged on the platter, his wings fluttering, and a smile plastered on his pretty face because he couldn't have known what was about to happen. Mateo let loose a belly laugh and most of the others joined him. One guess which beta didn't find it amusing.

He lowered his purple gaze on me, full of weight and judgment.

Glancing between me and Tristan, he shook his head. I could feel the disappointment in his stare. Or maybe I was seeing things and that came from my sense of guilt.

All day I'd pushed the thought of this moment to the recesses of my mind. I justified it to myself: I was just fulfilling my responsibilities to my species, securing an end to a means for myself. It was a job. A backup plan. Nothing personal.

I never expected to like the damn fairy.

Or almost sleep with him.

Shame curled its way along my spine.

It was wrong.

I knew that all along. But, could I do it anyway?

Mateo rubbed his chin. "I expected gold, but not like this. Are all gnomes as crafty as you?"

I nodded, knowing it could help my cause. Wells slid forward in his seat; shock written on his features. Mateo moved to dunk Tristan into the melted gold and chocolate dip. I went limp, shivering in disgust at myself.

I couldn't do it.

I couldn't literally feed Tristan to the wolves. "Wait! Stop!"

Mateo paused, curling his fist around Tristan, who was as still as a statue. He had to have figured out what was happening but was making no move to get away from the situation. Which made me feel even worse. Had my capturing him made him unable to flee? Shit. What had I done?

Mateo frowned, disappointed I'd interrupted his dessert. "This is the first thing you've said or done that showed me you may have some value."

The betas looked at one another, as a thick stillness settled, weighing my shoulders down. I had nothing. No reason to keep him from eating Tristan alive. "Um…"

I started backing away. I could grab Tristan from his fist and sprint for the backyard. I'd tunnel away before the wolves could move.

Maybe.

I inched forward, eyeing Tristan until a deafening buzz in my ear stopped me. I must have been having a stroke from the stress of it all. Then a tiny, but distinct voice whispered in my ear. "I'm fine, Babycakes."

"Tristan?"

Mateo cocked his head. "Who's Tristan?"

Tristan spoke again, whispering in Wind magic so only I could hear him. "Yes. That's not me in his hand. But you need to get yourself out of this mess or you're going to be dessert, not me."

He was right. All the wolves we staring at me and Mateo was clutching something that appeared to be Tristan, waiting for me to tell him why I'd stopped him.

I considered using Name Magic, but I doubted it would work on someone as powerful as the Conclave leader. Plus, I couldn't remember all the wolves' names anyway.

Shock was coursing through my veins. And adrenaline. I barely heard Tristan's directions. "Tell them that you learned the werewolves of old enjoyed eating fae because your grandmother read an ancient tome written by the King of the Summer Court. While it's not a practice followed today, you wanted to show your dedication to the petition. Tell him. Now, Terra."

I told him, the words tripping out of my mouth just as he'd said them. He'd used Name Magic to compel me, but at that moment, I didn't care. Mateo nodded, impressed. Then he dunked not-Tristan's feet into the chocolate gold.

I had no idea what was happening or how Tristan was doing what he was doing, but I watched in horror as Mateo shoved the fairy into his mouth. I turned my head and hummed a song my Gram used to sing me so I wouldn't hear the crunch of his skull as Mateo popped not-Tristan's head into his mouth like a bon-bon.

When I was satisfied, he was finished and I wasn't going to hurl, I turned back. Mateo was dapping the corners of his mouth with the gold silk napkin. Curls and Manbun were sticking their fingers in the melted chocolate gold and licking them. They hadn't eaten fairy, but they were sure enjoying the sauce as G-man—Gareth perhaps—side-eyed them.

Wells was peeking out of my Gram's so-old-they-were-no-longer-white lace curtains with his back turned.

"See? No reason to get bent out of shade. I told you it would be okay."

I wanted to scream and correct him: bent out of *shape*. But I knew that would arouse some suspicion. Somehow—even though I watched Mateo eat him—he'd managed to keep himself off the menu.

He was going to have to do a lot of explaining in a very short time.

Meal concluded; Mateo stood. There was conflict on his face. He wanted to say no again, but my fairy-flavored dessert had given him pause. Wells must have sensed his dilemma because he went right up to him, speaking in a whisper.

I didn't hear what he'd said but given the way he was boring a hole into me with his haunting purple eyes, I knew without a doubt, I was the subject. After a few moments of debate, Mateo shook his head in agreement and turned to me. "Conditions aren't right for me to grant gnomes membership in the Conclave, but my beta has informed me about a potential loophole. I could invoke Perception magic and give you a chance to prove yourself magically."

I'd never heard of Perception magic, but I knew that all kinds of magic existed in our world, hidden from humans and passed down from magic families. I got the short end of the stick in that department. If only my parents would've left an instruction manual before they died and left me, at two years old, with a grandmother who'd turn batty. Nope, all I got from them was a faded photo and a weird squiggle birthmark on my right wrist. "What is Perception magic?"

34

Mateo stopped short of scoffing at my naivete. I could tell he wanted to, though. "It's Wind magic and there are many uses for it: contracts, business ventures, and engagements are the main uses."

It sounded okay to me, but there were still a lot of questions in my mind. "Werewolves are Fire elementals. How can you wield Wind magic?"

Mateo gave me a 'poor little girl' look, then pulled a gold chain with a circle pendant from under his shirt. As he held it up, shimmering particles of light burst around the circle forming looping rays of magic that resembled translucent flower petals. "Not only does this Conduit key amplify Ambient magic, but it allows me to tap into all four Elemental magics. The Mage himself created it with Aetherian gold for the Conclave millennia ago. There are only five in existence and with it, I can perform many magics, including Perception magic."

"And what would this Perception magic do?"

"For our purposes, it would allow me to grant you provisional membership in the Conclave to see how you'd fare when faced with obstacles of our choosing. If you're perceived worthy, gnomes will be allowed in the Conclave. It's binding magic, so think carefully before you reply."

"So, it's like a trial basis?"

"Somewhat. Are you interested?"

After the day I'd had, it seemed like the best news ever. My commitment to getting to Aetheria was strong. I didn't doubt my ability to get past a few trials. "You bet. What do you mean by binding magic?"

He sighed and I felt like an idiot, but it wasn't my fault Gram was more interested in telling me nonsense than useful magical information. "Binding means that once I start the process, the magic takes control. There is no stopping it or amending it."

Okay, so I could work with that. Gnomes were worthy and I was tough and determined to make this happen. Like he'd said, I'd overcome plenty of obstacles in the past. Plus, if magic was in charge, then I figured I stood a better chance with it than with Mateo. "What do I need to do?"

He sneered, pleased with himself for whatever reason, which was dumb since Wells was the one to suggest this solution. "I need a candle and a handheld mirror—preferably with mirrors on both sides."

This was huge. I was halfway to getting to Aetheria. All I had to do was prove myself. "On it." I ran downstairs to grab Gram's antique hand-held mirror with faux ivory and gold inlay—thus, unpawnable—along the handle. It had mirrors on both sides, so it would work. Besides, it couldn't hurt to have a reminder of Gram there with me.

I glanced in the mirror. I think Gram would be proud of me for not following through on Tristan being dessert. She would've been disappointed in me for even thinking it, but I was desperate. Now I had a way out. I didn't know why Wells had suggested the contract, but I was going to take it and run with it. For Gram. And myself. Gnomes too.

I headed back upstairs and stumbled on Mateo and Wells whisper arguing about something. When they spotted me, Wells stepped away and dipped his head toward the two chairs they'd set up in the corner of the room. I took that as my cue to sit in one of them. He could've asked me nicely to sit, but no, he had to go with the silent head direction.

Mateo took the candle I'd taken from the curio cabinet and lit it. One of the wolves switched the lights off, causing a flicker of panic to tickle my insides. I had no idea what I was getting into. But I didn't have a choice if I wanted out of my current predicament. And while I was still mostly self-motivated, a twinkle of excitement rushed through me. There were many magical species not part of the Conclave, but gnomes had the largest numbers among them, and I'd feel proud if I was the one to get us in.

Mateo turned to Wells. "Are you sure about binding yourself to her?"

He nodded. "If it's okay with the gnome, I'm good."

It was the first time he'd strung more than a couple of words together and Mage help me, the low gravel of his voice made my stomach twist. Not only was he super easy to look at, but he possessed a voice that was a full-on sexual assault to my ears. I needed to get over that, pronto. "Okay with him doing what?"

"Perception Magic requires two people," Mateo replied. "The ritual will bind you until the final pronouncement. Whom you bind yourself with is your choice in this instance, but, once you commit, there's no going back. As I said, it's binding magic and will take on a life of its own once I invoke it."

Wells lowered his gaze on me, setting all of my insides on invisible fire. I considered saying no to this arrangement, but something told me risking it with one of the other betas would be less predictable and more dangerous. Wells had been judging me since before he walked in. And he'd suggested the crazy ritual after he'd seen me offer Tristan up on a gold platter, so maybe I stood a chance with him.

I nodded my permission.

As Wells took the chair opposite me Mateo started spouting orders. "You hold the mirror at the same time and position it where you can see your own eyes. Focus there. When things begin to swirl in the mirror, don't let it alarm you. It's part of the process."

I did as he asked. It was difficult because I could feel the warmth coming from Wells' hand as it curled next to mine on the mirror's handle. I knew he was looking into the mirror as I was, but it *felt* like he was staring at me. It made me want to dive under the dining room table.

I jumped when Mateo started talking again. "Terra Youngblood, do you promise to fulfill the conditional requirements and accept the consequences of your Perception judgment?"

"Yes?"

"Wells Payne, do you promise to be open-minded and judge fairly?"

Of course, his last name was *Payne*.

He nodded.

A snicker in the dark. "In sickness and in health, 'til death do you part, you may kiss the bride."

Wells reached out with his other hand, landing a punch in Curls' gut without looking up. Curls doubled over and coughed.

Mateo lit the candle and said some words I didn't recognize, probably fae tongue, the language of the Mage. Gram had once said it was easier to understand Klingon than fae tongue.

The candle's flame roared, almost reaching the ceiling. The image in the mirror began to twist, morphing into irregular patterns and shapes until I saw nothing but Wells' purple eyes staring at me through the mirror. They flashed, deep and amethyst, then faded back to their regular shade.

It was some weird magic mojo for sure. And disorienting to look into a mirror and see someone else's eyes. Pretty as they were.

"Wells, take her arm."

"Whoa. Why?" I crossed my arms over my chest, tucking them tight.

"For Mage's sake," Wells grumbled, and captured my arm with no effort whatsoever, locking our wrists together. His arm was longer than mine, so he wrapped his fingers around my elbow and the second we touched, I was overcome with a deep penetrating warmth that spread outward from my elbow to my fingers. He was warm. Like, feverishly so.

Before I could ask if I was about to pick up the flu from him, Mateo held up his circle pendant, directing it toward our clasped arms and blowing into the circle. A warm stream of wind swirled around our entwined arms in an intricate pattern, causing goosebumps to break out all over my body.

After the wind had died, Mateo dipped his finger in his water glass, then sprinkled droplets over our arms. The water seemed to come alive as it raced around the same path the wind had taken. Next, he took an empty wineglass from the table and held it over our clasped arms. I didn't even have time to panic about it as he tossed the glass up and it shattered, deconstructing into the sand it was made from. The sand rained down sand, brushing over our arms in the same way.

The Earth magic inside me tingled in warmth, recognizing its own kind. Turning glass back to sand was an advanced skill though. Never had done it and I doubted I ever would.

Wells' throaty chuckle drew my attention, and I looked back to the mirror and found him smirking.

Shit. We'd done Wind, Water, and Earth. His magic was next.

Fire.

Mateo took the candle and set it on Wells' arm. I screamed as the fire skimmed his flesh. He sat there stoic, giving no indication he'd even felt it. The fire jumped from his arm and licked across my wrist, chasing the same intricate path the others had. I gripped him tightly, my nails biting into his muscular arm as the fire kissed my skin in utter torture. I knew I had to hold on or this was all for nothing.

A light brush of Wells' fingers against my elbow drew my focus. It happened so quickly, I could've imagined it. But it distracted me enough to lessen the sting of fire, which seemed to dissipate as I concentrated. When I looked up, Wells was stone-faced and intense like he hadn't moved a single muscle.

Mateo said some more words in fae tongue and a stream of gold magic shot from his pendant, wrapping around our wrists. I felt it then second it solidified. We were bound together. There was no going back now.

Mateo announced Wells could release me. He dropped my arm like a stone, and I leaned back in the chair panting. Manbun scoffed. "That's some freaky bondage."

A snarl came out of Wells' mouth. It sounded more a feral beast than man. Manbun took a step back in response.

Mateo grabbed one of the gold napkins off the table and spread it out before us, nodding at Wells. "Think of the four trials you want to give her and put your hand on the napkin."

Wells smirked in my direction and a twitch of nerves skittered through me. He surveyed me like he was trying to dissect me into the individual atoms.

I'd thought maybe he'd make it easy on me, but the look on his handsome face was clear: he was going to be hard.

Fine. Bring it on.

He laid his hand on the napkin and Mateo placed his circle pendant over it. A flash of Fire magic burst from his fingers and words appeared, burned into the cloth. I'd used Etching magic on trees and in dirt before, but it was never permanent and generally just for fun when I was bored. The scent of burnt threads made this whole thing seem way more real and enduring.

When he moved his hand away, I grabbed the napkin to read what it said.

Heart trial — tunnel a specified distance in a specified time under the specified conditions.

"Well, that's vague. I'll need specifics to do the trial." I glared up at him with as much fierceness as I could muster. I wasn't going to be toyed with. There was too much at stake.

"I'll give details when I'm ready."

"So, I'm just going to go into this blind, then?"

He ran a hand over his jaw, scraping across the stubble that he probably worked really hard to groom into the sexiest look possible. "I'll tell you this now: your heart trial will take place one month from today."

"Month?" There I was thinking I could get this over with immediately.

"Yes. You'll need to practice to hit your goal. A lot."

This man was infuriating in so many ways. From his shiny dark hair all the way down to the manspread, and straight into the cocky way he looked at me, like he was my overlord. He was, in fact, but I didn't have to like it. I challenged him. "A gnome wouldn't need to practice tunneling."

The corner of his mouth kicked up in a sideways grin that seemed like it was borne of brimstone and sadism. "You will."

Mateo slapped a hand on Wells' shoulder and turned to me. "For what it's worth. I hope you survive this, Gnome."

Survive this?

Survive?

"Hold up. What do you mean by survive?"

He sneered, smarmy alpha dominance slid over his features. "I told you it was Binding magic. What did you think would happen if you fail to meet the conditions of the trials and he found you unworthy?"

"I don't know. Maybe I'd go on with my life, secure in the knowledge that I tried my best?" My voice was rising, in pitch and tone, as panic fluttered around my body. I was committed. I wanted it. I had no other options. But death was not something that even entered my mind. "You didn't say I could die from this. I feel like I entered this contract on false pretenses."

I glared at Wells, hoping he would help or explain that I was misinterpreting something. He didn't help one bit. "Didn't you know Binding magic means life or death?"

I didn't answer, but I got the feeling he knew I didn't have a clue what I'd done, given his eyeroll.

Turning back to Mateo, I was hoping for a reprieve or opportunity to back out. He was unfazed by my ignorance. "If you want in the Conclave, this is the way." He took out his phone, checking out the screen. The matter was done for him. It crawled under my skin that he was so callous with my life. "You should get your stuff together so we can leave. We've spent too much time outside the confines of our compound as it is."

And now I was leaving for four months on top of potentially dying? Gram's house would be in bank possession by the time I finished the process.

If I made it out alive.

Wells' arms were crossed over his chest, already judging my worthiness after a matter of seconds from getting the gig. "What have you gotten me into?" I whispered.

He scoffed. "You did this to yourself, Gnome."

After Mateo dropped his 'you could die' bombshell, he gave me fifteen minutes to pack my stuff and excused himself to make a phone call.

Outlook not so good.

I couldn't help it. A cyclone of fear swirled in my gut and my muscles tensed under the excessive weight of my decision. Forget about the ability to plan a months-long wardrobe. I was going to need more than fifteen minutes to accept what I'd done to myself.

The wolves didn't care about my processing. At all. "Come on, Alice. Wonderland's waiting." Curls waved his watch at me. "Get a move on."

I glared at him. We were not starting with that shit. If I had to fight for my right to live, so be it. I wasn't going to be the meek little gnome with these predatory wolves for the next four months. I may be lacking a lot of magical power, but I'd never been meek. I could thank Gram for that, at least. "My name is Terra."

He shrugged. "Okay, Terra. Move your sweet ass."

Huffing, I turned on my heel and brushed past Wells, arms folded over his chest.

He grabbed my arm, whirling me around to face him. His lilac eyes flashed as they settled on me. It wasn't just my overactive imagination either like I thought I'd seen in the mirror. They glowed for real. It was as beautiful as it was scary. "Pack light," he grunted.

I wrenched my arm from his grasp and headed for the kitchen, looking for Tristan. He owed me answers and just maybe he could help me out of this situation, but he was nowhere to be seen. Had he left? Could he leave without my permission? I had no idea.

Mage, I needed to educate myself. That was for damn sure.

Magic for Dummies, anyone?

Wells kicked the swinging door in and scowled. "We'll feed you."

I had to assume Tristan was fine and had the good sense to get out of Dodge. I had no choice but to pack, so I slid past Wells and trounced downstairs, not letting on how deeply rattled I was.

Pack light.

Whatever, Chickendick.

I slammed the door behind me and breathed a real breath for the first time since the wolves showed up. It was cool and dark in my room, a comfort after being in the spotlight under the unnerving eyes of the beta wolf who held my fate in his hands.

It was a lot of pressure.

This is your chance, Terra. No looking back. Aetheria or bust.

Just, stay alive.

After a few deep breaths, I got myself together enough to grab a duffle bag from the closet. Let's see. What does one wear to be judged by an overbearing werewolf? Sneakers and gym shorts or business casual? I opened the door and yelled up to the wolves. "Any tips on what clothes I'll need would be greatly appreciated!"

Silence. No response from any of them.

Assnozzles.

It took a few minutes of creative rolling to stuff some jeans and t-shirts in the bag with some leggings and tanks, sneakers, socks, and my favorite red beanie and I threw in the Magic 8-Ball too. Couldn't hurt to have some 'guidance from the Mage' with me, right? "Magic 8-Ball, am I going to pass these trials?"

Reply hazy, try again.

Didn't think it would help.

I tossed it in the bag and went to my vanity, grabbing hair ties, and a brush, and picking up my vial of soil, throwing it over my neck and tucking it into my sweater so the wolves wouldn't comment on it.

I took a deep grounding breath. The night had not gone the way I'd planned. I was now tied to a werewolf, for Mage's sake, and I could very well die. Tittering nerves aside, I should've been freaking out more than I was.

Instead, an overwhelming calm came over me.

It was right to do this.

Perhaps, I was going down the path Gram had traveled, and I was on my way to Bananas Town. Or maybe I was departmentalizing the fear and shutting it down. I don't know. But I didn't feel nervous. Not with my vial hanging around my neck.

"Thanks Gram. I hope you're not too disappointed in the fairy thing. I think he's still alive. I'll do what it takes to survive and get to Aetheria."

Calmer, my senses returned. I got back to business, going for the underwear drawer, rooting around, looking for comfy undies. It was nearing laundry day, so I had to dig deep for the panties, coming up only with the good stuff I tried to save for special occasions.

"Pack the nude ones. With the lace."

Wells. Taking up the entire doorway, staring at my handfuls of

45

underwear, and smirking like he didn't own underwear too.

Unless he went commando.

I gasped. At the sudden surprise, not the idea of his underwear.

Or lack thereof.

"Mage, you scared the crap out of me."

"The black ones are nice too, but I'm not a fan of the pink polka dots."

Like he had a say in my underwear whatsoever.

I tried to glare at him like he was glaring at me, but I knew there was no way I looked as menacing as he did. Since I couldn't match his brooding heat, I took the pink polka-dot undies and shoved them in my bag with a huff. I threw every other pair I owned in the bag but left the nude and black ones in the drawer.

His expression was unchanged. "We're leaving. Now."

"You gave me fifteen minutes to pack." I glanced at my phone. "I have five minutes left, so take yourself back upstairs while I finish getting what I need."

He huffed, then walked over, picked me up, and threw me over his shoulder like I weighed nothing. "Now means now."

"But—" I grunted at the sudden force of being thrown over his shoulder and barely managed to squeak the word out.

"But, nothing. We're not safe out here."

Wait. Not safe? In my little house smack in the middle of the Eugene geriatric community. That was stupid. Nothing ever happened here. And there were five werewolves in the building. Unsafe didn't compute. "What do you mean, not safe?" He went silent again, then headed for the door with me on his shoulder. "Wait!" I pounded on his back to make him stop.

His back was a solid plane of rock.

Was he part gargoyle? Had to be part gargoyle.

His chest rumbled, sending vibrations through me as the wolflike growl erupted from his mouth. "What?"

Yeah, that was said through gritted teeth for sure.

"I need my phone charger."

He sighed. I assumed he was going to put me down so I could get it.

Wrong.

He swung around in a circle, searching for it himself. Finally, he gave up. "Where is it?"

"On top of the dresser. If you put me down, I'll get it, Douchewipe."

He spun, stomping across the room. All the while, I was stuck on his shoulder, my face inches above his ass. I closed my eyes because I didn't want to see it.

Well, I didn't *have* to see it. Instinct told me that his butt would be just as hot as the rest of him, but I was not going to give in and look. It took a little effort because I was squirming as much as I could to spite him, but he kept one hand around my legs and managed to stuff the charger into my bag. I hoped anyway.

Then he stormed up the stairs, taking two at a time.

While he was carrying me.

Damn.

He was freaking strong.

"Wait, I need to get a few more things."

He ignored my request and dropped me at the top of the stairs. I landed with a thud. "We'll get anything else you need when we get there, but we're leaving. This second." He gave me a look that let me know he was serious. "Unless you want to come to your damn senses and forfeit this whole thing right now. All we have to do is smash the mirror."

There was hope etched on his face. Even though this was his harebrained idea, he wanted me to give up. I wouldn't have even considered forfeiting if dying hadn't been a part of it.

But it was.

I didn't know if I could go through with it. But I also didn't know where I would live if I didn't. There were no true options here. "What would happen if I broke the mirror?"

Wells must've read the indecision on my face. He huffed and spoke to me like I was three years old. "Since you seem to know next to nothing about magic, let me break this down for you. The trials will follow the four tenets of magic, which are…?"

Mage, he was testing me like he was a preschool teacher asking me to recite the alphabet. He was right, damn him. I didn't know a lot about magic, but at least I knew the answer to his question. "Heart, Mind, Body, Soul."

He stopped short of patting me on the head and giving me an apple juice. "Good. We're bound by those tenets, just like we're bound by the four elements of magic. As of now, the Perception magic has nothing to attach to. It's just swirling in the mirror and waiting for you to start your trial period. We break the mirror now, the magic dissipates, you go back to your little gnome life, and we never have to look at each other again." He paused, seeming to love that idea. I was with him on that. I didn't want to look at him, even as beautiful as he was. "Once you step a single gnome pinky toe over the threshold of your home, you're on your way and the magic will take effect. Smashing the mirror after that will mean I get to terminate you."

Get to. He was looking forward to killing me.

I put my hand on my hip. There *had* to be another way out of it. Though I wasn't sure I wanted one. I guess I wanted the option of a failsafe. "Surely Mateo could stop this with his Conduit key?"

"Mateo's too important and busy to concern himself with the nuances of Magic. That's where I come in. I study that shit constantly. And to answer your question, no. The magic is in control and even the key can't change it once it begins." He handed me the mirror and nodded toward the door with his head. "In or out?"

There it was—my jump off a cliff or not moment. Potential death or potential homelessness. Most people wouldn't think twice about it. Having no home was less of a bother than, you know, dying. But I wasn't like most people. I was half-gnome, half-human, alone, still grieving the death of my only family, scared shitless and single-mindedly tied to the one grand thought I'd had in the last two years— get to Aetheria.

Gram would've known how to manage this, but she was gone, and I was on my own with no prospects or help of any kind other than what I could do for myself. I heard her voice in my head when I was five years old, and she told me what I was.

Being a gnome won't change a thing in your life, but being a kind, determined, strong female will.

She would've wanted me safe and happy. And she would've expected me to make that happen for myself. Like she'd done when her husband ditched her with a baby and no source of income to speak of.

It was obvious what I should do. What Gram would've wanted. I'd done so much in service of the Conclave idea; how could I give up now? Not even death via werewolf could stop me. It was possibly, a bone-headed, misguided, and crazy idea, but it was my plan, and it was up to me to change my own life.

Wells examined me with fierceness, hanging on to what I was about to say. He wanted me to back out. I felt his reluctance as if it were a thick blanket pressing down over me.

But I didn't much care what he thought about it.

I tucked the mirror in the side pocket of my duffle bag, pushing past him and setting my pinkie toes and the rest of my body out the door and into the unknown without even glancing back. The second I crossed the threshold, magic hummed around me, inside me, through my bones, and down to my soul.

I'd done it. I was on my way. No going back now. Aetheria or bust.

I felt Wells' presence behind me, watching every step I took until I arrived at the cars where the other betas were gathering with Mateo.

There were two small black SUVs parked on the street. I stood there silently waiting for one of them to tell me which car to get in as they preened like peacocks under the waning moon.

Moonglow makes werewolves more beautiful and more deadly. Double the pleasure, double the fun! —Gram.

I snapped my fingers to get their attention. "Hello, which car?"

Wells nodded toward the back seat of the first car. Manbun called shotgun. Curls punched his arm before getting into the back as Mateo and...Godfrey—nah—went to the car behind us.

As he started toward the driver's side, I grabbed Wells' arm. He snarled and wrenched free. "Hands off."

So touchy.

"You said we were in danger here. I deserve to know why."

The wheels turned in his head, calculating what to tell me as he rubbed his hand along his stubbled jaw. He may have been ninety-seven and a half percent muscle, but he was a thinker too. And he studied magic? There was more to him than met the eye for certain.

"*You're* not in danger if that's what you're worried about." He scowled, then strolled around the car and slid into the driver's seat. I knew he wasn't telling me the whole story, but I had to take his word for it. What choice did I have? I got into the backseat next to Curls and hoped Wells wasn't bullshitting me.

While Wells fiddled with the air controls, I tried to be cool and get my bearings on this road trip. I took a breath to steady myself and prep for being surrounded by werewolves. For four months. "I'm sorry, I don't remember your names."

Manbun in the front went first. Right after he released a big, long sigh because it was just so bothersome to say his one-syllable name. "Ren."

Ren with an R. Not Ben.

Curls angled toward me, throwing his arm around the back of the seat, his curls brushing the tops of his shoulders. "I'm Mason, Mace for friends and orgasm purposes." My jaw dropped and he shrugged. "It's easier to scream a shorter name when you're right on the brink of com—"

"Got it. Mason."

Wells didn't bother to introduce himself again. I don't know if it was because he didn't want me to know his name or if he knew I remembered him already. He looked over his shoulder. "Do all gnomes have bad memories or just you?"

I didn't have anything handy to throw at him, so I flipped him off instead.

Remember that, Jerkface.

He seemed unmoved at my gesture, putting the car in gear, he took off.

I turned around to take one final look at Gram's cottage. I'd grown to love living there, in spite of being forced to do nothing but care for her for eleven years straight. Those should've been my formative adolescent and teen years, filled with friends and parties. Boyfriends.

I managed, but it wasn't typical, that's for sure.

It may have been worth it if she'd left her cottage home to me or made some arrangements to pay for it. I should've asked her before she died, but I was too busy trying to keep her alive. Though, I guess it wouldn't have mattered if she'd left it to me. The gnome half of me would've been incapable of hanging onto it anyway. Magic rules being what they were. I still had no clue how she'd possessed it for so long without repercussions.

As we drove away, I glanced at my neighbor, Mr. Rodriguez's roses. I'd helped him grow them as a tribute to his late wife and they were my babies, in a small way. I made a point to remember to go visit Mr. R if and when I got back from... "Where, exactly, are we going?"

Wells glared at me through the rearview. I picked up a 'you stupid woman' vibe from him. Ren answered me, giving him the first point in the which werewolf is my favorite game. "Wolf compound."

He would've gotten more points if he'd told me where said compound was.

"Which is...?"

"About an eight-hour drive. Hope you went potty before we left Ms. Daisy."

Point to Mason, but a deduction for being a smart ass, so he was still at zero. And thanks to impatient Wells, I didn't get to use the restroom before we left, so it was going to be a long drive.

No sense wasting it. I needed intel if I was going to make it through this and get to Aetheria.

"What's up with the warring species?"

I spotted Wells' cocked eyebrow in the rearview. "There are many Magicals. Some of them fight at times. Just like humans do."

He seemed quite fond of talking down to me.

"No, I get that. Which species and why are they fighting?" I knew from Mateo's reaction to my statement earlier, there was something going on.

Mason checked for Wells' permission before he answered. The sullen beta tilted his head upward ever-so-slightly, but it was enough to get at least part of an answer from Mason. "Djinn are the worst but just about every species has members that would slaughter people for their magic. The fighting isn't species against species—yet—but more like a rogue member or small number against another species."

Shock rippled through me. "Isn't the Conclave supposed to prevent sort of thing?"

Though I couldn't see it, I could feel Ren's eye-roll from the front of the car. "You're uninformed." He left an opening for me to confirm this, but I didn't, so he continued. "Lately, some asshats think it's cool to absorb magic from others, which is why you're not in danger and we're not. You don't have enough. We do."

Okay, that was good. I guessed. Probably not in terms of passing vague magic trials, but I had a month to worry about that. "How does one absorb magic?"

Mason got back into the conversation. "Depends on the species. Vamps suck it out, obviously. Trolls ring a bell in the person's ear to gain their magic. Elves cause an illness and take the person's last breath."

Ren added, turning in his seat to glare at me with intensity. "We'd have to wait for a full moon, but once we broke your skin with teeth or claws, your magic would be ours."

It was like they were spinning a scary story in front of a campfire. What they were saying couldn't be true. "You're shitting me, aren't you? Trying to prank the dumb gnome."

Ren and Mason laughed, and I was even more convinced it was all made up. But one look at the grim set of Wells' jaw and I knew they weren't. "We're headed back now, so don't be concerned. It rarely happens. You'll get a better understanding *if* you make it into the Conclave."

I got a sudden chill. There was so much I didn't know. I'd based all my decisions on a tentative grasp of my own reality and the knowledge from a mentally unstable person. That's a shaky place to be. I needed more information. "Let's say you, in your infinite wisdom, perceive me as worthy and grant gnomes acceptance in the Conclave. What would that get me, exactly? Membership card, secret handshake, fast pass to Aetheria?"

Had to ask. It was my sole purpose.

Ren snorted. "You're going to die."

Negative one hundred points to Ren. I cocked my head, asking him to explain with my expression. Even though I could see in his cold emerald stare that he didn't want to, he took pity on me. "The Conduit to Aetheria is closed. Why do you think people are killing others for magic? Our source has been cut off."

Slapping me in the face would have been less surprising and painful. I'd faced a whole hell of a lot of stuff in the past few hours, but this was the thing that gutted me. "*Closed*, closed?"

Mason chuckled, amused at my stupidity. "Closed, as in not open. Shut. Sealed. Do not pass go, do not collect two hundred dollars."

My world was growing rockier by the second. If I couldn't get to Aetheria, what would I do? I'd had it in my head for so long, I couldn't fathom any other routes in front of me. I was not going to cry in front of the wolves, but my entire body ached with the effort to keep the tears inside.

I rubbed my temples, trying to come to grips.

Maybe it was just a temporary bump in the road. There would be options in the Conclave, right? It existed for the benefit of magical species. Still. My world was titling out of control as the miles flew by out my window. What if everything I'd done so far was for nothing? I truly had no funds left, no options available to me, no hope whatsoever. The Conduit closing changed everything and it changed nothing at the same time. "Why is the conduit to Aetheria closed?"

"The better question is: why would you petition to join the Conclave when you had no idea what you were getting into?" Mason snickered. "Who wants to take bets on how long she lasts before Wells pronounces her unworthy?"

Ren turned. "I'm in for a hundred bucks. She won't last more than three days."

Ouch. Rude.

"I'll take that action." Mason turned sideways, eyeing me up and down. I had the urge to punch him, but I wasn't dumb enough to try. It would've been like a fly tickling him. "She's pretty sturdy. Three-hundred says she'll go a couple of weeks before Wells has to shut her down."

"*Sturdy?*" I screeched. I wasn't thin for sure, but I wasn't the least bit *sturdy* either. My curves had been well-appreciated by many men.

Okay, a couple of men.

And a fairy.

Sort of. If his Name magic advance on me even counted.

Turns out I was right. Punching Mason just made him laugh. "Simmer down, Mike Tyson. It was a compliment. I just meant that you don't look delicate."

There may've been actual flames coming out of my nostrils at that point.

Ren announced, "Wolves don't do weak."

Wells grunted, but at least he didn't weigh in on my sturdiness.

Or take the bet.

He just glared through the rearview with those damn haunting purple eyes. "She'll have a month to get the first trial accomplished before I have to judge her."

His pronouncement effectively changed the subject, which I thought was good. But, when they started talking about how awful it was to not have the option of visiting one of the famous fae brothels in Aetheria, I wasn't sure.

I glanced at my watch. Seven hours more to endure.

Great.

I really had to use the restroom.

JEWELS OF CLAY

If aggressive braking was any indicator of mood, Wells was in a bad one. He swerved into the convenience store outside of Portland like a maniac. I'd tried Name magic on him three times before I'd given up and made the actual request. Ten minutes later, he finally relented. "In and out. No lingering."

I saluted him, with my middle finger protruding. "Yes, sir." His audacity was off the charts. Would he have rather me wet myself in his car? Don't think so. As far as I was concerned, I was taking my potential demise and testosterone-heavy car ride in stride and being a perfectly pleasant person. One tiny request to pee wasn't much to ask for, in my opinion. He could've stopped in Salem, but nope. Kept on driving for another hour.

I held my breath and risked my life going into the nasty bathroom. It was gross, so there was no lingering there, but I'd be damned if I was going to hurry my ass back just because Wells instructed it. Instead, I browsed around, giggling to myself as I glanced out and found Wells standing next to the pump with his arms folded over his chest, watching me as he filled the tank.

Oh. So, he'd stopped for gas, not for my restroom needs. *Assjerk.*

I turned the corner and stared at the candy aisle. It was a crucial decision in my life at that particular moment. I had no control over what was going to happen to me, but damn it, I could pick my sugary snacks. I debated between candy corn and powdered donuts, choosing candy corn because getting powdered sugar on my black shirt in front of the wolves was out of the question. I went to the refrigerated case to grab some water, which would probably make me need to make another pit stop, but I didn't care. Wells was going to have to deal with it.

After I paid, I sauntered back to the cars. Wells grumbled something under his breath, which sounded a lot like 'slowpoke' then climbed back in, slamming his door with extreme aggression. I got a side-eye from Mason and a huff from the manbun, and we were back on the road. The tires squealed as the car careened forward and I immediately regretted not asking if I could switch vehicles and see if Gideon—Gideon! That was it—was as bad as the wolfholes I was dealing with.

The hum of the road—and intense desire to ignore the wolves—soon had me thinking back on everything. It was a slippery slope, for sure, because I started to circle back to the idea that maybe I succumbing to my Gram's disease and going out of my mind. She was a total nutjob at the end. But she had sporadic moments of brilliance that seemed to make perfect sense, like her insistence that getting to Aetheria was the answer to everything. She stated that idea more than any other. Maybe it was her way of taking care of me after she was gone.

Or, she was just insane and didn't know what she was saying at all.

I bolted upright. "Shit."

Mason turned his head. "What?"

"Nothing. I just…left something at home."

Wells glared at me through the rearview. "We're not turning around."

"I didn't expect you to." I threw myself against the seat, disgusted that I'd left one of my most treasured items at home. I stewed in misery for a long time over it. I assumed Wells had gone back to forgetting my existence, but after a few moments, through gritted teeth, he asked, "What did you forget?"

A flush of heat creep over my ears. I didn't want to tell them because I knew they wouldn't get it, so I kept mum. After fifteen minutes of them prodding me to answer, I caved. "Alright. When my grandmother got sick, her mind wasn't all the way there and she'd say ridiculous things all the time. I started writing them down in a journal to remember her when she was gone."

I hated myself in that moment. I couldn't believe I'd forgotten it. Wells had given me zero time to think before he pushed me out the door, so it was all his fault. I would hate him for that, if nothing else, though I suspected there were many other things soon to be added to the list. "I know you'll think it's silly, but it got me through her death. I just can't believe I didn't remember to bring it with me."

I had the 8-Ball, but it wasn't the same as her thoughts, her words and stories.

Mason shrugged, his expression seemed kind, but that could've been me hoping for the best and not reality. "If you make it through your trials, you'll have it when you get home, right? If you fail the trials, you'll be dead, so you'll never know. No worries."

Lots of worries. Many of them. One of which was that all my stuff would be auctioned off by the bank before I returned.

If I returned.

Nothing I could do about it at that point anyway.

Maybe someone would think it was funny and keep it instead of destroying what was left of my Gram.

Don't count on it.

I didn't know how much time passed. Enough for Ren to start snoring and for Mason to butcher five or six songs on the radio with his off-key singing. I'd managed to tune everything out, so it surprised me that I heard him because the low rumble of his voice was the softest whisper in the darkness. "People have done far worse things to cope with loss than keep a journal."

Shocked, I didn't know what to say. I appreciated his admission, but there was nothing I could do about getting the journal back. I just nodded at him and closed my eyes, trying to sleep the craziness of the night off and wonder why after hours of being a dickweed, he'd decided to give me just the teensiest bit of compassion.

I sat up when the car started to slow down. It was morning and the sun was beginning to cast a golden glow over the tops of the trees. It was early October, and the leaves were starting to turn bright orange and red, making the whole experience feel warm and hazy. Autumn was my favorite season, and I could nearly smell the pumpkin spice flavor wafting through the air. Normally this time of year I'd spend every available hour on the back porch curled up in a blanket with a book in my lap and hot chocolate in my mug, but I had a feeling there wouldn't be time for relaxation in my near future.

Once I was fully awake and banished all thoughts of lazy Autumn evenings from my head, it took me a second to get oriented.

Was I riding in a SUV with three hot werewolves?

Yup.

Had I learned that the Conduit that would take me to Aetheria, the answer to everything, was closed?

It appeared so.

Was I going to fail these unnamed trials and be eaten alive by a werewolf?

Concentrate and ask again.

My world had turned upside down, then upside down again, yet I still wasn't upright.

I made a quick check. Wells was glued to the road, hands at ten and two. He didn't even acknowledge me when I said, "Are we there yet?"

His answer was to give me whiplash by making a sudden left into the trees, slamming me into Mason. I scowled at him through the rearview. "Damn wolf, blinker much?"

He smirked in response. How he knew where to turn was beyond me. There were trees, then there weren't. It had to have been magicked. To keep humans away, I'd wager.

The road we turned on was more of a dirt path worn down from years of use and it was carved right into the expanse of trees like a hidden gem. My tension eased. Gnomes preferred dark enclosed spaces and this road was covered by dense foliage and a penetrating smell of rich earth. The path meandered through the woods for several miles before the trees gave way to an open field.

I stifled a gasp because I didn't want the wolves to know how thrilled I was that their compound turned out to be a converted campground with a lodge on the far right where the road ended. A massive open pavilion was on the left. There were several people sitting at tables in the shade while children were playing on the playground behind the pavilion. Beyond that, there were dozens of cabins, probably more that I couldn't see given the amount of people milling around, and other buildings too, all of them backing up to an expanse of woods that enclosed the camp in shadowy calm.

The perimeter fence was lined with colorful banners with different designs, none of which seemed to signify anything in particular. They looked bright and cheery fluttering in the breeze.

We drove in through a covered bridge gateway, though there was no water under it. The second we passed through, a surge of electric energy passed over that I knew had to be a magical barrier of some kind. Crazy that in the past several hours I'd experienced more magic signatures than I had in an entire twenty-two years. It signaled I was out of my depth, but I knew that already.

Wells parked the car to the side of the pavilion. Mason was the first to climb out. He released a sleepy yawn and said to no one, "Honey, I'm home!" Ren unfolded from the car next, retying his man bun. Wells grunted and slid out, making his way to the back and started unloading bags and crates of supplies.

Loudly.

I didn't know how I'd managed to fall asleep on the way, but now that I was fully awake and in a strange location, my nerves prickled. I knew nothing of these wolves or how they operated. It occurred to me that I may have found myself in the same situation that Tristan had. I could become breakfast to these creatures in the next five minutes.

I wondered where he was and if I'd ever see him again.

Mason took my arm. "Come on Dorothy, the yellow brick road is calling your name."

When I failed to move, Ren hooked his arm around my other elbow, pulling me forward, chuckling. "We don't bite."

Mason swiveled, positioned himself in front of me, blocking me from going any further. "Unless you're into that kind of thing."

That did not help. Not one bit. "I'm not."

I mean, I guess it would depend on the situation and partner, but I wasn't going to let him know that. He shrugged it off, but there was a flash of disappointment on his face.

Werewolves.

Wells shot Mason a quick death glare before he spoke to Ren. "You're up for babysitting duty first. Give her the rules and breakfast, but don't leave her alone for a second. I'll take her bag to cabin forty-two. You two can carry your own shit."

Was that chivalry or annoyance? The world may never know.

Mason shot a dazzling smile in my direction. "Welcome to Camp Boulderbrook." He and Wells took off in opposite directions and I was stuck with manbun. After he redid his bun again and huffed a couple of times, he motioned for me to follow him. I took a step, then stopped, slipping off my shoes and digging my toes into the soil.

It allowed the gnome part of me to read the energy of the earth. It had been a while since I was in new territory, and I welcomed the experience of new soil. And Mage knew I needed to ground myself in the worst kind of way after what I'd gotten myself into.

I connected with the richness around me, feeling how large the compound was, how the wolves respected what they had here. It felt...ancient, important, safe. That didn't take away the fear of what would come during the trial period, but it helped to ease my mind, just a bit.

Ren realized I'd stopped and turned. "What are you doing?"

"It's a gnome thing my Gram taught me. I'm connecting with the earth, feeling my surroundings, trying to get a vibe on you werewolves."

"Okay." He raised an eyebrow but didn't stop me. "What vibes are you getting, little Gnome?"

"Undetermined. And my name is Terra."

"Right. Terra. Come, while there's food left."

My stomach told me I'd better follow him, so I slid back into my shoes and ran to catch up.

The cafeteria was a separate building behind the lodge. I followed Ren inside and was hit by the most delicious smell. "Oh my Mage, bring me to the bacon." I was practically salivating.

Long wooden tables and benches sat in the center of the room, with a serving line in the front next to what I assumed were kitchen doors. I went straight in that direction, forcing my wolf bodyguard to keep up with me. He grabbed a tray and handed one to me. "Eat all you want, but when breakfast is done the fae have other duties until lunch."

It was a punch to my gut.

Fae. Serving meals. The irony wasn't lost on me. I wondered if they knew the alpha of this camp was okay with chowing down on their kind.

I lost my appetite. Even for bacon.

I had no idea where Tristan had gone. He could've stayed at my house or gone back to his fairy ring for all I knew. I needed, to speak to him about what he'd done, the things he'd said to help me out of the sticky situation. But it's not like I had his cell number.

That is, if it happened the way I remembered it. I mean, it wouldn't have been a far stretch to envision myself needing to cope with crushing guilt by hallucinating the whole thing. Maybe Mateo had eaten him after all.

I checked out the serving line. If Ren hadn't said so, I would never have known the three servers were fae if not for the small creatures twitting back and forth over the food and to the kitchen. "These fae are under the pack's control?"

He shrugged. "We found a fairy ring when the pack moved in years ago, so we captured a bunch and put them to work. The rest moved on."

Deep indignation coursed through me. I was about to put on my best Hermione G. "So, what you're saying is that you forced them to into slavery."

"Not me personally, no. It was Mateo's thing. But before you bitch me out about it, these fae have it good. Go ask. They'll say they don't mind doing the work because we compensate them well and they get time off whenever they want. It's not much different than working in a garden center, I'd say."

Point taken. A job's a job, I suppose. Still, I couldn't shake the ill feeling swirling inside me. Maybe I would ask them sometime and find out for sure. Though, my unease may have had something to do with how I'd treated Tristan. I shouldn't have left with the wolves without knowing what had happened to him. I owed him that much.

Ren helped himself to a huge heap of scrambled eggs and almost his weight in bacon, then I stepped forward. A pink-haired fairy smiled brightly at me as she explained, "It's self-serve. Unless there's something you'd like that's not on the menu. Just let me know."

Right. Of course. I was holding up the line with my guilt and shame. I hadn't even been able to go through with it—sacrificing Tristan—but that wasn't the point. I was awful and I didn't even get a chance to apologize for it. I picked a few slices of bacon from the buffet and turned to follow Ren.

"Try the pancakes. I think you'll like the special recipe, Babycakes."

Tristan's voice came from behind. I whipped around, dropping my tray with a clang that reverberated across the entire cafeteria.

Great.

Every wolf eye in the room was staring at me, the strange newcomer. There was nobody behind me, least of all, Tristan. Guilt was driving me to see and hear things and was going to screw me up and fail the Perception magic.

It is decidedly so.

"Sorry. Let me get this." I bent to pick up the remains of my precious bacon, and the plate of course, but Ren stopped me. "The fae will pick it up. Get another plate. We need to talk rules."

I swiveled, searching one last time before I grabbed some more bacon and pancakes too.

Shaking my head, I took a deep breath and sat across from Ren. He'd devoured half his eggs before I'd gotten there. He tore his deep emerald eyes from his plate, glaring at me. At least they weren't as unnerving as the purple ones. "Basics first. Don't attempt to leave the camp. Trying to break through the elf protection barrier will kill you. Or worse."

I wasn't sure what could be worse than dying, but okay.

"Second rule: during the day one of us betas will escort you everywhere you go. At night, you keep your ass in your cabin."

"What if I want a midnight snack?"

"Wait until morning. I'm in charge of security here and my guards *will* stop you."

Damn, I love me some nighttime nibbles. Oreos dunked in hot chocolate was my go-to.

"You're saying I'm a prisoner." I took a bite of pancakes. They were creamy, buttery, and covered in syrup just the way I liked. Though I hadn't poured any syrup on them. Fae magic. For sure.

"You're a guest and these rules are for your safety. Deal with it."

"But, what if—"

"Nope. Rules. Number three: you will be on strict motherfucking lockdown during full moons. No exceptions."

So, they *would* eat me.

Movement behind Ren's shoulder caught my eye where a fairy flew in figure eights in front of the window. As soon as I spotted him, he shifted, making himself adult sized. He saluted me and slapped his ass.

Mage Almighty.

Tristan.

So, I didn't imagine him escaping the fate I forced onto him. And I'm not going crazy. Relief flooded through me, and my muscles relaxed. I didn't know how any of it happened, but that wasn't important. He was fine and that took such a load off my back.

But I had questions for the manbun. "If you're in charge of security, what does Wells do? He seems pretty *grr* and bossy. Figured he was the muscle of your pack."

Ren took a bite of eggs before he answered. "Wells does day-to-day for Mateo. Gideon manages the business and finances. Mace is the morale booster of the camp. Playing with pups and making sure everyone is having fun when they're off duty. We have a responsibility to guard the Conduit and it gets intense at times."

My question answered, he went back to his duty, barely missing a beat. "Last rule: if any of the betas tell you to do something, don't ask questions, just do it."

The pack had no choice when it came to compliance, but I wasn't a part of their pack, and I didn't care to be ordered about. "What if I disagree with what I'm told to do?"

"Mother of the Mage, you've already broken the rule. Do it. No. Questions. Asked." He stared me down, a display of wolf domination or testosterone. Probably both. Power coursed from him like it was a tangible thing I could touch. I realized I'd need to do what he said, or he'd likely rip my head off.

I nodded.

Tristan zipped by, throwing his voice into my ear like he'd done at my house, "Meet me in the bathroom hall."

"Those are the rules. Save all your questions for Wells." Ren inhaled his entire glass of orange juice in one gulp. "I'm tapping out." He stood up and did that annoying male head bob thing toward the entryway.

I turned to find Wells there with his usual brooding glare, heat glowering from his purple laser beams all away across the room. This guy was a 'use stares, not elevators' kind of person.

"Wait, Ren. Just a quick question: where's the bathroom?"

6

I turned into the hallway where the bathrooms were located and closed the door behind me just as Tristan popped into his large form. I grabbed a jacket that was hanging from the coat hooks and thrust it at him, covering up his dude space, much to his disappointment. "You're no fun. Are you sure you don't want to take it to the next layer and hit this?" He gestured downward. At least he had the good sense not to try Name magic again.

I scowled at him. "How? Why are you here? Also, it's 'take it to the next *level.*'"

"No hi, how are you, I missed you?"

Hissing, I slapped his arm. "Tristan!"

"Fine. You captured me, so where you go, I go. Took me a minute to catch up with you, but those are the magical rules, forever and always, Babycakes. We go together like peanut butter and Jell-O."

Mage, he needed human sayings lessons. Especially if he was going to be with me forever. Liam the leprechaun did not mention that little detail at all. "No Dumbass, Mateo ate you. But you spoke in my head? What the infinite chasm happened? Talk."

He shrugged. "Oh that? I'm not an idiot. I figured out what you were doing as soon as you said his name and I saw what lengths you'd go to. I used ancient fae magic to make a golem. It wasn't me; it was a spelled figure made from flour. I really captured my essence, don't you think?"

He said that like it was an everyday thing that happened all the time. It didn't. And it was impossible as far as I knew, per Gram's *'thanks to the Conclave, fae in our world possess about as much magic as their tiny pricks have spunk.'* Gram loved a good penis reference. And didn't care for fae. Enough to tell me that the Mage was especially disappointed in his first creations and punished them far more than other species. "Fae don't have enough magic to do what you did."

"You're right. We're not part of the Conclave. A small number of us can amplify Ambient magic. Consider me special."

I was lucky to capture a powerful fairy. Not that it did me much good. "We're right here in the midst of the Conclave leader's den. If he found out, you'd be stripped of your magical soul. Shaded and left out of Netheria." I shuddered. No one deserved that fate, no matter how annoying.

Gram used to say *be afraid of the shade.*

"Like you care about me." He folded his arms over his chest—like someone else I knew—dropping the jacket in the process. Naked again. "Babycakes, you tried to murder me."

It hurt because it was true.

"I know and I'm sorry. I just—"

The door behind us squeaked and Tristan re-fairied himself, thank the Mage, because Wells was standing there looking less than amused for having to come find me. The look of derision was grand. "Who are you talking to?"

Crap.

"Myself."

He cocked an eyebrow, and I pushed past him, forcing him to catch up with me. Which took a total of one second thanks to his long legs.

"Did Ren give you the rules?"

"You're the big dog, so he had to obey when you gave that command, right?"

I marched out of the cafeteria door, having no clue where I was going other than it was away from Wells. His presence rattled me. I knew I needed to get over that since he was going to judge me. But at the time, I was at my wit's end because my plans to get to Aetheria had been blown to bits and I was facing some unknown trials just to stay alive.

I could go for a Magedamned nap right now.

Wells grabbed my elbow, whirling me around to face him. "Listen Gnome, until you end up a member of the Conclave or in a body bag, you're pack. And when Mateo isn't around, pack follows me. Don't forget that."

I doubted any of them would ever think of me as part of their pack. But hey, at least his eyes didn't glow that time. He let go of my arm and paced forward with long strides. "Keep up."

I had the significant urge to ask where we were heading, but I didn't want to give him the satisfaction of lording information over me. Instead, I kept my mouth shut and followed him.

Before we hit the playground, we veered right, moving deeper into the camp. Dense foliage hung from a large expanse of trees, making the ground below cool and shaded. I could get used to being there, lost in my thoughts and enjoying the atmosphere that made the Earth magic in me sing. I almost forgot I was following an insufferable jerk on my way to some mysterious trial period that could lead to my death.

We came to a fork in the path. Wells gestured to the right. "Cabins and lake, that way, lodge, offices, and medical, this way."

Worst tour guide ever.

He led me to the right, and we snaked our way past a couple buildings until we came to one of the only brick structures I'd seen on the grounds. It was two-story and strands of ivy covered the entire surface of the brown brick building, causing it to blend into the environment.

Wells pulled the door open and motioned for me to enter. As soon as I stepped, the strong scent of antiseptic and incense assaulted me.

A petite woman in scrubs sat at a desk a few feet inside the building. Though she could pass for human, I knew in an instant that she was an elf—luminous skin, bronze hair hanging to her waist in an unnatural silky ribbon. She had a sprinkling of freckles across her face and her big dark doe-eyes blinked as we approached. Everything about her signaled 'deer.'

Elves mate like the animal they favor. If you ever see one resembling a praying mantis, don't let them seduce you. They will bite your head off afterward.

As soon as she spotted us—correction, as soon as she saw Wells—she jumped up from her chair. "Wells!" She raced around the desk. "You're not hurt, are you?"

He chuckled and leaned on the desk with one hand. Mage, did he just flex his pecs? He did. He actually did. "When have I ever been hurt, Bambi?"

For the love of the Mage, she looked like a deer and her name was Bambi.

She dissolved into giggles as she twirled the ends of her hair in her fingers. I would almost kill for hair like that. My long brown waves were hard to control and, well, boring compared to her glistening locks. She leaned forward over her desk, her loose-fitting top fell, giving Wells an eyeful. An intended act if ever I saw one. "Never. Does that mean you've come to visit me?"

My head.

I would never be able to get this scene out of my head.

"No, it's business today. Bringing…her to Arlo. Is he in?"

Had he forgotten my name?

Dickweed.

Bambi stood and walked over to the door that was about, oh, four feet away. She swished that ass all the way over. Just for Wells. And you can bet he looked too.

She knocked on the door. "Arlo, Wells is here."

A voice from the other side replied, "Send him in."

Wells strutted to the door and Bambi made sure to touch him on the chest as he walked by. Midway through the door, he stopped and turned. "Are you coming, Gnome?"

I smirked. "Oh, my bad. I assumed I needed to wait over here while you banged the nurse."

He growled and I felt it in my bones.

Bambi giggled again, just to let Wells know she was down with my idea if he was. He might have done it too if I hadn't been the one who suggested it.

I sailed past him, whistling on my way into the room.

It looked like a standard doctor's office room, but instead of gauze and tongue depressors on the counter, there were potions, stones and various other magic-looking tools. But the most magical looking thing in the room had to be Arlo himself.

An elf, like Bambi the horny nurse, he was striking. His shoulder-length hair reminded me of a silver lion's mane, wild and wavy, with a black streak framing his face. His eyes had the same black streak, giving them a cat-like appearance. It was difficult to tell how old he was because elves had the best genetics when it came to being ancient, but he gave off a strong vibe that he'd been there and done a lot of that.

"Hello." He didn't look at me, he addressed Wells. "What have we here?"

Wells grunted and slung a thumb in my direction. "This one has decided it was a good idea to petition the Conclave for membership and I'm in a Perception magic contract with her, if you can believe that shit. Mateo wants you to give her a medical. And a stone."

He instructed me to sit down by glaring and tipping his head at the chair. I did it. Because of the 'you must obey my every command' thing. "If there's so much as one chestnut hair on her head that's off, I need to know." This time, it was Wells who was glaring at me and talking to Arlo.

"Does she understand the inherent dangers of what she's attempting?"

"I doubt she does, but here we are anyway."

I cleared my throat. "She *is* in the same room with you and can speak for herself. Yes, I understand if Wells perceives me unworthy, I'm toast."

Arlo laughed. "I apologize. This is a rare occurrence." He looked up at Wells. "I understand what you need. Give me a few minutes."

Wells shot me a warning with his laser beam stare. "Stay in this room until I come back." He left without another word.

Probably to go hook up with Bambi in a supply closet.

Arlo's shoulders relaxed the second Wells left the room. I couldn't figure out why an elf, for Mage's sake, was deferring to a wolf, even a beta. Elves were the most powerful beings in the Conclave on this side if you believed my Gram's *elf magic is like taking permanent Viagra—hard and ready to go at all times.* He could've eviscerated Wells, or any of the wolves if he'd wanted to. Instead, he bowed to him.

Arlo patted my knee in a grandfatherly way. "You must be special for Mateo to allow this. I didn't even realize he knew about Perception Magic."

"It was Wells who suggested it. I'm starting to wonder if I made the wrong decision." Saying it aloud made it more real. My brain had been pulled in so many different directions since starting this thing and it was distracting me from the real issue. Truth was, I was scared shitless about my trials. It seemed like I'd lived an entire lifetime in the past twelve hours. Out of my depth didn't even come close to capturing my feelings.

"Now that doesn't surprise me. Wells is a virtual encyclopedia of ancient magic." The affection he had for Wells shone on his face. "Don't worry. You're in good hands with him. He's a fine man."

I wanted to believe that was true, but I'd have to decide that for myself. Wells was part of a pack, and I was on the outside of it. That alone was enough for distrust to flourish in my mind. I couldn't imagine why he'd suggested the Perception contract and the more I rolled it around in my head, the more I suspected he had ulterior motives.

I wasn't very trusting. I'd never had the occasion to trust anyone other than Gram and when she went looney, I only had myself, so I wasn't going to just take Arlo's word on Wells' character.

Arlo turned and I wasn't expecting him to whip back around with a needle in his hand. "Roll up your sleeve, please."

Not until I get some of my billion questions answered first, thank you very much.

"What are you going to do with that needle?" The first question was the most obvious, but important, nonetheless.

His warm smile put me at ease. Not sure if that was elf magic or not, but in spite of his obvious deflection to Wells, he seemed to be a decent guy. So far. "I'm going to take some routine blood samples. Make sure you're healthy and who you say you are."

None of that seemed too heinous, so I rolled up my sleeve. Who was I supposed to be impersonating anyway? Mage knew if I were faking it, I would've selected a more powerful being than a gnome.

After he'd drawn three vials of my blood, he opened a drawer and fished a small gray rock from a jar. "Hold this in the palm of your hand until I ask for it again. Don't open your fist or drop the stone."

I closed my hand over the rock and as soon as I did, it began to vibrate. Not a lot, but enough for me to know it wasn't an ordinary rock I was holding. It seemed like my trial process had already begun even though Wells was nowhere near to perceive or judge anything about me.

Arlo pulled a glass jar containing a thick black substance that resembled tar from the cabinet and began shaking it. "If I may ask, what made you want to petition the Conclave? Most magical beings walking about in the human world couldn't care less about such things."

I wasn't sure I wanted to spill all my secrets to a stranger, but I couldn't ignore his question either. I decided to keep it simple. "My Gram gave me the idea. I think it was her way of trying to care for me after she died."

"I see." He shook his head like this was a sane event I was undertaking. After a moment, he continued. "I've known a few gnomes this side of Aetheria. They're all good people, so if you'll allow it, I'll give you some advice on their behalf: Perception magic can mess with your head and cause you to make unwise decisions. Don't miss the forest for the trees."

Say what now?

I nodded like he'd given me sage advice, not something scrawled at the bottom of a poster in a rando office. I wanted to ask him to explain himself, but he'd turned around and busied himself by pouring a vial of my blood into a small glass beaker. Next, he took the inky thick liquid and poured it into my blood. Just as it was about to reach the blood in the beaker, it turned to smoke and drifted upward.

I watched in awe as Arlo blew his breath in intricate patterns across the black mist and read its movements. He turned to me, bright with curiosity. "You're not a full blood gnome, are you?"

Embarrassment chilled my veins. I don't know why because it wasn't like I had a choice in my birth. That half-blood thing was always causing a problem. "No, I'm not. Will that be an issue?"

"I don't know." With a perplexed look on his pretty face, he licked the mist. Licked it. "What species are you, besides gnome, I mean?"

Before I could answer, Wells burst into the door without knocking.

Ignoring me, he addressed Arlo. "Well?"

"Your friend was just telling me what species she is, other than gnome, of course."

"My name is Terra, by the way. My mother was human." I gestured between Wells and myself. "And we aren't friends."

Succinct, to the point. And, oh so true.

Arlo shrugged, then he took a deep breath, drawing the black mist still hanging in the air above my blood into his nostrils. A moment later, the blood in the beaker went through about seven different colors before it turned clear. He mumbled to himself, "Interesting. I've never seen this before." He looked me in the eye, amusement settling on his face. "No, you're not human."

My entire life unraveled in a matter of seconds. "There must be a mistake. My mother was human."

Wells leaned against the wall and folded his arms across his chest. "What evidence do you have to support that claim?"

It wasn't like I was walking around with a human species membership card in my pocket. I had no way of proving it. I just knew. "My Gram told me. She was insistent that my mother was a human whore who went for my father when she happened to catch him making gold. In fact, she said if you looked up gold digger in the dictionary, you'd find my mother."

Wells huffed. "Arlo's never wrong. Your Granny must've lied."

She told me a bunch of nonsense about other magical creatures as she got older and sicker, but there's no way she would lie about my lineage. She adored her son, my father. It made no sense to deceive me. "Why would she lie?"

"No idea. But none of that matters now." He turned to Arlo. "We need to know what else is in her blood."

Arlo shook his head. "Understood. I'll let you know when I have the answer."

Not let *me* know. Let Wells know. I stood up to make my point. It was my blood. *I* needed to be informed, but Wells cut me off. He gestured to the door with his head.

Why did he do that all the time? Gesture with his head instead of speaking? He did that almost as much as he folded his arms across his sculpted chest. In fact, he did them so much I decided to consider them Gesture One and Gesture Two.

Since he'd Gesture Two'd us, Arlo and I followed him down the hall and out the back door into a clearing. Walking outside was like stepping into another world. The earth under my feet was different than what I'd felt from the rest of the camp—darker, denser, richer. Even with my shoes on, my magic tingled inside me as I stepped forward.

Earth magic.

Most of the trees in the camp were typical Pacific Northwestern varieties, but the trees lining the clearing were dead, charred. I couldn't even begin to identify the species. Gram would've been disappointed.

Two massive trees sat at the back of the clearing. They each had a main branch and a secondary one that grew toward the other, twisting and twining around to create a circular archway underneath. Broken and burned buds dotted the surface where blooms or branches once grew.

Beside the arch sat a huge boulder with water trickling from it. It flowed in two directions, making a circuit around the clearing, forming a trickling stream that connected to the same place it fell from. Humans would say it was an optical illusion, but I felt the magic surrounding it. It was no illusion. There was water coming from a stone. The name Boulderbrook clicked into place.

Water magic.

I got the feeling of reverence, from both Arlo and Wells. This place

80

was sacred to them.

"I agreed to come here and serve the werewolf pack because of this." Arlo bowed, this time deeper and slower. Wells tilted his head. Probably as close to a bow as he would ever get. Cocky sucker.

Arlo motioned me to follow him and as we walked toward the arch, a warm breeze caressed my face, though it didn't ruffle any of the surrounding trees and I felt a whisper deep inside my soul, like the wind itself was speaking to me.

Wind magic.

I reached down to sift the earth between my fingers, aching to feel the magic bound inside it, but Wells pulled me back, shaking his head. "Nope."

He led me beside the boulder where a small glass bowl hovered—yes, hovered with no visible means of support—on top of a fire. I bent forward to check it out and realized the fire gave off no heat.

Fire magic.

Up close. the bowl appeared to be carved from a crystalized rock like quartz, though it wasn't. How something could be more clear than clear, I had no idea. but it was. Hundreds of small colored stones lay inside the bowl. I reached out to pick one up, but Wells caught my arm and snorted. "Why do you feel the need to touch everything?"

As far as I was concerned, why bring me to the shiny stuff if I couldn't touch it?

Arlo stepped forward. "These portent stones represent every magical who's gone through the Conduit to Aetheria here at Boulderbrook. Consider them like payment, an exchange, something personal in return for safety in passage." He sighed. "That is, when it was possible to go through at all."

A nervous sense of foreboding overtook me, threatening to bring me all the way down. I had no idea where the feeling came from, but I wanted to tunnel out of the place and never look back. But Wells stepped behind me, holding me in place. He didn't touch me, but the heat of his body was so present, it felt like a caress. I addressed him without turning around. "This is the Conduit to Aetheria?" I knew it was, but I had to get the confirmation that all my wishes and dreams had turned to ash.

"Yes. All you had to do is throw a stone and walk under the archway created by the trees. Before anyway." Without warning, he reached down and pried the stone Arlo had given me from my hand.

Way to go me. I hadn't dropped it.

I grabbed Wells' arm, taking a good look at the stone for myself. It was no longer gray, but clear. It looked as if it were made of glass. Just like the bowl.

Freaky. I didn't feel anything happen when I held it. But looking at the bowl, it struck me that every other stone was a color of some kind. There were no clear stones. I glanced up. Wells was staring at the rock too, confusion written in his features. "Is there something wrong with my stone?" My voice was a bit shakier than I wanted it to be. Being there next to a strange magic arch made out of crispy, impossible trees was making me jumpy.

Arlo came over, taking in the clear appearance. "Just like your blood, your stone's interesting."

Of course. "What does that mean?"

He checked in with Wells before he answered, the two of them sharing a knowing look. "Time will tell."

Before I could throw a hissy and make them tell me, Wells took my 'interesting' stone and tossed it in the bowl. Like he was entering me in the Magedamned Triwizard Tournament.

"Why did you do that? You said the Conduit's closed."

Wells huffed. "It is. Casting your stone is more of a ritual now, a commitment to the pack who guards the Conduit. Which means us."

Commitment? "I haven't agreed to anything like that, Bud." Though I guessed I'd done just that when I entered into the Perception Magic contract with him. It seemed bigger somehow, to have my stone thrown in with the others and it mean I was officially in with the Boulderbook pack. Though it was in name only.

Without warning, the fire underneath the bowl surged, a giant flame roaring from beneath it, engulfing the bowl until we could no longer see it. Wells grabbed my waist, spinning me out of the way of the flames. He wasn't expecting that to happen. Neither was Arlo given the look of shock on his lion face.

Before I could ask for explanations, everything around us went sideways. Wind kicked up, twirling and mixing with the raging flame, creating a fire tornado that whirled around the perimeter of the Conduit trees. At the same time, the quiet trickling brook surged into a thundering waterfall, rushing over the boulder with fury and spilling over our feet.

Both Wells and Arlo wore confused looks, which I'm certain matched mine. "What's happening?"

Of course, they kept mum.

Until the ground started rumbling.

Wells snarled. "What have you done, little Gnome?"

Done? Me? I poked his rock-hard chest, punctuating my answer with my finger. "Not. A. Damn. Thing. Big. Bad. Wolf."

One corner of his mouth twitched. He was amused by my fury.

Donkeydick.

Arlo whistled, grabbing our attention. A hole had opened in the earth beneath the large stone. The boulder of Boulderbrook fame was now about half-buried in deep rich soil.

Had the tiny stone I'd held in my hand done that?

No way.

The brook bellowed, rising angrily with no sign of stopping. Magic surged through the water. Weird considering how an Earth elemental like me shouldn't have been able to detect Water magic at all. But this was the Conduit, so who knew what kind of crazy magic was there? Before I could make sense of it all, a huge swirl of wind blasted me in the face.

Wells stood firm, the beast that he was. It was like the magical elements being contained in the space were fighting for attention, each of them showing off what they could do. It was scary. And impressive at the same time.

On a whim, I had an idea. I shucked my shoes and stepped onto the freshly upturned soil near the boulder, trying to get a feel of the land that had just upturned and swallowed half a freaking monolith. It should've been easy for me to feel if something was wrong.

A shock of energy shot through my body like a bolt of lightning on steroids.

It was timeworn and deep, wrapping around my insides until I was drowning in it. I gasped, buckling under the weight of the energy. This didn't feel like any earth I'd ever known. All of my nerve endings caught on fire. There was no other way to describe it. I was being flooded by earth and burned from the inside out.

The water was still lapped around me too. I felt the rush in my ears.

I screamed, wracked in pain and shivering. Wells growled; the deep guttural sound bore into my soul on a primal level.

What the hell was happening?

Sharp crackles drew my attention upward. The flames had changed, morphing into blues and purples as they descended like a firefall, crashing into the soil and dissipating into smoke when they touched water.

I sensed movement behind me, but I was rooted to the spot and unable to move any portion of my body. A bright blur passed in front of me. I tried to reach out to it, to hold onto something, but it was gone in between heartbeats.

Sudden nausea overtook me, and my bare feet lost contact with the ground. Exhausted and buzzing, I felt myself being dragged away from the Conduit, sudden relief flooding in, setting me even more off-kilter.

I drifted in and out of consciousness, though I tried to hold on, to control what was happening to me. I don't think I managed to stay awake.

Snapping fingers woke me from my stupor.

Wells' stoic face was right in front of me, his eyes, glowing amethyst swirls. There was soft concern in them, but just for a second. The moment he realized I was conscious, he pulled away and went stone-faced. "Shit, Gnome."

I sat upright.

"There is no way you are going to pin this on me. All I did was hold a damn rock!"

Fear and fury are not a good combination.

I scrambled up, tried to get my bearings.

We were several yards away from the Conduit stone formation. It looked as it had right before I went heels up, but Arlo was standing there with a panicked look on his lion face, holding out his long arms and whistling. Wind magic. He turned to Wells. "The Ambient magic has been disrupted to a magnitude I've never seen before. Mateo will have to report this to the rest of the Five." The ruling body of the Conclave. I had trouble dealing with one of them, I shuddered to think how difficult five of them would be.

I looked over at Wells to get his response. Because that sucker knew what was happening. My jaw dropped.

He was wearing a towel wrapped low around his waist.

Nothing else.

Not even a shoe or sock.

He must have shifted into his wolf form.

First Tristan, now him. Why was I suddenly surrounded by men who'd ripped their clothes off all the time?

Not that I minded… Wait, yes. I minded.

My entire body short-circuited, and I flushed with heat as I took in his sculpted pecs and glistening abs that led to the sexy v-dip in his hips. I had to stuff my hands in my pockets to keep from reaching out and tracing that little line of dark hair running from his navel down to—

Stop it, Terra. Hormonus, controllus.

He straight-up had the most perfect body I'd ever seen.

Until he smirked.

He enjoyed watching me take in the surprise of him. It made me fume hotter in a different direction. So, yeah, he had a KILLER bod—all caps—but he was a cocky son of a bitch, and that canceled all the perfection.

I decided at once, I was not going to allow myself to be affected by his utter beauty. I couldn't. He was my overlord and judge.

Focus. You almost bit the freaking dust here, girl.

"Tell me what just happened." I took great care to make sure to phrase it as a statement and not a question because I had to know, and Wells was unlikely to answer any questions coming from my mouth. I knew things like this didn't happen every day, not even in super special magical places. I was certain of that.

Wells ran his hand over his stubble, trying to calculate what to tell me, which I knew would be a big fat nothing. "I'm starting to freak out here. Please, Wells." It was an admission I didn't want to make, but I hoped the Name magic I inflected would work to get some answers out of the beta.

His stern look didn't help with the freakout situation at all. He responded, half-exasperated and half-intrigued. "I don't know, but it'll be my job to figure it out." He paused. "Do you think you can manage these trials, Gnome, because from what I've seen, you're going to—"

A piercing howl shot through the air and interrupted him. Then, a second and a third. It was low and mournful, and it made me want to bury myself in the earth. Just not there at the Conduit. "What is that?" I whispered.

Because I wasn't sure I wanted to know.

Wells grabbed my wrist, pulling me along with him as he started jogging back to the area around the gate. "Warning signal."

8

W"arning for what?"

He didn't answer me, so I ground to a halt, forcing him to turn back and look at me. I was checking for signs he was about to shift again, to see if he was worried, something. I got nothing but stone-faced annoyance from the wolf before he went back to dragging me across the campground.

When we arrived at the gate, there were already several wolves gathered. Gideon jogged through the bridge and grabbed Wells' shoulder. "I was on lookout. It's the djinn."

"Not again." Wells growled, the animal in him rising to the surface. "I hate those fuckers."

Mateo ran from the lodge with wolf speed, even in his human form. He clutched Wells' arm in what looked like a death grip, then he bared his elongated canines at his beta. "I need one. Alive." The two of them had a stare-down that made me shiver. There were a lot of words and emotions passed between them that didn't come from their mouths.

Why would a person—a werewolf—*need* a djinn? Alive?

Aw shit. Could it be this easy? "Do genies really grant wishes? Because I could use one myself. It would change this whole deal right now."

Wells glared me into silence with his cold lilac gaze, then waited for Mateo to walk over to Ren and Mason before he swore under his breath. "Fuck. I don't have time for this nonsense." I must've had questions all over my face, but he ignored me, whistling and circling with his hand like a lasso. A sure signal of some kind.

I put my hands on my hips. Everything was spinning out of control. This was just as bad, if not worse than the Conduit area blowing up moments ago. I was halfway to tunneling out of the compound and never looking back. Perception magic be damned.

Answers. I needed them. "What nonsense?"

He turned his head toward me. I swear, he'd forgotten I was standing there. His eyes flared white before he opened the door to the nearest car that sat about five feet away. "Get in. Lock the door. Don't open it for anyone but me or the other betas. Capiche?" He helped me in the car by shoving me into the front seat. I didn't even have time to answer him.

I did not capiche. Not at all. But he waited until I locked the door then ran to the gate.

I glanced around the camp. The kids were being ushered into the lodge by adults. The number of wolves had multiplied, and they began to take up position along the fence. A sudden and violent wind blew the banners, ripping some of them from the fence. It was so forceful that the SUV I was sitting in rocked hard enough I thought it would tumble over any second.

Outside, the wolves stood at chilling attention. The whole scene was very unnatural. A few seconds later, some of the wolves began stripping. It took me longer than it should've to realize they were preparing to shift.

The closest one, a woman, pulled her shirt off but didn't bother with anything else. I gawked as she dropped to the ground and hair rippled over her body as she morphed, tearing her bra and the rest of her clothes into pieces.

After the hair, her body contorted into weird shapes and positions. It didn't appear to hurt, but how could I know? She craned her neck backward as her snout formed, ears poked up. Her tail was the last thing to change, erupting from her backside like one of those blow toys kids used to get at birthday parties. She finished off with a good shake.

The whole process took maybe fifteen or twenty seconds, but when she finished, she was a sleek tawny-colored wolf. She howled and the other wolves joined her in a haunting chorus that sent a chill deep into my bones.

Of course, I'd never seen a werewolf go through a shift before. I expected to be grossed out, but instead, I was fascinated with how smoothly it happened. I was so mesmerized by watching her change that I hadn't even looked for the betas until that moment. Ren, Gideon, and Mateo were still in human form, along with several others, but Wells and Mason had wolfed apparently. I scanned the bodies of the pack, wondering which one was which, but that became fruitless fast.

Just beyond the fence, a faint outline of a body descended from the trees. It was nothing more than a shimmer in the beginning, but as the wind carried him, her—I couldn't tell—the being became more corporeal. Literally. Bones manifested, riding on the wind like a skeleton surfer. In any other circumstance, it might have been funny, but I wasn't laughing.

Neither were the wolves.

Aberrant stillness settled over the camp as the figure descended from the trees. Muscle and tissues knitted into place over the skeleton, forming as it rode the wind. The skin was last, stretching over the body and covering it with a dusky bronze exterior that shimmered red when it moved.

By the time he finished, the djinn, male from the best I could tell, stepped onto the ground like he'd been walking and not…flying and forming into existence.

What had I gotten myself into? I wasn't prepared to go from the kiddie pool to the ocean in a day.

He jerked a banner from the fence and draped it around his waist like a guy would do to cover his privates. Only this djinn didn't have them. There was nothing in *that* area to cover up.

Suddenly, Gram's voice echoed in my ear. *Djinn. The "D" is silent for a reason, my jewel: they don't have one.*

The djinn just stood there.

Like he expected someone to thank him for his modesty.

He swiveled in my direction. Goosebumps spread over my arms as I locked onto his face, gasping at the realization he had no eyes at all. Two red glowing orbs of nothingness stared back at me.

I ducked down in the car, fear flooding my stomach with bile. Had to be a coincidence that he managed to look right at me—with no eyes—when there were all those wolves running around.

I peeked through the window. thank the Mage and all the stars in Aetheria, the djinn had zeroed in on Mateo as he started vibrating, for lack of a better word. He released a low-pitched rumble that grew louder and higher the longer it went. I put my hands over my ears and the wolves in the compound howled and winced in misery.

You cannot hide from werewolf ears. They'll catch your gasps, your heartbeat, the sound of your feminine lubrication rushing forth.

The djinn's sound stopped, and my mouth dried in horror as he split apart in the middle, like the mitosis Mr. Thornton had taught us about in tenth-grade biology class. There had been one djinn and between two heartbeats, there were two. Then four. Eight. By the time he was done, I couldn't count the number of identical djinn standing still and at attention right outside the gate. Each of them had materialized the same banner around their waist as the OG version.

What in the Eternal Flame?

This was the last thing I expected when I strolled—no, when I was dragged—into this camp. I couldn't comprehend how much my Gram had sheltered me from the magical world. It may have been for my protection at first, then because she'd lost her wits, but this is the kind of thing Magicals should be taught in Magic 101.

There should totally be Magic 101 classes. Maybe I could start one if I passed the trials.

Mateo started barking orders at the wolves. I couldn't hear what he said inside the car, but whatever it was, it made Ren shake his head in disgust behind him. A woman ran up to Ren holding long stick-like things and he passed them out to those not in wolf form. He and three others gathered at the gate.

Several wolves, a stunning white one, a gray one with a dark muzzle, and two rust-colored ones joined them while Mateo pulled out his gold Conduit key and directed it at the fence.

He was letting the magic barrier down for the wolves to get outside.

Why put up a barrier if you're going to take it down when an army of djinn clones with unspecified intentions comes knocking at your gate?

Werewolves.

The djinn moved in concert, each of them emitting a whistle. The wind around the compound picked up to twister level in seconds.

It took no time for objects, people, wolves to start blowing around like they weighed nothing. The car Wells had shoved me into for safety scooted, metal groaning against the force of the wind. I grabbed the 'oh shit' handle. Like it would do me any good if the car lifted and flew to Oz.

Ren and the other unshifted wolves retaliated by raising their sticks and shooting streams of concentrated fire at the djinn. I would've found it cool to see actual Fire magic in action if I hadn't been huddling in the car and praying for my life.

Thin shiny sticks materialized in the hands of each of the djinn. I thought they were made of metal, like silver or platinum, but the djinn raised their sticks in the air and jerked them back in one smooth motion. The sticks turned into whips that popped as they snapped them, air cracking with magic. Wind gusted from each whip, zeroing in on the wolves in shifted and unshifted form. Some of them made direct contact, throwing the people who were hit to the ground and causing them to gasp for air.

I was seized in terror as the wolves and djinn shot magic at each other, volleying fireballs and whipping wind competing for dominance. When Ren's fire hit one of the djinn replicas in the back of the group straight in the chest, it slowed the force of the wind, but not by nearly enough in my humble opinion. They'd have to hit a lot more of them to be effective against the djinn onslaught.

The shifted wolves bolted to the left where the djinn who'd been hit had paused, leaning over to suck in a breath. So, they were offshoots of the first djinn, but individual too. Hitting one djinn was not hitting all.

They launched at the isolated djinn, taking him down easily given the four-on-one matchup. The wolves latched onto his arms and legs. I braced myself to be disgusted, expecting one of them to go for his throat. That's what wolves did, right? Tear out the throats of their enemies?

The gray wolf shifted. It was Mason and I was thankful I wasn't close enough to see much of his now naked bod, other than a, well, nice butt. He grabbed the djinn around the neck and hauled him up over his shoulder so he could run instead of dragging him.

As they approached the gate, I turned my attention back to Mateo. He used the Conduit key to lower and raise the magic barrier and let the wolves back inside. In the split seconds between, a concentrated bolt of wind magic shot from one of the djinn whips right over the fence and straight toward Mateo. The white wolf shot forward, soaring over the fence and bounding toward the alpha, taking a direct hit, and knocking Mateo to safety.

"Wells!" I shouted though I didn't know how I knew it was him. I just did. Panic clawed at my throat. I didn't like the guy, but I didn't want him to die. Besides, what would his death mean for our Perception contract? We were bound together now, so his dying could mean I would go too.

Wind magic didn't possess the intensity of Fire or danger of drowning like Water, but it was lethal in a more gruesome way, according to my Gram. Wind magic would burrow into the point of contact on your body and take your breath from the inside. Being hit with even a small amount of Wind magic could rob the body of oxygen until it no longer had anything to make the lungs function. If that's what the Wind elemental wanted.

An awful and painful way to get to Netheria.

Wells yelped and rolled, his white fur covered in dust and debris. When he turned, there was no way of escaping the gaping hole the Wind magic had left in his back. He'd just saved Mateo's life. It was beyond me how he'd moved that fast or even why he'd risk his own life to save even his alpha. I knew something about how packs worked thanks to Gram. *No one is more loyal than a werewolf. Get yourself one of those and you'll have a friend for life.* To see it in action was breathtaking.

Wells sat up on his back legs and shook his head. He looked at Mateo and when he was satisfied that the alpha was okay, he bounded over to where Mason had carried the captured djinn out of sight behind the lodge.

How could he even breathe after the Wind tore a hole in his hide?

I opened the car door and stepped out. I intended to go after Wells, but I found myself inching toward Mateo and the original djinn who'd replicated himself at the start of this bizarre standoff. They were having a conversation over the fence like neighbors. I wished more than anything to know what they were saying.

I was drawn to them with unnatural force. I tried to stop myself, but I couldn't. My feet just kept on moving. The closer I drew to them, the weaker I became. It was like something was draining me. Of energy. Of my magic.

Mateo shot the djinn an irritated look. "Get off our land or we're going to have an actual fight on our hands."

Like what happened hadn't been an *'actual'* fight? I shuddered to think what that would be like. I doubted any of them, werewolf or djinn, would survive.

"Didn't you feel, it? The disruption. The tremor of magic zipping around the globe?" the djinn whispered. "We tracked the source. Imagine our surprise when it ended at Camp Boulderbrook." The djinn shifted his head, looking behind the lodge in the direction of the Conduit.

The djinn had felt the magic disrupting?

Mateo didn't answer his question, instead, he lowered a threat. "I could remove you from the Five. I could revoke djinn Conclave membership for this ridiculous attack alone."

"You say ridiculous attack. I say necessary fact-finding mission. Tomato, tomahto."

The djinn was the Wind elemental member of the Five, the ruling council of the Conclave? And he'd waltzed up and attacked some innocent werewolves who weren't doing anything at all. My head spun with the absurdity.

Another gust of wind descended. The leaves on the trees behind the djinn rippled and the wind became an arrow. I could see it, feel it. Not the leaves blowing in the wind, but the wind itself—distorted and shimmery. It passed over the djinn, grazed the fence, not even fluttering the banners left hanging there, then it whooshed forward, whipping around me, coiling tighter and tighter until I couldn't breathe. I tried to call out for help, but I couldn't choke any words out. I could only gasp.

I was about to have the literal breath choked out of me. Tears streamed down my face, and I stomped my foot on the ground, trying to get someone's attention. It was clear I was about to die and for some reason, all I could do was wish it weren't happening.

Then, as suddenly as it came, it left.

I heaved, sucking in a deep breath. Glancing around, it didn't appear any of the wolves or djinn had seen a thing. It left me feeling cold and vulnerable.

And attacked.

"Well, now that's out of the way." The djinn's voice grew louder, snapping me out of my haze as he began to shout at Mateo. "You took a part of us, alpha. Did you think we wouldn't notice?"

Mateo huffed. "Shall we talk about the werewolf whose head you put on that fencepost last week? You took a part of us too." He pointed and I couldn't help but follow to the fencepost in question. Nausea crept into my throat as Mateo rumbled at the djinn. "Tit for tat. Now get off our land."

The djinn balled his hands into fists. He looked around, his eyeholes grazing the group until he got to me. A shiver traveled down my spine. It seemed like he was delivering a promise to collect my soul at a future date.

Scary as fuck.

The djinn turned back to Mateo. "We've gotten the information we came for, so we'll be on our way. See you soon, *Conclave Leader.*" Yeah, that was dripping with sarcasm. These two had an issue.

Just like that, it was done. The djinn melded back into one entity and caught a gust of wind, flying right over the trees and out of sight. The second he was gone, I released a long shuddering breath. "Who was that assclown?"

I hadn't realized I said it out loud, but Gideon had come to check on me, I guess, and answered. "The djinn doesn't have a name. Or names, I guess I should say. They're one being but can become as many as they like. The red djinn is in the Five and the only local one that we know of, but rumor has it there are seven of those assholes in the world, but they're all linked together, so is there really seven or just one? No one knows. It's complicated."

"Understatement of the shitting century." I jumped at the sound of Wells' voice. And when I turned around, I gasped at the sight of him. He'd draped one of the banners low—very low—around his waist again. So, the banners weren't banners at all, but towels hung there for moments when they shift back from their wolf form. Smart. Thank the Mage and all his creations those towels were there.

Because he was shirtless again.

It was hard enough to ignore his gut-wrenching attractiveness. If he'd been completely in the buff, I would've come unhinged. I *had* to get over that.

Thank the Mage, Ren had joined us and I took a step toward him instead, putting some distance between Wells and me. "Is someone going to tell me what just happened here? Since I'm going to be here for months, I feel like I'm entitled to that information."

Wells ran his hands through his hair, and it fell right back into place like the hot boy hair it was. "Do you, now?" he sneered at me. I nodded and it didn't seem to make a difference to him. At all. "What happened here is none of your concern. You're safe and will continue to be safe until our business is done."

It occurred to me that while he was right and I'd been safe in the vehicle, others had not been safe at all. I saw him take a figurative bullet for Mateo.

Vows to stay away from him forgotten I couldn't stop myself, I grabbed his arm and swung him around, looking for the damage he took in his wolf form to be obvious on him somewhere.

There were no marks on his back.

Just smooth taut skin stretching across a muscled back that rippled in the best way when he moved. That defined line that scored his back in two was sharp and felt like it was pointing straight to his rounded ass. I pressed my hand between his shoulder blades where I knew the Wind blast had hit him. His skin was warm, and he flinched at the contact. "No touching." He spun around and snapped, "I'm fine."

"How are you fine?"

"Also, none of your concern." He stepped close enough so that I had to tilt my head back to see him. His gaze raked over my body, and I felt it like it was a caress, but not necessarily a nice one. His expression was all challenge and no understanding. "As I was saying before those djinn fuckers wrecked my already trying day, do you think you can manage these trials Gnome? Because it seems like you're a little girl who's scared shitless and in over her head."

I was. But you could bet the Mage's left testicle I wasn't going to let him know that. I placed my hand in the middle of his flawless chest. The warmth of his skin made my flesh crawl with the urge to explore his whole body with my tongue. I locked it down. Tight

"I'm neither scared nor over my head." I brushed my fingers against the light dusting of hair between his pecs. Not because I wanted to feel him, but because I wanted him to squirm. "And I'm definitely not a little girl."

He growled, low and guttural. The sound landed right between my thighs, before he removed my hand from his chest and Gesture Two'd in the direction of the cabins.

JEWELS OF CLAY

My mind was caught in a landslide of feelings as we walked to the cabins. He didn't think I could do this. Maybe he was right, but I wasn't going to give up and I sure didn't want to burst into a cryfest in front of the wolf who was judging my worth, so I swallowed about a million times to keep the sobs from spewing out, gasping when I rammed into Wells' back. He'd stopped walking and I was looking down in an effort to look anywhere but his towel-clad body.

He grunted and looked over his shoulder, his expression sharp. "You okay?"

Anger, piercing and sharp, flooded my veins. Was he serious? Nobody in their right mind would be okay after all of the mess I'd been put through.

"Let me see. Am I okay?" I paused, sucking in the deep breath I was going to need for the next part. "I've learned I'm not half-human, practically exploded the closed Conduit, witnessed a freaky-ass djinn attack, I've discovered I can't get to Aetheria like I'd planned, and don't forget the overwhelmingly stupid notion that I've entered into a Perception magic contract with a dickhole that may end in my death."

He turned to face me and I just kept on talking. "You wolves trudged into my life like a wrecking ball and you didn't even give me time to pack a toothbrush." I rolled on, poking his hard chest with my finger. "On top of all that—and honestly, this is just icing on the cake—I don't even have a clue where on this Mageforesaken earth I am other than eight hours from where I've lived my whole life. So no, Wells. I am *not* okay."

I'd always thought I was decent at keeping my shit together, but I could only take so much. He spun around, peering at me like he was seeing inside my soul.

I was milliseconds away from kneeing him in the crotch and laughing at the absurdity of it all when his stonewall features softened the tiniest bit. His eyes flashed a bright lavender. "Nah, you're fine. Worthy for now." He turned on his heel and began walking without looking back.

"I don't even know what the trials are yet and you're already judging my worth?" I was shouting. My voice was starting to crack. My mind too. Probably my heart and soul as well.

He shrugged. "How a person responds to adversity can tell you more about them than any elegant or calculating words they choose to say aloud."

I opened my mouth, but nothing came out. Damn him, he wasn't wrong.

He started walking but spoke over his shoulder. "You're going to drive yourself crazy if you obsess over the precise moments when I'm thinking about you—your worth. I wouldn't advise it."

I was ready to let him have a piece of my mind when he stopped again.

One more time, I ran into his solid back with a thud. Could that guy not talk and walk at the same time? "We're right outside of Vancouver."

A ripple of shock coursed over me.

Thank the Mage. He'd answered a question.

My breathing returned to a semi-normal rate. "See? Giving information isn't that hard, is it?"

He failed to answer me. Instead, he set off again like I wasn't even there.

We passed several cabins and veered back further in the property. When we pushed through some trees, and a pristine lake came into view. The water was a pure dark blue and the sun was up high enough to cast little dancing beams of light on the surface. It was nothing short of picturesque. "Please, please, please tell me I get to spend some time at the lake."

I'd beg for it if I had to. I'd never seen anything so beautiful and serene.

He shrugged. "Depends on how well you do on the trials." I held my breath, hoping he would take a hint and lead me there that very minute, but he didn't. Instead, he issued yet another rule. "Don't go down there unescorted."

Wells was bad at taking hints. "Why?"

Turning, he glanced over his shoulder again, taking more than a beat to answer. His unwavering violet gaze crept under my skin, leaving me warm and shaky. He had to know his epic glares effected people. Probably why he did it. "There's magic in places you'd never expect," he whispered.

There was a weight to his words. They sunk inside me and rooted there. We both stared at the lake a little longer, taking refuge in the coolness, before he broke the heavy silence. "I get it. My cabin's on this side too."

I could not let that go. "Well, well, Wells. Did you just share something about yourself? Shocking."

He stared at me, and I would've sworn he almost cracked a smile, but that would've been nuts. Not him.

Without any warning, he veered me away from the lake and we finally arrived at cabin forty-two, my home away from home. Thank the Mage the lake was still in view. The door squeaked as Wells opened it, then he was back to ordering me around like I was one of his pack. "If you need something, make a list and I'll have a fairy get it for you. My cell number is on the table. Call me if you want to leave the cabin or if you have any kind of trouble."

"Any kind of trouble? Like, if my toilet backs up?" I'd already gone through a fair amount of trouble when he was with me. I didn't want to think about what may happen in times when I was alone.

His eyes glowed an iridescent silver. He didn't seem to appreciate my particular brand of humor. Not that I cared. He Gesture One'd me with his arms over his chest and set his glare on one thousand percent wattage.

"I'll just go lie down now."

He agreed with a nod, then he was gone.

Bye! Don't let the door hit ya where the good Mage split ya!

At least I had some time to breathe. To process. To check out my cabin away from home. It was small, but cozy. And it wasn't like an ancient rundown shack laden with cobwebs and dust. Plaster filled the gaps between the logs, making it rustic, but civilized. There was a queen-sized bed covered in quilts and fluffy pillows in one corner. A large tub with jets in another. A door to what I assumed was the toilet was closed, beside it, a dresser and bookshelf, both empty.

Part of me wanted to unpack and make myself at home. Because I would be there for months. But another part of me, the biggest part, was bone tired from…well, every damn thing.

I had no idea what time it was. 'Still daytime' was the best I could do at that moment. Regardless of the time of day, I set my bag on the floor and crashed onto the bed, fluffing an insane number of pillows around me, creating a cocoon for myself with the final touch being the quilt over my head.

Stillness was not my friend.

Everything came rushing in.

But I would be damned if I was going to let it get to me. If I was going to survive this ordeal, I was going to have to be strong. What did the wolves say?

They don't tolerate weakness.

Trouble was, in the stillness of my new surroundings, I was as weak as a newborn bunny.

For comfort and just to feel normal, I pulled my vial of earth out and wrapped my hand around it, soaking in the feeling of home, wherever that was. Within moments, it had soothed me to sleep.

An annoying buzzing sound woke me from my slumber. I swatted at it, but it didn't go away. As hard as it was, I cracked an eye open.

Tristan was lying on my right breast like it was his own personal bed.

"Get off." I flicked him across the room.

He did a few backflips to recover, then enlarged to adult sized, shredding his tiny clothes in the process. He sat on the bed next to me and I shoved a quilt at him. "For Mage's sake. Cover yourself."

He side-eyed me like it was the strangest request ever, but thankfully did it. "I was hiding in the Ficus plant outside the alpha's office. You've got the werewolves crook, Babycakes."

"You mean shook. Why were you hiding in a plant?"

"Getting intel. I'm no dummy. I've survived this long because I always check my surroundings. Anyway, the hottest beta—with the purple eyes—he and the alpha were arguing over your special, one-of-a-kind, snowball blood."

"You mean *snowflake,*" I corrected. "What did they say?"

"The alpha said your magic and your blood were special. He kept using the word *fusion* while the stud argued against it, pointing out the alpha had denied your Conclave petition because you had such little magic in you, but the alpha ignored him. He was practically salivating over putting your blood through fusion."

"What does that mean?" I knew the basic meaning of the word, but not how it applied to magic and my blood. Was he adding something to it? For what purpose?

"How am I supposed to know? Sounds like a human word." Tristan shrugged. "I got the feeling the alpha was going to do it no matter what, which is why Wells was so pissed. The alpha even questioned Wells' loyalty to the pack. Said he was thinking with his dick. That's when Wells threw the chair."

None of this made any sense. Especially the part about Wells thinking with his dick. Not about me anyway. He could barely stand to look at me, let alone... "He threw the chair. At Mateo?"

"No. The wall. Broke into pieces, but it looked like a cheap chair to begin with. You know, I've always wanted to go to that Ikea place. Normally I don't do human stores, but I've heard that one's amazing. I bet he could find a new chair there. I could offer to go with."

I snapped my fingers in Tristan's face. "Focus."

He shook his head. "Right. Anyway, after the chair, Mateo whispered something I couldn't hear from outside the door and Wells stormed out, stomping his big feet down the stairs." He stuttered in the impending pause. "You know what they say about men with big feet."

"Yes." My mind took a little side trip for a second on that, then I snapped myself out of it. "We've got to find out more about fusion. You should snoop when you can and tell me what you find out. Okay?"

"Sure. I can do that for you, but there's just one problem, Babycakes. I don't have anywhere to live in this camp." He batted his eyelashes at me dramatically. What was I going to do, throw him out? Leave him on his own? I couldn't do that. I owed him already and he was going to help me.

"You can stay with me on three conditions." He clapped his hands like a little kid and the quilt fell to the floor. "One: keep your junk covered. Two: don't let the wolves catch you. They think you're dead. And three: stay off my tits and out of my bed. You can have one pillow to sleep on in your small form."

He repositioned the quilt over himself and placed a kiss on my cheek. "Yes ma'am. Oh, I wonder if they have tiny beds at Ikea."

I opened the door the next morning, not to go anywhere, but to let the cool fresh air in, hoping it would wake me up at least a little. Tristan had already gone Mage-knows-where, so I took a step outside, almost tripping over a paper bag that had been left there. I picked it up and looked around. No clue who'd left it there. Cautiously, I opened it, half expecting to find werewolf poop inside.

It wasn't werewolf poop or any other kind of poop for that matter.

Inside the bag was a toothbrush, toothpaste, shampoo and conditioner—my exact brand—soap, my brand, and bubble bath. Oh, that would be awesome in my giant tub. I found razors and vanilla and ginger lotion that smelled amazing. There were even pads and tampons of every size and kind in the bag, which I wouldn't need for couple weeks, but still. I hadn't even remembered to pack those.

This was Wells' doing. Had to be. I'd screamed at him about not having a toothbrush.

Well, I got the toothbrush and a whole lot more.

I tried not to think too much about it because if I did, I'd have to admit he'd done something nice for me. That didn't compute in my head at all. I tried to reconcile the kind gesture with the growling, menacing chair-throwing wolf and concluded he'd probably sent a female fairy to get these things for me. Only women would think to get tampons.

I brushed my teeth and stepped in the tub for a quick bath. The long bubble bath soak would have to wait until later. I'd just managed to get the towel wrapped around my body when someone pounded on my door.

I raked my hand through my wet hair and got halfway to the door as Wells kicked it in with brute wolf force. It whacked against the wall, then slammed back into place behind Wells, like he'd choreographed the whole thing to make a dramatic and angry entrance. I cocked my head to the side and attempted to calm my racing heart. "Can I help you?"

His gaze traveled down from my head to my toes and back up, then released a simmering rumble from his throat. The sound wove inside me like it was liquid fire intent on melting my bones. "I said seven a.m." He wiggled his wrist, showing me his watch. "It's seven-oh-three."

A flash of annoyance ripped through me. I wanted to strangle him, but I'd have to drop the towel to do so. That was not going to happen. "Listen, I've had a strange couple of days. You're within your rights to cut a girl three minutes' worth of slack."

He took a long stride, backing me up against the tub with his broad presence. "That's where you're wrong, Gnome. I can't cut you any slack. Even if I wanted to, which I don't."

Of course not. Why would he do anything merciful? Getting me a toothbrush was the upper limit of his compassion. And he probably did that to save himself from any potential hazardous morning breath situation instead of for me.

"Come on. I'm five minutes late. I can eat breakfast on the way to…what are we doing?"

He huffed. "You were supposed to start training for your Heart trial. Six minutes ago."

I came unglued when he started rifling through my bag, pulling out a pair of black gym shorts first, then some nude underwear. I yanked them from his grasp. "Hold it. I didn't pack those." In fact, I distinctly remembered shoving them back in the drawer because he said he liked them.

"No, I did." He offered me no other explanation than a smirk.

That wolfhole. He must've snuck those panties in when he had me over his shoulder grabbing my phone charger. It pissed me off but given the fact that I had very little wardrobe for four months, I'd have to wear them eventually anyway.

Next, he pulled out a black t-shirt that said *I've got a dig bick. You that read wrong. You read that wrong too.'*

He paused to read the shirt, grinned for an infinitesimal amount of time, then shoved it at me. "You have two minutes. I'll wait outside." The slam of the door was his punctuation.

Dig bick.

As much as I didn't want to give in to his unrealistic demands—because it would take me longer than two minutes to get dressed—I decided to hurry.

Though I would've done anything to sit in that tub and relax for about three hours, hot chocolate in my hand, lavender candle on the side, soaking my stress into oblivion, it didn't look like I'd get that any time soon.

But, training for my trials, meant I'd be given answers—praise the Mage—so I was all over the idea of hurrying. I managed to get out the door within the allotted time. Sure, I had to pull my shoes on and put my hair in the tie on the way down the steps, but I did it and I was proud of myself. Wells must have been too. If nodding in my general direction were any indicator.

We got a few feet past my cabin when the lecture began. "I don't think you have any idea how precarious your situation is."

I snorted. "Trust me, I do."

He continued like he hadn't even heard me, walking at his brisk wolfish pace, forcing me to catch up. "Because if you did, you'd be taking this a lot more seriously."

"So, being five minutes late is a reflection of my cavalier attitude?"

"Yes." It was a more of a snarl than an answer.

I ground to a halt, my voice got a little loud, spitting out what was simmering in my brain. I couldn't hold it in. I was tired and yeah, scared. "Do you need me to write down all the ways I've been deceived, all the insane things I've had to cope with since I met you wolves because I don't think you recall what I said less than twelve hours ago. In fact, you've not considered me once in this whole process, Mr. Three-Minutes-Late."

He took a thundering step toward me, and I matched him with a step of my own and continued my *thoughts*. "You're worried my tardiness will throw you off your schedule? What else have you got going on today: hooking up with slutty nurses at ten, strutting around in a towel at eleven, growling and brooding at one fifteen?"

The blinding white flare from his eyes was downright murderous.

Even worse was the tone of his voice. It was so soft, so breathy, lethal in its design. "Have you considered *me* in this—what did you call it— process?"

Suddenly, I was hyperaware of his nearness. It was a warm enveloping presence that threatened to choke the life out of me. I tried to step back, but he caught my wrist, wrapping his massive hand around it to hold me in place. "If you think killing an innocent gnome is high on my list of things to do, you're wrong." His lips pressed together in a thin line and his jaw clenched.

He was right. I hadn't given thought to the part he had to play in the contract. I couldn't imagine what it would be like to take a life. But he was a wolf. A beast. Killing was in his blood. He released my arm and the serious set of his mouth morphed into a bloodthirsty grin. "I could squeeze it in around four-thirty though."

It took every ounce of strength I had not to scream in frustration.

Dickhole.

I'd almost, *almost*, felt bad for him.

Do not be deceived, Terra. He's the enemy.

He'd already started walking again and wanting to be as far away from him as I could, I followed behind, simmering and stewing. By the time we got to breakfast, I'd made my mind up. No more feeling overwhelmed, or at least not letting it show to Wells or the betas. And no more being fearful about passing the trials. The wolves didn't do weak, huh? Because Gram had raised me, I was not weak.

My 'grr' was internal.

I marched into the cafeteria, cut in line, snaking around Wells, all three of the other betas, and a couple of other wolves, and grabbed a breakfast burrito. Next, I beelined to the coffee, pouring a steaming to-go cup. Wells stepped over to me, his eyebrow cocked when I added about half a bottle of the hazelnut creamer.

I took a sip and started walking to the door, looking over my shoulder. "Come on Slowpokes. We've got training to do, right?"

Wells glanced at his betas. They were amused, but he was about to spontaneously combust. He could sense the change in me, though I wasn't sure if it pissed him off or made him happy that I had decided to serious up.

He Gesture Two'd Ren to follow and caught up with me in about two seconds. He leaned down, his voice a low rumble that I, alone, was to hear. "Don't forget who I am, Gnome."

I shivered. I don't know if it was the sound of his voice or the thinly veiled threat. "How could I forget? You remind me every time we meet. You're the big bad wolf in charge. Fine. I got it." I took another sip of my coffee, for courage. And for dramatic pause. "You don't forget who I am either."

That eyebrow arched and he looked like he was about to chomp my head off. "Who would that be?"

"The bitch that's about to take these Magedamned trials down."

Wells and Ren walked with their heads huddled together, probably whispering about how they were going to torture me. I followed behind them with my newfound purpose keeping me company.

Until, distracted by my thoughts, I rammed into Wells' back with an oomph. Again.

He'd led us to an open grassy field on the far side of the campground that backed up to a dense section of woods. Wells dislodged from me and leaned against the metal door of a small storage unit; arms folded over his chest ala Gesture One. Why do hot guys lean so often?

The world may never know.

He cocked his head to the side as if he were trying to get a read on me. "Can you tunnel through the grass, or do you need to have a clear patch of dirt to go underground?"

I fought to keep a smile from my lips. I could tunnel. "Soil of some kind is best since you're asking. Though if I need to, I can dive through the grass." I could do it well, in fact, but I didn't want to show him all my cards at the get-go.

He dug a key from his pocket and opened the storage building, digging past soccer balls and nets, badminton equipment, tiki torches, and the like. They must use the field for recreation and sports, which made sense given the size of it. Wells produced a shovel, which he used to remove the grass from a small patch of ground, making about a four-foot-in-diameter square in just a few minutes.

Ren flopped down on top of the small stack of grass Wells had piled up. "I can't wait to see this. I didn't get as far as I thought I could when I tried. Working on it, though."

A wolf? Trying to tunnel? Why in the name of the Mage would he even attempt that?

Wells cleared his throat and when Ren looked up at him, he got an epic death glare. He wasn't supposed to tell me about his tunneling efforts. That much was clear.

Too effing bad. He'd already done it and I was beyond curious. "Wolves are Fire, they can't use Earth magic."

Ren shrugged. He'd gotten the message from Wells—tell nothing to the gnome.

Wells leaned the shovel against the storage shed. "Is this good enough for you to get started?"

I eyed the patch of earth. It was moist, free of debris, loosely packed. Perfect for tunneling. When I was a child and first learned what I was, it didn't take me long to figure out what soil was best for tunneling. Gram took me to every park in the city at night when most humans were asleep, teaching me to tunnel in different conditions and not just in our backyard. Though my yard would always be my favorite. 'Yeah, this'll work."

"Great. Get to it."

"You're just going to stand there and watch me dig a tunnel?"

He leaned back against the shed. "Yes. I want to see what you can do before I give you specifics of your trial."

Alrighty. If he wanted a show, a show he would get.

I walked over to the patch of soil and shrugged off my shoes. Nerves flittered their way through my body. Tunneling was a solitary thing.

Something I did when I was alone and wanted to feel the coolness and embrace of the Earth. It was odd to do it with werewolves watching. Wells had the same stone look he always had, but his body was tense, coiled like he was ready to strike at any second. Was it anticipation or anger? Who knew? "How far do you want me to go?"

"Up to you."

I stepped on the patch of dirt and my body hummed in response. There was nothing like the feeling it gave me. Harmony and peace were the first two words that came to mind to describe it, but it was deeper than that, etched into my DNA. Earth magic was grounding. It spoke to me, called out to me, even with the overbearing wolves standing there like two hot lumps of coal.

I raised my arms and reached inside myself, bringing the Earth magic to the surface and forcing the current from my fingertips. Like a diver going into a pool, I pushed off with my toes and leaped up, plunging into the Earth.

I held my breath as the Earth made way for me. The first few seconds of tunneling were the most dangerous. The moments before the magic created a bubble of space in front of me so I could breathe. I didn't know anyone who'd died from tunneling, but if I wasn't careful, I would suck in a mouthful of dirt and there would be nothing anyone could do to save me from the embarrassment of such a thing in front of Wells and Ren. Pushing my arms forward, I marveled as the Earth made way for me. My night vision kicked in and I was able to see about six feet in front of me, instead of the normal two or three.

I chalked it up to yet another unusual occurrence in Boulderbrook.

Magic in places you'd never expect.

The soil pressed around me, urging me to move, so I propelled myself, wiggling my body like a dolphin, redistributing the Earth around me. I slid forward with little effort.

Releasing my breath, I soared forward. When I inhaled again, I was overcome with the aroma. The dirt was rich, smelling of rain, pine, and held a sweetness like I'd never experienced before. It was hard to describe, but the word ancient sprang to mind. Not musty or old, but dignified, as if it commanded respect. I was possessed by it, and I sucked in several breaths just to get more. Yeah, tunneling here was going to be good and my magic hummed its approval.

I pushed my arms in a breaststroke pattern. The Earth shifted for me without having to consciously move it. After I'd made it about fifty yards, I decided to resurface, mainly to ask the wolves a few questions. Preparing myself to break through the grass, I moved my arms above my head and kicked my feet. I slithered up and out with minimal resistance.

Hauling myself through the hole I'd made, I collapsed in a heap. The Earth below me shifted into place as it had been. The only evidence I had been below was a divot of grass about my size. I reached over and pushed it back into place with my magic, making it look as it had before I'd climbed through.

Glancing over at the wolves, I brushed my fallen hair from my forehead. Then dusted the dirt from my shirt. "That good enough for you?"

They strode over to me. Ren offered me a hand and helped me upright. Wells Gesture One'd, giving me no indication he'd been impressed with my tunneling or otherwise. But I'd done what he asked. It was time for answers. "Now that I've given you a show, tell me everything, *everything* about my trials…and go."

He didn't like me telling him what to do. He almost huffed all the breath from his lungs as he counted on his fingers, glaring a hole into my forehead. "Four trials, four tenets. Your Heart trial will be to dig a specific tunnel, your Soul will be to master a magic rod, the Body trial will force you to push yourself past your physical limits, and your Mind trial will be

117

to produce gold. Easy peasy."

He knew it wasn't easy or peasy, given the sarcasm dripping from his words. True that most of the things he'd said were very gnome-specific, but I wasn't dumb. Trials were called trials for a reason. It wasn't going to be as simple as digging a tunnel or making gold.

Which I couldn't do. At all. Damn it.

I schooled my face so he wouldn't see how freaked out I was. I could do it. One thing at a time, right? "Can I just do the tunneling now and get it out of the way?"

The smirk was at least level one thousand. "Sure. Go from here to the edge of the woods where I hung the orange flag."

I looked over and damn, that flag was far away, but I knew I could do it in the welcoming Boulderbrook soil. A surge of confidence welled in me. Easy peasy, adjacent? Maybe.

He wasn't finished.

"You'll have one minute to get there,"

"You're kidding, right?"

"Do I look like a kidder?" In zero ways did he look like a kidder? I shook my head, no. "One more thing…" He paused and I wanted to crawl back into the Earth because I knew he was about to drop some serious shit on me given his expression. "You'll have one minute to get to the flag. And you'll have to take Ren with you."

I turned to Ren. He wiggled his fingers at me, grinning wide.

"That's impossible. Gnomes can't take other people with them. I'm half-human. I don't have the magic to displace that much dirt at one time. Not with someone who has no Earth magic too."

Wells laid a large hand on my shoulder. I swear it weighed five and a half tons. "Find a way to make it happen or you'll fail the Heart trial."

I wanted to scream that it wasn't fair because it wasn't, but I knew that was futile. Instead, I reminded myself that just a few minutes ago, I was determined to kick this trial's ass. I needed that fire to ignite in me again, pronto. "I get to practice? For a month if I need it?"

He sighed and ran a hand through his hair, just to make it tousle and shine. "Yes. I'm not a heartless bastard. We'll even help you train, but in the end, you have to fulfill the conditions specifically or the Binding magic will take over and…" He left the end of the sentence in the air. Though, I didn't need it or the throat-slicing sound effect he gave me either. I was dead if I didn't do it exactly right.

"You couldn't just watch me tunnel and be done with it, could you?"

"You do that all the time. How would that show me your worth?"

"So, the ridiculous time constraint and passenger-on-board request is the extra you need to judge me."

He booped my nose with his long finger. "Exactly." Mage, he was so proud of himself for devising the trials. Maybe he was up for killing me after all. "Good luck, Gnome. You better start practicing."

Fine. I wanted to get away from him anyway. I redid my ponytail, then bounced on my toes to get my blood flowing. When I started slinging my arms around, Wells released the most exasperated sigh I'd ever heard. Because of that, I added deep lunges and torso twists. I didn't need the extra warm-up. I just wanted to make him wait. When I finally stopped moving and raised lifted my chin, letting him know I wasn't going to be intimidated. "Time me."

He made a big show of taking his phone out of his back pocket and opening up the timer, glancing at Ren, he smirked, "Feisty."

I let my anger fuel my way, determined to make the one-minute mark. I'd never tunneled so fast before. It was a heady experience, the cool Earth begging me to slow down and feel her versus my drive to prove I could do what Wells demanded. It left me dizzy and disoriented. Still, I continued, using my hands to redistribute the dirt and my feet to propel me. I was like Michael freaking Phelps in that tunnel.

When I thought I'd make it near the flag, I burst up, pushing through to the surface, huffing and puffing for air and squinting in the sunlight. "Was that under a minute?"

"What? Can't hear you from over here." Wells' voice was a distant shot. I jerked my head around. He was fifty yards or more away from me, leaning against the tree with the flag on it in full Gesture One stance.

Oops. I may have gone quickly, but my path was crooked AF. I drug myself over to Wells, who hadn't moved an inch, forcing me to come to him, not vice versa. "I asked how my time was. Under a minute?"

The sun glinted off the surface of his phone as he lifted it to check my time. "No."

I huffed. "How long?"

Sneer.

"Three minutes, twelve seconds."

What? Impossible. I grabbed his hand, checking the time. I don't know why because I didn't bother to check the time before I began. He jerked back. "What don't you get about not touching me?"

That guy was so damn touchy, in both the literal and figurative senses. "You have no problem touching *me* without permission."

He raised his eyebrow and it read, "So?"

"So, this is a two-way street, Wolf. Don't touch me either."

His eyes flashed in their annoying way. This time bright violet. "Deal." We should've shook on it—I could see that he considered it—but, that would've required us touching. He cleared his throat. "I said it was three minutes, twelve seconds, so that's what it was. I hope you know some tricks to make you faster."

I didn't.

Defeat washed over me. How was I going to get quicker? "I don't know any tricks. Not long after I learned to tunnel, my Gram got sick, so it's not like I could get weekly lessons."

I'd hoped for sympathy, but I got none. "You'll have to figure it out yourself then. Dig straight next time. Missing the target will disqualify you."

Disqualify me? I was fighting for my literal life, and he was treating it like an Olympic event.

Signs point to Asshole.

I spied Ren lounging on the pile of grass. He'd put on some shades and was sunning himself, his sleeves rolled up to reveal the thick black ink covering his arms in intricate patterns. I set my sights on him and turned my body so that I'd go straight toward him this time. I nodded at Wells, and he reset the timer. "Go."

I dove in and this time I didn't allow any room for orienting. I just went. Long and hard and with extreme force. I could feel the dirt flying behind me, creating a wake of soil because it created solid blocks for me to push off from. I had no clue if it was making me faster, but it was making it a little easier. I didn't have to strain so hard to move forward. I erupted from the ground in the clear patch Wells had made for me, panting. Ha! Straight as an arrow.

Wells typed on his phone. Ren hadn't noticed my presence, so I picked up a clump of dirt and flung it at him. "Wells is texting you my time, Dickclown."

He flicked the dirt from his chest and checked his phone. "Three minutes, two seconds. You shaved off ten seconds. He sent the clapping hands emoji." I glared back at Wells who was standing in full Gesture One position, unemotional and unforgiving.

And sarcastic emojiing.

"I can do the math myself."

"Fine. Should I come along this time?"

"No, I prefer to tackle one problem at a time, thanks. I'll let you know when I'm ready to do the impossible part."

He chuckled and slid his sunglasses down and went back to the lounging position.

I hated those damn wolves.

I shouted to Wells across the field. "I'm going now, in three, two, one."

I dove back in and bolted my way through the tunnel. When I emerged at Wells' feet again, he frowned. "Three minutes, one second."

"Why are you so grumpy-faced? I cut my time down, didn't I?"

He huffed. "One. Second."

Frustration curled inside me. "Didn't you, oh mighty beta wolf, set the time stipulation on this? You could change it."

He stepped toward me, anger erupting all around me. "Believe me. I can't change anything about this." I was struck with the idea that maybe he wanted to change it. Had he thought about it and realized what a jerk he was being? Did he regret the inevitable fact he would have to kill me?

My limbs were growing heavy. I found it difficult to even gesture, but I managed to put my hands on my hips in righteous fury as I tapped into Name magic. It wouldn't hurt to try it, right? "Come on, make the trials easier on me, Wells. Pass me right now. Wells."

He cocked his head to the side. A clear sign he was gearing up to say something that would aggravate me. "One, that's several times you've attempted Name magic. Be advised, it won't have any effect on me. Two, how do you have a Wind skill?"

Damn. Didn't work.

My sources say no.

"I don't know. Gram taught me a few days before she died." He looked like he didn't believe me, but it was basically true. She'd called me over, put her hand on my chest and I felt a rush of a whisper whip through me. I started to freak out, but she assured me all Wind magic is like a whisper and that most Magicals didn't appreciate such a low-powered skill, but Name magic just might save my life one day. I continued, "I wasn't focusing on the magic at the time because I was worried about her health."

"And you've used it and had success?" He asked, his eyes laser-focused.

"Yeah, I landed my garden center job with it, got out of a speeding ticket once, back when I had a car, and..." I trailed off, not wanting to say what popped into my head next. Wells arched an eyebrow and lowered his icy stare. He wasn't going to let me get away with clamming up. I tried to think of something else, but my mind drew a blank. I took a deep breath. "Okay, I got a date from a human guy I was crushing on with Name magic."

I stared at my bare feet, which were now dirty. And I knew there was a blush across my cheeks, which I was certain were caked in Earth too. I felt like an awkward teenager in front of a hot teacher instead of an adult with magic coursing through her body facing an equal.

Wells lifted my chin with his index finger. A far cry from the laughter I expected from him. "Believe me. Anyone who can wield Name magic has used it to get dates. Did you make him sleep with you too?"

That was a very personal question. And his cursed finger was still burning a hole under my chin. So much for the no-touching rules. "No. As hard as it may be for you to believe, he did that on his own, thank you very much."

He took in every inch of me, slowly, deliberately, like he was deciphering my very existence with his intense stare. "Not hard to believe."

Well, well, Wells. Was that an actual compliment, or at least a compliment-adjacent remark? From him? Color me shocked. A leering half-grin appeared on his lips. "Most men are in a constant state of horniness. Name magic isn't necessary for sex."

I wrapped my hand around his, pulling his finger away from my face and not letting go, just to make him squirm. He hated me touching him. Maybe I could use the moment to discover a bit about my judge, jury and potential executioner. "Why are you always so warm? Are you sick?"

He dropped his hand and turned it over, like he was inspecting it before he made a fist. "The sun is out. It's Magedamned hot standing here watching you fail over and over."

A defensive stance.

An excuse.

And a lie if I ever heard one.

I wanted to press him but decided against it for the moment. I'd find out. Somehow. "Why doesn't Name magic work on you? Wells."

Can't blame a girl for checking. Just to be sure.

He scoffed because he knew I tried it again. "Because I'm special. Now, stop stalling and try the run again."

I knew sharing time was over. And even though I didn't get a whole lot of answers, maybe I'd made some kind of strange progress with him. We'd had an actual conversation-ish thing.

I dove into the Earth again, hoping and praying to the Mage I would shave some more time off. When I emerged next to Ren again, I looked over at the orange flag. Wells was gone.

Two days later I'd managed to shave a few seconds off my time, but it wasn't nearly enough. Wells was mysteriously absent and the only answer I got from Ren when I asked about him was "he's doing pack shit."

I was exhausted and ready for a bath and a good sleep, but as usual for us, when I bust into our cabin, Tristan was lying on my bed with a cocktail in one hand and some Hollywood magazine in the other. "What are you doing?"

He took a sip from his drink. "You keep correcting my phrases, so I figured I should read up on how to speak like a human. You know, be on the wall about it." I raised a finger, but he self-corrected. "Nope. On the ball. Right? I'm being on the ball about it."

His eyebrow lifted but I cut him off before he could say whatever he was thinking. "Don't make that dirty." He was disappointed, but left it there, so I went over and turned on the bath water. "Not that I don't appreciate you taking up my space and time, but I need a bath."

"I won't stop you."

"I'm not putting on a show for you, Tristan."

He grumbled but slid off the bed. "Fine. I need to refresh my drink anyway. I'll be back."

He wasn't lying. I barely had time to fill the tub with the bubble bath I'd been gifted and settle in before he came sauntering back through the door. This time with two drinks. I accepted mine and downed it in one gulp. I didn't know what it was or care. It was wet and sweet, and it hit the spot.

He sat on the floor cross-legged next to the tub, sipping his drink at a more civilized rate. "I organized your drawers earlier, FYP."

I shook my head. "FY*I*, not P. And why did you do that?"

"Bored. FY*I*, I like those pink polka dot undies."

I leaned back my head against the tub. I didn't want to talk about that particular pair of underwear. Or the stupid memory of Wells hoisting me over his strong shoulder that it conjured. He reached over and pulled open one of the drawers, removing Gram's Magic 8-Ball. "BTS, what is this thing?"

"BTW, for by the way. BTS was a K-pop band." I peeked through one eye. "It's a toy that belonged to my Gram. You're supposed to ask it questions, then shake it up and read the magical answers. I keep it for sentimental reasons."

He glared at the ball, then whispered to the part with the number on it. "What's for dinner tonight?"

"Yes or no questions only." I reached out and took it from him and asked the question I'd been asking since I arrived at the compound. "Am I going to pass the trials?" I shook the ball and then held it out for him to read the answer. It was the same it had been every time I'd asked.

Better not tell you now.

His laugh tumbled across the room. "I got it now. Let me try." He made a big show, jumping up and circling the room as the questions rolled from his lips.

"Is Wells in any way bisexual?"

Don't count on it.

"What about the other betas?"

Very doubtful.

"Aw. Couldn't hurt to ask, right? What about this: will Terra and I be BEF's forever?"

I sighed. "BFF's. Best *friends* forever."

Cannot predict now.

He frowned at me. "How rude."

"I didn't say that, the ball did. But like I said, it's a toy and not actually magical, so don't be so bothered by the answers you get. It doesn't know anything."

"So, we're BFFs then?"

"Sure." Why not? I had no other friends, not really. And it made me relax a tiny amount to think someone was on my side at Boulderbook. Even if I'd basically forced him into it by randomly capturing him and almost feeding him to the wolves.

He set the ball back down and plopped next to the tub. "Since we're besties, I'll make you a gift!" He practically hummed with excitement as he scooped a large handful of my soap bubbles and rolled it between his hands, speaking in Faetongue. "Don't look at this part. The magic won't work if you see it happen."

I wondered what in the world I was going to get, but I turned my head to look out the window. He giggled to himself as he alternately hummed and spoke in Faetongue. It took long enough for me to worry about what he was doing, but when I attempted to peek, he splashed me.

Finally, after five minutes, he declared it was time to look just as he set something on my bent knee. Reluctantly, I peeked and found a small fae-

129

sized replica of Wells. Right down to the purple eyes and broad shoulders with a tight white t-shirt stretching over his defined chest.

I glared at the top of his head, at what I thought was a weird beige beanie, but as I leaned forward and squinted, it became clear it wasn't a hat of any kind.

It was a penis tip. On top of his head. "What the actual fuck?"

"You like? You flick the cock up to turn on the vibrator function. There are only two speeds, but it's the best I could do with bubbles. I can make another Wells-flavored golem with more bells and whispers later when I have better supplies."

I let his mistake slide. Because I was staring at Wells with a peen on his head. "You made me a golem dildo. That looks like Wells."

He beamed. "Yeah, who else would I choose? Watch this." He directed a finger at the golem and the eyes glowed as it growled, deep and guttural, just like Wells always did. A second later, it raised a hand and waved at me. *Waved.* "I don't know what you're into, but if you get him to raise both hands while you've got it in your—"

"No, Tristan. Just, stop." I was afraid to move with the thing perched on my knee. "I can't believe you made me a golem sex aid."

He shrugged. "I can't believe you didn't pack one yourself, Babycakes. I thought maybe that 8-Ball thing could've been one, but I tried and got nothing out of it. Now you've got yourself a hot Wellsbrator. You're welcome, BTW."

I didn't know what to do, so I gingerly picked up the *Wellsbrator*—oh my Mage—and as soon as my fingers touched the t-shirt, it began to melt. Tristan shrieked. "My creation! No!"

He jumped up and blew on the golem, directing Wind magic into it, forcing the life in, I guessed. The more he blew, the worse it got, until the golem disintegrated into bubbles and dropped back into the tub. I scooted away from the offending bubble blob that used to look like Wells.

"Sorry?" I offered. I sure wasn't going to use it, but I didn't mean to destroy it either.

Tristan stared at his outstretched hands, flipping them over and over, trying to discern what had gone wrong. He quickly poofed small and then big, then small several times before he stopped and slumped over the ledge of my tub. "My magic is blinking."

"You mean it's broken somehow?"

He nodded, keeping his head down. "I can still resize, but the Wind magic in me isn't flaccid. It feels like shit, like part of me is missing."

The betas had warned me about this, that Aetherian magic was cut off and Ambient magic in our world dwindling. It made sense that those of us who had the least, the unConclaved like fae and gnomes, would feel the effects first since we had so little of it. I wanted to run out and check my Earth magic, but Tristan's clearly distraught mood stopped me. I put a hand on his back. "It'll be okay. You can still resize. And maybe if I get in the Conclave, I can help you in some way."

"I don't see how. What am I going to do? I'm nothing without my magic!" He sobbed, deep and hearty, then without warning, he jumped up from the floor and slid into the tub beside me. I had to swivel my legs to accommodate him. "I need to soak, Terra. I need to soak this misery out of me."

Understanding, I stood and wrapped my towel around me. He didn't even look up at my naked body. This *was* affecting him. I wanted to help, but I couldn't figure out any practical way to accomplish that, so I turned the tap to hot and added more bubble bath and let him try to soak it out. It usually worked on some small scale for me, and I hoped it did for him.

I went to sleep before he got out and when I awoke there was a note scribbled next to my 8-Ball that said 'Thanks BFF. I promise the next dildo will blast your mind."

Blow your mind, Tristan. Sheesh.

An aggressive knock on my door told me I had no time to worry about Tristan. I shimmied into my shirt that read 'Sarcastic Honor Society—Like we need your membership,' and threw open the door, expecting Ren. "I'm com—"

I almost swallowed my tongue.

Wells was standing there in total Gesture One mode. Wearing dark jeans that hugged his thighs, and a crisp white button down that was super-acquainted with his pecs. The top few buttons were undone, leaving a little more skin in view than his usual t-shirt. Just a few dark hairs were peeking out. I'll be Magedamned if my traitorous brain didn't go straight into *Wellsbrator* mode.

Damn it. No.

His hair was slicked back, the curly tamed into perfect submission. This was Wells on steroids. Wells plus. An extra bit of attention had gone into his appearance.

Why?

Concentrate and ask again.

He scanned me from tip to tail, eyeing the shirt I had cut and tied because it was way too big for me when I got it. A bloodthirsty grin accompanied his snarl. I swallowed, trying to get control over my twisting insides. "Where have you been the last couple days?"

He leaned against the door frame. Fucker. "Miss me?"

"Nope."

"Right." His tone told me he didn't believe it and he may have been close to correct. I'd missed his presence, not *him*. Surely. "I've been doing my damn best to avoid what's about to happen, but I could only hold them off for so long. Mateo's insisting. I have no choice but to obey my alpha." I raised an eyebrow, my blood pressure rising with it. He didn't look happy and that was concerning. I motioned for him to continue. "The Five are on their way. They want to meet with you."

I started to shout a barrage of questions in his direction, but I already knew the answers. They wanted to see the dipshit that upturned the magic Conduit. Not that I could give them any info about how or why I did what I did. I stepped toward the door. "Let's get this over with, then."

He blocked my way with his rock-hard body. "You don't want to change clothes? Meeting the Five is important. Especially when you're not even in the Conclave." He gestured to his own pristine look, and I looked away so I wouldn't stare at that triangle of skin peeking from under his shirt.

I considered it but dismissed the idea. "Nope. This is me, so this is what they get." He stepped aside and held the door open for me, but not before I noted his expression. He looked impressed. "And it's not a member of the Conclave *yet*." That made him chuckle. I was so glad my potential death still amused him.

We walked in silence to the Conduit in total silence. Thankfully, he didn't suddenly stop so I didn't bump into his back again. When we arrived, Gideon, Mason and Ren huddled together with Arlo next to the stone benches. They'd all cleaned up their appearance like Wells had. I was the only one who looked like they were about to shop Saturday morning garage sales.

Before we could even make it over to them, Mateo burst from the Infirmary door with four people in-tow. One of them, the creeptastic djinn. There was only one copy, wearing a long black robe that trailed behind, which was weird, but at least it covered up their not-privates.

His/their gaze on me all the way to the front of the Conduit. I couldn't help but release a whimper. Deep down in my soul I knew they were the reason for this meeting. Sure, the rest of the Five may have been curious about my little magical performance that day, but the djinn was eating it up like it was a deep-fried Twinkie dipped in chocolate.

Wells' deep voice slapped me to attention. He whispered so only I could hear. "Don't give them anything unless they ask specifically." I had no intel to give, so yay. He straightened up, putting his hand low on my back. I felt the heat through my shirt and for some damn reason, it made me shiver. "This is Terra," he announced to the Five.

Can a person be turned on by the simple pronunciation of the letter R? Because I think I was. The way he said my name was sexy. I went all Destiny's Child in my mind.

Say my name…

Focus, Terra. The djinn is looking right at you. Er, eye-holing right at you.

I shook myself out of it. Wells was still talking. "You already know Arlo's working on her DNA. You can see what happened here when she threw her stone. That's all we can tell you." He turned to address me. "You can go train with Ren now."

Clearly, he was trying to get me out of there. I appreciated that on a deep soul level. I took a step toward Ren, practically throwing myself at him to get away. Maybe it wasn't going to be so bad.

"Not so fast." Damn it. Too good to be true. It was the surly alpha who didn't want me to get away. "Walk us through it."

Wells clenched and opened his fist as I forced myself to speak loud and clear, not showing the fear simmering inside me. I retraced my steps as I spoke. "I held the rock Arlo gave me. Wells ripped it from my hand when we were standing here, he threw it in that bowl thing there. Took off my shoes here. Boom. Fire, Water, Wind, upturned Earth. I fainted. Woke up on this bench scared shitless and confused AF. Will that be all?"

One of the Five, a woman with radiant dark skin and badass afro, put her hand on my shoulder. "Tell us how you controlled all of the elements when you're half-magical and not even in the Conclave."

Not a question, a demand. My will loosened and I wanted desperately to give her the information she was seeking. She was so pretty, and she wanted to know so badly. I should help her by telling her what she wanted

134

to know. Then maybe she'd let me touch her hair. "I..I don't know." The woman's Conduit key amulet glistened against her chest as she stepped closer. My breath became shallow and everything around me started to swim.

Wells wrenched me from her grasp, pulling me against his chest. My head instantly cleared as he snarled at the woman. "Your siren magic won't work on her if she doesn't know how she did it, Jael."

So, she was the Water Elemental to the Five.

Sirens are as loud in bed as you'd expect, though their orgasms are silent.

Sirens could be dangerous, dragging secrets from people at the touch of their fingers. Though it pissed me off I was being manipulated, I supposed I was good because I didn't have the secret she wanted. Jael shrugged and lowered a 'can't blame me for trying look' on Wells.

"We could try something else." The sound of the djinn voice made me shiver. Though he'd loosened his grip on me a little, I could still feel Wells tense too. "She could wish the answers into being."

I wanted no part of the djinn suggestion. Nope. Not at all.

Sure, I wanted answers too, but not if it meant working directly with the djinn. There was something so not right about them. They were strolling into the camp like Mateo hadn't captured one of them, part of them, whatever. It was business as usual for him. For Mateo. It made no sense.

Mateo scratched his chin like he was considering it, but the way he and the djinn were staring at each other gave me the oddest feeling the whole thing was an act. He knew what the djinn was going to say before they said it. I was sure of it. There was more to the captured djinn too. I was going to send Tristan in search of them as soon as I could. Mateo shook his head. "Alright. Let's try it." Wells made a sound behind me that seemed scarier than a growl, but Mateo cut him off. "If the answers aren't inside her head, there's no harm in it. Unless she's lying. Step away from her."

It surprised me when Wells did just that. It left me feeling cold and alone and I didn't like it. Not that I could protest because the djinn stepped up and took my hand in his smarmy grip. "Make your wish. Seek the answers."

I tried as hard as I could to scrub my mind, but the wish materialized in my head without my permission. I couldn't stop it. It was just there.

I wish to know what happened the day the Conduit shifted. I wish to know how I did it, if I did it.

The djinn morphed into several copies of itself, and they branched off to surround the Conduit and boulder until there was a huge circle of djinn pressing in on me. "Interesting," they hummed in unison. My stomach clenched and I started heaving in breath so hard I thought I might hurl. The morning sunlight burned my skin like acid. It felt wrong. "Keep wishing," they urged. I concentrated on what I wanted to know, but everything in me hurt. Someone came close, but I couldn't figure out who because my vision had blurred.

I didn't recognize my own voice when I finally spoke. "I'm more than I am and less than I should be. I was able to disrupt the Conduit because of love, light, destiny, protection, and blood."

I sputtered and fell forward, but Wells caught me in his massive arms, pulling against his chest. Gideon stood behind me rubbing my back and Ren grasped my hand and squeezed like he was afraid I'd run away from them.

The betas had circled around me as the djinn sucked out my wish. I didn't know what to do with that. Because I wasn't accustomed to feeling protected. Warmth bloomed inside me, and I wanted to lean into that feeling more than I wanted to flee from it. That was a first for me.

Mason put a hand on my shoulder. "Way to be cryptic, Neo. I thought you were going to tell us we were in the Matrix next."

"I don't understand. How did I say those things? What do they mean?"

All the betas—save for Wells—stepped back and turned to the djinn who'd sucked themselves into one copy again. Their eyes glowed brighter than before and they were beaming. "We fed on your wish, which was tasty. And now we know, for certain, you affected the Conduit. But you kept the reason locked inside you."

"Not surprised." Wells' eyes were vivid fuchsia. He looked…amused. Proud? I couldn't tell. Whatever it was, it made my stomach swirl in the best way. His fingers trailed along my spine as he spoke. It felt like more than just supporting me or comforting me after the djinn rooted around my head. "Gnomes are guardians. It seems like you're guarding a big secret, even from yourself."

ells insisted I needed rest after that and the Five left to discuss what they'd learned, which was jackshit if you asked me, but they hadn't. I didn't argue because I wanted to be as far away from them as I could. I didn't like any of them, and I hadn't even heard the Earth or Wind Five members utter a word.

Though, I didn't get to rest like Wells had said. After the betas decided we couldn't know what my weird wish revelation meant, Wells said he'd be gone for a bit and shoved me at Ren and we were back at training. It was another week of grueling digging that left my nails broken, my body exhausted and my spirit weak.

When I wasn't training, I was thinking. That was a dangerous thing. In those moments I discovered a pattern to Wells' behavior that troubled me. Each time he did anything that resembled nice—like support me when the Five wanted to dive around in my mind—he vanished. He'd done it then and he'd done it after we'd talked about Name magic. Every time we got a teensy bit closer, he bolted, just to show up again later acting like nothing had happened. I couldn't figure out why. My heart told me it was because he didn't want to get close to the person he'd potentially have to kill. But my heart wasn't always right. Besides, I was happy when he wasn't around barking orders and snarling at me.

Right?

Concentrate and ask again.

Trying to figure him out was futile, so I poured everything I had into training. I pushed myself to my limit and beyond it, my sole focus to do whatever it took to get through the Heart trial. It had worked. I'd shaved eleven seconds off my time since the last time I'd seen Wells.

I pulled out of the tunnel and stretched, pleased with how I'd powered through, my muscles groaning with exhaustion. The sun had almost set, painting orange and pink ribbons across the October sky. It was tranquil until my stomach rumbled.

Remembering the last meal I'd eaten was breakfast, I used my Earth magic to cover the hole in the ground, eager to get some food. "I'm hungry."

Ren rolled his t-shirt over his head. "You tunneled through dinner. Can't help you."

"You can't just take me to the kitchen for leftovers?"

"I have somewhere to be." He checked his phone. "In five minutes. Hustle."

He unceremoniously dumped me at my cabin, then was off to his prior engagement. Which I guessed was hooking up with one of the multiple female wolves I'd seen strutting near his vicinity since I'd gotten to the camp. All of the betas had that effect.

I searched for Tristan, but he was nowhere to be found, so I paced for a good hour before I realized I wouldn't be able to make it until morning. I had to eat. I didn't want to do it, but I had no choice. I pulled out my phone and the piece of paper I'd wadded up and tossed too many times to count and added Wells' number to my contacts under the name *Wolfhole*.

He was at my door before I could finish running a brush through the hot mess on my head. "Were you just sitting around waiting for me to text you?" I asked.

The incredulous look he gave me was off the charts. "I'm the ancient magic expert. I've been in grueling meetings with Mateo and the Five, trying to figure out what your wished revelation meant for the past week—to no avail—so when they finally left and Mateo released me, I went to the lake to relax," he grumbled. "What do you want?"

Oops. I interrupted him at the lake. Too damn bad.

"Sorry to disturb you." I kept the *Your Highness* part in my head. "I'm hungry."

He released a huge breath, and it blew the curling edges of his hair from his forehead. His indignation was palpable. "Come on."

I followed him. Because he was taking me to the food. About four steps into our trek, I noticed what he was wearing: a tight white t-shirt and gray sweats that hung low on his hips. Not in that baggy douchey kind of way like some guys, but just low enough to make a girl wonder what lay beneath them.

I put myself in time out for those thoughts.

We'd just made it onto the main path when Gideon ran up, sweating like he'd been working out, but he still managed to have that effortless cool mixed with a healthy dose of swagger like all the betas. Why were they all really, really good-looking? It seemed like it was a Beta requirement. The whole camp was just a big distracting thirst trap.

Tension rolled from Wells as he whispered to Gideon. "How's *it* going?" Emphasis on the *it*.

"Not looking good. He's grown weaker in the past few hours."

Wells cursed. "Shit, poor Spencer. What's Arlo's opinion?"

141

"You know Arlo; it's all about the science, so he's giddy with all the notetaking."

"And our friend?" The way he said friend made it sound like whomever they were discussing, it wasn't a friend at all.

Gideon shrugged. "The iron's holding, but not sure how much longer he'll hang on."

They were being as vague as possible so I wouldn't figure out what was going on, but I was picking up things despite it. For instance, the direction Gideon came from and the mention of iron. It had to be where they were holding the captured djinn. Not that the OG djinn gave a shit, obviously. He'd been there at the camp for a week and did nothing about it as far as I could tell.

Wells emitted a breathy snarl that made my ears perk up. His sudden anger became a seething pit of rage circling in his body, trying to get out. He clenched his fists as his eyes flashed silver. "Fucking Mateo. This has to be the last time."

Yes, his sparking flashy peepers were definitely tied to his emotions.

Gideon put a hand on Wells' shoulder in an effort to calm him. "You know the fusion won't stop. Not unless…" he trailed off. Whatever the end of the sentence was, Wells understood it. And it made him look sick.

He ran his hand over his jaw, then Gesture Two'd Gideon back the way he came. The subject was closed. He set off for the cafeteria and I followed. As was usual for us, the walk was silent.

It was dark inside when we arrived. Wells flicked on the lights, and they hummed to life. We made our way through the dining hall, toward the kitchen, Wells was in his thoughts about whatever he and Gideon had discussed. And I was calculating how I would get away from a beta long enough to check out what was in the direction Gideon came from. We both slowed when we noticed a banging sound coming from inside the kitchen.

At first, I assumed it was just a fairy cooking or doing dishes, but the closer we got, the more I realized it was too even and repetitive. This was not the banging of pots and pans being cleaned. There was only one thing that sounded like that. "Is that—"

Wells kicked the swinging door open with his foot and froze in the doorway. "Mace, you fucking Manwhore!"

I peeped around from behind the mountain that was Wells and spotted Mason's bare ass. Over his shoulder—or underneath him would be the more accurate description—the pink-haired fairy I'd seen serving meals every day.

Oh wow. They were getting it on right there on the industrial chrome countertop.

I didn't want to think about the health and safety ramifications of the food being prepared right there where the fairy was sprawled out.

Wells picked up a plate and hurled it at Mason, frisbee-style. Since he had the werewolf speed gene and the fairy was a fairy, they both managed to avoid the makeshift shrapnel. But it made one hell of a crashing sound as it slammed into the wall and shattered.

The fairy poofed mini-size and disappeared faster than I could track. Mason turned to us, grinning and shrugging.

And doing nothing about his nakedness.

I swirled around and shouted over my shoulder at the wolf. "She's one of the fae working for the pack. Did you order her to…" I couldn't even finish my sentence.

Not that I had any ground to stand on when it came to being with a fairy. I reminded myself that Tristan initiated our brief encounter, so I wasn't taking advantage of owning him. I had no idea about this wolf, though. Tristan had told me that once a fae is bound, magic would force them to do whatever their master said.

Mason appeared in front of me. Still naked. "No way. I mean, look at all this." He pointed to himself, and I looked at the floor. I got a small peek first though. The fairy wanted to jump him for a good reason. "I wouldn't force anyone to do me, Ms. Sex Police. Don't have to."

Wells grumbled, picking up Mason's jeans and shoving them at him. "You're an idiot."

He wrapped an arm around Wells' neck, rustling his hair, which for the love of the Mage managed to stay perfectly tousled as if it would do anything else. "Yeah, but you love me anyway."

"In your fucking dreams, Man."

I was starving and debilitated from day-long tunneling and those two were standing there dude bro-ing.

I trounced over to a basket of crackers sitting on the far counter, away from the location of the sexcapades. I made a big show of unwrapping a package and shoving it in my mouth. They were dry as fuck, but it was something headed to my stomach. I took the whole basket back into the dining hall and made myself comfortable, leaving the wolves in the kitchen.

There was some clanging and rustling after I left, but I would be damned if I was going to go back and see what they were doing. They could've been screwing each other for all I knew. I just kept eating crackers and wishing for some water to wash them down with.

I was on my sixth package when they emerged from the kitchen, Wells holding a plate with a sandwich on it and Mason with a bottle of water. I batted my eyelashes. "For *me*?"

Wells gave me a look of derision, sliding into the seat in front of me. He cut the sandwich in half with a knife and took half for himself. "For us."

Mason reached over to grab the sandwich from him, but he knocked his hand away. "Make your own damn food." His obvious attempt at puppy dog eyes didn't faze Wells in the least. "And go clean up the broken plate, too." He looked like he was about to argue, but Wells gave him an 'I'm your superior' face, so Mason shrugged and trekked into the kitchen.

Wells slid the plate toward me. Still a bit too famished to argue, I took a huge bite from my half sandwich. Okay, I know it was just a sandwich—even I could make grilled cheese—but it was delish on a level that was…magical. I think I spoke with my mouth full. "This is amazing. What's in it?"

Wells shrugged like it wasn't a big deal. "Black truffle oil."

I'd had truffles before. Gnomes are great truffle hunters, obviously, but it was more than that. I side-eyed Wells, forcing him to give up his culinary secret. "The truffles came from Aetheria."

Magic truffles. I knew it. "How? You said the conduit to Aetheria had closed." He said nothing. "Fine. If you won't answer that, tell me what you and Gideon were talking about earlier." I looked through my lashes, issuing a challenge. I didn't think it would get me anywhere, but I had to try.

I'd assumed he wasn't going to answer me because he mulled it over for a long time before he took the truffle bait. "Before the Conduit closed, I'm told we had a trading system going with some of the troll clans in Aetheria. They supplied us with things like truffles from the forest outside a town called Aurelia, fae alcohol that will eff you up in the best way with no hangover—froth, they call it—and more potent magic rods made from magical sources, and other Aetherian magic objects like that."

My mind started to whirl. I never knew there were towns in Aetheria. I supposed it made sense given magical beings lived there. This fae froth sounded intriguing. "What did you send the trolls in return?"

A devilish grin crept across his face. "You don't want to know."

I did, but I didn't press him on it. It was trivial compared to actual Aetherian knowledge. I took another bite of my sandwich, so I had time to consider my next question. "If you still have truffles and things from this trade arrangement, the Conduit must have closed recently then?"

He finished off his part of the sandwich. "Depends on your perspective. The conduit closed on April twenty-first, twenty-two years ago. That's not even a millisecond to some magical species. To others, it's a quarter of their life." I stiffened, bits of sandwich crust still in my mouth. My breath became rapid as I grappled with what he'd just said. "Why do you look like that?"

Swallowing, I tried to be casual, but I was nowhere near casual. "That's my birthday." He shot me a vapid look. "No, you don't understand. Not just my birthday, but the actual day I was born twenty-two years ago. Don't suppose it shut down two minutes after midnight, did it?"

I was being facetious, so I laughed, but the accompanying look on Wells' face told me what I didn't want to know: I'd pegged the time. "Shit. That's--"

"—a hell of a coincidence, yeah."

In the following silence, I tried to myself that it was just that: a coincidence. But, when I lumped it in with the magical shitshow that went down when Wells threw my portent stone into the cauldron, deep down, I knew it wasn't. There was something going on with the Conduit and it had to do with me. The only good thing was that my connection to the Conduit seemed to have stumped the Five too.

I'm more than I am and less than I should be.

Mage, I was going to have to stamp that on my forehead I'd thought about it so much.

Wells stood, pulling me from the downward spiral my brain was taking. He picked up the plate. "I'm sure it's nothing. You need to get some sleep. You have dark circles under your eyes."

Thanks for the compliment. Needed that!

He'd given me an impossible task with an unrealistic time expectation, and my sleep schedule was all kinds of messed up. Of course, I had dark circles. It was a wonder I was standing up without leaning on him.

He took the plate back into the kitchen and when he emerged, he Gesture Two'd me to the door and said a sum total of zero words on the way back to my cabin. I scurried up the two stairs and turned toward him, hoping to glean something more from him. He took a step forward but stayed on the ground. That put us eye to eye.

We were close enough for me to feel the warmth radiating from his body, a nice contrast to the nip of the Autumn air. It was distracting for him to be so close, but I wasn't going to back down from our stare-off. Not even a little.

His eyes flared a deep violet hue. Even then, I didn't break away. I was drowning in the weight of everything I'd learned and done since I'd been at Boulderbrook. The moment there between us—staring like we were two boxers waiting to square off—it had a presence and form and while I didn't know what it was, I felt it in the depth of my being. Like we'd given life to this tangible thing, and it was staring right back at us.

I shuddered under the weight of it.

He broke the silence, dragging me back to reality. "I knew that lotion would be perfect for you."

My stomach looped like a roller coaster at the very intimate statement he so innocently dropped. "You're smelling me now?"

He took a deliberate deep breath. "I'm a wolf. What did you expect?"

"You and your nose can back the eff up." He smirked as I poked his rock-hard chest, attempting to move him out of my personal space, so he could no longer smell me.

"I picked the scent that best matched you. You don't like it?"

A vision of him standing in the personal care aisle picking up bottle after bottle of lotion flashed through my mind, followed by the Wellsbrator. It was very disconcerting. "I assumed you sent a fairy to get those things."

He flashed a bright smile, so damned proud of himself. "That was all me, Gnome."

It took me a second to spot it, and maybe I was imagining it, but behind that wicked broad grin there was something else—vulnerability. He stood there, watching, waiting for me to respond and I got the oddest sense that it was important for me to say the right thing.

Was I concerned about hurting his wittle wolfie feelings?

Reply hazy, try again.

"The lotion is nice. Thanks."

He nodded then slid right into Gesture One. "Good. I'll be here to get you at seven a.m." Then, he left, abandoning me to fight the chill in the air and wonder what had just happened.

I made a point to be ready before seven the following morning, but Wells didn't show. Instead, he sent Ren with a weak apology message, a strong cup of coffee, and sausage sandwich. When I made a snide comment about standing a lady up, Ren paused swinging around to face me. "Look, you're fighting for your life here and I respect that, but you don't *know* us. You should cut Wells some slack. He's a good guy and he's concerned about keeping all of us safe, including you."

I couldn't help it. I knew he *might* be right, but I was starting to feel the pressure come down on me in thick blankets. "*Where* is the slack he's cutting me?"

Ren smirked. "You have no idea."

When I questioned him further, he remained tight-lipped, refusing to discuss anything but the digging I was about to do. That was all there was about that.

Werewolves.

We made fast work of tunneling-slash-sunning. I tried to get more info out of Ren about Aetheria and the Conduit closing, but he ignored me until lunch, when I asked my zillionth question. At such time he uttered, "Do you think I have a death wish?"

So, Wells had made extra sure I would get no more information.

At lunch, I came face-to-face with the pink-haired fairy. She was serving mashed potatoes and didn't appear to be embarrassed in the slightest about her previous dalliance with Mason. Nor, did he, as he flashed her a big grin and got a second helping. He turned to me and wiggled his eyebrows. Screwing for food, it was.

A pinprick on my ankle snagged my attention. I bent down to swat at what I thought was a mosquito and found Tristan using my shoelace as a bungie cord. His voice materialized in my ear. "Meet me in the bathroom hall."

None of the wolves even looked up when I deposited my tray on the table and excused myself to the restroom. I found Tristan in the hall straddling the water fountain like he was a rodeo cowboy. He pressed on the button and water shot out the spigot. He stuck his head in and after he'd dowsed himself, he shook his head like a dog. I closed the door behind me. "What in the Perpetual Fountain are you doing?"

"I'm hot. I've been spying on Wells." He drew the l's out like he was purring, then proceeded to fan himself. The signal was so loud, people in Mexico heard it.

"So, Wells makes you hot?"

"Please. Wells makes everyone hot, but that's not what I meant."

I breezed over that comment. Wells did *not* make me hot unless we were talking about the angry kind. I mean, he was good looking, sure, and...nope. I shut that traitorous bastard of a thought out of my head and threw away the key. "What do you mean?"

"He and Arlo had a conversation at the Conduit. To hear what they were saying, I had to hide in the stones which are over a fire, so I was

150

being fried like an egg for you."

"Wait. That fire gives off no heat."

"Uh, yes it does. I almost burned my gonads."

Weird. Why was it that I couldn't feel the heat of the fire then? Yet another magical mystery. I wondered if there was a book I could pick up. Maybe Wells had *A Guide to Understanding Your Conduit* on his bookshelf. "What did they say?"

"You're welcome and I'm fine, by the way." He laid in the water left in the bowl of the fountain. Great. I added water fountain behind the kitchen countertop on the list of places that had been tainted by, well, someone's ass. "Arlo reported that their recent, and I use this word exactly, *fusion*, had been touch-and-go, but produced a success."

There was that word again. I motioned for him to continue. "Arlo was pleased to tell him that the source was alive and could be used in the future, but Wells thought the fusion was getting out of foot, because he got pissed and almost shifted over it."

That seemed extreme, even for Wells. I'd never seen him lose control of his wolf. The idea gave me the butterflies. "Is Arlo okay? And it's out of *hand*, not foot."

"Yeah, Wells pulled himself out of the shift and admitted he knew Arlo didn't have much of a choice in what was happening. Arlo accepted the apology and told Wells that, in fact, *he* was the only person who *did* have a choice. Wells was not amused by that."

The conversation sounded a lot like what Gideon had said. Wells had the ability to do something but didn't want to do it. "What do you think that means?"

"No clue. They moved on to the next subject. Want to know what Arlo and the hottie with the body said about *you*?"

I tried to play it cool, but I was a whirling ball of emotion. Arlo could've known what my other half was, and I was down to know about it. But, if I was honest with myself, hearing what Wells thought about me made me squirm. In the nervous, bated-breath, girl-with-a-crush kind of way. Which irritated me to the core.

"Arlo doesn't know what you are just yet, but he'd ruled out a lot of things. The list was too long for me to remember, but congratulations, you're not a vampire."

Thank the Mage. "What did Wells say to that?"

"He grunted. He likes to keep his thoughts to himself in case you haven't noticed." I had. It was frustrating. "But it was a positive kind of grunt."

Tristan stood up from his water fountain soak. He was drenched and for a moment I envied him. I hadn't even looked down at my clothes, but I knew they were caked in sweat and dirt. I grossed myself out. "Terra, my captor, my friend, my ride or fly, you should know, this man beast likes you. Liiiikes you. I sensed it before, hence the Wellsbrator, but now I know it."

I ignored the incorrect phrase and his sliding into thirteen-year-old girl territory and went straight to the unsettling part. "No, he barely tolerates me. You're wrong about that."

"I don't think so. I've watched the tragedy of *feelings* take over more times than I can count." A shadow passed over his usually jovial face. He'd been hurt in the past and I wanted to press him for the story, but he kept on talking about Wells. And me. Us. I shuddered. "I'd bet my life that he has feelings for you. He'll probably deny them until the day he dies—or the day he has to kill you—but, they're inside him. You need to give the guy a break."

First Ren, now Tristan. Everyone wanted me to give Wells a break. Sure, he was great at picking out lotion, but Wells had been rude, distant, overbearing. I had zero breaks to give him. There was simply no way Tristan was right about him. "So, your Team Wells now, are you?"

"No, I'm Team Babycakes, forever and always. Wells has a lot thrust on him. The Perception contract, djinn attack, whatever this fusion is, plus your portent stone causing the apocalypse, and monitoring your trials. He's got a lot of balls in the air." He paused, a wicked grin spread across his face. "Ooh. I bet his balls—"

I shoved my fingers into my ears. "Stop! We are *not* discussing Wells' balls!"

"What the fuck?"

I kept my fingers in my ears as I turned. Not that it would keep Wells from seeing me or erasing the last thing I just shouted at the top of my lungs. He cocked an eyebrow. "What were you saying about my balls?"

15

If there hadn't been a concrete floor and subflooring below me, I would've tunneled into the ground and never come back. How was I going to explain this to him? Not just the balls thing, but that Tristan was alive and well and living in the compound too. Wells might've wanted to do something awful to him. Mage help me, it may have an effect on my trials since serving him up to Mateo is at least part what got me there in the first place.

Wells was standing there waiting for an explanation and I was silent. For far too long. I needed to say something, but I was producing a big fat nothing. *'My bisexual fairy, whom you thought I fed to your alpha, is alive, horny, and wants to get up close and personal with your balls'* didn't sound like a good excuse.

A low rumble from Wells spurned me into talking.

"I was just...I mean...balls!" The last part erupted from my mouth, Bobby Singer-style, but I doubted Wells ever watched Supernatural and caught the reference. Why was my brain malfunctioning? I blamed the fucking Wellsbrator incident. Because now I was picturing that dang golem cock head with a set of balls attached.

"Terra. My balls?"

Mage help me. Each time he said it aloud made it sound funnier. Like it had lost all its meaning. I couldn't help it. I laughed. It started out as a little giggle, but when it mixed with my embarrassment and exhaustion from dirt swimming, it turned into an uncontrollable cackle. "Your balls!" I clutched my stomach, the muscles tight with strain.

He lowered his eyebrow and stepped forward, stopping inches away from me. He leaned in, the heat from his body pressing in on my personal space. "There's no way you were talking about *my* balls, because if you were, you wouldn't be laughing."

Damn.

That sobered me up in a heartbeat.

"I'm sorry. I'm just tired from tunneling."

He crossed his arms over his chest. Gesture One. "Mm-hm."

"Yeah."

"That doesn't explain who was on the other end of my balls..." He paused. On purpose, just to put the screws to me. Shit, this was getting out of control. "...conversation."

As he spoke, he peeked over my shoulder. I took a step back, but bumped into the water fountain, praying to the Mage that Tristan had gotten away while I was losing my shit over Wells' balls.

I had to stop thinking about his balls.

Don't count on it.

He reached around me and grazed my arm. Flustered, I lost my filter and blurted out what was in my head. "Mage, you're so hot." The corner of his mouth lifted but he didn't withdraw his arm. This encounter was going to kill me. I was certain of it. "I mean, not hot, warm. Your skin is always warmer than it should be. Why?" He ignored my question and snaked his other arm around my side. I was trapped in a cage of hot arms.

Warm arms. *Warm.*

There was movement behind me. "Gotcha little fucker." He raised his arms above and over me, Tristan caught in his grasp. To be honest the fairy didn't look like he minded at all. Wells studied him, recognition crossing his face. He barked at me. "Tell him to stay here and not fly away." Mage, he figured that out fast. And if the look on his face was any indicator, he was impressed that I'd pulled off keeping the fairy I'd fed to Mateo alive.

I released a slow stuttering breath. I didn't want to be part of Tristan's demise. Wells seemed to get that. He set Tristan on the water fountain. "I'm not going to hurt him. I just want to talk. Tell him not to lie."

He *did* know a lot about magic since he knew Tristan had to obey my command. I had no idea if Wells was telling the truth about not hurting him, but I didn't see any other way to end the conversation but to let him have it. And just something about the earnest look on his face made me trust him. In that moment anyway.

"Tristan. Stay put until we hear him out and tell the truth, please."

Tristan nodded. I wouldn't have been surprised if he offered himself up as a snack right there on the spot. I couldn't blame him. Wells put the *ugh* in *fuggable* and he was ramping it up to the highest level to taunt me and Tristan both.

"You're the fairy that Terra fed to Mateo. Supposedly. Was it your magic or hers that saved you?"

He should've known I didn't have the magic to have accomplish that feat, but at the same time, I shouldn't have blown up the Conduit formation either. Tristan beamed. "That was me. I used an ancient fairy golem spell and Wind magic to whisper life into my doppelganger. Nice, right?"

"Charming. Was there any way this golem or your magic would've hurt

157

Mateo?"

Wells was looking out for his alpha, which made sense until I forced myself to look directly at him. His lavender stare was more calculating than concerned. It was like he was searching for some hidden clue in Tristan's answer, in his magic. I couldn't imagine what.

"The golem was composed of flour, chocolate, and edible gold. Wind magic isn't designed to kill specifically, so it couldn't have harmed the alpha."

"Wait. Wind can kill. Gram said it can suck out your breath." I'd felt the djinn do it to me on the first day I arrived. I'd stopped myself from telling them about the attack because I didn't want anything to interfere with how Wells perceived me.

"Wind has more of a moral compass than the rest." Tristan continued, "It can be used to kill, but it takes a great deal of power to make Wind go against its original purpose to breathe life. It's the most noble magic if you ask me."

I smirked. "You're just saying that because you're fae and wield it."

He stomped his little foot at me, then whooshed himself to meet our size. Of course, his tiny clothes shredded on the spot, leaving him naked. I knew part of the reason he did it was to see if Wells showed any interest.

Wells didn't flinch.

Tristan turned and I focused on his face, not somewhere south of there. "No, it's true. The Mage created each magic with a purpose. Wind was meant to breathe life, Earth to ground life, Water to cleanse. It's Fire that kills and destroys."

It was beautiful when he put it that way. Wells didn't think so. "Fire does more than destroy. It protects and defends."

Tristan leaned against the wall. "Yeah, yeah. You're right. All I'm saying is that my golem couldn't have hurt Mateo unless someone else in the room added some Blood Magic. But how would they have known I'd created a golem in the first place? They wouldn't. So, Rob's your uncle. It was harmless."

"*Bob's* your uncle." I turned to Wells to interpret based on the side-eye he was giving Tristan. "He sucks at idioms and slang. You get used to it."

Wells turned his intense scrutiny in my direction. "You intended to feed the fairy to Mateo but didn't. Why did you stop yourself at the last second?"

Suddenly, it seemed I was on a quiz show and would win a million-billion dollars and a *brand new car* if I gave the correct answer. I tossed the question around for a few seconds, retracing the steps that led me to believe I could do it. "I was willing to do anything to get into the Conclave, but when the moment came, I couldn't sacrifice any life for my selfish needs. No matter what good came from a Conclave membership, I wouldn't have earned it if I'd done something heinous to get it. I would've hated myself." I swallowed, feeling both selfish and ashamed. "His name is Tristan, by the way."

Tristan put his hand over his heart. "I never said thank you."

"You saved yourself. I had nothing to do with it."

"Maybe, but when it came down to it, you couldn't go through with it and that's what matters."

Wells nodded. "Agreed. Mateo…"

He stopped himself short. I could tell by the look on his face that he'd almost let something out he didn't want out. I prodded him. There was something off about Mateo, including, but not limited to, his fae cravings and weird bromance with the djinn. "What about him?"

Wells squared his shoulders, stuck out that sculpted chest. "He's my alpha, that's what."

I wanted more, but I knew I had to tread lightly, or Wells would clam up. "So, if he'd told you to eat Tristan that night…" Tristan coughed, and it sounded like there was a *please* in there too. "…you would've?"

Wells rubbed his hand over his stubbled jaw, contemplating what to say that wouldn't appear mutinous. The guy was pack or die. It took him a while to answer. "No matter what Mateo's done for me, there are some lines I won't cross." The way he said it—whispering and tight—it seemed like he'd just realized it himself. There was something deeper in his expression than snacking on fae.

Maybe Ren and Tristan were right and there was more to him than I originally assumed.

Though he was still the tyrant and judge of my fate and that wouldn't change.

I glanced at Wells and our eyes met, his flashing bright violet. It lasted for just a second, but there was something familiar in that flash to me. Mage, I was getting used to it, and I still didn't know why it happened. I was about to ask, but he turned to Tristan with a devilish look on his face. "Now, what were you saying about my balls?"

Tristan lifted one shoulder, unapologetic in all his naked glory. "Are you willing to show me, so I won't have to speculate?" Mother of the Mage. I was going to have to teach him some common decency.

Wells shrugged his shoulder just as Tristan had done. Tristan kicked off the wall to close the distance between them as Wells emitted a low, sexy rumble that made the hairs on my neck prickle. He put a hand on the wall behind Tristan and leaned in super close. "Sorry. I don't swing that way, but I'll just let you know, so you can feel free to imagine what you will, my balls are spectacular."

Gulp.

Tristan laughed. "Am I free to go because I'm going to be thinking about that all afternoon? It would be better if I was alone while I did. If you get my swift."

Completely unashamed, Wells nodded, dismissing Tristan with Gesture Two. "It's *drift.* Enjoy yourself!" What had my life become?

Tunnel training was different the next morning. The entire complement of betas had shown up to watch me. Wells and Gideon had stationed themselves under the tree with the flag, Ren and Mason got the sunny spot. Tristan even showed up to meet the *squad*, as he called them.

After I'd corrected his first term: *quads*. Though when he said it, I peeked at their thigh muscles. He wasn't wrong. Still, I had no idea why he was there except for the eye candy. Once Wells had okayed him as long as he steered clear of Mateo, he set his sights on befriending the wolves. It took about twenty minutes before he and Mason were besties, considering how they figured out they had the pink-haired fairy 'in common.'

At least now I knew her name was Mona and she apparently lived up to that moniker.

I did my best to tune out the testosterone and focus on my digging. I still had half a minute to trim from my runs and while I was fully acclimated to the soil at Boulderbrook, I still got a charge of magic energy each time I tunneled. I'd hoped to channel that magic into faster times since I had the digging straight part down.

I dove in, the soil adjusting to accommodate my body, then sliding over the surface of my skin and creating a little pocket of air in front of me as I propelled forward. Even though I could tell where I was going thanks to gnome night vision, I always wished I could physically see the Earth magic pulsing from my fingers as I used it to move the soil.

When the wolves or djinn had used Fire magic, it was so obvious and tangible. I suspected Water magic was the same. Earth and Wind got the short end of the stick on that.

I shook the stray thoughts from my head and refocused, kicking my feet against the dirt behind me, pushing my body to move faster. When I emerged from the ground I found the betas laser-focused on everything but me, checking out the woods and the campground around us. I'd become accustomed to Ren's daily aloofness to my tunneling, but this was different. They were distracted.

The third time in a row that I emerged and found Wells' attention elsewhere, I picked up a stick and threw it at him.

He was supposed to be timing me, not checking out the flora and fauna.

The stick sailed into his hard stomach and bounced off. He pivoted his head at the pace of a snail on muscle relaxers. Meaning, I had a long-ass time to realize I'd made a crucial error in judgment.

He was on top of me so fast I couldn't process it. He was ten feet away, then boom, all up in my personal space. He grabbed my wrist and pulled me out of the soil with a swift jerk. "Ouch. If you want me to tunnel, my shoulder needs to stay in its socket, thanks."

This time, he started to shift, white wolf hair rippling over his arms as his golden skin began to stretch. I even heard some of his bones cracking.

162

Shit.

All because I threw a stick at him.

Because I threw a stick at him? He didn't even feel it. Not with those granite abs.

I sucked in a breath, and he got himself under control. After he almost rubbed all of the stubble from his jaw, he let go of my wrist. "Go again."

Chancing a look in Gideon's direction. He shot a pointed look to the hole I'd just come out of and back up at me. Message received: dig now.

Exasperated, I dove back in, but my heart just wasn't in it. I couldn't stop thinking about what was going on with Wells, with all of them. They seemed so alert and tense. Yet, they barely gave me a peep when I popped up from the ground.

I knew I wasn't doing a good job of shaving off time, so I decided to try and take advantage of the distracted beta squad. Knowing they had no way to track me other than when I popped up each time, I veered off-course, in the direction Gideon had come from when he gave Wells the super-secret and vague report mentioning fusion. It had taken me a while, but I knew I'd find the time to break away if I was patient. This was my moment.

I tunneled, fast and furious, speculating how far I needed to go to get out of the open field and into the seclusion of the woods. It was a risk. My heart was pumping like a machine gun, but some of it was from the excitement of sneaking away from the wolves and not the exertion of a fast dig.

I went as far as I thought I needed to avoid them seeing me when I emerged. When I broke through the earth, I was surprised to find myself in a cool green pasture. Several horses and loads of cows were grazing on the rich grass. One of the cows looked over and mooed, but other than that, they didn't seem to care that I was invading their turf.

There was a row of stables and a tattered old barn stood beyond the fence. A person passed in front of the open window, so I drove myself into the soil and tunneled right up to it. As I pulled myself from the earth shouting drew my attention.

I couldn't just let that go. I had to know what was happening in the barn nobody had mentioned to me before. So, I snuck around to the back and peeked between two rotting slats.

Cage the Mage.

The interior of the barn was nothing like the weathered and torn outside. Inside was sleek and sterile. No hay, no pitchforks, and no Farmer Brown in sight. Everything was clean and shiny, one side housing every kind of lab equipment you could imagine.

There were two wolves I'd seen at meals in the cafeteria. One on a computer, the other gripping a clipboard so tightly her knuckles were white standing beside an empty medical table with rumpled sheets. There were still dents in the pillow and covers.

What in the Mage's name was going on here?

The other side of the barn lab was much darker, but there appeared to be a cage of some sort along the back wall with bars extending from the floor to the ceiling. There was a faint red glow coming from the darkest corner and I tried to shift positions to tell what it was, but I never got that far.

I experienced Wells' familiar heat milliseconds before his hand slipped over my mouth. He pulled me away and forced me to crouch beside him out of view. I squirmed, but he kept his hand firm.

After a few terse moments of heavy breathing, from both of us, he put his lips to my ear. "This is life and death, Gnome. Stay quiet when I remove my hand. Nod if you understand." I didn't. Not by a long shot, but what the Eternal Flame was I going to do? Shake my head no and be stuck like that with him pressed against my back and his hand on my mouth?

I nodded and Wells released me, swinging me around to face him. I opened my mouth to ask the bevy of questions I had, but he put his finger to my lips.

We stilled. And we stayed that way for longer than was necessary.

Way longer.

Mage help me, I had the urge to open my mouth. Just a bit, just so I could taste him. But I pressed my lips together and convinced myself it was the adrenaline coursing through me causing the invasive thought.

A boisterous voice broke us from…whatever was going on. I recognized it at once. Mateo. "How did this happen, Amber? You better have a good excuse or you're both dead."

Wells flinched beside me. That was no empty threat.

Inside, Amber started rambling and I couldn't keep up with what she was saying. Something about 'him' being unconscious and them walking away to look at tests, and something about fusion doing unexpected things. I could tell by her tone she was nervous. They'd screwed the pooch.

I dared to stand up and take a peek. Mateo was fuming, half-shifting into an amorphous creature that was neither human nor wolf. He snarled at the poor woman, drool spewing from his snout and the clipboard tumbled out of her grip.

Wells grabbed the back of my neck and guided me down. "You can't let Mateo see you. Stay the hell down." At the force of his words, I half-expected Wells to go all shifty on me too. He stopped short of it and relieved, I nodded. I could stay out of sight. We could still hear everything Mateo was shouting in there anyway.

"I don't care that he's your friend, he's dangerous in this state!" After a few bellowing wolf sounds, he lowered a warning. "If he gets out of the compound, you know what the djinn will do to us."

Djinn. A shudder went down my spine. I had no desire to revisit the djinn. Twice was enough, thankyouverymuch.

A few minutes later, the shouting stopped inside the barn-lab. Wells removed his hand from my neck. The autumn breeze blowing sent a shiver through me. I wanted, no I needed to know why he was always so warm. I opened my mouth to ask him, yet again, but he grabbed my elbow and wrenched me forward, grousing and stomping away from the window. He was so pissed.

And I was going to die. I was ninety-seven-point-nine percent sure of it.

He dragged me back to the safety of the woods and checked to see if anyone had followed us. When he was satisfied, he turned to me and snapped. "Close your eyes."

Yeah, make that ninety-nine-point-eight percent sure of my death. "Nah."

Growl.

Ripple of hair.

"Fuck, Terra. This is serious." He lowered his voice, "Please." The tone of that one word burrowed inside me. It wasn't Name magic, it was a sincere and earnest plea. I didn't have much of a choice, I knew that, but part of me realized I'd been wrong about what Wells was angry over. It wasn't me. I took my chances of death down to seventy-six-point one and closed my eyes.

Wells stepped closer, enough that I could feel his breath across my cheek, warm and fluttering, causing my heart to jump. "You can open up now." When I did, his eyes shone silver, deep and haunting. I had to look away to keep from being overwhelmed by them.

That's when I noticed there was a ring of silver fire surrounding us.

He put his finger to my lips again. He needed to stop that. "Don't ask."

"But—"

"I can't and won't tell you what the fire is. Pack secrets. All you need to know is it's protecting us and keeping anyone outside from hearing what we say."

"Okay but what is it?"

A rumble erupted from his chest. "Do I need to repeat what I just said?"

"No."

"Good. Before you spout off a thousand questions, I'm going to break it down for you, capiche?" He didn't wait for me to answer. Did he ever? "One. Forget about the barn. What's in there *will* get you killed. Two. Stay as far away from Mateo as you can. Period. End of."

"I don't understand, he's your alpha. Why would I need to stay away from him?" I knew I should. Felt that in my bones, but I wanted to know why Wells thought so. There was a thing between them, and it ran deep.

His eyes flashed at my words, but he didn't acknowledge my question. "Three. If you *ever* run off from me…" He hesitated and the entire forest filled with the weight of his pause. "From us—again, I will judge you unworthy on the spot. Don't do that to me."

I was speechless. Sure, I had tons of questions, but the way he was looking at me, with his chest heaving, I *felt* his desperation, his disappointment in me, his utter desire to avoid being my executioner. I saw him in a new blazing silver light that matched the flame surrounding us.

I nodded. "I'm sorry. I wasn't trying to get away from you. Not really."

He stepped back and just as he was about to touch the flame, it dissipated. "Let's just get back."

When I looked down, the ground where the fire had been was untouched. I had no idea how he'd done it. I knew it wasn't a regular Fire magic skill. Like Tristan had said, Fire magic destroys. There's always something used up and burned in its wake. This fire hadn't left a single mark. The desire to ask him about it was strong, but it would just have to be something else to add to my ever-growing list of questions. I kept my mouth shut the whole way back to the field where we'd started the day. Anything else would have set him off, I was sure.

The intensity around him was off the charts. Whatever was happening in the barn, Mateo was at the apex of it and Wells was not cool with it. I wondered how that would work given pack dynamics. But that was the thing—it didn't work. And that was Wells' issue.

When we arrived back at the field, Tristan had vanished, but Gideon jogged up to meet us. "Situation contained." He glanced at me before his eyes darted back to Wells. "She's safe."

A niggle of warmth crawled inside me. Wells had asked the betas to stand guard as I trained, to keep me safe from the dangerous escaped patient, whomever it was. Because he was responsible for me. Until such time that he might have to off me.

Mage, our dynamic was weird.

Wells Gesture One'd. "Good."

Mason put his hand on my shoulder. "I see you located the fugitive." A grunt was all he got from Wells. "That was sneaky, but you know you'll never get away with it again, right?"

I sighed. "Yes."

Ren sauntered up, raising his sunglasses. "Are we back at it? There's another good hour of sun left." Did this man not worry about skin cancer?

I batted my eyelashes at Wells, hoping he'd cut me some slack. He did not. "Yep. She's got to make up for lost time now."

Wells Gesture Two'd Gideon and left Ren and Mason to time me.

Later when I crawled out of the Earth for what must have been the thousandth time, I was sweaty, hot, grumpy and my limbs were shaking from all the effort. I was about to refuse another attempt when Gideon showed up with a water cooler and some towels.

"Thank the Mage." Mason looked to me and released a long low whistle. "I mean no offense when I say this, but damn girl, you're a total Pigpen right now."

I ignored Mason and pushed past Ren, pouring myself a cup of the cold water. I downed it in one gulp. Ren side-eyed me. "Time for dinner. I'm famished."

"*You're* famished? From what, all the strenuous sunbathing?"

"I'm a werewolf. We like to eat...things."

I ignored the obvious double entendre. I was too worn out to protest. Instead, I got another cup of water and poured it over my face, relishing the coolness. "Let me take a quick shower first. Curls over there is right. I need one. It won't take but fifteen minutes."

Gideon glanced at his watch. "We don't have fifteen minutes."

That made no sense. "We can't be a little late for dinner now? You are the freaking kings of this place. You can't wait fifteen minutes for me to clean up? It's in your best interest, really." I glared at him, then shot a pointed look toward Mason. "Like you have no sway with at least one of the fae who cook and serve dinner."

Mason laughed. "Three actually, but that's not important. It's the second Monday of the month, so we have to be on time tonight."

"Is there a special menu?" I truly was not picking up what the big deal was, but the thought of something yummy made me salivate.

"No. You could go back to your cabin and shower, but you'll be stuck there the rest of the night. We have plans, Pigpen. Plans."

Gideon cleared his throat. "If you go back, we'll send food. We're not heartless." The jury was still out on that. "I think you'll be sorry if you don't come with us," he offered and the other two nodded their heads in a very conspiratorial way.

There was such sincerity on his features, and they'd poked at my curiosity enough that I was starting to get excited at whatever this second-Monday mystery was. Couldn't be worse than what was in the barn-lab. At least they weren't tense over it like they'd been with the escaped patient loose.

"Okay, but I'm not going anywhere like this." Without a moment of hesitation, I picked up the water cooler and dumped it over my head like I was a winning coach in the Super Bowl. I shrieked at the cold waterfall, but it did the trick to rinse the funk and sweat off.

All three of them started laughing. I ignored them and wrung out my hair the best I could. Then I reached up and pulled Ren's hair-tie right off his manbun and used it to secure my wet ponytail.

Gideon shook his head. "Baller move."

Ren nodded. "Yeah. I'll allow it. Once." He ran his hands through his long locks and did a little shake and, of course, it fell perfectly into place. It was an *'if you know, you know moment'* for him. He grabbed the towel and started dabbing my drenched shirt. Just as he was about to get to my chest, I stepped back. Way back. "Hey! I got it."

Mason laughed. Ren had the good sense to take a step back and hand me the towel. "Oops. I'll let you manage the rest."

Oops? *Oops?* "Yes, you will."

I did my best to dry as we walked, but I was still dripping when we got to the cafeteria, but at least I was somewhat clean. I piled my plate with pizza and headed for the normal table—Mage, I'd been there long enough to have a normal table—but Ren grabbed me by the elbow and dragged me outside to the porch. From there, we went down the side stairs that I hadn't seen any wolves use before. At the bottom of the stairs was a metal door that was rusted shut from disuse.

Mason leaned down and whispered something in Faetongue, blowing a breath and shooting a finger gun toward the lock at the same time. The door clicked and swung open.

Wind magic.

I stood there gaping at the Fire elemental using Wind but the only explanation I got was a cryptic, "You can call me Houdini."

These betas. There was something different about them. They definitely weren't like regular werewolves.

I followed them inside and down the stairs, surprised to find a warm, cozy converted basement space. There was a full bar, refrigerator, huge flat screen, lots of comfy recliners, and a plush couch; there was even a neon beer sign and a dozen sports-related knick-knacks from as many different teams. An octagonal cherry wood table with four chairs sat opposite the bar.

Ah. Man—werewolf—cave.

At said cherrywood table, wearing a black hoodie, gray tee combo and faded jeans with holes worn in the knees—his bare feet propped up and reading a book—was Wells. He was so engrossed, he didn't even look up when he said, "About damn time. Hurry up and eat so we can start, Dickheads."

Not the reception I expected.

"I know you weren't calling *me* a Dickhead, right?" I glared, daring him to repeat it.

His feet dropped and bewilderment colored his face. He scanned beyond me to the betas, raising an eyebrow. "Oh. She's here too."

He hadn't been expecting me, yet, if I were to always stay with a beta, he should've known I was coming. Unless he thought I was going to allow them to take me to my cabin at six-freaking-thirty and stay there until morning. Uh, nope. "Yes, *she's* here too."

He emitted a low growl that felt weighty and laced with irritation.

There was something different now between us since the thing in the barn. With my harebrained idea to tunnel away from him, I'd come too close to proving how unworthy I was. He'd come too close to realizing what he'd have to do if I failed. It felt just a smidge like we were in it together now. He took a moment to calculate and recovered fast, a wicked grin sliding across his lips. "She can play."

I didn't know what I was supposed to play, but I wasn't giving him the satisfaction of asking. Plus, I was starting to shiver from the A/C. My clothes were still wet, hair too. I couldn't ask to go back and change at that point. Shivering was a weakness, and I wasn't going to show any weakness. I was sure I'd be fine once my clothes dried.

Wells flipped the middle of the table over. It went from a cherry dining table to an obvious game table with green felt and slots for poker chips and drinks. Mason took a deck of cards from behind the bar.

Of course.

The challenge was written all over Wells' face. True, this wasn't an official trial, but he could damn well use this poker game to judge my worth. I had to win. I felt that thought deep down in my bone marrow.

Gideon made quick work with beers from the fridge. Everybody got one. Including me. I didn't even have to beg for it. And to my utter amazement, Wells rose from his seat and offered it to me. I managed to squeak out a thanks as he pulled a metal chair from the rack in the corner and sat it across from me. Backward. Then he proceeded to straddle that thing.

I did not need to focus on the man spread. I was out of my depth, soaking wet, in the middle of a wolfman cave with the thought of having to beat four men who played poker together all the time. The last thing I needed was another trip down Balls Road.

Outlook not so good. Avert your eyes.

I'd eaten half my pizza before I dared to look up. Everyone else was eating while Wells was unapologetically watching me. The intense way he was looking at me reminded me of a hawk eyeing its prey. I could sense him peeling back layers, reaching inside to discover what made me tick, the Perception magic swimming between us like he was forcing me to be worthy on sheer will alone.

The weight of it was unbearable. "What are you looking at?"

"Not sure."

"Direct your eyes elsewhere, thankyouverymuch."

He cocked an eyebrow, his eyes flaring lilac. "Yeah. No."

"Mage, you're so annoying with your flashy eyes." I spat. "Why do they do that anyway?"

"Do what?" Damn him, he was enjoying unnerving me. An angry snarl came out of my mouth and the corner of his lips kicked up in response. He shifted from predatory to amused. "Careful, Gnome. Certain types of growls signify specific things to werewolves. Don't ask for something you won't be willing to commit to, because right now, it sounds a lot like you want me to…"

He stopped talking, brushing a speck of dirt off his hoodie, but I didn't need him to finish that sentence. Not at all. "Jerkoff."

Wells shrugged. "If you're into it, sure." He laughed, deep and rolling, amused at what I'm certain was the blush his words incited. The rest of the wolves joined him, and they had a big ole chuckle fest until Mason shuffled the cards.

Wolfholes.

The guys took positions around the table, and I was the odd duck among wolves: certain to be eaten. Mason grinned as he began doling out cards. He paused when he got to me. "Do you know how to play Texas Hold'em?"

I'd watched more than a few old episodes of the World Series of Poker with my Gram when she was too sick to get out of bed. She was uncanny for being able to spot when Matt Damon bluffed, and she taught me how to read tells. After she died, I'd tried playing to make the funds for house payments, but I never could pinpoint the right time to cash out, then the gnome thing would kick in and I'd lose it all. I should've taken her to Vegas before she passed. "I can play, but if you bet with actual money, I'm out. Someone, who will remain nameless, but rhymes with Hells, didn't allow me to pack all of my stuff when I left." Not that I had any money to bring, but still. I glared across the table.

It had zero effect on him.

Mason cleared his throat. "Nah, we don't need money at Boulderbrook, per se, thanks to financial genius Gideon over there."

Gideon wiggled his eyebrows. "My charm goes a long way in helping me get away with what may or may not be considered legal in the strictest sense of the word." It didn't surprise me. The cool ease with which he did everything probably worked in a lot of ways on a lot of different people.

The whole lot of them snickered. "Don't tell me you play strip poker!"

Mason plunked a set of chips onto the table and doled some out to all of us. "Never have before, but maybe we should start tonight."

They all laughed, and despite my best efforts to be unaffected, my cheeks bloomed with warmth. I cleared my throat and began to stack and restack my chips.

"Cut it out. You'll scare her away." Gideon. My hero. Sort of.

I had a choice. I could bolt or I could face the gauntlet Wells had thrown down. There was no chance of me letting him intimidate me. Try again, sucker. "I don't scare easily. So, shuffle up and deal."

I ended up throwing several hands away to prove I wasn't going to be the chick who folded all the time. I took the time to watch how they played and check for tells. I figured out the three betas pretty quick, but Wells was tougher. He was a thinker, always calculating. He took his time and considered bets before making them and when he wasn't looking at his cards, he kept his eyes peeled on me. "Why were you so wet?"

"Excuse me?"

He pointed to the towel I still had wrapped around my neck and ran his finger up and down to indicate my whole body.

Oh. That.

I had mostly dried at that point, but his question reminded me that my hair was probably escaping Ren's hair-tie, releasing unruly waves and my clothes were likely clinging to my body. Not a great look for me. "Your friends wouldn't give me time to shower, so I improvised."

He glared at the betas, who all looked down to study their cards like they were prepping for SATs. Wells stood up and removed his hoodie, revealing more of the tight gray t-shirt underneath. The cut of his body was indecent. I couldn't stop myself from tracking him as he walked around the table and put the hoodie over my shoulders. "You should've said you were cold."

"I'm not cold." He bored a hole in my head with his obnoxious purple eyes, then made a pointed look in the direction of my tits.

Signs point to yes.

I pulled my own Gesture One, so the lot of them wouldn't stare at my nipples. "Maybe I'm chilly."

He chuckled, then pulled the hoodie off my shoulders and held it out so I could put it on properly. It was much warmer that way. I took a deep breath, reveling in the warmth and the scent. Sweet autumn rain and cedar, mixed sandalwood, and smoke.

Great. I did not need to know what he smelled like.

"Wolves have great ears, even in human form. I could hear your teeth chattering." He pulled the hood over my head, ducking down in front of me to tie the string. He leaned in, his lips grazing my ear. "And your pulse racing."

I leaned away from him. Did he say that to fluster me? Get me to lose concentration in the game? Mage, maybe they could all hear when I was bluffing. A glance and I realized he didn't give one flip about the poker game.

Across the table, Gideon cursed. "What the hell?" He waved his arms, whacking at a fern that was sitting on the bar behind him.

Ren shot him a withering look. "Why are you slaughtering a defenseless plant?"

"It attacked me!"

"The plant. Attacked you?" Ren questioned, obvious disbelief on his face.

"Yes. Something crawled along my neck. I reached up and the fern was stretching out, slithering over my arm. Going this way." He pointed to the empty chair just as Wells plunked himself back into it. "Look at the dirt."

He lifted the plant. The soil in the pot had exploded. There were bits of it around the bar, on the floor, even in Gideon's hair. Wells cocked his head, amused, but intense. "What did you do to make the plant angry?" It seemed like he was addressing Gideon, but he was looking straight at me.

Nothing. I'd done nothing.

Yet, I was the sole person in the room who would've been able to manipulate the plant. The only one with Earth magic.

Wells grunted. "Mm-hm."

Mason coughed. "Alright, let's just keep playing and forget about...whatever that was. Maybe you should move the plant since it's stalking you, Swamp Thing." Thank the Mage, he did, and Mason dealt the cards. Ren made the first bet, so everyone was diverted.

Except Wells.

He sat there with a smug look on his face like he knew something no one else did.

18

It took a minute to get settled back into the game, but I was doing well for myself. After a couple of hours, Mason had lost all his chips to Wells. He'd celebrated his loss with another two beers and a lounge on the couch. But it didn't keep him from encroaching on the game in other ways. "Since you're hanging with the big boys now and we know next to nothing about you, tell us about yourself, Newb."

Ridiculous nickname aside, I looked over and found him earnestly waiting for my answer. An uncomfortable queasiness swirled in my stomach. I had nothing to tell them. They knew I was there looking to get into the Conclave and go to Aetheria, which was off the table now. There was literally nothing else interesting about me to share. Mage, I was lame to myself. "Like what?"

"Favorite food? Favorite color? Favorite position?"

Mage, help me.

Gideon folded his cards and took pity on me. "Why don't you start with what do you like to do for fun?"

I couldn't help it. I laughed. His request was as crazy as Mace's sexual positions inquiry. "I took care of Gram since I was seven years old. I never had time for fun." I knew when it came out of my mouth it sounded like a joke, but it was truer than I could ever express. "We streamed a lot of tv shows."

Wells leaned over to throw some chips in. "You were close to her."

"Yeah. As close as you can be with a person whose elevator doesn't reach the top floor. She was funny though. Even in the end." I tossed a couple chips in. "I told you about my journal of Gramisms."

Gideon called the hand. "Give us one."

Warm pressure built in my chest. She'd been gone two years, but sometimes the hurt of missing her was palpable. Yet, it was so easy to think of her in spite of the pain. "She said vampires have long fangs to compensate for their small dicks."

Ren did a spit-take. "That's so fucking true. What else did she say?"

I must have read my journal thousands of times since she left me. All of her goofy ideas were ingrained in me. It didn't take long to think of something else Gramlike. "She said the Mage was her bestie for life, and also told me never have sex with a merman because their *parts* were too slimy."

The betas laughed. Wells slapped Gideon on the back. "Now we know."

"Ha. Ha. Very funny." They must have been referring to an inside joke. "What else did she say?"

"She said gryffins have eagle eyes, so they like to watch. They have lion tendencies too, so they like to dom just as much."

"Oh my Mage. Your granny was wicked, and I may be in love with her." Mason chuckled from the couch.

I searched my mind, trying to produce some other goodies. "Centaurs have horse dicks in both shifted and unshifted forms. I never met one before, but I thought it was a good thing to know. I put it between the recipe for her potato soup that I loved, and the warning about Blood Magic being facetious because it requires a sacrifice that no person should be able to make."

Wells raked in the chips from winning the hand. The rest of us around the table were looking at pretty low reserves, chip-wise. He cocked an eyebrow. "Anything else?" My Gram amused him. I felt the same way.

"Elves have the personalities of the animals they resemble. She also said, listen Jewel—that's what she called me, her jewel—when trolls want to have sex, they emit an intoxicating scent that makes them irresistible. Give in. You'll thank me later."

Ren smirked. "Accurate." I guess he'd hooked up with a Troll in the past.

"I wrote in that journal for years." I paused. "Which is why it sucks that I don't have it. But..."

I trailed off. It was hard to admit that I would have no home to go back to, even to myself. Wells Gesture One'd his arms across his pristine chest. "You'll get it when you're done here."

I had to swallow to tamp down the warm flutter inside me.

"About that." I took a deep breath. The beta squad was all staring at me. I wasn't sure how or why, but I got the distinct feeling I was safe with them. It had taken one night of poker to get me there. I didn't realize I'd allowed them into a small space in my heart, but Magedamned, they were there. And it made me feel better about sharing. "Gnomes are great at keeping valuables safe. But the magic BS that comes with that states we can't keep anything for ourselves. As a result, Gram's house is in foreclosure. The bank will have it and all the possessions in it before I finish these trials."

A heavy silence hung in the air.

"That *does* suck," Gideon said. It was obvious his wheels were turning trying to come up with a financial plan for me somehow. "There's no way for you to make money and keep enough to make house payments?"

"Nope. When I was young and Gram told me what I was, she said she was holding onto some very expensive jewels—like the kind they lend out to celebrities on Oscar night, you know? Very pricey with highly valued stones. I figured when she died, I could sell them and get around the magic, but she was a powerful gnome. I tried for years, I never found her hiding place."

Wells snaked his foot across the floor and touched my shoe. Just enough for me to realize he'd done it. He didn't say anything, but the look on his face was clear. He felt sympathy for me. I flushed and looked back down at my new cards.

Mason threw himself back down on the couch. "I feel like I could ace a Terra test now. And I'm filing a few things away for future reference. By the way, anyone know any female griffins?"

I tossed a poker chip at him, ignoring his question. "It was my Gram who had *thoughts* about humping centaurs."

He tossed the chip back and it landed on top of my remaining stack. How in the Eternal Flame did he do that? "Yes, but what you chose to write down says a lot about who you are."

Ren nodded. "True. You must be as naughty as your Gram."

"I am not!"

Was I?

Without a doubt.

They were all snickering and even though I should've regretted the whole thing, I didn't. "That's enough about me. What about you?" Since I'd shared a little bit of my life with them, I hoped to learn about where they'd come from or something personal.

Mason sat up and counted down on his fingers. "Sesame chicken, orange, and octopus."

Seconds later, Ren stated, "Pizza, black, and cowgirl."

Gideon cursed like he didn't want to, but he answered Mace's original questions anyway. "Lasagna, green, and sixty-nine."

What unholy hell had I unleashed?

My brain went into overdrive for several reasons: Trying to decipher what octopus position was, trying to avoid picturing them in these positions, praying to the Mage that Wells didn't answer, but praying to the Mage that he did at the same time.

I opened my mouth and snapped it shut. I had no response.

None. Zip. Nada.

This time, Wells pushed his foot forward and very distinctly, slid it across mine and didn't remove it. My eyes flicked up, narrowing on him as he purred. "Since you asked…"

"I didn't ask *that?*" My voice sounded like a screeching owl.

Turns out I didn't want to have that information in my head.

Mason laughed. "Wells likes eggplant."

Ren offered the next bit. "His favorite color is pink."

Gideon cleared his throat, side-eyeing Wells. "Going to take a guess here, due to your added strength: stand and carry."

Unfazed, Wells smirked. "One out of three sucks, Bros. I thought you knew me better than that." Before I could react, he laid down a winning hand, raking a lot of chips in the process.

It was another four or five hands before I could even look up at him. I was too busy trying to figure out which one they'd gotten correct. My guess was 'stand and carry,' but I didn't need that image in my brain. Because he'd carried me over his shoulder. I knew he was strong. Mage, I was going to need a serious brain scrub to stop my thoughts from going *there*.

Soon, Ren and Gideon were both working with the last of their chips. In that hand, Wells had folded, so it was down to me and two wolves.

The tension was mounting. Well, it was for me. The wolves seemed more entertained than anything.

It was my bet, and I was looking at a huge pot if I played it right. I was holding the best cards I'd had all night, but it was still a huge gamble. That's what poker is about, right? I pushed all my chips into the middle. There was a collective wolf gasp around the table.

Gideon looked from his cards to the pot, trying to decide what to do. I felt an obligation to help him decide. "You know you want to go all in, Gideon." Wells straightened in his chair, a grin stretching across his face. He knew I'd used Name magic on Gideon. And he was there for it.

Gideon flicked the corner of a card back in forth between his fingers. "Screw it, yeah. All in."

I turned in the other direction. "What about you? I'm sure your cards are good, Ren. All in for you too, right?" I paused to pour intention into the next word. "Ren?"

It took him longer to get to the decision, but the Name magic worked on him too. "Let's dance, Gnome."

For the first time since I'd gotten to the compound, I felt powerful. Sad that my power was coming from cheating at cards, but a girl's got to take what she can get when she can get it. Deep down I knew if I beat their asses at poker, I'd garner at least a little respect. Maybe not as much as I did with my Gramisms, but some anyway.

"What do you have, Gideon?" I batted my eyelashes innocently. He turned over a pair of tens. Oh, this was not going to go well for him. I flipped over my cards, revealing a flush.

Ren shook his head and threw his cards onto the table. "Damn it. I was bluffing. Can't even beat the tens."

I couldn't help but giggle as I laid down my three-fours and dramatically raked all the chips to my side of the table.

My head whipped sideways when Wells started slow clapping. "Well done, Gnome." I was riding high for a second. Until I realized what was about to happen. "I guess it's just you and me now."

Shit. I shouldn't have gotten so smug. If I was going to beat Wells, I had to do it on my own without Name magic. It wouldn't work on him.

While Gideon was dealing the cards, Wells slid his phone out of his pocket and made a call. "Hey Bash. Need a favor. Wheels up in an hour?" There was a pause for Bash, whoever he was, to answer, then "Thanks, Man."

I laughed. "Wheels up? Do you have a plane or something?"

"Yes."

I almost swallowed my tongue. I was kidding about the plane. "Wait. Really?"

"The pack has unlimited resources, including a private jet and pilot, all kinds of holdings, real estate, investments. Gideon's a fucking master mind when it comes to that shit."

"I have a head for it, I guess." Gideon shrugged, then turned to Wells. "Bash sober enough to fly you now?"

"Close enough. Not going far."

I wanted to ask about a billion questions, but Wells put on his stone face, and I knew I'd get no further information. Wherever he was going took a back seat as we had an epic stare down. Pressure started to build in my chest. I wanted to beat him so much. It was nonsense, I knew, but a deep desire, nonetheless.

He picked up his cards one more time and looked up at me through dark lashes. "Since I'm heading out and you need to be up to train in the morning, what do you say we both go all in and see what happens?"

Shivers raced down my spine. In a different circumstance, his words would take on a whole new meaning. I couldn't stop myself from dwelling there for a few seconds, thanks to Mace's positions conversation. But I shut that shit down because I knew my heart was starting to rev up about it. Why did he have to be so damned attractive? "Let's do it."

He smirked and I wondered if he was lingering in the potential alternate meaning of my words. "I call."

Mace jumped off the couch with his beer and wandered over behind me to check out my cards. "Get back, Jackhole. You probably have wolf telepathy of some kind." He shrugged, then went over to check out Wells' hand. It made him laugh. But was he laughing because I was going to lose or because Wells was? Was one of our hands good, bad, ugly? Who knew?

I took a deep breath. I was letting him get to me, which may have been what Wells wanted. I shot Mace the finger and laid out my hand. A straight.

Wells shook his head. "You got me." He threw his cards down and began gathering all the rest of them.

"Wait, you're not going to show me what you had?" I blurted out. I mean, I was thrilled with the victory, but it was hollow not being able to shame him for his chards.

"I had less than you. All you need to know."

He stood up and stretched, his t-shirt riding up as he did so. I hated myself for peeking at his abs. I only caught a sliver of skin, but just that did funny things to my stomach. I gave myself a good lecture in my head because it was getting out of hand.

Okay, Terra. Lots of people are good-looking, including every single dude in this room, so Wells is not that special. He's your overlord, your torturer, the person who's watching you struggle to meet the ridiculous trial goals. Get over his hot bod.

In an effort to distract myself from Wells, I asked an important question. "Winning is sweet and all that, but what did I win?"

Mace laughed as he went over and opened a closet door, pulling a huge wheel from inside. It looked like a vertical Wheel of Fortune spinner, but instead of money listed on each space, there were words and phrases. "Tell the audience what she's won, Gideon."

Gideon cleared his throat and went all announcer-voice. "Well, Bob, defeating the undisputed champion of Monday Night Poker, Terra has won herself one spin of the Magic Wheel of Victory!" All of the Betas, save for Wells, clapped, cheered, and made mock crowd noises. It made me grin despite myself.

It felt like I'd just experienced a night out with friends.

It was a sobering thought to realize it was the first in my life.

And they weren't friends, they were werewolves.

I walked over to the wheel with all its colorful spaces. "Somebody spent some time crafting."

"Guilty. You should appreciate the fine artistry. Took me fucking days." Mace beamed, but his voice took an ominous turn. "Be advised, there's a magic spell in place. No one can break the results or duck out of the duties placed on them by the wheel."

"You spin this every time you play?"

In unison, "Yes."

Big bad wolves using a colorful homemade spinning wheel for prizes. It was as cute as it was surprising. I chuckled and moved closer to read some of the titles. "Chef's Kiss?"

Gideon answered, "That's a good one. The losers have to fix dinner for you and a date. You get the whole romantic thing with candles and wait service. It works every time if you know what I'm saying. Wells is a great cook."

That much I knew from his Aetherian Truffle Oil grilled cheese.

But I had no potential person to date and wouldn't in a while, so I hoped I wouldn't get that space. I turned the wheel with my finger. "Catch and Release?"

Ren smirked. "That's a wolf thing. It wouldn't work with you. Unless you made it sexual." Wells punched his arm, hard enough to make him grunt in response. Okay, that's off the table.

"Laundry Detail is obvious. Night Watch? I assume this refers to guard duty of some kind?"

Mace nodded. "DJ means the winner forces the losers to listen to whatever music they want for twenty-four hours. You don't want Gideon to win that one."

"Hey. Boy bands are for forever, Man."

I laughed. Damn it, I was starting to like these damn wolves. "What about this one? King for a Day?"

Gideon grinned. "If the winner gets this space, the rest of us must do everything they say for twenty-four hours, big or small. It could be as simple as getting them a cup of coffee to sneaking into Mateo's office to steal something. The stipulation is that it can't harm anyone or put the pack in danger."

That one. That's what I needed. Wells stepped in front of the wheel. "You won, Gnome." I had. Even if I hadn't used it on him, I'd used Name magic to obtain my victory, so he was aware I cheated. He didn't say a word about it. He just Gesture One'd. "Are you going stand there all night or are you going to spin?"

Right.

I narrowed my vision on the bright purple King for the Day space—as if it would do any good whatsoever—and hooked a finger into the peg. I spun as hard as I could.

The clicking sound of the wheel seemed to reverberate around the room. Everyone was watching the wheel, but I couldn't help but focus on the dirt from the plant scattered on the floor. How had I done that without being aware? Did it have something to do with what happened at the Conduit or the enigmatic pronunciation I'd made? Was it a weird fluke because I was nervous? I didn't know how it had happened, but I knew I'd done it.

The betas held a collective breath as the wheel slowed. Click, click, click. I watched in horror as it slowed, coming to a stop on "Catch and

Release."

Nope. No way. Not a chance.

The Betas were raucous with laughter, but I wasn't going to let it happen. I took a deep breath and blew toward the wheel. It was stupid to think I could move it, but I didn't want to go through the explanation or subsequent sexual connotations of Catch and Release.

The laughter died when the wheel made one more click.

King for the Day.

I don't know how it worked. The wheel was heavy. I shouldn't have been able to simply blow it to the next space, yet I had. I expected Wells to cry foul, but he didn't. He just stood there smirking like he was proud of me. What was up with that? Was I growing on him—or worse—was he growing on me?

I didn't want to spend time thinking about it, so I grabbed a pen from the bar and crossed out the word King, and put Queen in its place.

I sipped my coffee, making a big slurping sound on purpose. "Bow to your Queen, Peasant."

Ren grumbled, lowering himself into a deep bow. Beside me, Tristan giggled. He had an uncanny knack for appearing by my side when the betas were gathered. He looked over at Ren. "Nuh-uh. Your Queen said to stay in the bow until she releases you. Bend over like you're sucking your own cock, beta."

Ren growled toward the fairy, then looked up at me. "You're taking this a little too far,"

Nah.

Gideon came jogging toward us, took one look at Ren, and executed a one-eighty. "Not so fast, Buster. I see you. Come here." He shook his head but came on anyway.

Was I taking the Queen thing too far?

Most likely.

"I'm going to need some cocktails this afternoon. You have booze here at the camp? Other than beer?"

His tone was playful. "Yas, Queen."

I motioned for Ren to stand up. The two shared a look, though it was more amusement, less contempt. "Great. I'm thinking…margaritas. Lots of them. I'll trust you and Mace to be here after lunch."

He bowed and scurried off before I could lower any other demands.

Tristan lit on Ren's shoulder and was removed with an aggressive flick. "I like how you think, Babycakes. But, have you noticed which beta hasn't bothered to grace us with his presence today?" Yes, I had. Hours earlier when I'd been escorted to breakfast on the shoulders of Ren and Mace. "Where is the hot, grumpy one?"

Ren retied his bun. "He and Bash aren't back yet. I'm sure we'll see him later."

"I see. He's avoiding me for fear of what I'd make him do as Queen."

Ren shrugged in a way that told me I was right. "Never mind him. I need to get some practice in. You ready?" He nodded and took his position in the sun. Tristan flew over to the tree and I was off and in the ground within seconds.

After a few runs, I'd shave all but four seconds off to make the one-minute goal. Sometimes I'd grumbled about having to dig tunnels all day but being in the soil was good for me. My muscles and my Earth magic were getting stronger every day and I *knew* I was going to pass the Heart trial.

Or maybe being Queen was going to my head.

I worked hard for several hours before I decided I needed to refuel and rest. I broke through the ground, punching a new hole an inch from Ren's resting spot. "The Queen says let her eat cake!"

"I wondered how long it would take you to get to that one today." He slid his sunglasses down his nose, checking out my dirt-ridden clothes and face. And hair. Everything. "You are too revolting to live."

Blunt, but accurate.

Even though Tristan hadn't been part of the poker game, he was enjoying participating in the shenanigans. He didn't bat an eyelash when I commanded him to get us some lunch so I wouldn't offend people in the cafeteria.

I plopped on the ground next to Ren. He'd turned over to sun his back, which was a nice view, for certain, but I'd realized he didn't do anything for me in *that* way. Yeah, looking at him was nice every day, but I enjoyed just hanging out with him because of who he was. He didn't even raise his head to speak to me. "Hey Queenie, you're doing well."

"You think?"

"I know."

I was overwhelmed with appreciation for the wolf. I didn't think he handed out compliments that often. "I like you, Ren."

He turned on his side to face me. "Go on."

"I mean, you're very direct. You just say what you're thinking and fail to care how other people feel about it. It's cool."

"Great. Do you want to fuck me now?"

"See? Very blunt. And, no, thank you on the sex." He smirked, but I continued. "Now, as your Queen, I'm ordering you to tell me something you like about me." I was messing with him, but as soon as the question popped out, a thread of nerves fluttered through my body. Did I care if Ren liked anything about me?

Yeah, I did.

I was new to this friend business.

He eyed me up and down, considering what to say. Finally, he came up with, "You're determined, and you don't take any shit. I'll give you that."

Okay, not bad. Flattering, even. "And...?"

He cocked his head. "If I had to say something else...I guess your eyes

193

are a nice rich color and your hair isn't terrible…"

"Aw, thanks. I'm blushing." I fanned myself, batting my eyelashes.

"…when it isn't matted with dirt and stuck to your head with sweat, that is."

"And, there he is."

He chuckled as Tristan arrived, normal-sized and clothed, carrying a picnic basket. Mace and Gideon weren't far behind with an orange cooler full of my margaritas. They made quick work of setting out a spread for us and we scarfed down our sandwiches because, like me, they were all about the margaritas.

I was on my second one when I spotted two female wolves walking by with their heads down, whispering. They didn't appear to notice us, so I called over. "Yo, do you ladies want a margarita?"

Mage, I was jumping on that friend train for sure.

Mace and Ren shared a look that I couldn't discern. I don't think they were trying to avoid the women, but something was up for sure. Maybe they'd slept with both of them for all I knew. Didn't matter. I was Queen and there was way too much testosterone around me.

The women approached. The blond one swished her braid over her shoulder and stuck out her hand. "If you're serving drinks, I want to get to know you. I'm Kelsey." She pointed to her sandy-haired friend. "This is Spencer." I shook Kelsey's hand, but Spencer hovered a little way behind her, looking at the ground more than me.

Spencer. I'd heard that name before. Gideon had mentioned it when he was talking to Wells. She was pretty with freckles dotting her nose and long athletic legs. I shot a look to Mace and tilted my head as if there were an actual crown on it. "Aren't you going to introduce me?"

"Okay." A gleam crossed his eye as took a big breath. If anyone could string together some nicknames, it was Mace. "This is Terra, Winner of Poker, Digger of Tunnels, Collector of Sex Anecdotes, Perception

194

Contract Participant, Master of Tristan, Troublemaker to Betas and Queen of Boulderbrook. All hail!"

The betas shouted a collective "Hail!"

Kelsey raised an eyebrow. "Dude, you forgot Distributor of Cocktails."

Mace handed a drink to both ladies. "Here, here. A toast to our Queen!"

The women took a seat, and I couldn't help but notice Spencer was staring into her drink more than consuming it. Gideon sat beside her. "How is he?"

My ears perked up.

She shrugged. "The same. Arlo says it's the best we can hope for at this point." I didn't want to ask, but I didn't have to. She looked up at me and I noticed dark circles under her pretty blue eyes. "My mate, Dominic, he's…under the weather."

I didn't know how werewolf mates worked, but I could sense the anguish emanating from her. It was like she was ill herself. For a moment, I was envious. To be able to feel so deeply for another person—a true mate—was a foreign concept. Gnomes didn't have mates and for a fierce moment, it made my heart ache for something, someone, whose life would be entangled with mine. To live and die with another person's heart inside yours was scary. And beautiful.

I'd never even had a real boyfriend before. I dated guys for a month or two at most. The closest I'd ever come to a relationship like Spencer's was the Perception magic that bound me to Wells. We were entangled, sure, but not in the good way that signified feelings and a longing to be together. Ours was business, a means to an end. "I'm sorry to hear that. I hope he recovers soon."

"He will." The booming voice came from behind me as his dark shadow passed over. "It takes time."

The betas and the ladies scrambled to their feet. Tristan poofed as fast as he could, leaving his man-sized clothes in a heap on the ground.

Mateo.

I stood up and dusted the dirt from my ass. Awesome. I looked like an idiot in front of the werewolf alpha. Mateo didn't seem to notice or care. He just stood there staring at me like he was trying to figure out what I was. "Miss Youngblood. Walk with me." A command. I mean, *he* wasn't Queen for the Day, so technically I didn't have to, but he didn't know. I didn't want to be the one to explain it to him.

It's not like I could say no to the alpha, so I followed him, my pulse starting to kick up as I remembered Wells telling me to steer clear of him. We walked in the direction of the barn and my magical hackles started to get all the way up. I forced myself to take calm even breaths, but I was feeling nowhere near calm walking in the direction I knew something sinister was taking place.

After a few minutes of excruciating silence, he spoke. "Wells said things are progressing with your training?" *Keep it together, Terra.* I nodded. "Good. Tell me, have you experienced anything else unusual since the day you first arrived and the Conduit…blipped?"

He called that a blip? I called it a magical inferno.

I recalled the night before during the poker game when the plant exploded and attacked Gideon. And the way I was able to blow the wheel to the space I wanted. Both small instances, but instances, nonetheless. There was something happening, whether it was to me or by me, I didn't know. Whatever the case, I was certain Mateo would want to know about it. And even more certain I shouldn't disclose it. "No. I've just been training, eating, sleeping. That's it."

"Good. Have you given any more thought to what you said after the djinn made you wish for answers?"

More than I am and less than I should be. Love, light, destiny, protection, blood.

I'd gone over it a million times and still didn't understand it. "No." I couldn't stand the tension raking through me as Mateo tried to stare holes into me like he was trying to pull the meanings from me with force. "Where are we headed?"

He smiled, but it didn't reach his eyes. They were cold, calculating, more wolf than man. "I want to run a little test. Nothing too invasive."

Whoa. Hold it there, cowboy. "Shouldn't Arlo be taking care of that in the Infirmary?"

My voice was shaky. Every step we took in the direction of the barn-lab ramped up my buzzing nerves. The overwhelming wrongness of the situation was slapping on the butt and telling me to halt, but I couldn't come up with a good reason to do so.

"Taking care of what in the Infirmary?

Wells appeared out of nowhere. This time, I don't know how he snuck up on us and I didn't care either. I was relieved to see him, even if his eyes were near silver and he was panting.

Wearing nothing but an aqua towel. Again.

So, he'd shifted. To get to us sooner? Or to torture me with his immaculate frame?

The world may never know.

Mateo ran his hands over his greasy hair, staring down at his beta. He bared his teeth, just a little, but it was enough for me to catch the elongated canines. A show of dominance. "Wells. You've been in wolf-form? Unusual?" His tone was light, but I was started to see the undercurrent in them, the way his questions were not really questions and they dripped with unspoken demands.

"I was on guard duty and needed to do a perimeter check. It's faster in wolf form."

A nervous skitter ran along my spine. He hadn't been on guard duty. He'd been somewhere overnight on a jet. Why lie to Mateo about where he'd been?

"Ah. Does the pack need to be concerned? No djinn presence?"

"No. A wayward bear shifter wandered onto our land looking to hibernate, but I took care of it. No djinn presence to report." Wells turned to me. "What did you say about the infirmary? Are you hurt?"

I opened my mouth to answer, but Mateo spoke for me. "It's time to explore further with her blood, since her make-up is in question, and she has a connection to the Conduit."

A lot of information was hidden in those few lines of dialogue. Not that I could interpret it.

Wells stepped closer to Mateo, his canines descending and hair rippling over his body. "She's had blood drawn. You don't need any more." He snarled at Mateo. The hair on the back of my neck took notice because it was way more menacing than any of the times he'd growled in my direction. "I promised Terra I'd show her the lake right now."

He promised no such thing.

Though I was going to demand it as Queen later anyway.

Mateo snarled. The two men stood chest to chest. I could feel the coiled anger rippling between them. I didn't know a lot about wolves, but I knew Wells stepping up like this, daring to confront his alpha, was a big deal.

It frightened me. Because I didn't want to watch them rip each other apart.

I put my hand on Wells' arm. Even in the heat of midday, I knew my touch was cool on his warm skin. It served to shake him out of whatever was happening. "Aren't we going to the lake?" His eyes returned to the normal purple color and both men took a step back. The stand-off seemed to be over.

But was it?

I faced Mateo, steeling my spine and trying to ignore how menacing he was. "See you later." I grabbed Wells' hand and started walking. Fast. After one step, Wells took over and pulled me along with him so that I found it hard to keep up with his long strides.

Behind us, Mateo gave his permission for us to leave, even though we were already yards away. "Go ahead. I'll perform the tests later."

Yeah, there was zero room for interpretation in that sentence.

I was more at ease with Wells beside me, but the foreshadowing vibe was real. Mateo wasn't going to let these tests go. And Wells wasn't going to allow them to happen. I just witnessed a legit confrontation between them. Over me.

"You're back. How did you know I needed you?"

Did I need him? In that moment, I had. That was a thought I wanted to shove back where it came from, wherever that was. I was bound by magic and relied on him for judgment purposes, but I didn't *need* Wells. I didn't need feelings about him crawling their way through me.

"I got back an hour ago and I'd just gotten out of the shower when Gideon texted me that Mateo came for you. I was worried he'd…"

"Don't leave the end of that sentence hanging. What are you worried about?"

Wells was still seething, his body taught, his breath shallow and rapid as he almost rubbed all the stubble from his jaw. "It doesn't matter. I'll take care of it."

I started to argue with him because his declaration to take care of it wasn't enough to quell the fear rumbling in my gut. But before I could, he grabbed my hand and pulled me along as he made huge purposeful strides. "Come on. We're going to the lake, but I have to get out of this towel first."

To my relief—and maybe just a *smidge* of disappointment—Wells dragged me to his cabin so he could change into proper clothes.

His cabin was nestled in an outstretch of the woods, surrounded by trees on one side, with a sweeping view of the lake on the other.

Oh, and it was a freaking treehouse.

I had a few minutes to look around while he went to change, so I took full advantage of the time. There was a thick hedge surrounding the perimeter of the massive tree that supported his cabin. The hedge was so tall, it had begun growing in and around the lower tree limbs in a beautiful natural way, linking the two and making the entire area below shady and secluded.

It had gnome written all over it. How mind-boggling that it belonged to a wolf.

I walked around the inside confines of the space and discovered the hedge going wider to make room for a sitting garden behind the tree. Well, what used to be a sitting garden.

There were a couple of wooden benches, small statues of magical beings like werewolves, dragons, fae, and more. Butting up against the back of the hedge, in front of a rotting wood trellis, sat a fountain that had dried up long ago. I could visualize how charming and peaceful it must have been in the past, nestled under the shaded expanse of the treehouse.

The entire garden area was covered in lush, fertile soil. I bent down and placed my hand over the earth. I was hit with an immediate and powerful feeling of love. It was so strong, I began to hum, to warm with overwhelming fullness inside of me. I couldn't help it; I thought of home.

I grabbed a handful of dirt and stood, crumbling it between my fingers just so I could get more of it with my Earth magic. As it fell to the ground, I picked up a deep sadness too. Not as strong, but there, nonetheless. It reminded me of the soil in my backyard after Gram died like it was missing a key component.

Wells' voice startled me. "This was my mother's garden."

I turned to face him; his eyes flashed a deep violet. He was wearing dark jeans and a purple V-neck sweater that looked like he had it made to match his eyes. I sucked in a breath at his intense beauty as he strode toward me and pulled me down on one of the benches. The sheer torment on his face told me things I didn't have to ask. I'd experienced it in earth between my fingers too. We lived with the same grief, he and I. "How did she die?"

He gave a rueful laugh. "Of all the magical dangers she could've run into in Aetheria, it was cancer that got her in the end."

"You were in Aetheria?"

He picked a leaf from the hedge, tossing it and watching it float to the ground. "I was born in Aetheria. There was an accident when I was three and my dad didn't survive, so I don't remember him. Mom thought she

202

could build a better life for us here, a quieter life, I guess. The pack took us in when we came through the Conduit."

He Gesture One'd, his shoulders tight as his muscular chest. "After she got sick, Mateo helped me build this treehouse cabin for her. I couldn't do it alone because I was an eleven-year-old pup who hadn't even had his first shift. I had no muscles and even less construction knowledge, but Mom wanted to live in the clouds. It was the best we could do in this place."

The lavender glint of love in his eyes made me flush. He'd never shared any of himself with me and it was overwhelming as it poured it out so freely there in his mother's garden. "She enjoyed looking out at the lake from the cabin upstairs, but down here ended up being her favorite spot. We would sit here in the garden for hours, reading books together.

"Mateo used to make fun of me for it. He wanted me to be strong, the kind of man who would take over as alpha one day. Not some studious nerd, as he put it." Wells cleared his throat, choking the emotion from his voice by force of will. "He was the only father figure I had. And I think he loved my mother."

Confronting Mateo like he'd done must have been rougher for him than I imagined. It wasn't simply a beta opposing an alpha, there was a deeper connection there. I took in the intensity of his stoic face, and I wanted to swoop him into a giant hug and take away his pain.

That.

Was concerning.

He was my judge, my tormentor. Not my friend. Not my...

He shook his head and blew out a breath that rustled his hair. "I should get rid of the flowerbed, fix the trellis. Just never had the heart to touch this place."

I could understand that. There was an entire house full of Gram's things that I'd refused to let go when she died. Mage, I was still carrying around her silly Magic 8-Ball because touching it erased some small pinprick of pain from my heart. It was like she was there with me. I knew I couldn't erase Wells' pain from losing his mother, but maybe I could do something similar for him.

Crouching down, I placed both hands in the soil and the magic inside me swelled. Apprehension threatened to stop me—I didn't know if I could do it—but I pushed back my fear of the unknown and dug in deeper, drawing out my magic. I needed to do this. For him. He'd just saved me from Mateo's experiments. I owed him.

Nothing more.

Wells slid off the bench and knelt beside me. He didn't say anything, but his presence was like cozying up to a fire on a cool Autumn night. I used that feeling. It seemed like I should. After a few moments, I looked up and couldn't believe what I'd done.

Deep purple flowers had sprouted in the flower bed, trailing up the trellis, and around the trunk of the tree. They were everywhere, growing from the soil under our feet, even nestling into the hedge. I meant to grow a couple of blooms, not explode flowers all over the place. I looked at Wells, eager to see if he was as shocked as I was.

He didn't look surprised at all. He was quiet. Still. "How did you know purple pansies were her favorite?" I don't think I'd ever heard him whisper in quite that way. His voice was breathless, full of awe, and had a fierce edge to it like he was clinging onto something.

"I just tapped into what was already there. I didn't do much. Just forced a little life into them." I shrugged.

"You're underestimating yourself." He stood suddenly, nipping a vibrant bloom from the trellis. He tucked it behind my ear and his warm thumb grazed my cheek, which made me shiver. "Thank you."

I wanted to tell him that I had no idea if the flowers would last. To make sure he knew I did it because of my own experience with loss and grief, but it felt too personal to connect us in that way, so I stayed silent.

In those moments I should've informed him I would *not* become the Boulderbrook gardener-in-residence or something equally business-like to put a cavernous distance between us.

But I didn't. I just said, "You're welcome."

He wrapped his warm hand around mine. "I promised you a trip to the lake."

He dropped my hand after we emerged from the cocoon around his treehouse, and we walked the winding path that led to the lake in silence. I went through about a thousand different things in my mind, most of them centering on Wells and how I needed to…not center on Wells.

In the past couple hours, he'd become more real to me. I couldn't keep my mind from comparing him to the few one-night stands and dalliances I'd had in my life. Those guys seemed two-dimensional now compared to Wells. It was probably more my fault than theirs since I didn't do attachments. Even after Gram passed. Mage, I had no clue if my last hook-up Trevor's mother was alive or not and we'd carried on for two months. But there I was, grieving the loss of Wells' mom like I'd known her.

I didn't like him crawling under my skin that way. He was still in charge of my fate. I needed to get my head on straight about Wells. It didn't help matters when he Gesture Two'd me to another bench that was nestled behind a patch of reed grass and declared. "Your throne, my Queen."

I sat and smiled in spite of myself. "You didn't forget."

"I pay my debts. You won fair and square."

"Except, I cheated, and you know it."

He shrugged. "I didn't know if you'd go so far as you did with the getting the right space on the wheel, but I had a reason to allow you to pull that stunt off." His tone had taken a sober turn. There was something prompting in the way he held himself. He was paused, on the edge of something, eyeing me for permission to continue. I nodded at him. He ran his hand through his hair, and it ruffled right back into place like it always did. The deepest desire to touch it myself tittered across my mind, but I shooed it out. Fast.

"I knew if you were Queen for the day, you'd make a hundred ridiculous demands, but eventually, you'd get around to asking questions, *forcing* me to spill the answers. The wheel's magic would give you what you needed to..." He titled his head, urging me to read between the lines.

Forcing him.

It was about the magic.

"So, because I'm Queen for the day, you'd have no choice but to answer anything I asked, no matter the conditions of the Perception contract? The magic in the wheel would override it?"

A quick nod. "Somewhat. I can't say..." he stopped to rub his temples, like he had a sudden fierce headache. "I need you to fill in some gaps here."

I rummaged through my brain, trying to pinpoint what questions I was supposed to ask. I decided to start simple. "As Queen, I'm asking this question: Would you really kill me if I fail to prove myself worthy in the trials?" Perhaps all of the hoops I jumped through were for nothing.

He huffed. "I'd have to. Not that. Different question."

Yeah, didn't think so.

"Okay." He started pacing in front of me, his shoes squicking in the mud as he trudged back and forth, stopping every few steps to look at me. Mage, he was uncomfortable. It was a very disorienting sight. He'd never looked anything other than smugly confident and in total control of everything. He pointed at me. His hand was shaking like it took effort. He wanted to talk about me.

"What do you think happened with the Conduit on the day I arrived?"

"My best guess—and what I haven't told Mateo yet—is that you poked a hole in whatever was blocking the Conduit from the other side. The Five don't see it that way because we still can't get through it, but you damaged part of the magic blocking it."

"Me? Damaging whatever was blocking Aetheria for years? The thing no one has been able to figure out?"

"Yes. You."

He motioned for me to keep going. "How?"

"Unknown. Your magic is different. That's all I know about it." He shook his head, clenching his fists as the pacing picked up. I interpreted it to mean try a different subject and hurry up with the questions. The two magics were warring in his body and it hurt.

"Mateo." He stopped in his tracks. Motionless, save for his chest heaving with each breath. "What does he want with me?"

That was it.

He slid onto the seat beside me, scraping the stubble on his jaw so hard I thought he'd rub the sexy scruff off and that would've been a shame.

Cage the Mage. He's trying to give you intel. Drool later.

His stubble was probably scratchy and not soft anyway.

His canines slid forward, and he bit his lip, drawing a little blood. It was clear he was about to say something he wasn't supposed to reveal, and the magic was interfering. When he spoke, his words clipped and sharp, like it hurt to say them. "He wants magic, power for wolves. Limited supply. Must take it from other sources. You have no family. No one to miss you. Disrupted the Conduit block."

It was starting to come together, but still made little sense. "He thinks he can get magic from me? A half-gnome? Not even in the Conclave?" I hurried to add on the "Yet."

"We don't know what you are yet, but he thinks you're…special. Didn't know it at the beginning or I would've never…" He switched gears. "He wouldn't blink an eye at killing you to get what he wants."

I'd known there was something up with Mateo, but it blew my mind to think I had anything of value to him. He said as much when I petitioned to join the Conclave. I was insignificant and held no power. But then, the Conduit went cuckoo for Cocoa Puffs and the djinn showed up the very day I arrived.

You are special, my Jewel.

Most grannies tell their grandkids they're special, right? She said it because she loved me.

But what if she knew I was more than that? All these weird things that I'd been writing off. Maybe it meant I was more significant than everyone realized. Everyone but Wells.

More than I am and less than I should be.

If it's true, then Mateo wants to take my magic and give it to wolves? But how? "Does this have anything to do with *fusion?*"

His eyes widened at the mention of the word. He tried to speak, but nothing came out. Frustrated, he ended up gripping his thighs and rocking against the bench. He was in real pain. And it hurt me on a physical level to see him suffering. "Has some kind of Magic prevented you from just talking about this?"

I could feel the relief flooding out of him like a damn had been burst. That's what he wanted me to ask. "Binding magic was used on the betas and anyone who knows about fus—" He stopped, tearing at the neck of his sweater like it hurt him to have it on. "He bound me in other ways too. When I'm near you and want to…" He didn't have the strength to finish that sentence either. Watching him slump over and whine was unbearable. He took a breath. "I'm getting better at breaking through that one though. Maybe soon…" He reached out, placing his hand on my thigh, but jerked it away after a few seconds. Like he'd been testing something.

I was grateful to Wells for giving me as much information as he had, but I couldn't stand to see him in misery any longer. I had more than I had started with and good idea who I could go to for more answers on fusion. Someone who might not be in intense pain from Binding magic.

"Thank you, Peasant. That'll be all the questions for now." He released a shuddering breath before I added, with a dramatic flourish, "I'm your Queen. Bow to me."

With the pain gone, he morphed into a different person. Back, was the smoldering, cock-sure guy with a sexy smirk hell-bent on torturing me. He dipped into a low bow. When he raised his eyes, they flashed deep magenta and he knelt before the bench, his laser-focus on me. "I don't care who he is. I won't let him touch you again."

He grazed my outer thighs with his hands. It was just a small shift in position, but infinitely more intimate. It was a promise that seemed miles beyond keeping me safe from Mateo.

A thick anchor was holding us in place, locking us into something we had no control over. I swallowed the quivering breath that vowed to betray me. He was so close and so warm. And I had an insane ache to know the feel of his lips against mine. He lowered his eyes onto my mouth, and I knew he was thinking the same thing.

This thing drawing us together us had to die. We had the Perception magic to deal with.

Wells shook his head, then walked over to the edge of the lake, allowing me to breathe for a second without giving my inappropriate thoughts away. Why did he have to be so *ugh*? I should've asked to bind myself to an fugly wolf. Though, I hadn't seen any at the camp yet.

He picked up a rock, skimmed it across the surface, making it bounce a few times before it fell. Seconds later, a plume of water erupted from the surface and shaped itself into a feather. I blinked to make sure I was seeing it correctly. The edges of the feather turned red as it hung in the air for a few seconds before it rained back into the lake.

I jumped up. "How did you do that?"

"Remember, I said there's magic everywhere? There's a water nymph spell from centuries ago in Lake Boulderbrook." He picked up a couple more rocks and handed one to me. "Try it."

I tossed the rock into the water. It bounced once before it kerplunked, but I guess it was enough to count. A huge water sprout gushed forward, shaping into a skull. It hung there in the air for about five seconds, turning black, then dropping into the water with a splash. "Mage Almighty, does that mean I'm about to die?" I sputtered.

He laughed. "Relax. It's not a portent. The magic takes what's on your mind, in your heart, and gives it form. Given what I just told you and the trials you're enduring, you've got to be scared as fuck."

It made sense. It was still unnerving, but I could believe the magic Water spell was picking up on my fear. I had enough of it to go around the entire camp. Wells dropped the rock he was holding in his hand and watched it as it thudded in the mud. "Didn't mean to scare you."

Something about the way he was staring at the rock in the mud touched me on a deep level. He looked…sad. I prayed to the Mage it wasn't regret for having shared something he wasn't supposed to, for daring to disobey his alpha. "Sure, I'm nervous about a lot of this, but I believe you when you say you'll protect me from Mateo."

He looked up at me, eyes flaring violet. "Good. That's what I wanted to hear."

I could tell it crossed his mind to throw another rock into the water, but he decided against it and dropped it in the mud.

He was uneasy and I wanted to ease his discomfort more than anything else at the moment. I couldn't let him just stand there and be maudlin after the ground we'd just covered. I liked him sharing things with me. "So, you were thinking about birds earlier? The feather?"

He grinned. "No, nothing that literal."

"Wait a second. Was it a fairy wing instead of a bird feather? Were you thinking about Tristan thinking about your balls?"

His shoulders relaxed and laughed. "Maybe I was. Sounds like you're a little jealous, Queen Gnome."

"What? Not even close, Peasant." I sat back down on the bench and crossed my legs dramatically. "I'm just going to sit here and enjoy the lake view. You and Tristan go and do whatever your little hearts and balls desire."

He sauntered over. This time there was no mistaking his intent. It was soft, playful. Smoldering.

Mage. Help. Me.

He leaned over, placing his lips right against my ear. "I don't think you could handle what my heart and balls desire." When he angled back, a devious grin spread across his face. He touched my cheek and I felt it all over my body. "Hm. I can almost touch you without consequences now."

"You mean to say you feel pain when you touch me?" Instantly I knew he was talking Mateo's damn Binding magic. He was trying to keep us from getting close.

That was a good thing though.

Right?

To assess further, he trailed his finger down my cheek, along my jaw,

213

tracing my neck and collarbone, then back up to my lips, testing to see what it did to him. *Shitfire.* Had the temperature gone up four thousand degrees? He bit his own lip, and I almost broke in two at the unadulterated heat that surged through me. He leaned in and purred. "It's almost sunset. I have to tuck you *in bed*, Queen, before the full moon rises."

He stood and Gesture-Two'd toward the main campground.

Did he just—?

He didn't.

Except he did.

That was…I was going to kill him. Murder him in his sleep.

Touching me, then telling me he needed to tuck me in bed. He trying to get a rise out of me. Again. He winked and turned back around. I followed behind, thinking of the various ways I could commit Wolficide.

My cabin was close, so I only got to imagine five ways to kill Wells before we got there. I was certain that number would reach into the hundreds before the night was over.

As I entered my cabin, he leaned against the door frame. Yeah, someone in his past had told him that leaning looked good on him. Curse, whomever it was.

I tried to reign in my emotions, but truth be told, I was ping-ponging between annoyed, appreciative, confused, and turned on. Wells managed to continue leaning as he Gesture One'd. "What are you thinking?"

"Nothing."

"Oh, it's definitely something."

"I was thinking that you're either a saint or a Douchehole. Jury's still out."

He sneered. "I'm not a saint."

No, he wasn't. But, as much as I wanted him to be a Douchehole, he wasn't that either.

I steeled my spine and marched over to the bed, grabbing his hoodie from the night before. "Thanks for the jacket." I shoved it at him, connecting with his stone-hard abs.

Back away now Terra. Do not let your hands in proximity to his torso. You will grab him, and it will not end well.

I took a step back. He smirked like he knew exactly why I'd shoved my hands into my pockets. His eyes slid from the tip of my head to my toes and my body almost burst into flames. He'd done that before—look at me like I was a snack he wanted to taste, but this time, it was primal. It zinged right between my thighs. "You keep it. It's getting cold at night, and you were right, I didn't give you much time to pack."

Damn it. It was so much easier to dislike him when he was just the hot dude who may or may not have to slay me. Now, I knew how much he loved his mother, and he was being…nice to me. Oh, I wanted that anger I'd experienced on the way to the cabin. Craved it. Yet, I couldn't summon it. Possibly—probably—because it wasn't real anger at all. "Thanks."

He Gesture Two'd me to the bed. A tingle of nerves swept through me until he took a spot on the edge of the tub. Okay. Distance between us was good. It was only three feet, but he was more than an arm's length away.

"This is important," he stated in his low rumbling voice that did things to my stomach. I nodded that I was listening. "The full moon's rising, so the pack will shift soon." My body went rigid. I wasn't sure I was ready for that event. "Most wolves will stay in the woods until after the moon crests, but you have to understand, only Mateo and the betas will retain full control over our wolves. The rest of the pack aren't that strong."

It occurred to me that I should've asked about werewolf shifting before that moment, but the werewolves had never seemed like wolves to me. Not really. They were just…them. "You're saying that if I encounter anyone besides the five special snowflakes, they'd eat me?"

"Eventually, but there would be a lengthy 'playing with food' situation first. You don't want to experience that."

I gasped. "Mage be damned."

"I won't allow any wolf near you, but…" He ran his hand over his jaw. I decided it was henceforth, Gesture Three. He did it when he was stalling and trying to figure out which information to leave out. "Never mind." He huffed and whatever he was thinking of saying stayed lodged in his mind.

I nudged him with my foot, but he shook his head and went back to business. "Arlo, Bambi, and the fae watch the kids who haven't been through puberty yet in the lodge. There are protection spells in place. You'll be safe there."

I hoped he was right about that. He seemed hesitant like there was a lot more he wanted to say, but when he stood and crossed to the door, I knew he wouldn't say it. "Stay here. I'll send food before the party, then you can head to the lodge."

"Did you say party?"

"Shit." He hadn't meant to divulge the party business.

"You should tell your Queen about the party. Now."

He sighed. "We gather together, as a pack, before the full moon shift. More of a tradition and less a real party. Nothing exciting." Shrugging, he was out of the door before I could ask if cupcakes were being served at the pack party. Though, in hindsight, I didn't know what kind of carnivorous wolf things may have been in the cupcakes, so I convinced myself I wasn't missing anything.

I opened the window to let the cool air in as I took a quick bath. Seeing the brown ring in the tub made me wonder how he'd stood to be close to me all day. I'd grossed myself out, but at least I was clean and shiny now. I'd put on my good black underwear and one of my kitschy garden gnome socks when there was a pound at the door. I assumed it was my dinner.

Grabbing the closest thing I could find—Wells' hoodie—I threw it over my head just as Ren, Mace, and Gideon burst inside, with Tristan flying behind them. "Whoa. Custom dictates that the knockee invite the knockers in before they open the door, Peasants."

Mace laughed and bowed low. "No time for that, my Queen." Before I could say another word, he scooped me up and threw me over his shoulder.

I yelped. "What are you doing?"

Ren passed my other sock to Gideon who put it on my bare foot. "Did you think we would allow our Queen to miss the party? What kind of subjects do you take us for?"

I laughed. They were turning out to be amazing subjects. "Wells said it wasn't a real party and then he said to stay here during the not-party, then go to the lodge."

Gideon walked around in front and bent down, making us eye to eye. He cupped my face in a weird brotherly way that made my insides warm. I was definitely getting used to these wolves. "Sometimes Wells needs help extracting his head from his ass. That's where we come in."

Tristan flitted in a circle. "Dibs! Dibs! Dibs on extracting things from Wells' ass!"

There was no limit to his libido. None.

Mace started out the door, but I wasn't sure I wanted to be hauled away to the party, especially since Wells had been so serious about me staying put. The beta squad didn't appear to give a single shit about that. And lying there, over Mace's shoulder with two other hulking wolves flanking me, I couldn't imagine any situation where I wouldn't be totally safe.

Plus, what kind of Queen would I be if I didn't at least share one drink with my subjects? "Okay, but I can't go like this. I don't have shoes. Or pants, for that matter."

A devilish grin spread across Ren's lips, as he reached around and lifted the hem of the hoodie. "You've got panties on. You're good." Thank the Mage, I did. My cheeks reddened, though, maybe that was because I was still hanging upside down on top of Mace. "Pants are overrated."

Said the person wearing jeans.

We left my cabin, the night air biting my legs. I guess I was doing this in nothing but gnome socks and a hoodie that came just short of mid-thigh. I mean, my ass was covered, but I was underdressed for a party. "I can walk, you know."

Mace swung me around like we were doing some kind of complicated ice skater moves, but I ended up in the exact same position as when I started, but on the other shoulder. "Nah, you'll get your cute socks dirty, Cinderella."

As we got closer to the pavilion, voices spilled into the night, laughing and talking. There was a warm camaraderie in the air, even before Mace set foot inside. This was what a pack was—more than shared experiences and history, pack was a feeling, a presence. It was light in the darkness.

I couldn't help but think back to all the lonely nights sitting beside Gram as she drifted in and out of consciousness. Nights when I knew kids from school were out partying or dating. Nights that I didn't regret, but still left a dark longing in my heart for something more than I had.

A twang of unease crept through me, and I felt like an imposter. This was *their* pack, and I wasn't a part of it.

Tristan flew in front of us, lighting on my nose like a gnat. I stopped myself from swatting him away because his presence made me feel less insecure. If a fairy that wasn't loyal to the pack was there, why shouldn't the Queen for the day be too? "I don't know if you're ready for this, Babycakes." I raised an eyebrow at him as Mace deposited me on the concrete. I steadied myself from hanging upside down and whirled around.

Tristan may have been right.

It looked like the entire pack was there under the pavilion, except the kids. I could count on one hand those who were fully clothed. The rest were wearing, well, very little. They weren't giving off a sexy, in-da-club vibe at all. It was just people hanging out, chilling.

In their underwear.

Mace kissed the top of my head. "See ya later, my Queen. *DJ Outer Mace* has a job to do."

Mage, he was ridiculous.

He ran over to a stand behind the picnic tables, grabbing a woman around the waist and slinging her around. She yelped but wasn't mad at him. In fact, she looked like she was about to tear his clothes off. In response, Mace ripped his navy t-shirt down the middle and howled.

The rest of the wolves, every stinking one of them, howled back.

A smarter person may have been scared, but it made me laugh.

I turned to Ren. He grinned and held up his finger for me to wait. He ran over behind the pavilion and half a minute later, he reappeared holding three red plastic cups with a yellowish drink inside. He handed one to me and passed one over to Gideon, whose eyes went wide. "Are you sure this is a good idea? Maybe she shouldn't."

"She should." He nodded at me. "Drink up, Queen."

I put the drink to my nose. There were notes of pineapple and honey, mixed with an earthy spice, which made it sweet, but not too cloying. There was a foam on top like beer. "Fae froth?"

"Yep. You'll thank me later." He took a huge swig of his drink, then ran off like there was an urgent meeting he had to attend.

Beside me, Gideon murmured. "Maybe, maybe not."

I looked around. Practically every wolf had a cup in their hands. I had to admit I was curious and tempted to drink it because it smelled so amazing. "Wells told me about this, but he said it was from Aetheria. Does it age like wine?"

Gideon took a swig. So, he was of the *me*-no-drinkie club, but he could consume half his cup in one swig? Dick move, Gid. "No, the original batch came over centuries ago, but fae can use magic to create more from a single drop. As long as we have a fairy and don't let the supply dry up, the froth flows free."

Say that three times fast.

Tristan lighted on the rim of my cup. "More like a sourdough starter, than wine." He helped himself to a slurp of my drink. "Mage, I've missed froth." He took another swig and I had to swat him away that time or there would've been none left for me if I decided to drink it.

Ren appeared again. Wherever he'd gone, somewhere along the way, he'd lost his shirt. He looked like a model about to pose for a naughty photo shoot. Especially given the way he was smiling at me. He was already wasted.

And even though a blazing hot dude was standing there in front of me, a tantalizing thought of Wells crept into my mind. I hated myself the second it happened, but I wondered when he would show up. And when he did, would he be pissed at me for being there?

And would he have on clothes?

Mace switched songs: "Bark at the Moon." I rolled my eyes as he bowed to Ren, who was raising his cup, urging me to join him with a look. Before I could talk myself out of it, I raised mine and clinked his cup.

"To our Queen!" He checked his watch. "For a few more minutes, at least. I hope you pass your trials!"

It had been a few hours since I'd remembered what I was actually at the camp for. There was no better reason to get drunk on froth than that, so I tipped my cup.

Froth tasted cool and bright, thicker than it looked. The pineapple flavor was there, but there was something I couldn't place laced inside it. And Mage, the spicy kick at the end was insane, like a little jolt of electricity.

My mind whizzed straight to the memory of me playing Red Rover with my classmates at recess. It was as clear to me as the day it happened. One of the boys had challenged us to go as fast as we could. We were laughing and running until we fell over and had to suck in breaths that scratched our throats. I was so happy that day. I ran home to tell Gram about it, but she was asleep in the middle of the day. It was the first time I knew something was wrong with her and the bubble of joy I'd experienced with my friends at recess popped forever.

I hadn't thought about that day in years.

Ren was eyeing me with a look of expectation. He reached up and ran his thumb along my lips. "Foam."

"Thanks. I just had the most vivid memory. Did the froth do that?"

Gideon shot me a sheepish grin. "Yep. I guess you'll be okay with this. Have fun, my Queen." He bowed and kissed the back of my hand, then skirted away, shouting at Kelsey across the pavilion. When she looked back, it was clear that he was getting laid in the very near future.

I tried to take another tentative sip of the froth, but Ren laughed and tipped my cup back, forcing me to guzzle it. Before I knew it, I'd chugged the entire cup. My head, my senses, began to reel in response. I was lightheaded, but not like with human alcohol. I was aware of what was happening around me, but I was loads more relaxed and holding a wealth of warm memories inside me.

A birthday when Gram got me exactly what I wanted, my first paycheck, first kiss, then Wells' deep throaty chuckle, as he knelt in front of me and said he'd protect me from Mateo at the lake.

When Ren handed me a second cup I took it, eager to see what my brain and the froth would conjure up. He conquered his cup and when I looked over, he was leaning against the column of the pavilion, panting. I wanted to ask him what he was feeling, but I wasn't sure it would be a good idea, given the look of pure desire on his face.

The froth had made him remember having sex with someone. I was sure of it. Not a bad thing, in my opinion. In fact, it made me consider a third cup, but DJ Mace changed the music and I decided to hold off. "Who Let the Dogs Out?"

Who. Let. The. Dogs. Out.

Most of the wolves jumped up and ran to the middle, dancing together in a big mob of people. Ren stood upright and kissed me on the cheek before he ran into the fray.

Werewolf kisses all around.

Except from...

Nope. Lock it down, Terra.

The throng of wolves were having so much I wanted to jump in and join them. Some of them had even started dancing on top of the picnic tables. I couldn't help myself. I started singing along.

Because who didn't know "Who Let the Dogs Out?"

Tristan appeared again and he was in full size. Thankfully with a Boulderbook towel on and handing me another cup of froth. We ended up sitting at one of the tables at the perimeter of the pavilion, away from the group. I was fine to sing along to Mace's music but jumping up in the middle of them seemed intrusive.

Their pack. Not mine.

Tristan leaned in. "What are the odds that the betas who randomly ended up together in this pack all happen to be fuckable?"

Testify.

"Wait. They weren't all born in the same pack?"

"No. I've been talking with the camp fae to get the play of the land."

"*Lay* of the land."

"Lay, huh? Should've gotten that one right." He laughed. "Anyway, you've heard of lone wolf, right? Most of the wolves at Boulderbrook were either lone wolves or left their home pack for one reason or another. They all ended up here together with Mateo as their alpha, guarding the Conduit to Aetheria."

I was shocked because from what I'd seen this pack was as close as they could be. Especially the beta squad. Knowing their bond was cultivated and not due to being born into it made me like them even more. An odd spring of hope welled in my heart.

But the formation of the pack didn't line up with what I was learning about Mateo. He wasn't the warm and fuzzy type. He was taking magic through fusion, and I suspected he was there at the Conduit for the sole purpose of draining all the magic he could. And he was using lone wolves to help him do it. None of them could do anything about it because he'd placed all sorts of Binding magic over them. It was chilling.

The music switched again, causing all the wolves howl in delight. It took a few seconds, but I recognized the old funk song, *"Atomic Dog."* With the first beats of the song, the wolves morphed into a frenzied horde. They formed a long line across the pavilion, some of them on top of the tables, each of them spreading their legs wide, stomping and thrusting in time to the music. There was some back-to-back, some back-to-front, all of them whooping and moving together. It wasn't a line dance, per se, but it was coordinated moves built from years of parties like this.

A red bra sailed across the pavilion and landed on my head. Tristan leaned over to pick it up and say something, but I was swooped off the bench from behind. I reached out, failing to grasp anything but air, and in a move drunk girls everywhere would've been proud of, I managed to hold on to my drink.

I should've panicked at being pulled away without knowing what was happening, but I was feeling too good to do that. Besides, I didn't recall the djinn having tattoos on their arms.

Ren deposited me on top of the picnic tables and jumped up in front of me. I had to laugh as I tried to pick up the dance they were doing. I wasn't much of a dancer, but the steps weren't dance steps either. It was just swaying, stomping, and grinding.

And stopping to take occasional sips of fae froth. Because every time I did, a steamy memory cropped up. It must have been all the close dancing or maybe I'd just sort of steered my mind in that direction. Whatever it was, I was getting hot in more ways than one.

Ren put his hand on my waist, maneuvering me, helping me figure out the dance. He glanced at Gideon, who raised his own cup and nodded his approval.

Maybe I didn't suck at dancing after all.

Or the fae froth had something to do with it. I was feeling heady and buzzed, and oh, so carefree. Knowing I wouldn't have a hangover made it even better.

I backed up, proud of myself for doing it in time to the beat. Ren moved his hand to my back. He turned me around, keeping in time with the music as I pressed into his solid frame, but not close enough to feel inappropriate. We weren't like that. Though glancing around at the rest of the wolves, I struggled to determine what would fall under inappropriate with the pack. They were very affectionate with each other.

There was another guy, wolf, in front of me. He had on a green and blue plaid flannel shirt that stretched tight across his broad shoulders, with a built-in gray hood that he'd raised over his head. The dude had a nice ass, and he was moving to the music like a professional. His own cup of fae froth was raised and he howled along to the song. He was having a damned good time.

So was I. Fae froth was the best thing ever invented.

I put my hand on his waist like the other wolves, connecting the long line of bodies together as we ground together. The guy turned to face me, gripping my hip.

I gasped.

Of course, it was Wells. Who else could it have been?

The human Pope? Batman? Kanye?

Ren was going to pay for this.

Wells' shirt was unbuttoned, revealing his insane torso and those feverishly low-slung jeans with the top button undone. There were definitely more than six in his pack. And, mercy Mage, his defined pecs made my stomach do a loop. The way he was dancing…there were no words.

Well, there were words. All of them were naughty.

If he moved like that when he danced, how in the Mage did he move when he—

Nope.

I stood there motionless. And if I stared at the V-dip in his hips any longer, drool would've come out of my mouth.

Get it together. You're having a physical reaction to his body because of the froth. He's smexy now, but tomorrow he'll be back to barking orders and owning your ass. Don't go there.

His eyes were closed, and he had a crooked smile on his lips. For the first time since I'd met him, he seemed relaxed. He reached down, pulling me close and pressing his pelvis against me as we danced. I sucked down the rest of my froth, hoping it would help drown my hormones.

It did no such thing.

The moment the froth passed my lips, I conjured a memory like none other I'd had all night.

It couldn't have been.

We'd never kissed.

Mage be damned. I shouldn't be thinking about him like that. I needed to scram, but before I could remove myself from the dire situation, he thrust his hips forward to the beat of the song. He was just the right height to graze my stomach with his fly. And he had to go ahead and jerk me against his hard length in the process.

Kill me now and bury me in the morning.

I stumbled back, bumping into Ren, who shrugged and stepped away like I had the plague. *Jerkhole.* Wells reached out to help the poor bumbling klutz who couldn't dance without falling. His eyes flew open. The adorable lopsided grin disappeared, his back went rigid, and his cup of froth splashed on the ground.

It was the biggest record-scratch moment I'd ever seen. He'd been dancing and enjoying himself, but he'd turned to stone at the sight of me.

I thought we'd had a breakthrough earlier. Mage. I'd just fantasized about kissing him and he stood there, inches away, gripping my waist, looking repulsed by my presence. He focused on the froth in my hand, then shot Ren a glare so violent, coffin salesmen everywhere started salivating.

The music was pumping and everyone but the two of us was grinding in time as I calculated my next move. Should I laugh it off and blame it on the betas who dragged me there? Should I apologize and go back to shaking my ass? Should I lick his chest?

Never drinking fae froth again.

I opened my mouth to speak, but he beat me to it. "Where are your fucking pants?"

I'd forgotten I was half naked, but so was everyone in the entire camp and he didn't seem to have a problem with them. "Why do you care?"

He kept his hold on me and torpedoed off the table with me in tow, taking us behind the pavilion, away from the pack. He leaned against the logs like the stud he was, twisting the fabric of my hoodie—his hoodie—into his fist as he skimmed over my bare legs. The look he served me was predatory and seductive on a level I'd never experienced.

He may have been concerned about my pants-free look, but it wasn't because he was protecting my honor. No. The naked desire on his face sent goosebumps over my body and the raging hard-on he was rocking was the final clue; he *liked* seeing me without pants.

This was potentially bad.

Potentially good too, based on the size of the bulge.

Nope, it was bad. And I needed to snap myself out of it.

With the hoodie still clenched in one fist, he Gesture Three'd with the other hand. He was standing there, sex incarnate, sporting a hard dick, trying to decide what to do or say. Why was he always thinking all the Magedamn time?

In my fae froth haze, I decided it would be a good idea to unburden him from his ever-present brain gymnastics. So, I stepped forward, slid my hands up his chest—damn near shuddering apart at the feel of his taut skin and the simmering heat of his flesh—until I reached his neck.

Then I kissed him.

This was no chaste kiss either. I laid it on him and pressed myself against him, forcing him to open his mouth for me. A tremor of shock coursed through him, but only for a moment. In the next second, he dropped the hoodie and both his hands slid over my ass. He caressed my back, softer than I imagined he was capable of, as he met my tongue with enthusiasm. I was suddenly drowning in the feel of him, the smell of him, the sound of that low rumble in his throat. He pulled back, whispering. "Finally broke the Binding magic."

"Good." I shivered. I expected someone who looked like him to be a great kisser, but I'd gravely underestimated his prowess. His mouth was hot and hungry, and I was instantly under his magnetic spell as his hands roamed and my body arched into the hard lines of his chest. I yanked his hood down so I could get my hands in his hair while he moaned his approval into my mouth, pulling me closer and pressing his arousal against me.

He broke our kiss, and I gasped as he moved to my neck, kissing and licking his way up my throat to my ear, his words half-growling, half-moaning whispers laden with fire as his stubble scratched against my jaw. *Soft, not scratchy.* "I've wanted... I need to taste every inch of you."

I was swimming so deeply in sensation, of potent, pulsing desire, I could barely get the words out. "Yes, definitely." And he did just that, running his tongue over my ear, back down to the hollow of my throat, kissing my collarbone as my hands trailed over his chest and I relished in each defined ridge, every ripple of muscle, all the little dips and valleys that twitched under my fingertips.

His body was more wonderous than I could've dreamed and when he stopped touching me long enough to yank his shirt off, I took a second to stand there and gawk at his utter perfection, damn-near salivating. His eyes flared magenta. "If you keep looking at me like that, I'm going to devour you."

I had zero problems with that.

We collided into each other, frenzied and greedy like we were an all-consuming fire of need and desperation. Every place our bodies touched—hands, mouths, flesh—burned in the most exquisite way. His hands trailed from my back, raking across my stomach with slow delicious torture until he grasped my breasts. He groaned as he squeezed, offering me relief from the swelling ache he'd created in me. I was ready to combust under the weight of his desire. Of my own.

Until he came to his senses.

It was like a flash of lightning struck and the electricity went out as he pulled his hands out and literally pushed me an arm's length away.

Outlook not so good.

Had he not really broken the Binding spell? I dared to look into his eyes, and I knew that wasn't it. He was choosing to put distance between us.

Never drinking fae froth again.

He blew out a long breath, regret written all over him, from the look on his face to the arms folded across his chest. "You should've stayed in your cabin."

I shivered at the loss of his warmth. Of the heat coursing through our bodies as we kissed. Sure, I could see it could've been a bad idea to throw myself at him, but there was no denying we'd both dug it. I took a tentative step toward him, but he matched it, stepping away. "You aren't safe now."

A chill ran up my spine. Being in danger had been nowhere on my radar, not after he'd touched me and kissed me like he had. Why was he thinking about that then? The whole pack was out there with us. "What do you mean? You said you and the betas would protect me from the pack when they shift."

He glanced down at my legs again and I felt it as if were another touch from his warm hands. "We would." There was a flicker of silence before his next words. "I will."

"Then what's the problem? Don't say it's the pants. I have shorts shorter than this. And you're showing as much skin as I am." I pointed at his bare chest and undone fly, which made my stomach clench, despite my effort to stay unaffected by his sex-god body.

I had to get a grip. He'd pushed me away. What did I care if he no longer wanted to touch me? I didn't do relationships or feelings or anything that formed connections. Never had. Though a deep, lingering, gut-wrenching thought crept into the tiniest place in my brain: maybe with him, I could.

I squashed the idea like a bug as he took a step to the side, putting more distance between us. "If you don't put on pants or get out of here, I don't know who will protect you from me, Gnome."

"You said you'd be in control."

"Of my wolf, yes. In my human form, with my hoodie barely covering your fine ass? With your lips wet with froth?c When you kiss me like it was your deepest desire to unravel me and ruin me at the same time? Unsure."

A crackle of electricity passed between us, causing us both to take heavy quick breaths. We stayed there for several seconds, neither of us wanting to move or break whatever magic was happening between us. At least it felt like magic to me. Warm, inviting, scary. Wells shook his head, his hair falling over his sexiest feature. "Fucking fae froth. It gets in your head and makes you do and say stupid shit every damn time."

The statement cut me.

Dumb didn't even come close to how I felt. There wasn't a connection between us, it was drunken lust and nothing more. And I'd had a temporary thought that maybe there was something more there. Something deeper.

Never drinking fae froth again. Never drinking fae froth again. Never drinking fae froth again.

"By stupid, do you mean kissing me like you were trying to burn the feel of your mouth onto mine? Or referring to me having a fine ass?"

He smirked. "No, I think your ass is perfect on the daily without the froth." Then he shrugged just enough to cause me to wonder if he actually meant it or if it was the froth talking again.

Maybe he was right, and I shouldn't have come to the party, but I couldn't have known that. Though the betas likely did, and they brought me anyway. Shitholes. I straightened my back and pulled the hoodie down my legs as much as I could. This—whatever it was or might have been—was done. "Okay. I'll go then."

He glanced at his watch. "Good idea. It's time, thank the Mage." He took another heated look in my direction before he turned and unzipped his fly. My body reacted to the sight of him by taking a giant step toward him, close enough I could feel the heat radiating from his tanned skin. His beauty was a palpable thing that I longed to wrap my hands around him again, but I stopped short of grabbing him. Without turning back, he roared in the predatory way of his, then took off running toward the woods and I was left shaking my head.

It was the most frustrating conversation I'd ever had, and I was already dreading the next one.

Cannot predict now.

I was about to make one of the betas interpret Wells for me, but the music stopped, and the crowd went silent, save for Mace. "Here we go, pack…in, sixty, fifty-nine, fifty-eight…"

Ren appeared, whispering in my ear. "You and Tristan should exit."

"Fifty-four, fifty-three…"

I turned to face him, still reeling from, well, every damn thing. Ren had stripped down to his black boxers. The other wolves were undressing too. For a second, it appeared there was going to be some kind of wild wolf orgy, but then my brain came back to me. They were shifting.

Fae froth was the devil's urine.

Tristan tugged my arm. "We should think about going…away, now, Babycakes. I'd love to be eaten by any of these wolves, but not in the literal sense."

"Thirty-one, thirty…" Mace was still counting down as he was removing his underwear.

I focused on the sky. The full moon was a beacon, illuminating the inky darkness of night.

"Nineteen, eighteen, seventeen…"

I knew what Wells had told me. I knew Tristan was right and we should go. But I didn't want to leave. There was a solid immovable thought in my mind: stay.

I'd watched a wolf shift when the djinn had come on my first day at Boulderbrook, but she was just a woman moving around the camp. I didn't *know* her. These were my friends. They were becoming important to me, and I wanted, no I needed, to watch them and experience them shift, firsthand. It was who they were.

I turned to Ren. "Can I see you shift? Then I'll go." He nodded and shot me a grin. I think he understood my desire to feel a part of the pack, even if it was from the fringes. I needed a connection now that Wells had severed ours.

He leaned forward, doubling over, as hair erupted on his skin. He reached out as his arms and legs changed, positioning himself to properly on all fours. The cracking of his bones didn't gross me out like it had with the other wolf. They were more like sounds of strength. I felt a power and connection to him, just because he was allowing me to observe his shift. The Ambient magic in the air flared to life. I could feel the surge in the air.

Ren's face was the last to change, bending his neck back as the snout of the wolf grew, then he shook his head like he was shaking off water. It was done. He stood there, a handsome black wolf with a tuft of long hair. For him, the process appeared to be as simple as changing clothes.

The rest of the pack shifted, some of them ripping their clothes as their bodies changed, others getting naked first. The change was so elegant, so vital and life-affirming, I was jealous I couldn't do it myself. One of the wolves stalked toward me, but when Ren growled a warning, he bounded way.

I watched the wolves disappear, one by one, into the dense trees until one wolf remained, hovering at the tree line. White and majestic, he waited, watching for his pack until the last of them turned.

To me, he seemed more alpha than Mateo ever had.

He jumped, yipping at the brown wolf who was the last to make it to the woods. Then he paused, looking right at me. He was far away, but I could still detect the flash of violet.

Emotions. Of some kind.

He let out a gruff, intimidating bark. He wanted me to move, to get to the lodge, so I Gesture Two'd Tristan and we started walking.

I checked back one more time as I opened the lodge door. Wells jumped, turning a circle, which made him look more like a cute family pet than a menacing werewolf. He released a long mournful howl and escaped into the woods.

JEWELS OF CLAY

The main space of the lodge was warm and inviting with golden beams stretching across a cavernous room and a massive chandelier of deer horns hung in the center. No doubt the wolves had hunted and *disposed* of the deer themselves. Tables and chairs were pushed to the side, leaving a massive space for the pack's kids to run and play in. By my count, there were twelve of them and they were taking advantage of all the room. I'd just made it inside the room before a small boy ran up and latched onto my waist. "Base!"

An older kid, this one partially shifted, but still on two legs, ran in and slid to a stop in front of us and touched the boy on the top of his head. "Arlo said people can't be bases. I got you, you're it!"

Arlo joined us and scared the kids away with what he likely meant as a stern scowl, but given the laughter as they ran off, they didn't perceive it as such. "You throw a great party."

He released a long breath, and the fringe of his lion-mane hair flew up. "Pups have a lot of energy. It's like this every Mageforsaken month."

His eyes darted from group to raucous group, and I got the strongest feeling he wasn't as grumpy about pup-sitting duty as he was making out. "I want you to know I've eliminated a lot of particulars in your DNA, but I haven't found the key to your genetic make-up yet. Wells told me I could let you know as much."

I didn't want to talk about Wells. At all. Maybe never again. As far as I was concerned, he could stay out there in the woods permanent wolf-style, and I'd be peachy.

Maybe my feelings were a little hurt by our strange interaction.

A lot hurt.

He was into kissing me, then boom, 'froth makes you stupid.'

Wolfhole.

Arlo cursed. "Damn, fae." I followed his gaze to a set of double doors on the right of the room. Six small-sized fairies were flying into the room holding a unicorn-shaped pinata on strings. He shouted at the group, "What did I tell you about this? The last thing they need is sugar. They'll be up all night!"

He took off to reprimand the fairy brigade but ended up standing underneath the pinata, helping the fairies position themselves on each string so it hung low enough for the kids to reach. He was the one who handed the girl a brass candlestick to whack the pinata with and even used the handkerchief from his own pocket as her blindfold.

I spied Spencer sitting across the room, sipping a bottle of water. I went over and pulled up a chair. I had questions she may've been able to answer, but mostly, she looked like she could use a friend. "You're not shifting tonight?"

"No. Once werewolves perform the mating ritual, it's impossible for one to shift without the other. It's like we're two halves of a whole. Since Dom's sick…" She trailed off, letting me fill in the rest.

It was easy to read her despair and fear in her words. "How is he?"

"Improving. I think. It's hard to tell. Like Mateo said, it takes time."

The bite in her voice when she mentioned the alpha's name was palpable and I knew I was right. She'd be the person to ask about fusion. "Would it be rude for me to ask what illness Dom has?"

She beamed at the mention of his name. "There isn't a name for what's wrong with Dom." I knew it was the time to ask, but to my shock, I didn't have to give voice to my questions because she spilled without them. "Wells told me to make sure to talk with you tonight, which I thought was strange because, of course, I'd chat with you, you gave me margaritas for Mage's sake. Then I realized what he was saying."

"To tell me about fusion." She tapped her finger on the side of her nose. "You're not under the Binding magic?"

"Not me. Mateo bound Dom from telling me anything about this, so he didn't think it was necessary to bind me too." She made a wistful laugh. "He underestimated Dom's stubbornness and the depth of our mating bond. Hell, the fact that Dom told me everything may be the reason why he's not recovering from what Mateo did to him."

"Fusion?"

"Fusion."

The constant pinata whacking and uproarious laughter seemed to diminish in the heavy air around us as I waited for her to continue. "Fusion combines the blood of two species. In Dominic's case, adding djinn blood to his werewolf."

Blood Magic, the darkest, most disgraceful offense to the Mage in existence. It shouldn't have been easy to perform it without consequences, but I guess if you possessed a Conduit key, anything was possible. "Dom agreed to the fusion?"

"No way. None of them have. But wolves do what the alpha commands or lose your place in the pack." She picked at the edge of the label of her water bottle with her fingernail. "We could've run, but I didn't have a chance to ask Dom before the Binding magic was in place. Now, I can either break the mating bond, leave him behind and find another pack that might be willing to take me in and live without love for the rest of my life. Or stay here and love my mate no matter what he's like on the other side of this. If he survives at all."

I knew from the tone of her voice that some of Mateo's fusion experiments didn't end well for the wolves. I prayed to the Mage that Dominic would survive his experience. I liked Spencer and my heart went out to her.

We sat for a while in silence. She seemed to be allowing me to think about what she'd divulged. Two things kept running through my mind as I tried to piece everything together. "Why is Mateo doing these fusion experiments?"

She reached up with her wolf speed and snatched a piece of wayward candy as it flew toward us and popped it in her mouth before the girl who was charging to get it could reach us. "Think about it. With the Aetherian Conduit closed, magic is finite. Conclave membership is a source to obtain magic, but once the Conclave's magic and the reserves dry up in our realm completely, what do you think will happen?"

I hadn't allowed myself to see much past my potential spot in the Conclave. I wasn't doing it for the power anyway. But alpha species like wolves, vampires, djinn? There was no telling what they'd do to keep from losing their power. The betas had even broached the subject on the way to the camp when they'd explained how other species could leach magic.

My stomach roiled and I turned to Spencer. "Throwdown imminent?"

"Bingo," she said. "Wolves are already strong, but add in the magic of other powerful species? A pack like that would be unstoppable."

Cage the Mage.

An unstoppable pack would be capable of taking every speck of magic and have a virtually unlimited supply of Magicals to take from. The magic would be unbalanced and the consequences devastating, even to humans, given the sheer number of Magicals in the world. My mind whirled with the unbearable inevitability of the upcoming war over magic. Unless the Conduit could be opened or Mateo convinced to back off his Dr. Moreau impersonation, we were all doomed.

I had the what and why of it all, but I had one more question for Spencer. "What made him try Mateo try this in the first place?"

She looked like she was going to give me an answer, but Tristan came careening into the room from the same double doors the pinata had come from. He released an insane whistle that should not have come from his tiny body. "The djinn are here!"

25

The fae and Bambi the horny nurse corralled the kids into a big lump in the middle of the room, taking up positions around them. I knew they didn't have much magic in them, but Tristan had surprised me on many occasions since I'd met him, so I hoped they had enough in them to protect the children.

That left Spencer, Arlo, and me.

Against the djinn.

I glanced at Spencer. "Guards?"

"In the woods. We have no control over the shift unless there's a weird situation like mine. I'm all you've got for the next few hours."

I didn't doubt she could do damage in her wolf form, but I knew one werewolf, one elf, and a half-gnome, half-question mark would be no match against the djinn if they wanted to hurt us. My stomach took a dip as my breaths became shallow shaky things, but I took another look at the terror on the faces of the young wolves and grabbed Arlo's arm. "We have to take this outside."

We barreled into the night. A chilling breeze whipped my hair around as the djinn landed in front of me, sending a shiver rocketing through me. Their voice was cold. "There you are, our precious."

Were they seriously going Lord of the Rings *on me?*

"I'm not your precious."

Arlo surveyed the fence and the fact that the djinn just sailed through it. We both scowled. "You guys may want to think about calling the repairman on your magic barrier."

He shook his head. "I raised it myself. Not to toot my own horn, but I'm the most powerful elf on this side of Aetheria now. The barrier should've held firm." There was genuine fear in his voice. It seemed the wolves didn't have a plan for this kind of thing since Arlo should've been able to make a barrier strong enough to keep any threats out. It didn't make sense that the barrier was shredded upon impact. Unless there was more to it.

I glanced around for Mateo, thinking of his shiny Conduit key, but he wasn't around that I could tell.

As the djinn divided into dozens upon dozens of copies, my body went rigid, a cold trickle of terror ran along my spine. They were standing right there, glaring at me with crimson death holes.

Wind whooshed around us as Arlo whipped his rod from his jacket pocket. It me feel a teensy bit more at ease with the situation, but the rods had barely made a scratch on the djinn the first time we encountered them.

My mouth dried. The only time I'd ever experienced that much terror was when I walked those few steps into Gram's bedroom after I knew she'd died. When my life shifted from one thing to another.

As the djinn multiplication process went into full effect. I lost count of the number of copies. Especially when they started branching off and moving into different areas of the camp, the whip rods cracking the wind as they walked. I hoped one of them would amble close enough to the woods to alert the pack, but they seemed to be aware of the full moon and steered clear of the trees. It was precisely why they'd chosen this moment to come back.

I Gestured Two'd at the woods then stepped toward the djinn, hoping Spencer would catch my meaning, as I tried to distract the djinn. "Yo, this is a private party. I'm going to have to ask you to leave."

The djinn sneered, their eyeholes glowing with fire as they turned their attention back to me. They shrugged, their naked bodies glistening in the moonlight. "We won't be long."

We were at their mercy. There was no way the three, now two, of us could go up against the powerful djinn collective, even with Arlo's magic rod. Still, I couldn't just stand there and let them creep all over the campground while the pack was off frolicking on their full moon sabbatical, unaware of the danger. I took another step. Man, it was hard to do. "Leave, you freakazoid!"

All the hands of djinn in raised in my direction in eerie unison. "It's amusing that *you*, of all beings, would call us freakazoid, little girl."

I was about to protest being called a little girl, but something else they said hit me like a frying pan in the face. I marched up to the original djinn and squared up eye-to-place-where-the-eyes-should've-been. "You know what I am?"

"You haven't figured it out yet?" they asked, power dripping from their mere words, slithering inside my brain. I had the most intense urge to shake him and force the information from him. More than anything, I wished to know what I was. I felt it deep in my soul like it was a living entity.

But standing there in the cool dark, the more I thought about wanting, no needing, to know what I was, the weaker I became. My magic drained from my body, though I couldn't explain how or why it was happening or where it was going. "But you'd like to know, wouldn't you?" they probed, before they licked their gross lips and gave something they probably meant as a smile, but it wasn't. It was a distorted grimace with a twist.

Was it possible the djinn might have figured it out what I was when they forced their wish on me that day? I asked the question with my eyes. Arlo shrugged. It made me sick to do it, but I turned to the djinn and nodded yes.

Mage, I couldn't believe I was initiating a conversation with those assbags.

"We see," the djinn hissed, considering my answer. "You're going to be stupefied when you discover your roots, little girl, but we won't fulfill that wish today. Though, it was quite a scrumptious morsel." Their bodies glowed, telling me they'd absorbed my wish to know what I was and turned it into magic for themselves.

This time, I was not having it. Powerful anger shot through me, enough that I temporarily forgot about how weak I was and how little magic I possessed. "I'm not a little girl, you shit-eating, ugly-ass copy machine!"

They laughed. It ate at my insides.

A wolf's howl broke me out of my head, so I turned to find a half-dozen wolves and Spencer running toward us with her rod. One of the wolves I recognized as Ren, but the others were indistinguishable to me, though I noted none of them were white. Spencer raised her elegant copper rod at the nearest djinn and shot a stream of concentrated fire into his chest.

He laughed as he absorbed the fire like he was sucking down a milkshake. "We're made of fire, so we're immune to Fire magic, silly girl." They paused and a malevolent grin passed over their thin lips as they swiveled toward Spencer. "Such pain and torment inside you. Allow us to grant that wish in your heart."

All of the djinn raised their hands and a trickle of electric red magic passed between them. Spencer's face crumpled in confusion.

Same, girl. Same.

She bent over, howling in pain before she toppled to the ground, panting and heaving like she had no energy inside her. Maybe no magic. With that, the wolves snarled and attacked as one unit, descending on the djinn, ripping and gnawing at the throats of as many as they could. At the same moment, Arlo lowered a blast of Wind magic on the main djinn, knocking it back a few feet, but nothing more.

Helpless, I wished more than anything to have enough magic to do some damage to the djinn collective, but they were so strong and indestructible as far as I could tell. Maybe I was special like Wells and Mateo thought, but I'd be damned if I knew how to use whatever that quality was in the situation.

A howling yelp drew my attention, and I screamed as a small blonde wolf body rolled in my direction, stopping at my feet. I jumped back as the wolf body shifted back into human form.

Kelsey.

I threw myself on the ground and checked for a pulse. It was barely there, but present enough to know she was still alive. Spencer screamed. Wolves howled, tearing at djinn throats, locked in bloody battle with the djinn who just stood there deflecting attacks with very little effort.

Anger, deep and vicious, rolled through my body. I lowered my hand, tapping into my Earth magic. A rumble erupted from the earth as the soil undulated, creating a wave that trembled toward the OG djinn. He stumbled, looking up at me in surprise.

I sent another shockwave forward, but it was weaker. Just like I was. I guessed I'd used most of my magic on the first blast. I didn't have a lot to start with. The magic would replenish shortly, especially if I was connected to the earth, but I didn't know if I had long enough to wait for that to happen. I wrapped my hand around my vial and dug deeper, pushing everything I had into the ground.

Violent shockwaves spread across the camp. Gold erupted along the tips as roots broke through the earth, tumbling toward the djinn and reaching for their throats. The gold surprised me. I hadn't even been trying to produce gold, but I'd take it. Maybe I was making a difference. It was all I wanted.

"Stop! Please, Terra. It's Dominic." I whipped my head around to Spencer. Her sweet face was contorted in fear and panic as she rushed behind me. A blonde guy was hobbling toward her, using one of the djinn as a crutch. The crest of my earth blast rolled toward them, causing them to stumble. "Are you okay, Babe?" she cried. "I can't believe you're okay. All I wanted was for you to be safe." He grabbed her face in his hands with a tender look, then collapsed into her arms.

The djinn he'd been using to walk slumped over. He wasn't as *formed* as the others around us. He'd been the one captured by Mateo on my first day at Camp Boulderbrook. The nearest copy of the djinn wrapped his arms around the weaker djinn, and he reabsorbed him.

Just like that, it was over.

The djinn had been toying with us. They could've wiped everyone out the second they'd arrived, but they'd allowed the wolf attacks to continue while they rescued their captured brother. Or copy. Or part. Whatever. Djinn existence was confusing.

The group of them slid back into one and the OG djinn stalked toward me as goosebumps erupted over my skin. Mage, I wished I could hurt those damned psychos. "Now that we've collected our brethren, we'll be on our way." His voice was so pleasant, so civilized. So utterly wrong. "Please, let us know once you've sorted yourself. We could fill you up with all manner of djinn magic. It would be divine." He was up and

248

walking on air before I could say another word.

Arlo stuck his rod back in his pocket, then scurried around, checking on Kelsey and the wolves who'd been in the battle as I got the story from Ren who was a little beaten up, but okay, thank the Mage.

Mateo had ordered Wells and Gideon to stay in the woods to protect the pack, while he'd gone to check on the djinn captive. Obviously, he failed to keep him in the cage. Ren and Kelsey had been ordered to come to the gate with us, along with three other wolves I didn't know.

None of it—*none of it*—was effective. The djinn had reclaimed their copy and Kelsey was nearly a casualty of the fight. The only good thing I could tell was that Dominic was alright. At least in appearance. Spencer kept mumbling about her wish coming true.

I was glad for her, but nervous that something else sinister would happen thanks to the djinn's visit.

The golden morning light streaming in the lodge windows woke me from my fitful sleep. I'd only gotten an hour, tops. It's hard to sleep when you're in danger of constant threats attacking you for no Magedamned reason.

I stroked the hair of the little girl who'd ended up curling into my lap in order to get comfortable and I envied her innocence. She stirred and turned over and I was able to slide out from under her without waking her. I grabbed my shoes and left the lodge without rousing anyone. Even Tristan had conked out after he'd allowed some of the kids to chase him as he flew around the lodge. At least they had never known what was going on beyond the walls.

Everything outside looked as it had before the djinn had come. Peaceful morning dew rested on the grass, and I allowed the cool breeze to fill my lungs as I walked to the barn.

I wasn't even sure why I was going there other than this deep-seated need to make sure the djinn was truly gone. Like, there wasn't some tiny little scrap of him left lingering in the corner of the cage.

They'd planned the rescue for the full moon when the wolves would be otherwise engaged, though the thought plaguing me was the djinn didn't need to wait at all. They could've gotten him the day the Five visited, or Mage, obliterated the whole camp with their freaky powers any time they wanted. I couldn't figure out the timing at all. That made them the most powerful magical beings in our world with the most questionable ethics and unpredictable means. That was a heinous combo.

As I made it to the barn, I tried to shake the attack off, which was hard since they seemed to be fixated on me every time they were here. The entire area around the woods was a ghost town. Sighing, I glanced out the window, searching for… Well, I didn't want to admit who I was searching for.

At the edge of the trees, I spotted a large gray wolf and a smaller deep brown one. They chased each other, nipping and yelping, like they were playing. Before I could look away, the gray one lunged forward, and, I would never get the image out of my head.

He started humping that wolf right there at the edge of the woods.

"Mage, Mace. Can't you ever keep it in your pants?" I muttered to the empty room.

"No, he can't."

I whirled around and found Mateo entering in human form, dragging two people with him. The man whose neck was being practically broken in two by Mateo's grip was hissing, his fangs dripping with blood. Vamp.

The woman being dragged by her arm wasn't resisting. I couldn't gage her species, but she was small and delicate, and I instantly feared for her. Tears streamed down her face as Mateo wrenched her forward, throwing her into the iron cage first and stuffing the vampire in after her. They shared the same look of terror that was likely on my face at the time.

"What are you doing?" I knew full well what Mateo was doing, but I also didn't want to get Spencer or Wells in Mateo's bad graces for telling me about his fusion activities.

Like he had any good graces.

"It's no concern of yours, but I'm glad you're here, Miss Youngblood. Saves me the trip to find you."

I schooled my face to look innocent and unafraid, but I started backing my ass toward the door like it was a magnet, my eyes flying around to look for something, anything, I could use as a weapon. "What do you need me for?"

Almost there. Just a few more feet.

Mateo pulled his circle amulet out and a gust of wind slammed the door shut. "I just need to take a little blood, remember?"

Cold sweat beaded across my hairline as I spotted the only thing in the room, I could possibly use to defend myself. "Yeah, sure, uh, can we do that a little later? I just survived a djinn attack and I, uh, have to pee now." Not my most valiant moment or excuse, but I was panicking. More than I had when I faced down the djinn.

He moved toward me at werewolf speed, blocking my exit. "It won't take but a second."

Before I could protest any further, his hand was around my bicep, and I was being dragged toward the iron cell where the two new prisoners were held. He slammed my face against the bars and pulled my hair away, revealing my neck. "Don't worry, you won't turn unless you drink his blood." He offered, like it was a consolation prize, right before he bellowed at the vampire, "Drink. Now!"

The vampire looked like he was about to throw up, but as soon as he got close, he was entranced by the throbbing pulse of blood in my veins.

He leaned out between the bars and bit into my neck like Mateo had commanded.

I screamed.

It was *so* not what I pictured Mateo meant when he said he'd take some blood.

Blinding pain coursed through me as the vampire sucked the blood and magic from me. He was a greedy sucker and the more he drank, the weaker I became. I swung my arms at Mateo, but it was giving off the effect of a mosquito fighting off a velociraptor. His hold on me didn't budge.

And the vampire didn't stop.

Deep dread filled my lungs and I slumped against the cage. If I didn't act soon, I would have nothing left. I summoned everything in me, pushing my Earth magic from my fingertips. A wayward strand of ivy that had pushed between the slats from the outside responded to my call. It grew, stretching down the wall, across the floor, over my leg, finally wrapping around the vampire's neck and pulling him away from me.

He collapsed on the floor as Mateo released a gruff laugh. He picked up the strand of ivy and attempted to rip it apart, but I threw all my magic into it, and he failed to break it. He glared at me. "What are you playing at?" It took all I had, but I pushed my magic into the vine, and it snaked its way to Mateo's throat. He looked from the ivy to me, amused. "Let's see what magic you've got, then."

He dropped his hands and allowed the vine to curl around his neck. I put every effort I could muster into the strand, twisting it tighter and tighter, my head spinning in the process as a dusting of gold broke out along the vine. My vision blurred and I was certain I was going to pass out in the effort it took to restrain Mateo.

Until an explosion of something—light, fire, energy, I couldn't tell— roused me. I managed to raise my head enough to track Wells stalking toward Mateo. Naked. Pissed. Ready to throw down.

Did I mention naked?

My eyelids fluttered, opening and closing against my will as the two wolves growled at each other. The sound was so deep and rough, it seemed Nether-worldly. Arms wrapped around from behind me and raised my head. The woman in the cage was trying to help me up.

I braced against the bars and though my legs were heavy and uncooperative, I managed to work my way up to standing. I had no magic left inside me and it was the hollowest I'd felt in my life. I'd need hours inside soil to replenish my store of magic. There would be no defending myself against Mateo for a while.

The vampire was huddling in the corner of the cage in the most unvampire-like way imaginable, weak and desolate. The woman though, she was serving looks at Mateo and I was there for it. I addressed her. "Thank you. I promise to get you out of here."

I sucked in a deep breath and took a step forward. The wolves were standing inches from one another snarling. Mateo was even spitting, his mouth foaming like a rabid dog. Wells' back was to me and curse the Mage for my stupid hormones because I took precious seconds off my impending getaway to check his ass. Damn, son. It was perfect.

As if he sensed me ogling him, he spoke, never breaking his standoff with the angry alpha. "Can you walk?"

"I think."

"Go. Now. Gideon and Mace are outside." White wolf hair erupted over his arms. "I have some business to discuss with my alpha."

"But—"

"Terra." The growl he made when he said my name leveled me. A tightness coiled in my stomach, and I had the urge to run over and hug him. Once again, he'd shown up when I needed him. Not that I liked the damsel in distress role on me at all, but I wasn't dumb enough to think I was any kind of threat to Mateo. Wells was. I could read it on Mateo's face.

I needed to go like he'd said, but every muscle in my body was locked tight as the two wolves bared their teeth at each other. Wells stepped toward his alpha, bumping his chest aggressively. "It's over, Mateo. You're done playing Mage with the lives of our pack."

Mateo laughed. It was deep, sinister, maniacal. "Stand down, boy. I'm your alpha. You're bound by my magic, and you don't tell me what to do." He raised a hand, flicking his fingers and Wells' knees buckled and he grunted under the weight of his alpha's binding magic hitting him.

He was only down for a second before he set himself upright and steeled his shoulders. The power, the magic emanating from him was like a warm glow around the barn. He was not going to be subdued anymore. It was fucking beautiful. "You don't deserve to be alpha of this pack. Not anymore." He turned, peeking over his shoulder, addressing me with soft lilac eyes. "Go, Terra. Tell them to get the torches."

I didn't know what it meant, but Mateo sure had. Shock flickered across his face, then he lunged at Wells, snarling and going for his throat. In human form.

Human form.

Wells used his wolf speed to jerk away right before Mateo connected with his throat. Before I could scream or do anything helpful at all, Wells grabbed Mateo by the back of the neck and slammed his face into the ground. Blood spurted from his nose, and he moaned from beneath his boot. "Lucky strike. You won't best me again, boy. You're too weak and too emotional."

How could someone be so wrong about a person they claimed to love? Wells was strong and his emotions were the reason why. Wells leveled his silver gaze on me. One final rumble and I got the message, hightailing it out of the barn as fast as I could go and stumbling into Gideon's arms.

He tumbled backward into Mace. "Wells said to get the torches. I hope that makes sense to you and I hope that means you two are going to go in there and help him."

"Shit. Okay." Gideon's handsome face paled. "I had a feeling you would make this happen. Let's go."

Mace wrapped a hand around my arm and pulled me along with them. "Wait. Aren't you going to help him?"

"We are. This is pack business. Let us do it."

A hundred unanswered questions later, I was dumped at my cabin. They swore they'd explain everything to me in time and I vowed deep in my soul I would make them. Mateo and Wells were fighting in the barn and the betas were off gathering torches for some unknown reason. Something was about to happen. I had no clue what it was, but deep down, I knew things were about to change.

26

Had I gone from being a potential prisoner in the barn to an actual prisoner in my cabin?

You may rely on it.

Mace had the decency to look sheepish about having locked me in my cabin under a magic barrier he shouldn't have been able to create, as he stood there apologizing an hour later. "I know. I'm sorry It was the quickest and easiest way to keep you safe while we did what we needed to do."

"Which was, what? Help Wells?"

"In a way. He's got to do the hard thing now. Though, I think I'm doing the most difficult part by dragging you along. He's going to kick my ass for this."

He led me out of the cabin and when I noticed the usual beam of sunshine that seemed to accompany Mace wasn't there, a gnawing sensation crawled up my spine. "Where are we going?"

"I want to get this off my chest first. Long story, short, in case you haven't figured it out yet, I've been through fusion. Mateo gave me elf blood." He waited for it to sink in for a moment before he continued. "It was the absolute worst thing I've ever gone through and, believe me, I went through some shit growing up. But now that I'm on the other side of it, I'm thankful I have Wind magic now."

It explained so much: opening the poker room door, flying poker chips, spelling the poker wheel with magic. "Why? Thankful you can lock your friends behind magic barriers?"

He shrugged. "Don't blame me for that. It was the only way we could get Wells to calm the fuck down. He was about to go John Wick on Mateo for what he'd done to you. We needed him to do this by the book, or it would've been for nothing."

"Do what by the book?"

We made it to the field where I'd done all my digging, but it had been transformed. I don't think there was a wolf at the camp who wasn't there, kids included. Tiki torches were lit and spread into a wide circle in the middle of the field. The wolves assumed positions around it as they crowded in to look on.

The woman next to me bent down to pick up her young child, pointing to the pavilion where a huge black banner hung. The ominous way it whipped in the wind caused a shudder to rip through my body.

Tristan appeared next to me, poofing into big-sized. Mace handed him a pair of sweats. Apparently, they'd planned the meeting. "Hey, Babycakes. Something's down."

"Something's up." I looked to Mace because Tristan wasn't wrong. "What's happening?"

The other two betas flanked us in a tight circle and Gideon shook his head, glowering at Mace like he'd done something heinous. "Please go back to your cabin, Terra."

He attempted to take my elbow and pull me away, but I wrenched out of his grasp, bumping into Mace on my other side. He snarled at Gideon. I'd never seen any of the betas mad at each other. It made me nervous. "She should be here. You know that."

Gideon scoffed. "You want her to see this? To watch him...?" He trailed off like Wells had done so many times and my head started to ache with the possibility of the words he didn't say.

"He wouldn't be here if it wasn't for her. She has the right to witness it." Mace's voice was more subdued than Gideon's and while he appeared to be arguing for me to stay, I could tell he didn't want me there any more than Gideon did. He just thought my presence there was important.

My tone was much firmer the next time. "Somebody needs to tell me what's going on."

Both Gideon and Mace spoke at once, shouting their arguments at each other, but Ren stepped in between them, pushing them apart. "Let her fucking decide for herself."

He turned to me, his green eyes full of more emotion than I'd ever seen. He gripped my shoulders and I braced myself. Ren would give it to me straight. He always did. "Wells challenged Mateo as alpha of the pack. In a minute, the two of them are going into that circle, but only one of them is coming out alive."

A river of emotion coursed through me, threatening to come out in the form of a scream. What was he doing? I wasn't sure if I spoke it aloud or if I just made a squeak. I *was* sure I was about to pass out.

Gideon put his hand on my shoulder and squeezed. "Wells found a spell to temporarily transfer the Perception magic over to me for now. If he succeeds in challenging Mateo, then the Binding magic will transfer back four hours after we performed the ritual, which was about half an hour ago. If he fails..." He paused to swallow. I didn't like the sound of that any more than he did. "...the Binding magic will stay with me. It was the best way to make sure you'd have a fighting chance no matter what happens here. He wouldn't have done this any other way."

An icy shiver went down my spine. How *dare* he?

Dare to change the contract without asking me, dare to challenge someone stronger and more experienced than him, dare to do everything behind my back like it meant nothing to him? Like I meant nothing. Raw, coursing, pain erupted from inside me. I didn't recognize my own voice when I snarled. "Where is he?"

Mace wrapped his arms around me from behind. "It's too late. The banner's hung and you can't stop it, Terra." My gut wrenched. He'd given me dozens of ridiculous nicknames since I'd met him, but he picked that moment to call me by my real one. It punctuated how wrong this whole thing was.

How could he? Why?

I couldn't stop my tears.

Tears of anger. Of terror. Of some deeper emotion that I'd been denying.

I swiped the tears away and Gesture One'd myself. "I'm not going anywhere."

The Betas flanked me in a circle of protection. My heart would've swelled with the expression if I hadn't been so worried about what was about to happen.

A calm came over the crowd as Mateo slithered in from Mage knows where. None of the wolves looked like they were on his side. No one looked him in the eye. He was their alpha and I didn't have to ask to know a challenge like this didn't happen very often. At least not in this pack. He'd been alpha since the beginning.

And he'd experimented on them, tortured them, ruled them with an iron fist and Binding magic. Still, they abnegated to him because he was their alpha. Most of them probably had no idea what he'd done.

The pack deserved so much better.

He was already shirtless, exposing his tanned skin and muscular build, dripping in coiled power. He entered the circle of torches, his golden amulet gleaming in the fire glow. He was an imposing figure with a twisted sense of morality, and it hurt to look at him after what he'd done to me, to countless others. He needed to be stopped. This couldn't be the only way to do it.

Intellectually, I understood it; emotionally, I couldn't wrap my head around it. Every life was valuable, every mistake could be overcome, opinions changed, actions given consequences.

Right?

Death wasn't the only way, was it?

Right there at the moment, I think I would've preferred to kill him myself instead of Wells having challenge his father figure and leader.

Mage, what did that mean? For me to care that much about it?

Movement from behind drew my attention. Wells parted the crowd and made his way to us. He snarled in Mace's direction. "Why is she here? I said keep her locked up until this is done."

"You know why."

Wells looked any and everywhere but at me. I reached out, but he turned away from my grasp, then put his hand over his crotch, addressing Tristan behind me. "If I fail, feel free to have your way with my balls before they haul my corpse off."

My heart stuttered at the word *corpse.*

Tristan laughed, then did a few tumbling loops, landing on Wells' shoulder. He whispered something in his ear which made Wells chuckle. "You could try." Tristan looked like he was keen to try whatever it was.

Wells turned and clapped Ren on the back. The no-nonsense beta visibly swallowed, anguish coloring his features. He was as bothered by this as I was. "Are you sure about this, Wells? Your theory's untested."

"What better time to give it a whirl?" I didn't know what his theory was, but Wells' voice was forced. Like he was trying to be casual, but the hum of intensity beaming from him was anything but. He squeezed Ren's shoulder. "You know what you have to do if I'm wrong."

Ren nodded. "Yeah. Don't fucking make me do it."

Wells smirked. "That's the plan."

Wells looked to Gideon next, though they said nothing, the affection and respect they had for each other was obvious. He'd trusted Gideon with my mirror. It spoke volumes and I could admit the anger it had caused had vanished as I stood there watching him interact with the betas. Like it was the last time he'd see them.

Mace wrapped his arms around Wells in in bear hug. "I know you threatened to kill me, but since you're already mad at me for bringing her. I'm telling her everything. Hey, Terra?"

It wasn't until I said "yeah" that Mace let Wells go. "Poker night? He had a full house."

So, he *had* let me win. Wells slapped him on the back of the head, his curls went flying and he turned around. So that no one would see his tears. I was sure it.

My hands trembled. I did not want to be next in Wells' farewell tour.

"Wells." It was all I said. I couldn't figure out how to put words to my emotions.

He seemed to understand anyway. "It's going to be alright."

I wanted so much to believe him, but Mateo was so strong and so ruthless. "If not, I'll kick your ass, Jerkface."

"Don't worry." He smirked. "I'm more scared of you than him."

"Good. You don't want to tangle with this chick." The lump in my throat was large and in charge. I had trouble choking out my words.

He leaned in and I smelled his warm sandalwood scent. "Tangling with you is all I think about, Gnome."

My breath hitched.

Damn him for saying that now.

Before I could respond, he squeezed my hands, then walked to the edge of the Tiki circle. And I was left to dwell in what-ifs and if-onlys.

My blood chilled as Mateo started in on him, taunting and smug. "Are you sure you want to go through with this, boy? Renege and I'll make sure you have somewhere to go when I kick you out of my pack for daring to challenge me."

Wells ignored him, remaining stone-faced. He was good at that.

Since Wells had refused to take his bait, Mateo skirted around the edge of the circle, trying a different approach. "I knew you'd challenge me one day, but why now? Is this really about the girl?"

A low rumble emanated from Wells, and he took a step forward. "You know why."

"I don't, son. Explain it to me."

Wells snapped at him. "I'm not your son. And the one explanation you get is that I won't allow you to hurt people I care about. If it means the pack ends up with no power when magic dies, so be it. You won't take another life." His eyes glared silver. "Especially hers."

Mage almighty.

Mateo grinned, flexing his massive muscles. "Think of the good we can do with more magic. It's worth risking a few meager lives if it means we can protect the Conduit better. She's unimportant and she makes you weak. *You* make the pack weak."

"No." Wells stepped forward, jutting his chest out and rising to his full height against Mateo. Even at his size, he was smaller, but when you factored in the determination in Wells' eyes versus the smugness in Mateo's, it seemed like an even match.

I clamped my hand around my vial of Earth. *Mage, help him.*

Wells peeled out of his white t-shirt. Wrong time, wrong place. But. I was never going to fail to have a visceral reaction to his body. He dropped his jeans, revealing gray boxer briefs. When he stepped behind the tool shed to remove his underwear, I figured it was for my benefit and not the wolves. As I'd seen, even the wolf children were used to the human body and none of them raised an eyebrow at nakedness.

Not that I wasn't interested in what was under his boxers. I was. Times a thousand. But I appreciated his modesty because I didn't want the first time, I saw what was in his boxers to be in a crowd of people when he was about to kill or be killed.

My head started spinning. When did I conclude that there would be a first time for me to see what was in his boxers? Maybe after he told me he wanted to tangle with me?

Or maybe, probably...definitely before that.

And now, if Mateo had his way, I would never know.

There were things we weren't saying. I felt them in the air during every conversation, every heated look, each time his scorching touch grazed my flesh. And now it could be too late to say any of them.

Wells' white wolf stalked from behind the shed. I sucked in a breath. In this form, he was way more menacing up close. From far away, I hadn't noticed there were splashes of red and black on the tips of his ears and tail, like fire lighting his edges. He circled the outer perimeter of the torches, eyeing Mateo and growling in a way that seemed equal parts regal and domineering.

Mateo shifted into his dappled brown wolf, then lunged, baring his teeth and chomping. The crowd made a collective gasp. The brawl between them was immediate and vicious, and my body locked in rigid tightness as Wells got ahold of Mateo's scruff and shook him from side to side. Mateo, though, was nimble and twisted out of his grip.

He whipped around and bit into Wells' back, flipping him up and over his head. I wasn't just me who screamed when Wells skidded across the field. He jumped up and shook himself. Blood seeped from his back wound, trickling down and coloring his fur in crimson.

Mateo made another aggressive move, nipping at Wells' head, snapping his jaw across Wells' muzzle. Blood sprouted like a fountain. I couldn't help myself, I tried to bolt to him. It took Mace and Gideon to hold me in place. Shaking, I grasped Ren's arm and he put a hand over mine. He was trembling too. All of it seemed so wrong.

Wells went on the offensive, howling as he leaped up and came down on top of Mateo. They rolled together, snapping teeth and swiping claws, as they skidded into one of the torches. Mateo was distracted by the impact, so Wells chomped down near the top of his hind leg, making Mateo whelp and jump away, limping.

Mateo used the distraction to his advantage. He sunk his teeth into the wound on Wells' back, shaking and gnawing at the spot using gravity to flip him. Wells landed on the ground with a massive, thundering thud that soaked into my bones and would probably never go away.

He didn't get up.

My head spun. This was not happening. He said it was going to be fine. Beside me, Mace grunted as if he'd taken the hit himself. "Come on, Wells. You need to fucking get back up like you're a character in the MCU."

As blood pooled on the ground under Wells' body, Mateo began pacing back and forth, eyeing him and waiting to make his next strike.

We were all waiting.

My heart beat harder with every second that ticked by.

After what seemed to be a lifetime, Wells lifted himself, but his legs were weak, and he tumbled back to the ground. This time, he didn't rise.

This was it.

Gideon whispered, "Shit."

Mateo pounced, leaping up and going for the kill. Everything inside me burned. The Tiki torches flared. Wolves howled. Time seemed to stand still and in that frozen moment, I realized what he was starting to mean to me. Even after all the ways he endlessly tortured me through the trials, maybe I was developing real feelings for him.

And I was about to lose him.

Wells must have sensed what was happening because threw himself sideways to avoid Mateo's attack. He connected with the torch, almost dislodging it. It hung there crooked, dripping small droplets of fire. Even in his wolf form, I could somehow read his expression. Something occurred to him in that instant. His eyes flared bright platinum.

He knocked the Tiki torch to the ground with his body and it landed near Mateo, orange flames igniting the grass around the wolf. Mateo rolled out of the way, and I gasped as Wells laid his paw into the flames. Fire surged, shifting from orange to silver as it engulfed Mateo.

The silver flames burned faster and hotter than any fire I'd ever seen, the heat licking the air from yards away. Mateo whined, trying to escape, but the blaze consumed his body in a fierce torrent. It took a matter of seconds for the flames to devour his wolf form. The crowd was speechless. Someone threw a jacket over Mateo, dousing the fire, but it was too late. He was already gone.

Wells stood, his legs wobbling. He hobbled away from the circle and behind the shed. The betas took off after him, but not before Ren told me to stay put. Which I did for about four seconds. When I got there, the betas were crouched around Wells, looking grim. Ren's voice was cold and sounded like it was miles away. "He's not breathing, and I can't find a pulse."

I shouted. I'm not even sure what I said. Gideon looked up and barked for Tristan to get me out of there.

"Come on Babycakes. You shouldn't see this." His grip was strong, and he managed to pull me to the front of the shed before I collapsed, unable to make my feet walk any further away.

266

I don't know how much time passed, but I'd laid on Tristan's shoulder, holding my tears back with sheer force of will, when a bright silver light flashed from behind the shed. Trembling, I jumped up. "What was that?" It wasn't fire and too bright to be a flashlight and it came from the spot where the betas had been tending to Wells.

Tristan couldn't hold on to me that time. I whipped around the shed and froze.

Wells was standing in his human form, leaning on Mace and Ren. He had his boxers back on and he was covered in cuts and bruises. But he was very definitely breathing. Utter and complete joy rushed through me like a cool wave. "Wells."

Gideon looked at him, relieved, but concerned. "You'll heal faster in your wolf form."

Wells wrenched away from the others and took a shaky step in my direction. "I know. I just wanted her to see I was okay first."

I ran over to him, afraid to touch him because his body was eaten up with wounds. "What was that light?"

He smirked. "Pack secret."

"A pack secret you had to hide away from the rest of the pack. Try again."

I didn't get a smartass answer the second time. "I'll tell you, but not now. I have to appear in front of the pack. You understand." I did understand because the whole time I was sitting there thinking he may have died, the rest of the pack had stayed put and grieved right along with me.

He took a few more steps and the crowd of wolves parted, making way for him and bowing down on one knee when he stepped among them. He raised his hands. "Thank you, but don't do that for me again. I'm your alpha now, but I'm not your overlord. Those days are over for us."

They all stood, clapping until he quieted them and continued. "This pack has been tasked with guarding the Conduit for years and we're going to get back to it. And beyond that, we're going to get it open and get the magic flowing again so we won't have to fight over it."

He glanced at me. If I truly held the key to it, I wanted more than ever to figure out how and why, so I could help him keep his promise to the pack. Looking at him as he stood and spoke to his people, I knew he was born to be this pack's alpha. I hated how it happened, but he was going to do things for the pack that Mateo never dreamed of.

Wells stumbled a little and the betas flanked him. "These guys will be my betas, of course. I'll appoint a fourth soon, but for now, I need to heal. I'll be in the office as soon as I'm fully healed."

The crowd cheered again, and I ran over to catch up with him as he leaned on the betas. Tristan met up with them. "Oh, oh, chicken soup coming up, Alpha!" He poofed away and my heart fluttered. He was just as much of the pack as I was, and I loved hearing him use Wells' new title.

I took a giant step toward him. "At least tell me we get tomorrow off for you to heal."

"You don't get a day off, Gnome. And I'll heal overnight because I'm highly motivated to be fully functional for a lot of reasons, all of which have to do with you." My eyes went wide, and he chuckled. The sound burrowed down inside me and rooted there. "Get some sleep. I'll see you tomorrow."

I admit, I watched them walk him all the way to his cabin before I turned and went to mine. He appeared to be fine, but I'd heard them say he had no pulse and wasn't breathing. I *had* to be sure for myself. There was a thing there between us now, other than the Perception contract. I didn't want to name it or give shape to it in any way, but it was there.

Back in my cabin, I expected sleep to allude me, but as soon as I was tucked in and had my hand wrapped around my vial, thanking the Mage and everything in Aetheria that Wells had survived his challenge, I was out.

◯

Right after I woke and dressed in a t-shirt with a Sasquatch figure and Hide and Seek Champion underneath it, Ren knocked on my door. He yawned and managed to sigh at the same time, boredom written in his stunning features. "We're training. Let's haul."

Yeah, not so much. "Hold it a second, wolfhole. Is it back to business as usual after what happened last night?" Part of me craved the idea of the routine, reveled in getting the trials behind me, but a bigger part of me was dying inside wondering how things would change with Mateo gone. *If* they'd change.

Did I want them to change?

Nerves clawed their way through my body, prickling me with itchy heat. I was going to have to face Wells again soon. The only explanation I got was "It's the way of the pack." Then he shoved a croissant in my hand, and we made the walk to the field like we did every day. The second we arrived, he shucked his shirt, flexing in the early morning sunshine. So yes, business as usual for Ren.

I shrugged out of my shoes, eager to dive into the Earth and work out some of the nervous titters I had at the thought of seeing Wells after our froth kiss and after he'd killed Mateo, but Ren caught my wrist in his hand, swirling me around. "Wells said it was time to show you."

"Show me what?"

He smirked, then reached down and put his hand on the grass. The earth rolled under his touch, shifting and opening a decent-sized hole. He stood back up and I stared in disbelief. Ren was a werewolf, he wielded Fire magic, yet he could perform Earth magic too. Everything started to click into place. "You've been through the fusion process too?"

"Yes. All of us betas are fused. Many more too, some who didn't survive. It hurt like a sonofabitch to go through it, but I'm as much troll as I am wolf now. Thank the fucking Mage no one else will have to experience it." His words were full of gratitude for his new alpha. His friend. And they weren't made out of Binding magic or coercion. It was respect, pure and simple.

Wells was making things better for his people. Maybe he wasn't the cold hard ass I'd assumed in the beginning.

Ren wiggled his fingers and the soil rumbled, shifting and moving until a single white flower grew from a small hole in the ground.

Wow.

Ren was part troll.

Staring down at the hole he'd created, I got the urge to tunnel with him. If he could move dirt in any capacity, he wouldn't slow me down like I'd assumed he would. My heart stuttered when I considered that Wells had known that too. He'd given me a task that appeared impossible, but in reality, might not have been. I banished the thought tugging at my heartstrings. "Let's see what you've got, Trollboy." I sailed into the earth, and he dove in behind me.

"Well, that's not sticking."

We tunneled together for a few hours, beating our times frequently. It was different tunneling with a person, but the Earth magic the troll had given him made him more of a partner and help, than a hindrance. My confidence soared. I even kept on tunneling when he declared he had to take a piss and left.

I was going to do it. I was going to get us to that flag in under a minute. I pushed myself as hard as I could until I had to take a break for fear of passing out. The second I burst into the sunlight, something tapped my head. I looked up and found Wells leaning against a tree with a bamboo stick in his hand.

He arched an eyebrow, rapping on my head with the stick again. The third time he did it, I sailed out of the ground and grabbed it from his hand, breaking it in two over my leg as I spat out his name. "Wells."

Without turning or breaking eye contact, he reached behind him, produced another bamboo stick and proceeded to hit my head again. "Whack-a-Mole."

Was he kidding me?

I peered behind him and found a whole pile leaning against a tree. As much as I wanted to break the next one over his head, I stopped myself. I could tell he was enjoying this little game, whatever it was. I didn't want to give him the satisfaction.

I Gesture one'd and would stay that way until he talked.

His eyes said he was about to say something smart ass, but as soon as I saw the vampire puncture wounds in my neck, he shot toward me with lightning speed, grazing the marks with his heated fingers. Tingles went from that spot, all the way down my body, pooling right there between my legs.

No. He hit me with a stick. I'm mad at him, not turned on. For real, body. For reals.

"I underestimated Mateo's desire to have your blood. He could've…" He trailed off, the look on his face was simmering disgust mixed with sincere regret. "It doesn't matter. He's not a problem anymore."

I couldn't stop the current of sadness sweeping through me. He'd done what he had to do, and it had cost him his only father figure. I couldn't imagine how difficult it had been for him. The anger I'd felt a few seconds earlier dissipated like the wind. "It must have been difficult to challenge Mateo. Do you want to talk about it?"

A flutter of surprise passed across his face at my question, then he went straight to Gesture Three while he decided what to share with me. "He was a good guy before the fusion experiments but went too far and wouldn't stop no matter what I said or did. I had to forget the memories and the history between us. I didn't *want* to do it, but it was necessary to keep the pack safe from him. To keep *you* safe."

"This is beyond taking blood samples and vampire biting. You really thought he was going to hurt me."

He grazed the vampire bite with his thumb, then shook his head like it disgusted him. "The minute I saw you on the floor with blood dripping from your neck was the minute I knew I had to do it." He tucked a strand of hair behind my ear, and I melted under his touch. "You're too important."

"But I'm nothing. Half-magical at best. I don't get his obsession with me. He didn't even want me here."

The growl from his lips curled my toes in the best way. "You are far from nothing and always have been. *I* want you here. I did what I had to do. End of."

His words were heavy with emotion. I touched his cheek, just for a second, just so he'd know I understood how hard it was for him. And that I appreciated him. "No one else could've challenged him?"

"No. Even if I hadn't been the one strongest enough to pull it off physically, I would never have allowed any of the betas to be in the position to have to kill him. They're my brothers."

His resolute fierceness about his betas made my heart flutter. He was an ass sometimes, but he loved deeply. I didn't want to know that. It made me feel things. Things that swirled around in my stomach and created a deep-seated heat that bordered on pure desire. There was something else lingering too. Something I needed to fight if I had any hope of passing these trials.

I couldn't fall for the man who may have to kill me. No matter how tempting he was. "Sounds to me like you were alpha way before you were alpha." The word fit him as if he were born to embody it. He looked up through his lashes, directing the million-watt smile that people rarely got in my direction. "So, what now alpha?"

I didn't even know what question I was asking him. It felt bigger than just asking him what we would be doing in the next few minutes. And he took it that way too based on the heated look he lowered on me. "Next, we get to the end of these trials, so I can..."

Trailing off again. Damn him.

I'd been bitten by a caged vampire, threatened by djinn, and I still didn't even know what I was, but all of that took a backseat to the trials. I looked up. "You that eager to kill me?" Probably. Since I'd froth-kissed him and he hated it.

"Eager, yes. But not to kill you." He shook his head like he was dislodging a thought, then took another stick from the pile, spinning it around in his hands, above his head, around his back, all over the place like a ninja. "Let's see what you can do with an elemental rod."

He smirked at his own double entendre and his eyes dipped down to my breasts where the stick he was calling a rod landed. "Where do you get those ridiculous shirts?"

The stick spun with a hollow hooting sound as I backed away from him. "Thrift stores mostly. You don't like them?"

Shrugging, he whipped the stick forward and a plume of fire erupted from the tip, burning a few leaves, then fizzing out. Showing off his Fire magic. He took the hem of my shirt and balled it in his fist. "Yeah, they suit you."

I inched backward until I hit a tree. My heart thudded in my chest at his nearness. His sweet sandalwood and fiery smoke wafted around me, and my breaths became ragged because I was trying not to inhale and inhaling at the same time.

Wells pressed the stick against my jugular and my pulse spiked as he leaned in. I went up on my toes, just to close the distance and force his lips to touch me. Thanks to my raging hormones, I didn't give two craps about where on my body they were. Anywhere would do.

Bad decision alert: It would've been better if I'd decided to eat a week-old tuna sandwich that had been left in the sun than giving into the feel of his lips.

He exhaled, his breath tickling my ear and another place way below my ear. "Fair warning: All the Binding magic placed on me when I was a beta is gone now."

"What does that mean?" My voice was a whisper because if he was saying what I think he was saying, I was in trouble. Deep.

"It means I get to make my own decisions and act on them accordingly."

He'd answered my question. Without answering it at all.

I tried to scramble away, put distance between us, but he caged me against the tree with his other arm. He made a sound that was somewhere between a growl and laugh. I had to force my hands into fists so I wouldn't reach out and touch his chiseled chest. He moved, less than an inch, but it was enough to seal our bodies together. The heat bouncing between us was unbearable. When he licked his lower lip, I almost shattered into flames.

Damn him. I had to get back in control of my senses. And my situation. He was supposed to be training me, not eye fucking me. I shoved his chest, pushing him back about a millimeter. "Teach me how to use the elemental rod."

He laughed, amused at my discomfort, then handed me another stick. He positioned himself behind me, guiding my arm as I swung out. "Don't worry about the magic yet. Just get comfortable using the rod as an extension of your arm."

His body twisted as he helped me swing the stick. He pressed into me, showing me how to move without even saying a word. The hardness of his body, the intimacy made my stomach turn to jelly. I had to distract myself. "I get that maybe I could use a rod against someone in a fight, but these things did nothing against the djinn."

"If we don't get the Conduit open, the djinn may be the least of our worries." He ran his hand from my wrist to my shoulder, adjusting the position of my arm. He could've just swung my elbow out, but no, he had to go for the long draw of skin-to-skin contact that set my nerves alight.

"You're stiff. Don't force it."

I tried to relax my body, but I was a coiled wire of solid steel thanks to him. His voice was a purr in my ear. "Think of it like this: fighting with a weapon is like sex. Close your eyes. Feel the movement, lose yourself in the dance between partners. Allow your body to buzz with the anticipation of what comes next and meet it with equal action."

Fuckity frick, frack, fuck.

I was losing myself, alright. Him talking about sex didn't help one teeny bit.

And he knew it too. *Asshead.*

He placed his hands on my waist and turned me as I moved the stick, growling as he gripped me a little more than he needed to. He caught himself, cutting off the sound, but that didn't stop him from sliding his hands forward and resting them low on my stomach. Any lower and— well, I didn't want to think about that because I would lose my mind.

I somehow managed to hold it together as we sliced at the air until he stepped back and allowed me to move the stick myself. All I was doing was waving a stupid stick in the air, but something about it made me feel powerful. I concentrated and tried to use the correct body positions and movements he'd shown me.

"That's good. Now strike at me, use your Earth magic."

Goody. Now we're getting somewhere.

Focusing on his voice to pinpoint his location, I whipped around and flexed my wrist, slinging the stick toward his shoulder and summoning my magic. He sidestepped the strike and dirt exploded around him.

He shook his head to dislodge the soil and his hair fell right back into annoying place. "Faster. More magic."

I turned back and tried again. The stick swooshed through the air as he ducked under the spray of dirt. "You're telegraphing your moves. Don't let your eyes give you away. Look at me, not where you're aiming to strike."

I huffed in frustration. "I'm trying to hit you, so do I look at you or not? You're sending mixed messages."

So, so many mixed messages.

He shook his head and took the stick from me. "Watch me."

I prepared myself to be whacked on the head or sliced on the neck again, but it didn't happen. He held the stick in front of him and I locked eyes with him. His flared and I was sunk. Pop. Sting. He'd whipped my ass. Thank the Mage he hadn't used his Fire that time. "Damn it, Wells."

"See? My eyes never left yours and still I managed to land a strike."

"And it hurt, Dickwipe."

He laughed and handed me back the stick. "It grazed you at best."

Determined, I focused on his pretty eyes. I mean, if I had to look somewhere it may as well be someplace pleasant. I took a deep breath and flicked the stick, landing a blow to his right side. I couldn't stop myself from doing a little victory dance, raising my arms and shaking my hips in a circle.

"You look ridiculous."

Come on, I deserved a celebration. That guy was all business when it came to playing Whack-Me-With-A-Stick. Though, his look said something completely different than his words. He was staring at me like he wanted to jump in and dance with me instead of admonishing me for it. He set his feet apart, anchoring his stance. "Stop moving your damn hips like that and come at me again."

If he insisted.

I looked directly at him and struck a blow. He countered, but I was able to defend myself against him, throwing a column of dirt in front of him and backing him up. He was right, moving from my shoulder and anticipating his moves made my strikes more powerful and graceful. And the magic was flowing a lot better because I was able to use not only soil, but roots and branches from nearby trees.

Within minutes, I managed to pin him against a tree with a branch across his chest. He grinned, proud of me for following through and picking it up so fast, but I couldn't let him distract me. I lunged forward, meaning to hit him on the ass like he had me, but I telegraphed a little too much. He managed to catch my stick and throw it to the side. The branch bounced back into place with a whipping sound. "Don't get cocky now."

"You'd know all about being cocky."

His chuckled response was low and intense, and I had to shake it out of my bones. Had to put some distance between us. Something, anything to get him to stop looking at me like he was. "I cornered you."

"I could get around you." His eyes swirled magenta as he shrugged. "I could get over you, under you, inside you. Anywhere I wanted, anyway I desired."

I had no response because I was picturing him over me. Under me.

As I see it, yes.

He bit his lower lip, then kicked off the tree, pushing me aside and Gesture Two'ing. "I just had a thought. Come with me."

I had no clue what he was up to. His newfound alpha forwardness was becoming an issue because I liked it too damn much. He wasn't wrong. He could get me in any position he felt like and I wouldn't have protested.

That was disconcerting.

He led me to the courtyard around the Conduit and made me close my eyes. For a second I thought things were about to get smexy, but when I considered we were out in the open with other wolves milling around, I figured I was safe. Which was as comforting as it was disappointing.

When I opened my eyes, the whole area was surrounded by the same silver fire that circled us in the barn. "Okay, I have to ask. What is this fire?" I don't know what possessed me, but I reached out to touch it. I was drawn to it for some reason, and I just *knew* it wouldn't burn me.

Wells grabbed my hand before it connected with the flame. "Don't. If you have to touch something, you could always put your hands on me."

I whipped my head around. "If I recall, you told me specifically not to touch you a long time ago."

"Yeah, I did. Binding magic made me do it. Never would've on my own." He stepped forward and I had the urge to do exactly what he'd suggested, but I balled my hand into a fist instead, resisting. He chuckled. "All you need to know is this is ancient Fire magic, dangerous to anyone who can't wield Fire."

"Okay, I'll keep my hands to myself. Now, tell me why we're here."

He Gesture Three'd. "We need to start working on the Conduit issue. The Five aren't going to sit around and do nothing after what happened your first day. Three of them have had the mind to try and bleed you dry over the Conduit to see if your blood does something to open it. We need to find another way."

"But aren't you their leader now? Can't you just order them to leave me alone?"

"I'll have some control, yes, but even I can't keep them off for long." He placed a hand on my shoulder. "We may not even need your blood. Since you're a gnome with Earth magic, what if you tried going under it."

I laughed. It seemed so ridiculous, it just may work. "You want me to tunnel to Aetheria."

He shrugged. "Yeah. Maybe you loosened the lid on the jar that first day and now you can break it open. Try and see what happens."

My curiosity was piqued. I was some super special thing that affected the Conduit, then maybe it would work. And if I did, all my problems would vanish. Well, not the sexy, brooding, purple-eyed, marble-chested man who I couldn't seem to stop picturing shirtless problem. That would take more intense problem-solving skills.

I slid out of my shoes and took a second to retie my hair as Wells shifted behind me. I almost jumped out of my skin when he leaned in close, heat radiating from his body and giving me a fuzzy feeling. Maybe that was why he was so warm all the time. He could control the ancient Fire magic. "I'll be right here with you."

It took a second to move after that chilling statement, but I got it together, hopefully before he noticed me lingering in the ache of his body heat. I dove headfirst, pushing my Earth magic to the surface and out of my hands. The moment I connected with the soil, my vial of earth around my neck hummed to life, buzzing in what I would swear was contentment.

Weird.

I shook it off and pushed forward, pressing the dirt back and breathing in the rich, ancient aroma of the soil around me. It took mere seconds to cross the distance, passing right under, or through, the Conduit. The moment I knew I was past the tree arch, the dirt became littered with tiny flecks of gold.

The further I pushed, the more gold I discovered in the dirt. It was like they were guiding me, showing me the path to take. Excitement buzzed in my veins. I might just be arriving in Aetheria in a matter of minutes.

I kicked it into high gear with my legs, swimming forward toward my goal, following the concentrated flecks of gold as they veered to the left. Instinct told me to follow the path, so I did. Several seconds later, a flash of blue light passed in front of me. I froze, trying to refocus my night vision and figure out if there was something down there with me or if my excitement over Aetheria had taken over my brain.

A second, a third, a fourth blue light whizzed in front of me. The blue lights whizzed all around me, hissing and flickering. They skirted over my body then stopped in front of my face, wavering like little blue-flamed birthday candles with almost-faces.

I didn't feel fear, but I also didn't feel safe either. I was more curious than anything. "What are you, little guys?"

The lights vibrated in unison and the whisper of an answer floated by, though I couldn't make out what they'd said. I lifted my finger to touch one and I swear it giggled. The flame didn't burn though. I decided to try my luck. "Is this the way to Aetheria?" I mean, I wasn't some man who refused to ask for directions when needed.

The cute little blue flames roared into one big blue fireball, merging together and creating a wall in front of me. I didn't so much hear their whispered response as I experienced it inside me. It was like broken shards of words and incomprehensible phrases, crunching into my brain from within. "Untime. Buildinger building. Clay unformed. Aetheria unopen."

Reply hazy. Please try again.

Untime and buildinger were not words I was familiar with, but at least I got clay and Aetheria. Though untime and unopen were just different ways to say not now and closed. "I don't understand."

Their response was swift. Flames shot around my body, enclosing me in a fiery blue tomb. Their crunched-up little faces grimaced, and their tiny angry voices pricked inside my head, louder than before. "Unopen. Untime. Return."

It wasn't time to go to Aetheria?

Made as much sense as anything.

The blue fire surged around me and when I started to feel the heat. I got the picture. I spun around and tunneled back the way I came, blue lights following me like some magical cop car on my tail until I hurled myself up from the ground, panting. Wells pulled me up by my arms and laid me down beside the Conduit. "You're okay. I've got you."

He brushed a strand of hair from my face and the warmth of his hand calmed my frayed nerves. He looked at me expectantly and I knew he was waiting for intel on what I'd seen, though I didn't know what I learned, not for sure. "There were specks of gold in the soil, like a hidden pathway. I think it was the way to Aetheria. But I didn't get far because little blue flame creatures who spoke in broken words took issue with my presence. They blocked me from going further."

He Gesture Three'd. "Bluecaps?"

Gram had told me about bluecaps though I wasn't even sure they really existed when she mentioned them. They were supposedly distant cousins to gnomes and fae. Smaller and less corporeal, the Mage created them to tunnel and mine in crevices and crannies that trolls and gnomes were too big for.

Bluecaps probably get blue balls because you can't mate with something that has no physical body.

They're rare because they hold both Earth and Fire magic. And sentient, but barely, which kind of vibed with what I'd seen. "Could be. This was my first attempt. Maybe next time I can find a way past them."

The corner of Wells' mouth kicked up. "I like how you think, but don't go down there again unless I'm here with you, capiche? Can't be too careful."

He was right. The bluecaps may have looked cute, but they were formidable. And even though I hadn't gotten far, the path to Aetheria seemed closer than it had been before. Hope spread through me like sunshine, and I was kicking myself for not trying sooner. Maybe I could open the Conduit eventually. With his help. And as much as the thought of needing him scared me, I liked the sound of him being there too. "Capiche, master. Anything you say."

His eyes softened into the palest lavender. I almost got whiplash when he took my face in his hands, brushing his thumbs along my jaw. "Don't say that because I want to take you up on it. I'm tired of..." Trailing off again, biting his lower lip, making me quiver. "I want to..."

My mouth salivated under the intensity of his gaze. I was sick of battling over him in my own head. He was warring with the same thoughts in his. We were both fighting, just not with each other for once. "Would you just finish a Magedamned sentence? What do you want, Wells?"

I shouldn't have asked him. Because he would answer and when he did, I would have to face the feelings that I'd tried so hard to keep under control. His voice was like smoke in my veins, warm, enveloping. "I want you."

There it was out there in the open. There would be no denying it or twisting it to mean anything other than the simple, raw aching truth of what it was. I tried to respond, but he stopped me by running his thumb over my lower lip. "You're brave. And beautiful. And stubborn. And so damned frustrating because I want nothing more than to claim every supple inch of your body, heart, mind, and soul for myself. But now that I'm alpha and I could, I know shouldn't." He growled and I felt it between my legs. "I can't figure out what to fucking do about it." His eyes flared magenta as he zeroed in on my lips. "I shouldn't…"

Swim after you eat? Commit tax fraud? Run with scissors?

I stood there entranced by his enthralling eyes, reveling in the feel of his warm hands on my face. Every nerve ending in my body tingled as he pulled me up to an invisible cliff with his eyes alone, daring me to jump off with him.

We shouldn't.

Without a doubt.

His eyes flared and between two heartbeats, his mouth was on mine.

He kissed me hard, grasping my neck and pinning me against him in a firm grip that was somehow gentle too. And there was no froth anywhere near either of us.

I'd tried so hard to resist this. Resist him. In that moment, I couldn't remember why.

I tangled my hands in his soft hair and gave in to him, opening my mouth and moaning when he deepened the kiss. I wrapped my legs around his waist as he lifted me, spinning me around and pressing my back against the boulder. His hands slid over my hips, locking me in place underneath him.

Like I would go anywhere else.

He pulled back to look at me, his lilac eyes glowing with desire. "I have responsibilities to the pack now that I didn't have before. And, Mage, I'm trying to do the right thing here, but you have no idea what you do to me." He pressed his hips against me as he cradled my ass in his hands. The hard line of his arousal causing tremors between my legs. "I'm supposed to be deciding your fate based on some damn magic trials when all I want to do is bury myself inside you so deep you know without a doubt how worthy I think you are."

I gasped at the strength of his words, the sincerity of them.

The promise.

It was a dangerous thing, this. My raw desire for him was on a collision course with our Perception magic contract and I knew I should stop this, but I couldn't make myself. Not when it felt so right to kiss him like this. To feel his hands, to experience the hunger of his mouth, to sense the depth of his desire. I knew if I let him, he would squeeze the life out of my heart.

Never before had anyone felt like this.

He drove his mouth against mine, pressing just enough to feel the sting of his stubble against my cheek and make me want to beg for more. His tongue flicked over mine and I whimpered.

How could I let myself get into this position?

To be honest, I'd get in any position with him—even octopus if I figured out what that was.

I gripped his waist with my thighs as moved his hands to yank my shirt over my head, exposing my blush-colored lace bra, which was sheer

284

enough to see through. His eyes flashed as he swore. "Fuck, Gnome."

Diving down, he ran his tongue over my nipple, making it hard through the thin fabric. I arched my back, encouraging him to continue and moaning when he gave my other nipple the same treatment. "That feels…" He bit down and the rest of my sentence dissolved on my tongue. I writhed beneath him, grinding against his hard cock as he sucked my taut nipples.

He raised his head. "I can finish *that* sentence. It feels fucking right."

It did. There was no other word for it. I'd lost myself in the feel of him and I didn't want to be found ever again.

I grabbed his collar and pulled him up, seeking the heat of his mouth and the feel of his tongue against mine. He groaned, giving me everything I wanted as he kissed me, palming my breasts in his warm hands.

There was liquid fire in my veins. He was both the cause and the solution, and I hummed with need for him, ached with it. He growled my name and the sensation wove through my body and rooted there in my bones. I knew without a shadow of a doubt, I would never be able to dislodge it.

Suddenly, I stilled as a buzz vibrated against my leg, short-circuiting my desires.

Outlook not so good.

I don't know how I did it, but I pulled away from him. I was panting like a damn dog, but I managed to squeak words out. "Your pants are buzzing."

He pressed a kiss low on my neck, then trailed up with just the tip of his tongue until he reached the sensitive spot behind my ear. "You have no idea."

Mage Almighty.

I did. I was vibrating from head to toe.

He ran his thumb along my bottom lip as if he were signing his work like an artist. Yeah, he was the Picasso of kissing.

It took him even longer to recover from what we'd done. He sat there Gesture Three'ing, scrubbing his jaw while his thoughts tumbled in his head. "I...shouldn't have let myself get so carried away," he whispered, his voice low and gruff as he took me in with a heated gaze like he couldn't bear to stop looking at me, but knew he had to.

"Maybe. But I didn't mind." It was the plain and simple truth. We shouldn't have, but we did. And it was fucking phenomenal.

He dug his phone out of his front pocket, then looked at me through those dark lashes after he took a few seconds to brush dirt from his shirt. I had no clue how it had gotten there. "I know."

My emotions slammed back and forth with the dilemma we'd put ourselves in. I'd allowed it and that was on me. My stupid heart needed to calm the fuck down. He sensed my discomfort because he looked down and cupped my face. "That was...enjoyable. *Very*. Maybe not the best idea, though."

Enjoyable?

How about spine-tingling, earth-shattering, and panty-melting?

Enjoyable.

He may have botched the description, but he was right about it being a bad idea. It sucked so much, but he was right. What did Arlo warn me?

Don't miss the forest for the trees.

Even attractive trees with a rock-hard chest and sexy smirking ability.

I had to do it: I had to be an adult and see reason, no matter what he did to my hormones. The kissing, the touching, was over for good. It was nice while it lasted. Who was I kidding? It was perfect while it lasted. But it couldn't happen again. Maybe if I passed the trials and things calmed down... "You're right. With the Perception contract, we shouldn't..."

Now I'd picked up his habit of railing sentences.

He seemed to get that though. "Yeah. I need to remain partial, keep you at a distance. It's best for your trials. For you." His eyes flashed and I swear they were red this time. "Let's take this one step at a time. First, we focus on passing your trials. Then…"

He paused, long enough for me to know he was calculating what to say, weighing the consequences on some invisible scale in his head. "Then what?"

"Then we'll see what happens when I *do* let myself get carried away."

He switched gears, handing me my shirt, his shoulders squaring as he delivered the next bit of news. "Come on, The texts were from Arlo. He finally has answers."

I was numb as we tracked straight to the Infirmary and entered the same exam room, I was ushered into on my first day at Boulderbrook. So much had happened since that day and I felt like a different person completely. There was so much riding on what I was about to hear. Yet, at the same time, no matter what I found out, nothing would change. The Perception contract was still in place and Wells was still my judge.

When Arlo entered the room, Wells slid an arm around my waist, like he was bracing me for impact. "What did you discover?" he demanded. Like it was his news as much as mine. I suppose it was now that he was alpha, and we were all banking on me opening the Conduit some way, somehow.

I swallowed.

Without taking his eyes off Wells, Arlo answered. The weight of his response crashed down on my soul like a boulder. "I'm afraid you're a golem, my Dear."

utlook not so good.

    Gram used the word gobsmacked all the time. That's what I was—gobs-fucking-smacked.

I'd seen two golems in my life: a sex toy made of bubbles and a decoy made of flour, chocolate, and gold. There was no way I could be the same as those things. I bled when I cut myself shaving. I'd puked my guts for days when I had the stomach flu. I had a period each month! I glanced over at Wells. I *felt* things like attraction, anger, lust. How was it possible that I started life inanimate?

I tried to formulate everything in my head into a sensible question Arlo could answer, but when I opened my mouth, nothing came out. I just stood there with the room spinning, trying to stuff the anger and confusion I felt into a box in my heart. I gripped Wells' thigh for support and when I did, he growled at Arlo like he was the enemy. "Explain."

Arlo smiled, trying to ease the blow. "The djinn used a peculiar phrase—they'd fill you with djinn magic. I would likely have never thought to test for it otherwise. To my knowledge there's no other being capable of being *filled*."

Filled.

Like a doughnut or cookie with a cream center.

My head spun and I would've sworn the temperature had dropped twenty degrees. Arlo just kept on talking. "I know of no being in our realm with enough power to make something, someone, as complex as a golem with total sentience. It would require all the magic we have left."

Wells traced circles on my back, sending me silent comfort as he tried to reconcile what Arlo was telling us. "You're saying she was created in Aetheria?"

Arlo nodded. "I suspect. There are several Wind beings—elves, cupids before they were all banished to Netheria, some fae royalty perhaps—who would possess this amount of power. But they'd have to be in Aetheria to have the magic."

I clutched the vial of earth around my neck, desperate to ground myself in some small way. I may have been born, *created*, in Aetheria—the place I wanted to return more than anything. None of it made sense to me.

Arlo gestured to my vial of Earth. "May I try something?"

Yearning for answers, I handed my vial over to Arlo. He poured a small amount of soil into a beaker and set it aside. Next, he plucked a hair from my head—ouch—and placed it inside a second beaker.

He added a thick black liquid to each and spoke in Faetongue over the vials, the tension in my body coiling to the Nth degree. Beside me, Wells was rigid and focused as the seconds ticked by, but he didn't stop touching me.

The beakers went through multiple colors and finally, a white mist erupted from each of them, curling into the air with a sweetness that settled inside my lungs. Arlo handed my vial back, his lion eyes full of wonder. "I can definitively say your make-up is the same as the earth in your vial—Aetherian clay."

I clawed at my wrist, trying to see if I'd crumble if I scratched too hard. Wells took my hand, threading his fingers through mine, which felt oddly more intimate than his tongue on my nipples earlier. "Don't. Nothing has changed here. You're more than just a golem."

More than I am and less than I should be.

More than a gnome, less than real.

Okay. Okay. Okay.

Reply hazy…

It was too much. I had to get out.

I bolted.

I realized I needed to know more, but I feared if I heard one more syllable, it would break me. And I knew Wells would kick my ass later, but I left him in the dust, running out of the Infirmary and past the Conduit and to the closest patch of earth I could find. I tunneled in, letting the cool earth surround me.

I stopped after a few minutes of fierce digging. My muscles began to relax as the Earth hummed to me with a gentle caress. In here, I was safe, protected, not a freak of nature. I allowed myself to cry. Just a couple of minutes. The emotion spilled out of me as I tried to come to grips with my identity.

Golem.

An empty shell. A puppet.

I wonder if Gram knew.

Golems are more than empty clay vessels. They're powerful tools capable of the deepest magic imaginable. Or they can be great housekeepers in in pinch.

I dug into my memories trying to capture some clue that would lead me to more answers. I tried for a long time, but still produced the same childhood memories and life experiences as I had before this whole thing started. Frustration built in my heart, my mind, my soul. Were those experiences real or implanted by the person who created me for some nefarious purpose? I might never know.

That was the kicker. With no clear path to Aetheria, I was stuck. Even if I passed my trials, which I was still determined to finish, and somehow unlocked the Conduit like Wells wanted, I was always going to have this big question mark over my life. Who made me and why?

I wrapped my hand around the vial of soil around my neck. Was I even still part gnome? You were either made or conceived. I was...both? It made no sense. And I started to feel like my very soul had been ripped from my body.

If I even had a soul, to begin with.

I don't know how long I stayed in my tunnel, but I realized that there were no answers in the earth around me. The only way I was going to be able to deal with that shit was to come out and deal with it. It was tough, but I forced myself forward and crawled back into the light.

When I breached the surface, Wells was there, sitting on the ground and leaning back on his hands. The sun had almost set and there were orange and pink ribbons painting the sky behind him, covering him in a golden glow. He was striking, no matter the light, but like this, he was luminous. He held out his hand and I let him pull me up. "How long have you been sitting here?"

He shrugged. "As long as you've been in there."

I laid back in the grass, close but not touching him. "How did you know where I was?" He pointed to his nose. I looked down at my clothes. I was a dirty, sweaty mess again. "You smelled me? Gross."

I moved to scoot away from him, but he caught my arm and pulled me closer. "I happen to like dirty." He took a long predatory glance over my body that I felt way down inside my atoms. If golems had those. "And you smell fucking edible."

Before I could react to that comment—because wowzah—he shifted and went from sexy dirty boy to nice guy. "I won't ask if you're okay."

If he had, I would've broken down in front of him. The very last thing I wanted to do. "Thank you."

"Do you need anything?"

"I'm sure I must, but I can't tell you what it is." It was the truth. I felt…hollow, which was hysterical considering what I was. Golems were cavernous creatures with no beating heart or blood coursing through their veins. But as I glanced over at the stunning man beside me, I felt my blood was flowing. He was the reason. He filled my emptiness, and I didn't know what to do with that.

"Fair enough. If you think of something, you'll let me know?"

"Sure."

He laid back like I was, watching the sky turn before he spoke again. "You're managing this better than most people would."

"Trust me, I'm freaking out on the inside. But I can't change anything, so I have to be okay with it, right? What's the alternative?" I turned on my side and rested my head on my hand. "This won't affect my trials, will it?"

"No." That was good. I still wanted to be a part of the Conclave. And…not die.

Wells started to say something but stopped himself. I wanted to pull it out of him, but I decided I shouldn't. He'd tell me when he was ready.

I was impressed with my own maturity. Or maybe my golem shell was full to the brim with information, I couldn't hold anymore.

Wells looked at me for a long time, studying me, trying to discern how I worked. Hell, if I knew, Buddy. The seconds ticked away, and in the quiet span of time between words I was grounded, just as if I had been surrounded by the hushed whispers of the cool Earth. It was him. He made me feel that. Hours ago, that might have unsettled me, but in that moment, it made me feel stronger.

Not because of the way he'd kissed me. Because of the way he'd taken up residence at my side during the worst moment of my life. He finally broke the silence. "You know you haven't changed, right? Fuck DNA. It's not what you are that matters, it's *who* you are." He pressed his hand to my heart. "Who you are is incredible." His eyes flashed plum, and I melted because I knew under the growling, alpha exterior beat the heart of a man who cared deeply. And he was sharing a piece of that heart with me.

He licked the tip of his thumb and raked it across my jaw. If anyone else under the sun had done that, I would have been grossed out and slapped them.

I didn't slap him.

He continued running his thumb along my jaw and it curled my toes. His touch was soft and when he wrapped his hand around the nape of my neck, I was certain I would need a cold shower or a little alone time. I should've told him to stop.

I didn't.

He stared at my mouth, and I couldn't keep from licking my lips. I had become a burning flame of nerve endings and desire and I wished he would kiss me again. That desire became a tangible thing between us. I could feel it pulsing with energy and possibility and I know he could too. Just when I thought I might go up in flames, he pulled away, leaving me cold and breathless. "You had a little dirt on your face."

I shook my head. It was all I could do.

We weren't doing this. No kissing, no handsies, no inappropriate shenanigans with your judge, jury, and executioner. Stop thinking about the feel of his mouth on yours. Golem. Conduit. Trials—all more important than your developing feelings.

He jumped up. "I have something I need to do. Let me walk you back to your cabin."

294

Right. He was alpha now. Pack first.

As it should be.

I followed him, turning over everything in my head as we walked without saying anything. He appeared to be doing the same thing, though I doubted we had the same things sloshing about in our minds. Though, it felt like our silence was part of us now. I enjoyed the feeling of it.

We weren't far from the cabin, so it took us no time to get there. I opened my door and took a step inside. "Terra?"

I turned back. "Yeah?"

He startled me by taking a giant step forward and pulling me in close in a tight embrace. At first, I stood there like a wood plank, but I realized that was foolish. He was standing there offering me comfort in his warm grasp. So, I wrapped my arms around his back and there we were.

Hugging?

Hugging.

He moved his hand up my back and twisted my hair in his fingers for a second before he squeezed harder. "You're okay."

He let me go and he was off again.

I wasn't sure if he was telling me or himself. The only thing I knew was his warmth was clinging to me and it left me dying for more.

I didn't have the heart to face anyone in the cafeteria and explain my tear-streaked face and bad mood, so I stayed in my cabin. Tristan had brought me some amazing chicken parm he'd made and, despite the deal we'd made early on, he was stretched out in my bed like he owned it. Fine by me. I was having a good ole time wearing a hole in the floorboards with my pacing. "Tell me, again, the golems you make can have memories implanted?"

He let out an exasperated sigh. He was growing weary of my incessant questions but was answering them, nonetheless. "Yes, Babycakes. If the creator is powerful enough, they can implant memories as well as commands. The whole point of the golem, in the first place, is to do something the maker can't or doesn't want to do themselves, i.e. become werewolf snack food." He paused and I shot him a look. I'd already apologized for that. Multiple times. "My Wellsbrator aside because my magic is dying, the golem I made for Mateo was dumb because I just had to fool them a few seconds, but if I'd needed it to go on longer, I could've breathed more life into it, made it sentient, and think what I wanted in order to accomplish the task."

Super.

I'd just discovered my body wasn't what I thought it was. Now my mind was slipping away too. I had to understand more.

Golem History for two hundred, Alex.

"Do golems die when their task is completed?"

Tristan flopped over on his side and hugged my pillow. "Not always. I guess you can consider this the upside: golems can be immortal. The key to their power and life force is in Name Magic. When a golem is created, the maker writes their name somewhere on the golem and breathes life into it. I signed the Wellsbrator across his perfect ass, but I scribbled my name on *my* golem's cock. Because, well, it's fantastic, you may recall."

"Is it now?" Wells had appeared, back from wherever he'd gone and leaned into my open window like it was a photoshoot for a new brand of tight t-shirts and masculinity. "Should we compare?"

Tristan reached into his pants like he was going to pull it out and show Wells. "Nope. Stop. Let's keep everything in our pants, shall we?" I turned to Wells who was smirking like he'd won the showdown anyway. "Tristan was just telling me that people who make golems write their name somewhere on the body."

Shrugging, Tristan removed his hand and continued, "Yeah, some use a necklace the golem wears, but to me, that's risky. What if the clasp breaks or it gets knocked off somehow? Wasted golem. I'm guessing the one powerful enough to make someone as intricate as our Babycakes here would make a permanent mark, so they could retain control for as long as they needed."

I considered my vial of Earth being the Name object but threw out the idea. I'd taken it off hundreds of times and I didn't...cease to exist. As I fiddled with the necklace, I got another idea. "Something like this?"

I held out my wrist so Wells and Tristan could see my birthmark squiggle. The interconnecting ovals or swoops looked more like spring than anything, though that was stretching it. Wells ran his thumb over the mark, and I felt that touch zing all over my body. We shared a heated look and the feel of his hands, his mouth, every time we'd kissed came sailing back into my mind.

We shouldn't. Don't get distracted by the pretty.

Tristan coughed, breaking up the moment. I wasn't sure if I should be upset or grateful. "Yeah, that could be it. Though I have to say, your fabricator has terrible handwriting."

I squinted, trying to glean some meaning or intent from the mark. I got nothing.

Wells dropped my hand and Gesture Two'd toward the door. "I need a moment with Terra."

"Oh, that's no problem. I'll just poof down and take a little nap while you talk." When he miniaturized, Wells grabbed him out of the air with his wolf speed and flicked him out of the window.

I started to protest the abuse of my fairy, but he stopped me. "He's fine. He loves it when I manhandle him." That tracked. "Come out here."

When I made my way outside, he was leaning against the side of my cabin in full Gesture One glory, pale green tee stretching across his chest. I had to bite my lip to keep myself from telling him how hot he looked. He shot me a wicked smirk and I knew he'd figured out what I was thinking, damn him. "I hope you don't get pissed about this, but I have something for you."

I couldn't understand what I was looking at for a moment. I was lost in the hazy thoughts of how well that shirt suited him. But the second I drew closer, I was gobsmacked once again. "Is this Gram's cane?"

He twirled it in his fingers, then handed it to me. "Your new rod."

I closed my hand over the smooth hilt of the cherrywood cane. It was worn from years of use, carved by her gnarled fingers. "I didn't have the heart to part with this when she died. It was such a part of her." I shook my head. "But it's just a cane."

He slid his long fingers over the surface. I trembled at the sudden surge of magic coursing through it. "It may have been just a cane, but when I saw it lodged in the corner of your dining room, I knew it would be the perfect rod for you. Your connection to her will amplify the magic."

My head spun. The cane had been in my house, and that was an eight-hour trip one way. It wasn't just a nice thing to do. It was a gesture full of meaning. I was a tide of overwhelming emotion and tears were threatening to spill from my eyes. I'd never, in my life, been given something so thoughtful. So meaningful. "I don't understand. When? How?" I left the question of why out. I didn't think I could manage his answer to that one.

"That night after we played poker. I had Bash take the plane to Eugene because I couldn't stand to think of you losing so many things that were important to you." Having felt his love for his mother, it was clear why he felt this way. He understood. "I got a few other things while I was there, but we'll get to those later. Right now, I wanted to prove that you'll be fine. And I just thought you needed a piece of home."

I focused on the cane because I wasn't at a place where I could add more to the mountain of implications lying at my feet. "I-I don't know what to say."

"Don't say anything. Try it."

I raised the cane, directing it at my cabin window. Standing there with my Earth magic flowing between me and my new rod, I'd never been less hollow. Everything about being a golem, a vessel for some unknown entity, seemed to vanish in wake of the overwhelming gratitude I felt in that moment. For him. For Gram. For the pack of wolves who'd become friends. It was all coursing through the rod.

I released a blast of Earth magic. The ground hummed, rumbling and rising until a burst of purple pansies burst out, trailing along the windowsill. Wells plucked a flower, inhaling the scent that I knew reminded him of his mother, then held it out to me. "Look." Inside the pansies, were glittering flecks of gold. I'd never made gold of any kind and I tried so many times.

"I did that?"

He tucked the flower behind my ear, like he'd done before but this time it seemed laced with meaning. He ran his finger over my ear, and I melted. "I knew you were special from the first day I laid eyes on you. Terra, this is only the beginning. I feel it in my bones. You're the answer."

I didn't know what I was. The answer, a golem, a gnome, a girl who was falling for a werewolf she shouldn't be. None of that. All of it? The only thing I knew for certain was that I had never felt fuller.

JEWELS OF CLAY

30

I crawled out of bed as the sun rose over the lake, took a hot bath which eased at least some of the tension in my muscles. To avoid thinking too long about what clothes to put on, I stuck my hand in the drawer and pulled out my royal blue sports bralette with the zipper front and my favorite black yoga pants. When I was dressed, I paced until the knock on my door at seven. Just as Wells had said.

Werewolves were punctual. I needed to add that to my Gramisms.

When I opened the door, the betas were standing in a semi-circle, each of them holding a rod in their hand. Except Mace. He had his between his legs like he was riding a broomstick.

No wait. This was Mace. He was pretending it was his penis a moment before I opened the door. They greeted me in near unison. "Good morning."

"Wow. You guys are a little early for trick or treating. Come back in a couple of weeks. I'll have Butterfingers."

Mace laughed. "I'm taking you up on that. Wells is on his way to meet us. Now, get your rod and move your ass, young Padawan, time to learn some things."

"Before breakf—"

"Here." Ren handed me a paper sack and I found biscuits and bacon inside. "Eat while we walk."

As I bounded down the stairs, nippy October air filled my lungs. At the last second, I ran back into the cabin and threw Wells' hoodie and my red beanie on for warmth, then I shoved a biscuit in my mouth and trailed behind the long-legged freaks as we made our way to the field.

To my surprise, the beta squad led me through the field and into the woods beyond. It was exciting to explore a part of Boulderbrook I hadn't seen before. We were a few yards into the dense foliage—I hadn't even been able to look around yet—when a huge crack reverberated in the air. I ducked in defense.

"Damn, Mace, give us a warning next time, you ass." Ren had crouched down too and had his rod drawn for combat.

I looked up and found Mace holding his rod up, pointing toward the top of a tree. A huge branch had fallen at his feet. Putting two and two together, I realized he'd used his rod to break the branch. I went over to him so I could learn as much as I could about the magic weapons. "May I see your rod?"

As soon as it came out of my mouth, I knew he was the absolute worst person to ask that question of. "Sure, but I'll have to take my pants off first."

A stream of silver fire blasted over his head.

Wells had appeared, brandishing his rod and looking like he'd been on a weeklong spa vacation, glowing with contentment and virility. The gold circle amulet hung from his neck, gleaming against the tight, white V-neck tee he wore.

Yeah, alpha looked good on him.

Not that it mattered. It didn't.

Shouldn't.

He shot Mace a look that matched the fire that almost singed his curls. Mace handed me his rod. "Sorry. I'm not used to hanging out with women I'm not actively trying to bone. It'll be an adjustment. Here you go."

Though it didn't sound like it, there may have been a compliment in there.

Mace's rod was bright silver, but I knew that couldn't be right. Werewolves and silver didn't gel. It wasn't iron either, obviously. "Platinum?"

"Yep."

I twisted the rod in my hand. It had an intricate swirl pattern down the—Mage help me—shaft with a huge diamond stone on top and it was telescoping, easy to conceal. I handed it back. "It's pretty. And if that diamond is real, you are a rich son of a bitch."

"Eh, the diamond's from Aetheria. Those things practically grow on trees over there. This rod belonged to the elf whose blood Mateo used in my fusion. I needed something that channeled Wind better than my old copper rod, so I decided to use his in memoriam. Fore!" He sent another Wind blast over his shoulder and a single leaf drifted to the ground.

Something stirred behind me and turned to find Wells staring at me with intensity. "What?" I asked.

"Nothing."

The look on his face? That was not nothing.

It was unadulterated smolder, and it was being aimed at me.

Ren cleared his throat, then raised his own rod and attempted his own shot, pointing his rod made of what looked like polished ebony wood, toward the ground. A stream of dirt shot up and grazed a nearby branch. A single leaf tumbled from the tree. I could manipulate Earth, but how Ren had the precision to do that was a mystery.

It was Gideon's turn next. He shrugged and held his glass rod up. It was simple with a long single twist around the shaft and curved at the handle, like waves. He released a single focused stream of water overhead. As the leaf dropped from the tree, the water splashed down on Mace's head. He shook his curls like a dog. "Thanks, Ariel."

Gideon huffed. "Mace thinks it's funny to call me Ariel because I was fused with a water elemental. But, for the thousandth time..." he raised his voice. "I'm not a merman, I'm part sea dragon now. Much scarier and more deadly, you wannabe Legolas."

I had to laugh. Even after the horrendous things Mateo had done to them, they'd embraced their new identities. It didn't excuse anything, but it made me feel good to know it didn't break them. It had, in fact, made them stronger. Which was an unsettling notion considering how it was Mateo's reason for the fusion in the first place.

Not to be shown up, Wells lifted his rod. It was thicker than the others, made of copper with scrolling fire etched along the sides. There was some sort of winged figure on the handle that glinted in the sunlight. The rod was gorgeous. As was the manhandling it. "Ahem," was all he said.

Silver flames shot from the rod and licked along the surface of a branch without setting it on fire. A single leaf drifted from the tree, wafting down and landing near Mace. He picked it up and held it for us to see the artistic cock and balls burnt into the leaf.

Yeah.

I'm not ashamed to admit that was the most inappropriately hot thing I'd ever witnessed, and I was there for it. Wells blew on the end of his rod, settling the contest and declaring himself the winner. "If we're done measuring dicks, can we get serious? She needs to be able to use her rod."

I raised my Gram's cane and faced him with a challenging grin. "Bring it on, alpha."

He whacked my rod, but I held firm. We volleyed for a few minutes until he swirled around backward and surprised me with an attack on the other side. "I fully intend to bring it and you're not going to know what hit you, Gnome." The look on his face told me he wasn't just talking about sparring with our rods.

We stood there; our rods locked with charged electricity coursing between them, between us. His eyes flared and he didn't even try to hide the way he was looking at me from the others. It was pure, unadulterated desire.

And I was serving it right back to him, despite my best efforts not to.

"Um, should the rest of us leave? I saw a wood nymph porn once that started just like this. Only there were a couple of centaurs and a dwarf too. I could get down on my knees to simulate if you want." Mace said, giggling to himself.

Wells shot a stream of fire that singed the top of his sneakers. "Nope. We're good."

I shook off the heat zinging between us. I needed to focus. "I don't know if I'll be able to channel magic and do hand-to-hand at the same time. It takes too much concentration for both."

Wells turned to me, grinning. "Your magic will come naturally if you focus on your opponent. Watch them spar, see what I mean."

He Gesture Two'd the Betas. Gideon and Mace each raised their rods and before I could blink, they were fighting. It looked like a cross between two kids playing with plastic swords and two professional fencers. But, as they continued to spar, I began to see patterns in what they were doing. They used magic to distract or disarm the opponent, then went in for the strike in the wake of the magic.

When Mace's platinum rod and Gideon's glass one touched, a charge of magic was released. Zaps of wind and water flew around them. Gideon spun and struck at the same and the concentrated stream of steamy water ended up making a small hole in Mace's t-shirt. He snarled at Gideon.

"Oh, that's how we're playing? Let's do this, Vader."

Mace deflected Gideon's rod, then thrust his forward. A thin surge of air shot from his rod and hit Gideon right in the crotch. He went down and Mace did a little victory dance until Wells sent a swish of rod fire over his head.

Wells placed his hand on the small of my back. I jumped at the sudden contact, then leaned back into him almost as quickly, reveling in the simmering heat of his touch. "Ready to try?"

I wasn't afraid of using my magic. I was worried I wouldn't have enough to be effective at all, which gave me an idea. Probably, a stupid one, but it was just a matter of time before I would need to perfect the rod thing for my Soul trial anyway. It couldn't hurt to try it. "Since I'm a golem, technically a hollow being, do you think you'd be able to fill me with some of your magic?"

Gideon coughed. "Have you learned nothing? You can't leave Mace an opening like that."

Mace thrusted his pelvis. "Oh, he'll *fill* you with his *magic,* alright! Fill you all night long." Ren punched him in the arm to shut him up.

I turned to find Wells surveying me like I was a puzzle to solve. I guess I was. It was an insane idea. Magicals couldn't just share magic. If they could, Mateo wouldn't have designed a way to steal it. But maybe a hollow being could hold someone else's magic. What if that was my purpose? Even if it wasn't, I might be able to use it to help me with these trials.

"I've never read anything magic sharing like you're proposing, but I've also never had conversations with golems who have smart mouths and sweet asses before either. Let's give it a shot." Before I could react to his statement, he slid his large hand inside the hoodie, resting it over my heart, the source of Elemental magic. His warmth overwhelmed me, and my pulse kicked up. He smirked because he felt it.

The Conduit key around his neck glistened and power sparked

through my body like a wave, flooding my veins with the electric hum of foreign magic. It was like meeting someone for the first time and clicking instantly with them—new and familiar at the same time. "I feel something."

A glimmer of surprise passed on his face and his eyes flashed deep amethyst. "Damn, Gnome. I didn't think it would work and I really didn't think it would feel like this."

I sucked in a breath. "Like what?"

He hesitated, then splayed his fingers, grazing the hollow of my throat with his pinkie and swiping the swell of my breast with his thumb. A shockwave of shivers went through me. "It feels magnetic. Seductive. Like you're drawing me in slowly, inch by excruciating inch and all I want to do is drive my magic deep inside you." He released a moan, and I felt the rattle in my bones. Mage, he sounded so turned on. "What do you feel?"

I closed my eyes and concentrated on the warmth of his hand on my chest as magic flowed from his fingertips. "Like I've tunneled through the richest, most inviting soil down to the center of the earth and I'm floating in liquid magma without getting burned." A sigh escaped my lips at the same time as his growl. I opened my eyes and found his swirling in lavender, his expression full of awe.

The magic moved from my body into my rod as he slid his rod along mine, slowly circling, turning me as he moved. He took his hand from my chest, and I groaned at the loss of warmth, damn near gripping his hand and putting it back for him.

Taking advantage of my momentary loss of concentration, he jerked his rod away and came down on mine, almost smacking it out of my hand. I shook myself out of the magic-sharing stupor and remembered why we were sharing in the first place.

I drew my rod back, twisting it and raising it at the same time. When it connected with his, magic flared, and dirt went everywhere. I sputtered, spitting the remains from my mouth. I looked up and Wells was shaking his head, dislodging the dirt from his hair, which fell into place with a flick of his head. "Sorry."

He frowned. "Don't apologize for wielding your power. Not to me. Not to anyone."

"Okay. But you don't hold back on me. I need to be able to truly defend myself."

He nodded in agreement. I stepped onto the dirt patch and removed my shoes in order to connect more with the Earth magic I had. I was getting used to the warm buzz the rod gave me and I tried to tap into that feeling and coax the magic out as I planned my attack. Wells' rod came down and I blocked his advance. Behind me, the wolves clapped, and Ren shouted, "Yes. That's it. Don't forget the trees."

"Say what?" I turned and Wells took the opportunity to zap my butt, searing a hole in my pants and allowing a tiny patch of butt cheek to feel the breeze.

I swiveled on him, and he shrugged. "You said not to hold back."

"These are my good pants!"

He surveyed my lower half in one long heated look. "They *do* make your ass look perfect, but they'd look better on my floor."

A collective "oooh" came from the peanut gallery and my entire body flushed with heat.

He thrust his rod underneath mine and flicked upward, trying to knock it out of my hand, but I used the momentum to spin around, lowering my body. I shot a spray of dirt in front of him, blocking his view as swung and went for his legs, clipping them just below the knee. He tumbled backward, landing on his back. "*You* look better on the floor, Wolfhole."

The betas went insane, shouting and cheering.

Wells shot me a smirk from the ground, like he was happy to have been knocked on his backside. "You're getting the hang of this." He whipped himself off the ground, which was, wowzah, hot.

Until he shot a stream of fire at my feet. I barely sidestepped it, but it served to remind me that he and I were using different magics. Suddenly Ren's hint made sense. Squinting, I focused on the ground beyond Wells, coaxing roots from the tree behind him. They jutted up and I directed them with my rod, whacking him right on the ass and pushing him down, pinning him underneath them.

Confidence swelling, I went over and stood in front of him, ready to taunt him. He used his rod to produce of curtain of fire before I could get close. When the fire dissipated, he was upright again and that wouldn't do.

I pointed my rod at the soil in front of me. A surge of magic coursed through the Earth. The unsettled ground tunneled forward, then broke the surface right in front of Wells. As my dirt bomb exploded around him, I directed my rod at the branches above his head. They bent to my will, pushing him down from behind in a smack of force. His rod slipped from his hand as he fell.

He crawled from the ground at a snail's pace. For a split second I thought I'd made a huge mistake. The man had killed his alpha hours ago. He bit his lower lip and brought his hands together.

Slow clapping.

He was slow clapping me. Again.

Douchehole.

"You're going to do fine, Terra." He shot a sultry expression my way, but then morphed into alpha between heartbeats. "Ren, manage the seating."

Ren clapped his hands together, and for once, he looked giddy. It was weird on him. He walked over the large tree beside him and placed his hands on the trunk. After a few moments, the ground under my feet started to vibrate. I shot Ren a questioning look, but he kept his hands on the tree and his mouth shut.

The earth around us spattered, shooting up clods of dirt as it rolled. I yelped when a tree root broke between my feet and curled. Wells yanked me to his chest to keep me from being skewered by it. "I told you there was magic in the most unexpected of places."

I was starting to see that. In a couple of different ways. I didn't want to admit it to him or even to myself, but *he* was magic.

The tree roots wrapped around themselves, creating stump-like seats for the five of us. Ren plopped into one of the makeshift chairs and beamed at me. "It's dryad magic. Anyone who touches the trees can create whatever they envision. I'm just better at it than them."

Gideon slid into another tree chair. "You say that like it's a talent you've honed over years. It's the troll blood." Ren shrugged as Wells Gesture One'd, a serious grim settled on his features and he wasted zero more time getting down to business.

erra's trials are a non-issue as far as I'm concerned, so I'm focusing on other things." His confidence in me passing all the trials was disarming. And hot. I gave him a grateful look as he continued, "Long term, we need to formulate a strategy for magic diminishing and if we can't get the Conduit open, we'll have to prepare for war over it."

He gave it a second to settle in and I wished it could've, but that statement made the reality of our situation weigh a ton. The Conduit opening was going to fall on me. The bluecaps had stopped me before, but I vowed to find another way past them. Maybe Tristan could help me with that. They were related to fae, after all. Whatever it took, I would get that thing open.

Wells' booming voice pulled me back into the moment. "The djinn are the immediate problem."

I hadn't thought about the djinn in days, and I cursed myself for it dropping my guard. "They're coming back, aren't they?"

He nodded. "I've been going through Mateo's email. They had a deal from the start—he could use the djinn we captured to attempt fusion for two weeks. In exchange, he was going to share the process with them, but when they discovered you, Terra, the deal changed."

Great. "Me?"

"The djinn knew the potential you possessed as a vessel, to use their word." He stopped long enough to growl his annoyance. "Mateo wanted to create more golems like you and had begun experimenting on ways to use them to harness power for the pack. The djinn would help him for an equal share. In the end, it would've been them and us wielding all the magic in this world. Ambient magic, included. And when they needed more, they'd take it from all other Magicals, even those in the Conclave, effectively destroying it."

"Thank the Mage that won't happen now," Gideon said, placing a hand on my shoulder.

"Yes, but the djinn have it in their heads. They'll be back for Terra and when they come again, it'll make the other attacks will look like holiday visits from sweet Aunt Clara."

"Shit." Ren and Mace together.

"Shit doesn't cover it. We have to be ready for them because they can't have our gnome." He was still calling me gnome. I swallowed to combat the lump in my throat, knowing all of what was going to happen after this discussion was going to be for me, to protect me from the djinn.

I'd never have believed it before, but I knew it in the depths of my soul in that moment—I was pack, a part of them, and they would do what they had to do to keep me safe. Not because I may be able to open the Conduit for them one day, but because they cared about me. And I felt the same for them.

A prickle of a tear streamed down my face, not a big one, but enough that all of them smiled, returning the emotion they saw in me. We were in this together. Not just Wells, all of them. "How do we do that?"

Wells lowered himself to the ground in front of my tree seat and squeezed my knee, warmth spread under his touch. "We prep for a djinn attack. Rods and elemental magic will slow them down if we use them as a unit in force, but their strength comes from wishing and rods won't help us there."

I raised an eyebrow. "Like what they did to me at the Conduit, to wish what happened out of me?"

His voice grew serious. "Yes. Everyone has wishes, most of which are basic mind or body wishes, like 'I wish I had a million dollars' or 'I wish I had a big juicy steak for dinner.' Yeah, it's fine to want those things in the moment, but those are wishes made from our bodies or minds, what we *think* we want."

Mace mumbled. "I could go for a blonde water nymph right now." Wells glowered at him, and he straightened up. "That's a body wish, I guess, huh?"

"Yes, Dumbass." He continued, keeping his hand on my knee, tracing circles with his thumb to the point it was distracting me. "The issue is the heart and soul wishes, the things we want that drive our inner desires." He glanced at me, telling me in a swift look exactly what he desired. It failed to scare me that time.

"When we wish for things on a deep level, they carry a tremendous amount of power for the djinn. Their power and their defense is to force us to make soul and heart wishes in their presence and when we do, they take the magic of those wishes for themselves and turn it back on us."

Each time the djinn had been near me, my magic waned because they were pulling my wishes from me. They didn't need to attack with force. They could slide the magic out through wishes. "Outlook not so good."

He nodded. "If a person faces a djinn and thinks about their soul or heart wishes, it could have disastrous consequences. Say a woman wished to save her dying son. Not just a heart wish, but a soul wish too, a deep desire that's more than fulfilling a physical want. The djinn could force that wish to the surface, even if she wasn't trying to think about it.

"Then they siphon the wish and convert it into magic and power. The woman's magic is drained, and the wish gets some bastardized fulfillment. Like, the son getting a miracle cure to save him, but the mother contracts a fatal disease."

Oh, my Mage. My heart thumped against my chest like a beating drum. He was telling his own story. This is why he hated and feared the djinn so much and why he was trying to prepare us for what could happen. I reached out and placed my hand over his, squeezing to offer what comfort I could. His lips closed into a thin line, suppressing the deep emotion he felt.

Ren rested his hand on Wells' shoulder. "We thought your mom just got sick. You never told us." He wasn't angry. His tone was more surprise than anything.

Wells shrugged. "I know. I'm sorry. I don't like to talk about it. It's too painful, knowing I was the reason."

"But you weren't." I whispered.

"It's always felt like I was." His eyes flared silver, then faded quickly.

"Dude," Mace said brightly. "None of us here in this circle had good mom experiences, but I'm pretty sure good mothers would trade their lives for their children. It's how they're wired. Yours was a good one."

Wells' voice was tight, but he smiled. "Yeah, she was."

We sat in silence for a few minutes, absorbing what Wells had said, and giving him a moment to harness what he could in his heart. I ached for him. And wished I could ease his pain, even just for a moment.

Gideon finally broke the silence. "It makes sense now. Spencer said when the djinn attacked all she did was wish for Dom to be released from Mateo's clutches. She said she couldn't stamp that thought from her head and grew weaker and weaker. Suddenly Dom was up and free and she was relieved she'd gotten what she wanted."

I cleared my throat because it had tightened up. "But?"

"But he's not the same as he was before Mateo injected him with djinn blood. Something with the mate bond isn't right. She didn't elaborate and I didn't think it was right to ask." He paused as the group grappled with the ramifications. "It seems like she got her wish, but not like she wanted it. He may never love her the same way again."

"Damn," I uttered. "It's like *Fantasy Island*." Ren shot me a look. "What? My Gram had cable."

"Not a fantasy I'd be interested in." Wells squeezed my leg. "You've all seen it; we can hold the djinn off with rods for a time, but our real defense is to keep our wishes from coming to the surface. The djinn will tug on them to get them out, but we need to shut that shit down as soon as we can. And make sure the whole pack knows to shift because thoughts are less complex in wolf form. It's the only hope we have for saving the pack when the djinn come for us."

I cleared my throat. "Um, I can't shift."

"You have to tunnel. Promise me, Terra. Tunnel away as soon as you see them. Try the Conduit, go past the barn, wherever you can find. Just get away." He pinned me down with the earnest flash of amethyst. It wasn't until I shook my head in agreement that his eyes returned to normal. "We have to be strong and prepare because it's coming."

He jumped up and held out his hand to help me. Which I took. Of course. "I sent a few emails to the Five on behalf of Mateo, trying to stall and keep them away. But as soon as they find out, Mateo's dead, they'll act. We have to keep this internal. No going for supplies or talking to anyone outside the pack."

Mace mimicked locking his mouth with a key, then tossing it over his shoulder.

Wells nodded. "Now, someone we know has a trial tomorrow and she needs to spend the day resting and preparing for that. Because I wish, well, I hope I don't have to kill her."

As if the djinn problem wasn't enough to unsettle me.

My heart ramped up. Wells had casually mentioned my impending death like he didn't believe it would actually happen and I hoped, no I wished, it were true. The fact of the matter was, I could've had less than twenty-four hours left in my life.

It was an overwhelming thought and I banished it to keep from freaking the freak out.

Good practice for avoiding wishes, right?

We all walked together to my cabin. It was natural to be with them now. The camp was starting to feel like home and making me nervous because a deep soul wish threatened to force its way to the surface. I tapped that sucker down. Far. Camp Boulderbrook was not my home.

Did pushing the wish out of my mind work?

Reply hazy. Try again later.

I trudged up the steps, eager to take a day off as Wells had said. I turned to say goodbye and found Wells all up in my business on top of the steps. He made zero effort to be quiet with his next words. "I'll make dinner for you tonight. In the meantime, you might want to start thinking about all the body wishes you can muster. And for the love of the Mage, don't change clothes."

Damn.

Shit.

Fuck.

I didn't know how to respond, so I closed the door and slid down the backside, releasing a wistful laugh mixed with a sigh. On the other side, he rapped on the door twice and chuckled.

32

I should've known the frenetic knock at the end of the day wasn't Wells. It was too timid. And not even useful because a man-sized Tristan barreled in without me bothering to answer. "You, Babycakes, have been summoned."

"To...?"

He surveyed me up and down. "First, a question: have you changed clothes since this morning?"

I'd removed the panties that Wells had blasted a fire hole in but kept everything else on as he requested. "Nope."

"Then if you'll be so kind as to accompany me to the alpha's treehouse." I was amazed that he'd sent Tristan to get me. Those two were getting tighter each day and it made me happy. "BTW, he refused my input on this meal of his, so it may be awful."

Nervous titters threatened to take over my entire body as we left my cabin. On one level, Wells had been *very* clear about what would happen when we were together next. As panty-melting—literally and figuratively—as it was, he'd also been adamant we shouldn't mix the business of our Perception magic contract with anything else. I had no idea if I was in for more scorching kisses or torturous training for my trial.

Which was one hundred percent the way he wanted it.

Halfway there, Tristan interrupted my thoughts. "So, the alpha thing gave Wells a blow job, huh?"

I screeched to a halt. "A what now?"

He shrugged and kept walking. "You know when someone has a significant change to their appearance, from looking ordinary to looking amazing? Though he was never ordinary."

"Glow up. You mean a *glow up*." Mage almighty. He knew what a blow job was. Of that, I was sure. "You're not wrong. He seems more *more* than he was. It's…"

We'd made it to Wells' treehouse cabin and we both froze in place as Wells descended the stairs, barefoot in black jeans and pale pink V-neck that had to have been two sizes too small. I'd berate him for it—the color and the fit, both— but when you know, you know. He damn well *knew*. Tristan gulped and licked his lips. "Um. I stand by my original statement. Blow job, it is."

Mm-hm. The word was right there on the tingling tip of my tongue.

Alphuckable.

The corner of his mouth kicked up, as his gaze roamed my body, approving of my clothes and making me squirm with heat. "I like that you take direction well."

My mouth went dry. I had no response. Tristan, on the other hand, did. He raised his hand like he was in school. "Oh oh oh, give me directions! I'll do anything you want."

The alpha growled and it went straight between my thighs. Damn. It was going to be a long night. He turned to Tristan. "What I want from you is privacy. Say in your cabin all night. Don't come out, capiche?"

Tristan cocked his head. "All alone? That'll be *hard*. If I give you this valued privacy, what do I get in return?"

"I never said you had to be alone. Just away from us." He Gesture Three'd, producing a reward for my crazy fae friend. Then, in a move I would never ever be able to forget as long as I live, Wells turned around and offered his ass to Tristan. All he said was, "Once."

The gleam in Tristan's eyes was manic. He reared back and slapped Wells' tight butt with a whack. Just once. He poofed and was gone.

I gulped. "Oh, my Mage."

Wells shrugged. "He'll relive that all night and won't even think about bothering us." He took my hand and tugged me behind the tree into the sitting garden. "We have a few minutes before the sauce is ready. I thought you'd enjoy sitting out here, gnomestyle."

He wasn't wrong. Even though I'd only been here once before, it was my favorite place in the whole camp. The love and the sense of home it gave me was reason enough. I tried to tamp down any other reason that may have been trying to niggle its way in too.

I sat on the bench, and he leaned against the tree. With the last remnants of sunlight dipping behind him through the hedges, he became a dark silhouette. The shape of him—defined, hard, masculine—it hurt on a physical level. Every part of me ached for him. But we couldn't allow whatever this was between us to screw up the contract. I didn't want to die, and I didn't want him to have to kill me. I needed to contain this fire threatening to consume all the oxygen around us. "You're different now that you're alpha."

He tilted his head. "Am I?"

Guh. I led myself right down this impossible road. Should've kept my trap shut. "You've been a cocky bastard from day one, but now you're more—aggressive isn't the right word—"

A predatory sneer spread across his full lips. "—forward?" Thank the

321

Mage he stayed close to the tree because I wanted him closer. But we couldn't. Shouldn't. I had to fight my urge to run over and jump him. "Is my forwardness a problem for you, Gnome?"

My reply is no.

"Maybe. You should try to tone it down some." He arched an eyebrow, knowing full well I was lying. I scrambled to explain. "Like you said before, we have a Binding magic contract, and we shouldn't do anything that might be…"

Mage, I was picking up his habit of trailing off.

"Physical?" He raised his hands. "You're right. And I *do* feel more powerful as far as the magic goes, but my feelings, desires, my wishes—" he paused because we both knew those were dangerous words in dangerous times. "—those have stayed the same. Besides, even though we shouldn't, doesn't mean we won't."

Heat blossomed all over my body. "It doesn't mean we will either."

"True. You know, emotions and sex are two different things. What remains to be seen is if we can separate them." Just the mention of the word set my hormones into overdrive. It was tempting to just let him follow through on it. Sex without emotion. That's how I rolled. Right?

Cannot predict now.

I ran my hand over my heart, clutching at it like I could squeeze the feelings out like a tube of toothpaste.

A wayward vine from the garden wound around his ankle, inching up his thigh. He looked down and grinned before he plucked it away, zeroing in on where his hand had laid over my heart earlier. "Do you still feel my magic inside you?"

A simple question, but the way he groaned the last two words made it far more complicated and I'll be damned if I didn't automatically feel the pull of his magic, of him, in that moment. "A little. It's mostly faded though." I wouldn't tell him how I laid in my bed praying to the Mage it wouldn't diminish all afternoon, then feeling weak and a little broken after it had. I didn't want to give him that much of me. I couldn't tell him how good his magic had made me feel. How complete and powerful.

"So, I should tap you off?" He raised one shoulder, feigning innocence, but there was nothing innocent about him, whatsoever. "If you wanted more magic, I mean."

Mage. Tap me off?

"I suppose. But I don't think now is a good time for that." A hundred different things it would be time for ran through my mind. Most of them involved us having no clothes on. Damn my lusty brain to Netheria. I had to stop doing that to myself.

He chuckled, angling himself so that a vine with purple pansies stretched across his stomach, wrapping around his waist. "You know, your magic gets away from you sometimes. Especially when you're turned on."

I took a second to consider that and I knew he was right. It's what happened when we'd played poker. And when we'd kissed on the boulder.

Now.

Another vine trailed down the tree, over his neck, down his immaculate chest and scraping over the zipper of his jeans. He arched back and let it happen, groaning like he liked it.

I clenched my fists and tried to tamp down the Earth magic coursing through me. I was losing control and it was veering all over him like the blush I was certain I had across my cheeks. Which he noticed. And smirked about. I cleared my throat. "I'm not turned on. Now, what were you saying about being alpha?"

Thank the Mage, he took the bait, dropping my horny vine issue as he removed the offending foliage from this fly and twisted it in his fingers, somehow making it more sensual. "The alpha magic doesn't override the Perception magic. I still feel that when I think about you, which is a whole fucking lot, in case you're wondering."

I swallowed. I did not need to know he thought of me when I wasn't standing in front of him. He leaned against the tree like it was grown for the sole purpose of cradling hot-guy ass. And he just kept on talking and twisting the stem of flowers in his long fingers. "Earlier I was thinking about how you look when you burst from the ground after you tunnel. Like a feral cat, savage and untamed. I'm just not sure, yet, if I want to tame you or let you run wild."

There was silent siren blasting in my head.

Danger, danger, danger.

I hurried to find something else to say. "The alpha magic? You were saying…"

He ignored me, his eyes lighting like an amethyst Christmas tree. "Sometimes I think about is the curve of your ass, and I wonder if your cheeks bloom that luscious pink color when you come."

Awooohga. Awooohga. Mage help me.

"Mostly I think about the look on your face when you think you're hiding your feelings. Because I have to break it to you, Gnome, you're not."

How long can a golem hold their breath? Let's find out, shall we?

He chuckled and it struck something deep in my nether-regions. "Did I go too alpha there? Oops."

He did not oops. No oops whatsoever. Not at all.

I had zero defense against his newfound allure, his bold advances, not when there were vines and flowers wrapping themselves in knots around us. He knew what he was doing to me and for the fucking life of the Mage, I wasn't mad about it. I loved his alpha forwardness, which was almost as much of a surprise to me as the fact I was a golem. I wanted him to keep talking to me like that. I longed for him to back his words with action.

He surveyed me with a heated look, then kicked off the tree, checking his watch, then Gesture Two'ing toward the stairs. "I'll behave. Now, let's eat before the sauce gets cold." I followed him, but cold was a million miles away from where I was.

33

Wells' cabin was like him: warm and masculine. Evening light streamed through the massive bank of windows facing the lake. It had two separate rooms off the hall which I assumed to be a bathroom and small bedroom.

The door was flanked with bookshelves, stacked with ancient books and beautiful painted landscapes of the grounds tucked inside. A moss green couch faced the window, unstructured and soft, like it would be the perfect place to curl up and nap. There was a neatly-made bed in the corner next to a small fireplace and kitchenette beside the door that led to the other rooms. I had the immediate urge to run and examine everything, but I stopped myself when the most delicious aroma hit me.

Wells Gesture Two'd me to the small built-for-two table in the kitchenette. He grabbed his rod to heat a pot of spaghetti to boiling with it and I laughed as he explained, "Perks of having Fire magic." Within minutes steam was clinging to the edges of his hair and I had to grip the table to keep from going over to brush my fingers through the damp locks.

He turned his back to stir the sauce and suddenly it was dinner and a show. His ass could star in its own production.

C-ASS-ablanca, starring Wells' firm and rounded butt cheeks.

Thank the Mage I didn't have a lot of time to think about that because he'd stepped behind me to pour sauce over the plate of pasta he'd set before me. I took a deep breath. "This smells—"

"Familiar?"

I cocked my head, questioning him, but he Gesture Two'd at the plate. I picked up my fork and dug in, not even worrying how unladylike it was. It smelled divine.

Tasted even better.

I couldn't believe it. I was certain my tastebuds were lying to me, but the flavor of the sauce sent me reeling back to my childhood. I groaned as I swallowed. "Well, well, Wells." I took another two bites just to be sure. "This is just like my Gram's. How?"

"You should be warned: it's a complete turn-on when you say my name like that." He took a bite, laying the suspense on thick until he wiped his mouth. He reached over to the counter and drew out a paper bag. "Where do you think I got the tomatoes? I couldn't believe they were still growing this time of year. Cool, by the way."

I had trouble processing what he was saying. He'd taken them from the garden in my own backyard. I found myself overjoyed and grateful. Again. I shrugged. "Perks of Earth magic."

He reached in the bag and pulled out what I assumed would be tomato evidence, but it wasn't. My breath hitched as he handed my journal over. "I hope you don't mind, but I copied the recipes because your Gram seemed to be a damn fine cook. Though, I can't imagine there'll be a vampire vertical sixty-nine scenario in my future, so I skimmed over those parts."

328

I snorted. Mage, I missed her.

"I can't believe you did this." He smiled and it was…too much. I jumped up, wrapped my arms around him and rested my head against his chest. His heart thrummed in my ear. "Thank you. Again." First, he brought me her cane, then her journal. His thoughtfulness was overwhelming, and I had no idea what to do with it in my mind.

His hands went around my waist and heat spiraled in my core as they trailed up my spine. When he tangled my hair in his fist, I stilled. A few weighted seconds passed before I forced myself to pull back. The look in his lavender eyes told me he didn't like it, but he didn't force the issue, which I appreciated. I just had to keep him at arm's length the rest of the night.

Don't count on it.

I picked up the fork, handed it to Wells and went back to my food. I didn't stop eating until the pasta had disappeared.

"Do you want dessert now?" A pregnant pause gathered momentum, enough that I knew it was purposeful. "Or later?"

What kind of dessert are you talking about?

"Later. I'm stuffed."

Dang. Why did everything I say sound dirty now?

He shot me a smirk that told me he'd caught it too, but quickly picked up the journal and Gesture Two'd me to the couch. He flopped into one corner, and I forced myself to sit in the middle. Away from him. Still, he slung his arm over the back of the couch, grazing my neck and sending shivers through me. "Read something for me."

I mean, he could've read the whole journal himself, but the fact he asked me warmed my heart and various other places on my body.

He was keen with interest as I flipped through the pages, trying to find something good. "Gargoyles walk around with semis all the time but can't stay hard unless they're on top."

A melodious laugh tumbled from his lips, deep and raspy. Sensual. "I wish I could've met her."

"She would've loved you. Though…"

"Mace would've been her favorite."

"For sure. I think they would've been soul mates." I turned the page. "Here we go: Shades can operate like Patrick Swayze and Whoopi Goldberg in Ghost—weird but satisfying." He smiled and I wanted, more than anything, to draw another one from him.

"I remember this one, right before she passed. It was in the middle of the night—I slept in a recliner in her room during those days—and she called out to me. When I jumped up to see what she needed, she grabbed my shirt and pulled me in. Her eyes were cloudy and wild, and I thought she was about to die right then, but she didn't. She said one sentence and then went right back to sleep."

He leaned over, twisting his fingers in my hair for a second, then letting it go. Thank Mage. "What did she say?"

"Always remember this, my jewel: Team Jacob."

He leaned back to laugh, and his shirt rode up, revealing his sculpted stomach and his low-fitting jeans. I slammed the journal shut. Suddenly reading about sexual positions and gratification seemed like a gigantic mistake.

"Of course, Team Jacob. Vampires suck."

These wolves and their Dad vampire jokes.

"Yes, I recall." I reached up and touched the place where the vampire had bitten my neck. It would heal, but the wound would stay fresh in my mind for a long time. As a reminder of what Mateo had done in his attempt to control magic.

Wells brushed my hand away, tracing his finger over the spot, electric warmth flooded my veins. I tried to focus on something other than what just the tip of his finger was doing to me but failed fantastically. "I'm sorry I didn't step in sooner with Mateo. I should've—"

"Forget him. It's over. Besides, I have more pressing things to be concerned about."

He drew back his hand, his voice was commanding in a way that I felt in my core. "Don't worry about the trials." He was so certain. So sure of what he was saying.

"Yeah, I don't know how I can help that. Are you itching to kill me or something?"

I meant it to diffuse the tension coiling inside me, the thick pull between us, but he didn't take it as such. He leaned in, curling his hand at the base of my neck. "I'm itching to do many things to you. None of them involve killing. Unless you count death by mind-blowing, spine-tingling, gasping-and-screaming-my-name orgasms. *That* would scratch my itch."

Cage the Mage.

I couldn't take it anymore. I was finding it hard to think or breathe or feel with him talking like that. "Stop. This isn't a joke."

His eyes flashed, bright and intense. "On what level do you think I'm joking?"

I sighed, frustration weaving through me. To be there with him like that, was a colossal mistake. I needed to get out, get my bearings, and focus on the job at hand. Yet, curiosity filled my mind, rooting me to the spot next to him. Inches away now. "How would you do it? If I screw up tomorrow and you find me unworthy. Would you shift and take me out like you did Mateo or kill me with your rod? Snap my neck with your bare hands? I want to know."

I didn't know where it came from. Possibly the part of me who was falling under his spell, the part who saw him as more than my judge. The part that feared as much for him as I did myself.

331

He grunted. "We're not discussing that."

"Yes, we are. I want to know what to expect. Tomorrow you could—"

He jumped up, grabbed my hand, and pulled me off the couch, effectively cutting off the rest of my sentence. "I can't answer that because I don't know. The magic is out of my control. What I can say with certainty, Gnome, is I have never—not once—considered you unworthy, so I'm not concerned with what will happen tomorrow or at the next trials."

The roaring silence in the room was palpable. We were both breathing heavily as he pulled me flush to his chest. My body and mind were turning loops in and over and around themselves. I wanted to believe him because I could see he believed it himself. But as he reminded me: he was not in control of the magic. No matter how bad we both wanted him to be.

He ran his hand through his hair, something he could control. "Do you think you could stop worrying about the trials until tomorrow?" In a way, he wanted to control me, to make me feel like I had nothing to worry over. Another gift he was giving to me, even if he didn't realize it. I wished more than anything I could accept it. I wasn't going to lie to him, though. I owed him that much. "I doubt it, but there's nothing you can do about that."

After a few more excruciating moments of intense scrutiny, he grinned. "That's where you're wrong, Gnome."

Without saying another word, he led me out the door and we walked silently, hand-in-hand, to the woods where we'd practiced our rods earlier. Where he'd given me his magic. "Close your eyes."

"Why?"

He Gesture Three'd. "Because there are things about me that I can't share now. I want to tell you. Just not tonight. You're my focus now." He paused. "Please."

The sincerity in his voice made me ache, so I did what he asked without further questions. And when he instructed me to open them again, we were surrounded by the ring of silver flames. They gave off the faintest light, feathering his features in shadows which made him look even more striking. He'd tell me about the flames one day. And maybe why he was so warm all the time. But I'd have to wait. I was weirdly okay with that. I was too mesmerized by what else he was doing.

He walked over to where two trees stood close together and placed a hand on both of them. The branches groaned and cracked as they bent, reaching out and twisting over each other until they joined together in front of him. "What are you making?" It certainly wasn't chair stumps like Ren had made earlier.

He wiggled his eyebrows. "You'll see."

More branches stretched from the trees, weaving themselves together and forming a net pattern as leaves suddenly sprouted along the surface of the net. In a matter of seconds, the entire thing was lined with soft leaves, creaking as it swayed gently.

Like a hammock.

Wells released the trees and prowled toward me. "It's probably not as nice as the one in your backyard, but maybe it'll do." It was a statement, but there was a clear question in his voice. He wanted me to like it.

And I did.

I'd gotten the hammock to help Gram stay close to nature, near the trees and garden. She'd nap there for hours and wake up more focused and refreshed. I always enjoyed laying on it too, my toes skimming the earth beneath it, recharging my magic.

That hammock had come to be a place of healing for us both. And while the one Wells had formed from tree branches wasn't made of the same material, I knew before I even put an inch of my body in it, I would feel the same in it. My voice was a whisper because of the lump in my throat. "How did you know?"

He tucked a lock of hair behind my ear. "I have a confession: when you petitioned the Conclave, Mateo sent me for recon first. We were supposed to take turns watching you, but after the first day, I insisted I be the only one to trail you."

"Why?"

"You had me under your spell before I even met you." I sucked in a breath, and he licked his lips like he was remembering the taste of me on them. "When you swung there in that hammock every night, you looked so peaceful. It made me crave you in a way I didn't understand then. I do now. Hop in."

He steadied me as I ungracefully lowered myself into the branch cocoon.

I shucked my shoes and dug my toes into the soil, pushing myself backward a touch and letting the nest swing. "It feels like I'm always thanking you for one thing or another. But, thanks. This won't make me forget the trials, but it's nice."

He frowned and moved behind the swing with his wolf speed. Before I could even catch my breath, he leaned down and whispered in my ear, his stubble rubbing against my cheek in the best way. "Don't thank me yet. I'm just getting started." He pressed his hands onto my shoulders and my entire body went rigid. "If you won't relax about the trials, I'll just force the tension out of you until the only thing on your mind is me and what I'm doing to you."

Blood of the Mage.

That sounded like simultaneously the best and the worst idea ever.

He worked his hands into my shoulders, and I went limp at the feel of it. His hands were incredible, and I didn't want to deny myself the feel of them. Of him. "You're putty in my hands, Gnome. Don't talk. Don't think. Don't try to define this thing between us because…"

For once, I knew what he wasn't saying at the end of his sentence: if

334

we thought too much about each other, we were in danger of turning body wishes into something else. Something the djinn could feed on.

I could do that. Maybe.

He leaned in, pressing himself against my back as he massaged my shoulders and neck. I bit my lip to keep from groaning as the defined ridge of his cock brushed against me. "Shut off. For now. Please."

It was the *please* that got me.

I nodded. I wanted nothing more than to let him do what he was doing. He may have had to kill me tomorrow, but tomorrow was hours away. Mage be damned with the consequences of the foolish decision I was about to make.

My eyes closed of their own volition, and I knew that moment, I was in.

Deep.

The more he worked my shoulder muscles, the more aware I became of his hands. He knew what he was doing, using just the right amount of pressure to make the first knot of pain turn to pleasure by the time he finished working it. I wasn't even aware that I'd made a sound until he commented on it with a low sexy growl right in my ear. "Was that a purr or a moan?"

Heat crept across my face, my embarrassment fleeting because he moved his hands, pressing his thumbs along the base of my neck, reaching in to touch my bare skin instead of the hoodie. I sucked in a breath at the electric spark that ran from my neck straight to my lady parts. I dug my fingers into the branches holding me up, just to grip something.

"That was a good gasp, right?" He followed up by working his hands into my hair at the top of my neck, so I couldn't even formulate an answer to his question. I nodded, whimpering. "Thought so."

Overconfident bastard.

But it was time for me to face it: the cockiness was well-earned.

He touched a sore spot and I winced. Understanding, he pressed harder, until parts of me started to go numb at the relief of it. He hummed into my ear, the deep baritone of his voice sending shivers through me. "Trigger point."

My wicked mind reacted to that. All I could think was that I wanted to pull *his* trigger.

I was letting it get out of hand, but I *so* did not care. It felt good. And not because of what was happening, but because of who was making it happen. A fleeting thought zinged through my brain.

Better not tell you now.

I shouldn't let him affect me like this.

Maybe I could forget about…whatever it was he wanted me to forget. I'd already forgotten.

He slid his hands down my neck, skimming my collarbone with a soft graze of his fingers as he released some of his magic. Heat flooded every vein in my body and my stomach tightened in the best way. When he dug his fingers deep into my hair, pressing a soft kiss where the vampire had bitten me, that was the moment it went from one thing to another.

If I were going to stop him, that was the moment.

In no way, did I stop him.

I was one hundred percent flames as he worked his way up my neck, planting breathy kisses and running his teeth along my neck, like he couldn't decide between kissing me and feasting on me. By the time he got to the most sensitive part right behind my ear, I was trembling with desire, a physical need manifesting inside me. I was struck with the urge to tell him to kiss me like that all over my body, but I kept from saying it, hoping he'd never know how deeply I wanted him.

He liked the way I trembled, grinning as he licked the top of my ear, his breath hot and ragged, telling me he was as turned on as I was. "Say the word if you want me to stop." He froze on the precipice, hands, lips, body, right where they were as he waited for my answer. Of all the things he did for me, to me, giving me a choice may have been the sexiest.

He'd told me not to think or define this, but my brain and heart were not very good listeners. Both of them were in overdrive and he was making me feel things. If I allowed myself one more second of hesitation, I might have told him to stop.

My future self would have to come back and bitch-slap my past self for the crappy decision.

My next thought threatened to flatten me under its weight, but I wouldn't let it.

No matter what would come from the trials, I was safe in Wells' hands. I trusted him. And I didn't want what was happening to end. I wanted to feel him. I wanted him to want me. To make me forget everything but him. I let the rush of feelings in, landsliding in my acceptance of them and hoping I didn't regret them later. "Don't stop."

He released a predatory growl that slid right inside my soul. "Thank the fucking Mage." With one hand still in my hair, he reached around with the other and unzipped the hoodie. Each individual tick of the zipper echoed, in slow delicious torture. "You look sexy in my jacket, but it's in my damn way."

He planted steamy kisses along my jaw, making his way back to my ear as he peeled me out of the hoodie, stopping for a brief moment to run his thumb over my birthmark. I hungered to turn around and kiss him, but the way he kissed everywhere but my mouth was scorching and so arousing. "When I saw you this morning…"

He left the rest of the sentence in the air because he got distracted placing his hands low on my stomach, sliding them up in a delicious leisurely pace that made me ache and crave what came next. He was the artist, and I was the clay as I arched my back just to get some relief from the anticipation of what he'd do next. He chuckled, low and deep. "So eager."

It is decidedly so.

I nodded because I couldn't speak and because he was right. I couldn't wait.

"In that case, allow me to help you with that problem.'"" He yanked my bralette zipper down with wolfish speed, exposing my breasts. He growled as he palmed me from behind, licking and dragging his canines along my neck. Mage help me, it was so fucking hot when he sounded feral. It made some kind of beast rise in me too.

He stepped over the hammock, pausing with one leg on each size. He peered down with an animal grin, biting his lip, before dropping to his knees in front of me. I had no warning. It was like the best kind of attack like he couldn't wait a millisecond longer. He took a nipple in his mouth, sucking until it pebbled under his hot tongue. I leaned back, giving him access as his tongue lid across to the other side flicking the other nipple and sending a torrent of gratification through me.

He pulled back and his ragged breaths were as heavy as mine. "Now I can't decide if I like your ass or your tits better." He moved one hand to my breast, massaging the fullness there, licking the other until I was moaning and panting underneath him. "I'll dream about those sounds you're making from now until the end of time."

I tried to speak, but it was difficult with my breaths coming so quickly. "Your. Fault."

He chuckled. "You're welcome."

I was probably in trouble.

Definitely.

I was feeling things. And not just in my body. He was Magedamned perfect and my utter need for him was debilitating. I shouldn't...

He short-circuited my thoughts when he suddenly lunged forward, cupping my face and lowering his mouth to mine. His tongue darted

338

inside, and I grabbed his neck, holding him in place as our mouths moved together. It felt like we were devouring each other, and our need amplified as we both groaned into the searing hot kiss.

I wished it would never end. The world could crumble around us, magic could fade out of existence, and we would be perfectly fine as long as we stayed glued together, searching tongues and roaming hands and deep, all-consuming fire scorching between us.

I gasped when he trailed the tips of his fingers inside the waistband of my pants, stopping when he realized that was all I had on. "Naughty girl. I expected to find those pink polka dot panties just to spite me."

"You burned a hole in them this morning, but I can run and put some others on, if you like." I teased.

"Fuck no." His eyes were glued on me as his hand dipped inside my pants, raking his way slowly, finally brushing against my center. The touch wasn't much, but enough to make me see stars and thank the Mage I chose to forego the underwear.

I arched into his fingers as he stroked me, gently pressing on the sensitive clit, while he dove forward and claimed my mouth again. It was too much, but it wasn't enough. I lifted my hips, rising to meet his blazing touch as I panted his name against his lips "Mage, Wells. I don't know if I can take this."

"Trust me, you can." He pressed harder, making tight circles over my clit. I was starting to quake, but I didn't want to let go. I didn't want it to end.

It was magic. Where I least expected it.

From him.

I don't even know what kind of sound I made next. I couldn't contain it because he had one hand on my breast and the other rubbing just the right spot between my legs. Whatever it was, he liked it. A lot. "Fuck, Terra. What do I have to do to make that sound come from your fucking delicious lips again?"

I didn't know, but that didn't mean I didn't want him to try. "I'm sure you'll think of something."

"Challenge accepted."

I kind of set myself up for that one.

Oh well.

He thrust a finger inside me to meet the challenge, biting on my lower lip at the same time. I cried out as pleasure rolled through me, gripping his shoulders as he pumped until I was a writhing, moaning, aching pile of nerve-endings and hunger. He purred as he thrust his finger deeper into my heated pussy. "You like this, don't you?"

"Without a doubt." I was caught in a web of pleasure and emotion, my legs, inside me, my breasts, my neck—I couldn't even process where his hands, his tongue were. I was riding on a wave of bliss like I never had before.

I lifted my hips, and he pressed a second finger inside me. He pumped faster, spreading his fingers wide as he drew them all the way out. He knew I was on the edge because the sneaky bastard circled his thumb on my clit until I nearly blacked out from pleasure. He leaned back on his heels, his eyes flashing bright. "That's it. Let go for me. I *need* to watch you come."

Utterly destroyed at his words, I gripped his shoulders as I shattered into so many pieces I didn't know if I'd ever find them all again.

But he didn't relent, not until he squeezed every bit of ecstasy out of me that he could. His hard-on pressed against my waist as he leaned in, searing me with a rough kiss, his mouth ravenous and hot, his desire laced in his moan.

He finally pulled away, pinning me to the spot with fuchsia gaze that read like he was as satisfied as I was. Then he removed his fingers from inside me achingly slow, licking them, one by one. I panted, fresh tightness coiling in my stomach already. When he finished, he chuckled darkly, and it turned into a growl of pleasure. "I fucking knew you'd taste good."

Magedamn.

Hottest thing I'd ever seen.

I collapsed against the makeshift hammock, no longer tense. And no longer caring about how dumb I was to let him touch me or how tomorrow would end. What came next, I had no idea. And I didn't care that I had no idea.

Damn him. It worked.

He ran his finger over the swell of my breast as he rezipped the hoodie, frowning when I was completely covered. "Scoot over."

I moved to accommodate him. He fell into the hammock, pressing me against his side and placing a short kiss on my forehead. The hard ridge in his jeans did not go unnoticed. I couldn't wait to get my hands on him. I reached out, but he caught my wrist before I made contact with his cock, grazing his thumb over my birthmark. "This was about you, not me."

"But—"

"Trust me, there'll be another time for me. Especially now that I have the taste of you on my tongue, scent of you in my lungs and the sound of you coming in my memory." He wrapped his arms around me, and my hands landed on his muscular chest. Confidence oozed from his very being. "That worked," he declared.

I spread my fingers, brushing against his hardened pecs and peeked up through my lashes, "Eh."

His eyes glowed and his deep sensual laugh had me quivering. "Whatever you have to tell yourself, Gnome. You can't hide the truth from me. Now I know just which dirty little buttons to push now, and I intend to push them all. In fact, I have a whole list of places in this camp where I'm going to make you come." He counted off on his fingers. "The bridge, the picnic table under the pavilion, your bathtub, my shower, the stables, under my treehouse, the desk in my new office…"

I was about to ask him to get on with his plans, but a small rock sailed over the silver fire that surrounded us, landing at our feet. A few seconds later another came. Then a third. We both sat upright. Someone was out there trying to get our attention and with the sound barrier, we couldn't hear them. Thank the Mage, they hadn't heard me moaning.

Wells leapt up from the hammock—leaving me swinging—snarling as he prowled through the ring of fire, and it dissipated. "Mage help whomever is out there if this interruption isn't life or death."

Out of the dark, Ren stepped up to him, chest-to-chest. "I wouldn't be here if it wasn't important. I'm not that Magedamned stupid." He shot me a raised eyebrow before he turned back to Wells with a worried look. "It's Dominic. Arlo thinks he's rejecting the djinn blood." My heart seized and all I could do was think of Spencer. She must have been worried sick.

Wells nodded. "I'll be right there."

Ren hurried away with wolf speed as Wells turned back to face me. I jumped off the hammock and the trees shrunk back into place and creating a little well of sadness in me. I ran my hand over Wells' stubbled jaw, hoping to ease some of the tension that had set in with Ren's news. "Is there anything I can do to help?"

He took my hand and placed a warm kiss in my palm. No one had ever kissed me there and until that moment, I never realized something so innocent could feel so important. I let it settle into my skin.

"Not with Dominic, but you could do something for me." I was ready willing and able to do whatever I could for him. He'd done so much for me already. "Stay in my cabin tonight."

I opened my mouth, whether it was to protest or question his motives, I will never know. "You have a big day tomorrow and my bed's more comfortable. Besides, Tristan will hound you all night if you go back to yours."

He wasn't wrong about that. I had a sneaking feeling Tristan would be able to detect what Wells and I had done, and he'd want graphic details I wasn't willing to share. He continued his plea, "I'll be gone awhile, so there's no danger of us getting into a repeat performance, if you're worried you couldn't handle any more tonight." I tried to school my face so the disappointment wouldn't show. I must have failed. "Mm-hm. But you should know, next time I'm not going to be content with just a hand in your pants."

Neither am I.

"Thanks for the warning. Wait. How am I supposed to sleep *now*?"

"Not my problem, Gnome" He winked and was sped toward medical before I could formulate any response.

I went to Wells' cabin like he'd asked, lingering in the door in a moment of indecisiveness that quickly passed, before I crossed the threshold. Something had definitely changed and as much as I wanted that to be no big deal, I knew deep down that it was. I wasn't going to define it. He didn't want that either, but it felt like something between us was growing and taking shape right under my nose and against my will.

Shaking it off, I may way to the kitchen, opening cabinets to search for the dessert he'd promised me. I had to laugh when I found at least five different varieties of Oreos inside. Figuring he'd put a little more effort into it, I swung open the fridge and found a tray of chilled ball-shaped cookies drizzled in white chocolate. They looked like perfect little round bon-bons, and I moaned when I bit into one, relishing in the cool chocolatey goodness until a sizzling bite of spice hit the back of my throat. Spicy Oreo balls?

Well, well Wells. You are *a good cook.*

I popped a few more off the tray and enjoyed them as I spent a few minutes checking out the painted pictures—all signed by Thea Payne, which had to be Wells' mom. Checking his bookshelves I discovered he liked historical information and magic. Some of the texts looked so ancient, I didn't dare to touch them, let alone open them.

Finally, the day started to catch up with me and my bones craved sleep. I padded into the bedroom and flicked on the light. The bed was full-sized, and the duvet was covered in pink and purple flowers. It definitely didn't feel very Wells.

I scanned the framed photo of a pretty woman with long dark hair and man who bore a striking resemblance to Wells. A small toddler was holding their hands and looking up at his mom with bright eyes.

This was his Mom's room. And it hadn't changed since she died. My heart squeezed. I'd left Gram's room like that too. Pain washed through me, but this time it wasn't my own.

I turned off the light and back out into the great room where the other bed was. There were more than a few moments of hesitation, but when I allowed myself to pull back the covers and sink into the welcoming gray sheets on this bed. It was comfortable, like he'd said, and it smelled like him: fire, heat, deep sandalwood musk. I fluffed the pillows just right and pulled my journal into my lap, thumbing through the pages. One of the last entries I wrote made me smile and tear up at the same time.

You, my Jewel, will open many doors and shine brighter than the sun. Your life will be filled with more treasures than you can imagine if you remember who you are.

I wiped away the tears from my face.

I'm more than I am and less than I should be.

My heart swelled. Her love for me shone through her insanity and even though she was gone, her presence was with me. I closed my journal and tucked it in my arms as I settled in. Thinking about her instead of the other things on my mind helped me to drift off in hazy sleep.

B right rays of sunshine glistened through the large windows, dragging me from my deep sleep. I rolled over on my side, burrowing back in the sheets, inhaling the deep scent of man and wolf.

I bolted upright.

I was in Wells' bed.

And I needed to prep for my Heart trial.

After I got in a good stretch, I was surprised to find Wells sleeping on the couch, ancient book in his hands and peaceful slumber on his face. He was shirtless and a blanket was draped over his lower half, allowing me to get an unfettered view of his sculpted abs and the sexy indentions of his hips.

I couldn't stop myself, I tiptoed to where he was sleeping, mesmerized by the way his chest moved as he breathed. I reached down and gently touched the part of his hair that had fallen over his eyes. Realizing the very small action was about to take me down a road I didn't need to travel,

I started to back away.

He reached out and grabbed my knee, locking me in place, though his eyes were still closed. "Morning."

Dang. Even his sleepy morning voice was sexy.

"Good morning." When he released my leg and sat up, I took the opportunity to back away and sit back on the bed and prayed to the Mage he would stay on the couch.

And put on a shirt.

Or remove the blanket.

My brain and body were warring even before I'd had coffee.

"Is Dominic okay?"

"It was touch and go for a while, but he made it through the night." He ran his hands through his hair and bed head never looked so good. "I hate what Mateo did to him, but I'll be damned if we might be able to use it."

"What do you mean?"

As he stood and stretched, the blanket fell away. I had to hold my breath because I was afraid he'd be naked under there and it was too damned early for resisting that temptation. He was wearing gray sweats, thank Mage. "The fusion is different for each species and what Arlo assumed was a rejection of the blood turned out to be Dom synthesizing it and incorporating it into his system. He said he had vivid dreams while he was in and out of consciousness. Arlo thinks it may have been the djinn blood trying to communicate with the hive mind."

"So, Dominic might know what the djinn are thinking?"

"I don't know if it'll be that specific, but maybe." No wonder Wells looked less tense than when he'd left the night before. It seemed like we may have a defense against the djinn.

He brushed his hands along my back as he walked over to the kitchen, retrieving the bag he'd pulled my journal from. I was starting to enjoy the feel of his hands on me. Way too much. "I have something else for you."

"Haven't you done enough? You brought me Gram's cane and journal. You cooked me a fabulously sweet and delicious meal. And you…"

He cocked an eyebrow as he finished for me. "Made you come so hard you almost passed out? Yes. I did. Come here." He Gesture Two'd me to the kitchen table, which had been cleaned. I guess he'd cleared everything away when I slept. I'd been out cold.

Relaxation will do that to you.

"I didn't almost pass out."

"Beg to differ."

I was shocked when he pulled out one of the kitchen towels from my house. He smirked as he unrolled it, revealing a diamond-encrusted choker, a massive emerald ring, ruby drop earrings, a gold necklace with ginormous sapphire pendant, and a rope-like bracelet covered in differing sizes of purple jewels. "What are these?"

"The better question is: where did I find them?" His grin flashed about a million watts as I nodded. "After I picked the tomatoes from your garden, I took a seat on the hammock. Something glinting in the sunlight high in the tree caught my eye. I thought it was a bird, but when it didn't fly away, I climbed the tree to investigate."

I laughed. "I didn't know werewolves climbed trees."

"I live in a treehouse."

"Fair point."

"Anyway, I climbed up there and found all these jewels inside a plastic reusable storage container, along with this." He pulled out a piece of folded paper and handed it to me. Tears sprang to my eyes as I recognized Gram's shaky handwriting.

I kept these jewels for a dear friend, but she passed on to Netheria. Give them to whomever you deem worthy, but they're not yours to keep. Understand me. You cannot hold them, yourself. You must give them away. I'm certain you'll place them in the right hands. I love you, my jewel. Gram

Something about the purple beaded bracelet drew my attention, so I picked it up and placed it over my wrist and it seemed to come to life, humming and warming me in the strangest way. Wells grabbed my hand, twisting it so the light hit the stones. "It suits you. And I know you like purple."

Confused, I looked up at him and his eyes flared. Oh yeah. They were purple. "Why do your eyes do that? Does it have anything to do with the silver fire?"

"Yes. And I've already promised to share everything with you. Soon."

I wanted to drag it out of him, but I was preoccupied with the jewels I'd searched so long for and never found. "I *do* like purple."

I took the bracelet off and placed it on the rest of the jewels. Wells looked confused. "I know I'm not just a gnome anymore, but Gram was clear in her message for a reason. We're meant to guard property, not keep it ourselves. If I treated these jewels as mine, bad things would happen. Gnome magic is very specific about that. Like I said when I beat your ass that night at poker, it's why I can't keep her house or have any kind of savings account. Why I want in the Conclave so much."

"First, I let you win. Second, maybe the gnome magic won't work the way it does for others since you're a golem."

"That's not been my experience. I just know I can't keep these or any money I may make from selling them. Besides, Gram asked me to give them away."

He Gesture Three'd, long and hard. On a whim, I grabbed his hand away and placed mine over his stubble instead. He smiled and kissed my palm. That was quickly becoming my favorite place for him to kiss me.

So far.

He smiled. "Here's how I see it: I found these jewels. Since we have no way to trace any potential next of kin to give them to, I declare, by the law of finders-keepers, they're mine."

I laughed. "I don't think that's an actual law."

"Shh." He wrapped the purple bracelet around my wrist and fastened it. "These jewels are valuable and dear to me. I'd like you to keep my pretty purple bracelet safe please, Gnome."

Mage, I *was* in trouble. Deep, deep trouble.

It is certain.

Things were simpler when he was rude, overbearing, and distant.

I twisted my wrist, spreading flashes of purple light as the huge stone glinted in the sunshine that streamed through the windows. The small beads that circled the rest of the bracelet were dull in comparison. I ran a fingernail across one and small purple particles fell over the table. "I think the small beads are made of clay. Like me."

He huffed, irritated I was comparing myself to a lump of clay. "The big one's an amethyst. My birthstone." He ran his fingers over the beads, then along the sensitive part of my wrist, bringing shivers in their wake "I like how it's two things in one: earthy and exquisite at the same time." His eyes flashed as bright as the amethyst on my wrist. "Like you."

He pushed out of his seat and stalked over the hall, raising his hands to the top of the door frame and occupying the entire space there, his arm muscles flexing. I had to clench my thighs together to tamp down the desire. Mage, that was smexy. "What I don't get is how you didn't see the jewels after the leaves had fallen in the Fall. Did you keep it in full bloom like the tomatoes?"

"Always. She chose the perfect hiding place. Wish she'd clued me in before she passed though. It might not be here if I'd been able to work around the magic."

"In that case, I'm glad she didn't tell you. I wouldn't have met you otherwise." I swallowed down the lump his words had created in my throat. He lowered his arms in order for him to Gesture One. "Now, I need to get ready for your Heart trial. Shower's big enough for two."

Signs point to yes.

"I'm about to tunnel in dirt. I'll clean up after."

He pinned me with a predatory look. "I'm sure I'll need another one later too."

"I'm sure you need to clean your dirty mind."

"No, I don't think you want that at all." *Busted.* "I'll see you in an hour."

I headed straight for the door because I knew once I heard the water running, I would find it very hard to leave.

35

I changed into my black leggings and tank. I didn't need the vivid blue bralette reminder of my night of questionable decisions distracting me from the job at hand.

Everything looked different in the bright light of day.

Did I regret it? *My reply is no.*

Did I want it to happen again? Hells yes, but it couldn't unless I passed the trials. Last night had worked to distract me for a while, but it was temporary. What happened next between Wells and I was secondary to what I was about to face with this trial.

I gingerly pulled the mirror from my duffle bag and when I held it up, Wells' pretty purple eyes were staring back at me. So much had changed since we'd bound ourselves together that day. I'd pegged him for a cold-hearted beast who had no problems with murdering me in cold blood, but I was wrong about that. Sure, he was a beast at times, but he cared deeply and had done so much for me. I knew with every inch of my being that he didn't want to kill me any more than I wanted to be killed.

I was different too. Wells, the wolves, Tristan even—they'd changed me, and I liked the person I was becoming. I wanted, more than ever, to pass this trial and the others that would follow. I had so much more to lose now than just my life. I never thought I'd find anyone to care for her after Gram died. She would've been proud of me for attempting this crazy trial. And would've loved my wolves.

I tugged at my vial of earth, and I warmed as I felt her presence there with me. The purple bracelet she'd left in the tree, glimmering in the early morning sunlight.

I felt grounded. I _was_ grounded. And for the first time, I felt the earth guiding me forward. To my Heart trial and beyond.

Pounding on my door made me jump. I opened it and Ren handed me not one, but two apple Danish pastries. I side-eyed him. "Figured you might need two in order to replace some calories after last night."

Heat spread across my cheeks. "I don't. I mean, we didn't…"

He laughed. "Look. Mace is one of my best friends, so I stopped judging people over their sex life a long time ago. Besides, whatever you two did last night was good for my alpha—my friend—and you look like the fucking cat who ate the canary right now, so I'm cool with whatever happened."

Okay then. I was cool with it too. I think. I really needed to focus on anything other than the way his fingers felt when he—

No, Terra. Don't be distracted on the most important day of your life.

My focus renewed, I enjoyed both of my flaky treats on the way to the field. When we arrived, there were a lot of people hovering in anticipation of my trial. All the Betas, Tristan in big-boy form, Arlo, Kelsey, and Spencer who gripped Dominic's hand like she feared he would run away.

Gideon and Tristan approached me, each kissing a cheek. "You've got this in the butt, Babycakes."

My eyes widened and Gideon groaned. "In the _bag_, Tristan. Not the butt. Mage."

I couldn't help but laugh as I started to bounce on my toes in anticipation. Across the field where the finish flag was, Mace bounced on his toes in the same way. Then he switched into a grinding dance and his hand shot up. A warm blast of air whipped through my hair. I felt strangely supported by it.

Ren laid a hand on my shoulder and squeezed. "We can do this."

The fact he'd said *we* and not *you* made me tear up. I wasn't alone. I hadn't been since I arrived at Camp Boulderbook. A bloom of grateful warmth spread across my chest. I could think of one word to describe that moment, with those people surrounding me, it was *pack*.

Wells came strutting toward the field dressed in the green Henley he'd worn the first day I met him. It continued to be the hottest thing I'd ever seen. I couldn't help but stare. He was sex on wheels.

Do not drool over your potential murderer in front of all these people.

Wells pulled his phone out of his pocket, pressing the clock function. "Let's do this."

I froze like a deer. I wasn't ready. I may never be ready. "No pomp and circumstance then? Just, go right now."

He raised an eyebrow as his eyes raked down my body. "The quicker we get this over with, the quicker you and I can…"

My heart began hammering in my chest and I decided I could use the end of that hanging sentence to add fuel to my fire, so to speak. "Okay." It was all I could make my mouth say.

Sensing he was hitting the exact right nerve, he leaned in, his breath tickling my ear. "Tell you what: take this trial down and I'll make you think last night was chaste."

Holy Mage, father of all magic.

My mind blanked for a split second before very naughty thought I'd ever had came racing in at once. I looked up. He was dead serious.

He smirked, then Gesture Two'd Ren and I to the patch of dirt where we would start. Ren removed his shirt and stood beside me, his tattoos glistening in the sun. Wells and the rest of the group began walking to the orange flag finish line.

I pulled my hair up and then started fidgeting with my vial of Earth. If ever I needed a little grounding, it was that moment. Wells gave me precious little time to think as he raised his hand and shouted across the field. "When I drop my hand, you have one minute to get both of you here, Gnome." Pricks of nervous energy crawled over my skin. Just when I thought my body was going to explode from apprehension, he dropped his hand.

I sailed into the ground, summoning my Earth magic and forcing the soil to move at my will. I'd learned a lot from the torturous practice digs and I knew, without a doubt, I was going in the direction of the target. Ren was close behind, his Earth magic shoving me forward. We made a good pace, so my body started to relax. It advanced us even more.

I was feeling good, but about halfway through the run, my knuckles cracked, and pain rocketed through my hands. I was stunned and certain I'd broken at least one bone in each hand if not more.

Reply hazy. Try again.

A rock was blocking our path.

No, not a rock, a boulder.

I looked back to see what Ren was doing, but it was so dark I couldn't make him out, even with my night vision. He urged me forward, blasting dirt around us, trying to help me, but no matter what, we were not getting through the boulder.

Ignoring the throbbing pain, I reached out, searching for the edges so we could go around. I ended up veering way off course, so I knew a real boulder hadn't been plunked in the middle of our path. It was a magic barrier of some kind. I went twice as far as I'd already dug trying to get us around it, but there was no getting around it. I pushed against the barrier, and it didn't budge.

My pulse raced. Something wasn't right.

My breathing became choppy and real sheer panic consumed me, squeezing my heart until all I could hear was its thundering beat. I was going to die because I couldn't pass the first trial. Magic was going to force Wells to kill me.

I tried to choke down a sob, but I couldn't. Tears streamed down my face, mingling with the dirt that was already there. My knuckles were pounding, and I was close to passing out from fear, frustration, anger, pain.

I couldn't let this thing beat me.

I steadied myself by wrapping a hand around my vial and as I did, my fingers grazed the amethyst stones circling my wrist. The ripple of a pulse shot through the stones under my touch and a surge of magic shot threw me.

What the Mage was happening?

I jerked my hand up and a flash of purple light blasted from it, tingling and warming my fingers. I reached up and found the magic barrier was gone. Obliterated. I'd somehow blasted it out of my way with a jeweled bracelet Gram had hung in a tree.

I didn't have time to stop and wonder about what had happened. I'd lost precious time, so I grabbed Ren's arm and pulled him with strength I didn't possess. We pushed forward as fast as I could go, much faster than we had been as I used my newfound purple bracelet magic to blast through the earth like it was air.

I broke through the ground, startling Tristan who jumped back with a stunned look on his face. Ren climbed out of the ground behind me, and we collapsed together in a heap, panting and sweating.

A dark shadow passed over us and I looked up to find Wells standing over us blocking the sun, with a smug expression on his face. He turned his phone so I could see it.

One point three seconds left.

"We did it?"

Ren reached over and patted the top of my head. "*You* did it."

I jumped up, wobbling and weak. Wells caught my elbow before I fell over. "How? That had to have been more than a minute."

Tristan stuck his pinkie finger up toward me, a move that I'm certain was meant to be a thumbs-up. "No, Babycakes. It was fifty-nine seconds. I was counting in my head."

Wells circled his thumb in the sensitive spot at the crease of my elbow, bringing me out of my shock and into a different direction. Still, I scowled at him. "Why didn't you tell me there would be a barrier?"

"What do you mean?"

"The barrier I took out with my magic…?" I didn't know what had happened under there and the more I questioned it, the less confident I was in remembering. It was like it was disappearing as the words formed in my mouth. I gestured at the crowd of people looking at me. "You saw it Ren, right? It was like purple lightning shooting from my hands?"

What a ridiculous statement. I wasn't in the middle of a superhero movie, for Mage's sake. Mace was probably about to call me Storm or something.

Ren shrugged. "I couldn't see anything but your ass down there." Wells snarled. "Relax, man. I was behind her. What else was I supposed to look at?"

The group glanced at each other like I was going crazy. Maybe I was. Finally, Arlo stepped in. "We couldn't see anything under the ground, but if you say there was a barrier, then perhaps the Perception magic created an obstacle for you to overcome?" He paused, stating the obvious. "You overcame it."

356

But how?

"Damn right, she did." My fingers were throbbing in sheer agony. Barrier or rock or whatever. My hands had hit something and I'd broken them. Wells noticed. "Arlo, I can't look at her hands like this. Go fix her, please."

I started to follow Arlo to the Infirmary, but Wells held me in place. "I knew you'd do it. Congratulations, Gnome." He pressed a kiss on my temple and handed me over to Arlo. "You're going to love the victory celebration I have planned for us."

After a whispered confab with Tristan, Arlo examined my hands, declaring three fractured bones and a bunch of bruising. "We can fix that up in a jiffy."

I slid the bracelet off my wrist and set it on the table, anxious for the healing to begin. My hands were on fire. Before I could ask how long a jiffy was, Tristan ran in with his hand over a beaker containing a soft orange cloud. Arlo took it from him and blew the cloud in my face. I went straight out. When I woke, I flexed my hands and found them back to normal. No pain whatsoever. "Whatever that orange stuff is, I'd like to order a crate of it, please."

Arlo laughed. "We're fortunate. I'd used fae haze many times, but none of the fae at the camp knew how to make it. If it weren't for Tristan, you'd be in some pain now. He's very gifted for a fairy on this side." I looked around, intending to thank my BFF, but he wasn't there. Arlo explained, "All I'm allowed to say is that he's on a secret mission."

I knew better than to try and guess what he was up to. I just prayed to the Mage it wasn't another Wellsbrator. I swung my legs over the table and Arlo wrapped the purple bracelet over my wrist. "Wells told me about the origin of this bauble and while you were recovering, I studied it, if you're interested."

The bracelet seemed to click in place, like it was a part of my arm. While it seemed felt like it was supposed to be there, I was crazy unsure about it. Arlo lifted my arm and twisted it in the light, nodding like he'd proved some hypothesis. "What did you find?"

He tugged at the bracelet and we both gasped when we realized it wasn't coming off. I didn't really want to take it off anyway. "The small stones are made of the same thing as your vial of earth, as you—Aetherian clay. But the large stone contains something entirely different: think of it as a non-sentient life force, a spark of magic embedded within the stone."

Reply hazy. Try again.

"See here." He twisted my arm and I squinted at the bracelet. As I focused in, a tiny spark of light flashed inside it. Much like the lightning that had obliterated the barrier in my Heart trial. "I put the bracelet on myself, for testing purposes, and it didn't respond to me. It seems bonded to you. I can't say if that's due to your grandmother's influence or your golem nature."

I swallowed. The news was difficult to take. His words were light but the weight of them was crushing my soul. "What are you saying?"

"I believe this bracelet was meant to be yours and now that you have it, you may just possibly be the most powerful creature this side of Aetheria."

"How? Why? What does that even mean for me?" I was having a little freak out moment, but I felt it was earned.

Arlo placed a hand on my shoulder. "No one at Boulderbook would be a threat to you, but as magic dwindles in this realm, there are those who would seek to obtain what you have. Like the djinn. Many others too. Food for thought."

Food for throwing up was more like it. I didn't want to have a bigger target on my back. It was bad enough the djinn knew what I was. I jumped off the table and did a few laps around the room, trying to absorb the information as Arlo's phone buzzed. He glanced at it and a fierce blush broke out on his face. "Oh dear."

Dread made my stomach sink. "What?"

"It seems the alpha needs you for a very specific reason." He handed me his phone and as soon as I read the text, I knew why he'd chosen to hand it over and not to read aloud.

Are Terra's fingers functional yet because I need to feel them wrapped around my cock ASAP.

I glanced at Arlo, my blush matching his. Another text appeared and I held my breath as I read it.

Never mind about her fingers. Just make sure she's not in pain and send her to my cabin. Her mouth worked fine earlier. That's all I really need. Well, that and her pussy.

My brain stopped working and my mouth dried. The alpha aggressiveness was definitely one of my favorite things about him, but this was a whole new level. I'd never in my life been pursued so hard.

Hard.

Bad word choice? Nah. Exact right word choice.

A third text.

You should send her now because if you don't, I'm going to come take her right there on the medical bed in front of you, elf. Capiche?

Cage the Mage. I handed his phone back. "I'm just going to go now."

He smirked and shot a quick text back to Wells. I didn't even stop to read it. I shot out of the Infirmary like I was a cannonball and ran all the way to Wells' cabin and taking the stairs two at a time.

Not that I was in a hurry to see him.

Okay, I was.

I needed to get used to the idea of not pushing him away. These feelings were new to me. I'd never allowed myself to feel this before. It was scary and I was riding high on passing the first trial. I had another month to go before the stress of another one overtook me. I couldn't help but think of the lengthy list Wells had given me about all the places in Boulderbrook he wanted to...

I stepped inside and found him lounging on the couch in his gray sweats and nothing else, looking every bit the predator he was. He glanced at his watch and smirked. "That was fast. You must've been in a hurry to see me."

Busted.

I should've wanted to smack that smirk right off his face, but he wasn't wrong. A deep heat traveled all over my body when his eyes flared magenta. "Before we...heads up: Mace and Tristan have planned a big celebration for passing your trial—heart balloons, Tristan making a heart-shaped cake, and a huge batch of froth—but I told them you were mine for the next several hours and I would rip anyone apart who dares to interrupt us."

It was sweet for Tristan and Mace to do that, and I fully intended to appreciate the gesture later. But there was something more pressing to deal with first. I shot over and pushed Wells back against the couch, placing my legs on either side to straddle him. "You thought sexting Arlo was a good way to get me here?"

He shrugged. "You can't hide from me, Gnome. I could see on your face that you like dirty talk. And your phone was in your cabin, so I used Arlo's. He was fine with it." He showed me Arlo's reply and I blushed in response.

She's coming. Or, she will be soon, I assume.

He shrugged. "I needed you here. Now." The word came out as a growl as he grabbed my ass, pulling me close enough to feel the hard length of him between my legs. I ground against him, unable to keep the pleasure bubbling inside me from my throat, as he devoured me with his gaze, his hands sliding up and down my thighs. "I'm done fucking around. I don't give a shit about the Perception contract or my role as your judge. You're going to conquer the other trials like you did the first. And until we have to deal with the Soul trial, I'm going to possess you in every way I can imagine, Gnome. Is that okay with you?"

He nuzzled against my neck, then raked his tongue over my throat, along my jaw, tasting my skin before he pressed a kiss on the side of my mouth, giving me a chance to answer him. Chills erupted along my spine. "Yes."

"Good answer." He grasped my neck, kissing me like he was doing just that—owning me with abandon and fearlessness, like it was inevitable, and he was lost to it. Our mouths moved together, and we seized what we'd both denied for so long.

When we broke apart, I was throbbing with need. Though, it wasn't just physical desire. Yes, I wanted him, ached to do all sorts of things to and with his body, but it was more than that. My heart, my mind, and soul were crying out for this man too.

And I wasn't afraid.

The moment I realized it, I felt a complete fullness like I never had before.

I glanced down and spied the hard line of his cock as it swelled against his sweatpants. I bit my lip and he chuckled. "See something you want?"

"Without a doubt."

"Then take it, Gnome. It's yours."

I needed no other encouragement. I brushed my hand over his sweats, tracing his thickness as he tilted his hips to meet my touch. The groan he delivered sent tingles all over my body. I wanted to coax even more from him.

It was a thrill to have a beast like him under my fingertips but stroking the fabric of his sweats wasn't enough for me and he knew it. He pulled at his drawstring, and I dipped my hand inside his sweats, wrapping my hand around his big cock. When I stroked his smooth, warm flesh, he purred. "Do you feel how hard I am for you?"

"Yes."

His eyes flashed deep plum as he ground against my hand, panting as I pumped his shaft. "This feels so fucking good, but I'm going to need a little more, Gnome."

You may rely on it.

I picked up the pace as I leaned forward and flicked my tongue between his hard pecs like I'd wanted to do since the first time I saw him shirtless. I licked my way up his chest, along his neck, savoring the fiery taste of his skin, aching for more.

We both needed more.

I was going to give it to him too. Until a piercing howl echoed across the cabin. I recognized it instantly as a warning howl, like the ones the pack had made the day the djinn arrived. Something was wrong.

Icy terror flooded my veins, replacing the lusty heat that had raced there seconds ago. Wells grunted. He pulled my hand from his sweats, then placed a sweet kiss on my palm. "To be continued," he murmured, then stood up with me still wrapped around his waist. "We should see what's going on."

ells grabbed his rod that was stashed next to the door, and we rushed down from his treehouse and headed to the bridge leading into Boulderbrook. It seemed like the whole pack was gathered there. Several wolves had shifted and were standing guard along the fence, others who were still in their human form were holding rods.

My attention snapped as Spencer and Dominic raced around the lodge toward us. She was wearing a t-shirt that hung mid-thigh, which was more than Dominic had on—blue boxer briefs and nothing else.

Mace snickered, but he stopped cold when he read the wild look in Dominic's eyes. "I feel them. They figured out how to access my head and they know Terra just passed her first trial. The djinn are coming for her before she gets powerful enough to stop them."

I glanced at Wells. He'd never said anything about gaining more power or magic with each trial. He shrugged. "I didn't know, but it makes sense. Getting into the Conclave will give you access to more magic, so I guess you get a little bit with each trial you pass."

Time seemed to speed up and slow down all at once. A hazy blur of motion drifted around me. Wells barked at Arlo to make sure the barrier shield was in place and Arlo threw up his hands, checking the field. I gasped when I realized Tristan and a few wolves had gone over to the other side of the fence.

A flicker of concern threaded through my heart. Tristan's magic was failing, and he'd have no defense against the djinn. "Get out of here now," I shouted. He hesitated for a second, then poofed away to Mage knows where. I didn't care as long as he was safe.

With the barrier in place, Arlo ran off to contain the kids. Around me, the betas began to strip out of their clothes. I turned to Wells, who was standing far too still and wearing way too many clothes for my liking. But not for naughty reasons, for once. "What are you waiting for? Shift!" I screamed at him. My heart banged in my chest as an aching need for him, for them, to be safe overwhelmed me.

His eyes blazed red. "Not me. I won't leave you alone and unprotected." He pressed me against him in a tight hug. "You have to tunnel under the Conduit. Force the bluecaps to let you through."

"No way. I'm not leaving *you* unprotected."

We stared at each other, heat and electricity coursing between us. He leaned in, his blazing warmth sliding over my skin as he growled. "Don't you get it, Gnome? I won't be able to suppress my deepest heart wish if you're near me."

He'd said he wanted to possess me, and I'd convinced myself he meant physically, but reality was standing there whacking me in the fucking face. He already *had* possessed me in the most important way. He had my heart. And somehow, I had his.

The sudden realization took my breath away. I cared for him. Deeply. It was the most real I'd felt in my life. There was no way I could be hollow, not with him in my heart. "Wells—"

A murderous cackle took the rest of my sentence from me. We turned and found the djinn landing like they were Peter frigging Pan. They wasted no time separating into twelve different versions of themselves.

And strutting right through Arlo's barrier like it was nothing.

Wells snarled, white fur rippling over his arms. He kept his voice calm and steady, but he was seconds away from going full beast on them. "Get out."

"Now, Alpha. I suspect you realize we won't do that." He paused, lowering a possessive scowl in my direction. "We won't be long. Just a tick."

Deep, penetrating cold swept through me. My mind went straight to Wells and the way his hands were always so warm, the way he'd touched me, how he'd given me gifts from my Gram, and helped me find myself despite being a golem. All I wanted to do was make sure he stayed safe.

A leer spread across the djinn faces. "Oh, how sweet. I think she likes you, Alpha."

Wells shot him a murderous look. "Yeah? That hardly ever happens, so I think I'll keep her."

Shit. They'd just pulled a wish from me like it was nothing. I should've been practicing training my mind every second of the day instead of tunneling or eating or being with Wells. I had to do better and keep my mind under control.

It turned out to be near impossible to school my mind into thinking of things I didn't wish for.

Cold sores, war in the Middle East, pickle-flavored latte.

Watching the pack die.

The djinn prowled toward me. All of them. The wolves went on the offensive, lunging and attacking. Slick horror slid through my veins as I watched all three betas latch on to the scruff of a djinn figure with their teeth, snarling and tearing at it with their incredible enhanced power. But when the djinn looked like they may go down in the fight, they pulled the copies into the original djinn and separated back again, leaving the wolves disoriented and unable to counter.

A blast of silver fire soared over the OG djinn, Wells bellowed behind them. "Listen, you motherfuckers, if there is one hair on anyone in this compound's head damaged, I will reign unholy fire on you and everyone you ever cared about. You will *wish* you were dead." Emphasis on the word 'wish.'

Magedamn, that was hot.

He was trying to lure them away from me, from the pack.

It didn't work.

The djinn raised their hands, aiming at Wells. I saw or heard nothing, but Wells buckled over in pain as the djinn laughed. "Tsk. Tsk. Such a graphic mind you have there, Alpha. Does she know you want to do *that* to her?"

After a few precious seconds, Wells was still bent over, trembling from weakness. They'd drained some of his magic. It was evident in the renewed red glow emanating from their eye sockets. The djinn stepped toward him, and I allowed, for just a second, a wish to pop into my mind. I wished they were all dead. I had to get them away from Wells or he'd lose all his magic and the djinn would be too strong to resist. I shouted at the djinn, "Whatever graphic thing he was thinking, I'd probably be down for it."

The djinn whipped their heads, abandoning their pursuit of Wells in favor of me.

Good.

As they approached, a profound icy chill sailed through my veins. I turned my head and spied the pavilion. I was overwhelmed with the memory of dancing on the tabletop to Atomic Dogs. It hit me like a brick.

What I truly wished for was a home and friends, a place where I belonged.

The djinn broke me from my revelry. "Oh, that one tasted delectable. What else do you wish for?"

Ask again later.

And all around me, the wolves were buckling as the djinn suctioned magic via their wishes, their eyes glowing more crimson with each wish. Out of habit, I reached up and twisted my Earth vial, trying to grab comfort where I could. As I did so, the amethyst stones on my wrist seemed to come alive.

Arlo had said the beads had a life force in them, but if that force held some magical properties, I didn't know how to wield it. I wished I'd had time to figure it out.

One of the wolves howled, but it was clipped and mournful. Whomever it was, he was in pain. I looked over and caught Wells latching onto the fence, trying to raise his rod, but couldn't get it up.

A snicker threatened to leave my mouth. Mace would not have been able to let that statement go. Mage, I had to save him. Save all of them. I just wish I knew how.

My magic took a huge dip. I could feel it sliding from my veins, but I whipped my head up as the djinn finally said what I knew they were there for. "Come with us and all the suffering will stop."

"No, Terra. You can't." Desperation dripped from Wells' voice. "Don't."

If I had amplifying power of any kind, it would be lethal in djinn hands. They'd siphon the entirety of magic in our realm in a matter of weeks, if not days if they could create more golems like me to hold the power. I couldn't go with them. But I couldn't let the pack lose their magic either. I couldn't let them die because of me.

I don't remember the thought itself forming in my mind. It was more of a whoosh of understanding spreading across my brain, but in my gut—

369

no, in my mind, heart, body, and soul—I knew what I had to do to stop the djinn.

I had to take away what they wished for most.

I looked over. Wells could barely lift his head, but his eyes flashed gold, a color I'd never seen them turn. It opened up an aching chasm in my chest. He tried to speak, but he was too weak to form a single word. I wanted to shout at him, share my feelings, express my gratitude, but I didn't have time and it would've given the djinn more power if they accessed my biggest heart wish.

I couldn't give them that. And I couldn't do what Wells had asked and tried tunneling through to the Conduit either. It wouldn't have stopped them from pursuing me. And it wouldn't have kept the pack safe. If they were making a play for all the magic, it would just be a matter of time before they wanted control of the Conduit too. The wolves would've been in their way.

I turned away. Even though he was in his wolf form Ren clearly had figured out what I was going to do, based on his annoyed growl. I imagined him calling me an idiot in that blunt way of his. I dipped my head toward him, and he lunged for one of the djinn copies, chomping on his flesh, trying to tear it to pieces so I could use the precious moment of distraction to do what I had to do.

With the djinn fixated on Ren's attack, I threw myself into the ground, tunneling into the earth, forcing my way under the compound, racing toward my cabin. When I arrived, I hurled myself forward and jerked open the door. Taking my duffle from the bed, I glanced out at the lake and a wistful longing surged through me.

I'd never know what the feather Wells' water magic had conjured meant.

And I'd never know why he was always so warm.

Of if he felt the same way I did.

So many possibilities would disintegrate into ashes.

But I didn't have time to grapple with lost longings. I had to get back to save the pack.

I grabbed what I needed from my bag and sailed back into the ground. I knew where I was going, but I wasn't sure where the djinn would be when I got there. I took a chance and shot up through the ground where I hoped to land.

Wells released a mournful howl. He was hanging on to the fence, some of his color returned, but he was nowhere near full strength. The djinn must have been playing with Ren while I was gone.

"Don't," he whispered. I would've been okay if he had yelled it or growled it in my direction, but he had to soften his voice and make it feel like a caress.

I placed a quick kiss on his cheek before I stepped away.

My stomach lurched when I realized I'd been correct: Ren was laying on his side, whelping, the black tuft of hair matted with dirt. Beside him, Gideon had shifted into his human form, pointing his rod at the djinn as clouds of steam wafted over them. Nothing they were doing was working to harm the djinn predators.

"Yo, djinn. Will Smith called and he's not happy with your life choices. You're giving genies a bad name."

The djinn swiveled, barreling toward me with lightning speed they hadn't yet shown. They were gaining power. The still bodies of the pack littering the camp were evidence.

Tears trickled down my cheek as I pushed my deepest wish into my mind. The heart, mind, soul, and body wish that had wrapped itself together in my head before the individual bits and pieces had names. When I broke it down, I'd already gotten what I longed for most—a place to call home and people to share it with. What else more could I need?

Nothing. And that's what made the sacrifice worth it.

I looked over at Wells one more time and my heart cleaved into pieces. He would bear the brunt of my sacrifice too—the absolute worst part of it, but I knew he could. He was far stronger than even he knew. "I'm sorry for this."

Sunlight gleamed in the mirror as I held it up, slicing into pieces and scattering reflections that felt like my heart. My voice was steady as I announced to the djinn, "What I wish for most of all is to be admitted to the Conclave."

The pull of the djinn's power drew the wish from me at a slow torturous place. Fear, pain, and resolve coursed through my body and the hollowness of my chest that someone had created became a living breathing entity, filling with energy and magic as I smashed the mirror into the fence, shattering it into pieces.

Magic shot from my hands, projecting forward and bouncing across each of the djinn bodies, connecting them blazing purple lightning. They fell, one by one, sizzling and sputtering and unable to fight against whatever flowed from the bracelet through me. Several seconds ticked by and none of the djinn stirred. I looked down at the broken pieces of mirror, sucking in a deep breath.

The bracelet was cool against my wrist, like it had done its job and was resting. Maybe that's what I was doing too. I'd done it. I'd overwhelmed the djinn, taking them out with my most powerful wish and a well of magic I'd only hoped was within in me.

It was over.

Over.

A low growl, rumbling and horrifying, reached my ears and tumbled into my chest. I looked up, trembling as a set of elongated canine teeth and bright white fur closed in on me. He lunged forward, but stopped suddenly, like he was tethered to something behind him. His head cocked to the side as he studied me, eyes turning silver and that predatory noise erupted from his chest.

He was trying to fight it, holding himself back, but looking at my throat like it was his next meal. The magic was in charge of him, even if he was holding off with sheer willpower. I knew without question he'd lose the battle.

My hands gripped his soft fur and I whispered into his ear, as thick saliva dripped from his mouth. "I did this for you, for the pack. Don't grieve me and don't feel guilty. It was a choice I'd make again and again for them. For you."

I felt the moment that the Perception magic won the war over him. I screamed as teeth tore into my neck, the same place he'd kissed me so many times before. I felt myself leaving my body and everything around me went black. The last thing I heard was the anguished howls of the pack.

Author's Note & Acknowledgements

Think of this as a "fusion" of back matter.

Hey there Readers. (Capital R because you're that important to me.)
Yes, that ending was a bit cliffy. I'd apologize but I'm not that sorry. There's much more in store for the characters in this world, things you probably think you know and other things that may make you even more angry at me in the future. But, since this is my debut and you haven't had time to get to know me yet, I'll tell you I'm a real believer in the HEA. That's all I'm going to say about that. We'll get there, eventually. But first, there's going to be this awful...

Better not tell you now.

When I became an avid reader way back in Jr. High, I always made a point to read the acknowledgments of each book. I was curious about every little detail that went into making these worlds that I adored, and I read these sections as voraciously as I read the books. As such, I've been writing acknowledgements in my head for a long ass time. Now that I'm finally tasked with putting my thoughts down, I'm at a loss on where to start.

All stories have a beginning, so I'll begin there. Thanks to my parents, my family, and friends. You know who you are. I'll probably name you in the dedications of future books if you don't tick me off before then. I want to thank my editors, Erin Bledsoe and Roxana at proofreadebooks.com for helping me beat this world into submission and put out a jewel of a project I'm proud of. And I simply must thank my borrowed PA for coming in that the clutch moment. I don't even know if I used that phrase right because it's a sports term, but I appreciate all you did to help me with last minute things.

This book would not exist without you, Mandy O'Dell. (Y'all should go read her YA books. They're great!) You've been a critic partner, a sounding board, a therapist, an enabler and instigator, and most importantly, a friend. Thank you for all of it. I'm thrilled to share a brain with you. And to Lori, for being my biggest cheerleader from the get-go, way back when I was writing inoffensive YA that never saw the light of day because of my crush on Four. I hope you're not too disappointed in the smut. If so, probably don't read the next one. I love you and your support is one of the main things that kept me writing over the years.

Thank you to the readers who took a chance on an unknown indie author. I hope you love these characters as much as I do. I'd also like to thank Henry Cavill's chest for the inspiration and Scott Speedman of *Underworld* fame for my obsession with werewolves.

Lastly, to every aspiring author who's read this to the end because you have the same intense desire to publish your work as I did. In case you don't have the network of support I've enjoyed, let me take this moment to say this: The world's full of people who stopped before they had success. Don't let that be you. Keep writing. Keep reading. Keep going. There are readers for every story and stories for every reader. Let yours be one of them. Love and werewolf howls until Book 2.

--Cat

About the Author

Cat Collins is a collector of stories, weaver of words, and unofficial Diet Coke swilling champion of the South. She's been writing since her debut, "Kermio & Piggiet," her ninth grade Shakespeare project earned her accolades (A+) that sparked her love of words and deep affection for spinning tales. You can bet Miss Piggy wasn't dying for that fool, Kermit in that story.

Cat's romance stories are full of humor, heart, and heat and she digs creating swoon-worthy guys for fierce main characters who may or may not be a little broken.

When she's not writing or reading, Cat likes to travel, watches way too many foreign shows on Netflix, and can be found hanging out with her two cool kids, two unimpressed cats, and one patient husband.

Magic 8-Ball:

Will this reader sign up for Cat's newsletter to be kept up to date on new releases, get bonus content and other fun things?

Signs point to yes.

Sign up at CatCollinsBooks.com

You can find Cat on all the social media platforms @CatCollinsBooks

OTHER BOOKS FROM CAT COLLINS

Find the magic with the <u>complete</u>

DIMINISHING MAGIC SERIES

Jewels of Clay

Flames of Gold

Guardian of Whispers

Ripples of Glass

REINDEER GAMES SERIES

Spicy & irreverent "Why Choose" Romance featuring one of Santa's naughtiest reindeer shifters. Each one is standalone.

Fixin' Vixen

Not So Stupid Cupid

CURSE OF BETWEEN SERIES

Spicy Urban Fantasy series featuring two overlapping stories: one light with rom-com vibes & one dark with triggers. Each book is standalone.

Read Between the Grinds

Between the Sheets

RE-MEMBERING SERIES

A satirical spicy novella series featuring Dr. Frankenpeen & his "Hard-core" surgery.

Each book is standalone.

Wood

Book 2 coming soon